HEREIN

EYE OF THE SERPENT

SECOND CHRONICLE OF AELWYN

A Tale of Old Enmities and Fresh Deceits and of
the Power of the Great Art and Its Makings

Robert N. Charrette

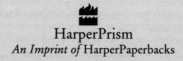

HarperPrism
An Imprint of HarperPaperbacks

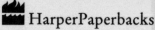
HarperPaperbacks
A Division of HarperCollins*Publishers*
10 East 53rd Street, New York, N.Y. 10022-5299

This is a work of fiction. The characters, incidents, and
dialogues are products of the author's imagination and are not to
be construed as real. Any resemblance to actual events or
persons, living or dead, is entirely coincidental.

ISBN 0-06-105499-2

HarperPrism is an imprint of HarperPaperbacks.

HarperCollins®, ®, HarperPaperbacks™, and
HarperPrism® are trademarks of HarperCollins*Publishers*, Inc.

Cover illustration by Jean Francois Podevin

First printing: September 1996

Printed in the United States of America

Visit HarperPaperbacks on the World Wide Web at
http://www.harpercollins.com/paperbacks

❖ 10 9 8 7 6 5 4 3 2 1

THE ATTACK

Friend or enemy?

Out here there seemed only one likely answer.

Yan reached in his shirt for his *claviarm*. He had no weapon but his magic. Just then, a drakkenree, jaws agape, burst from the foliage. Yan ducked under the outstretched arms, but was caught in the ribs by the attacker's pumping leg. It was like being struck down by a battering ram.

The drakkenree stood over him, its wedge-shaped head drawn back. The gaping jaws were studded with a single row of teeth. The creature wore a sword but hadn't drawn it; instead, it held its clawed foot out, ready to gut Yan. A brown leaf was already impaled on the outermost of the three toes.

How strange, Yan thought, to be calmly studying one's own killer. . . .

THE CHRONICLES OF AELWYN
by Robert N. Charrette

Timespell
Eye of the Serpent
*Wizard of Bones**

Published by HarperPrism

*coming soon

For all those who have traveled under the three moons, but especially for Bill C., a longtime traveler and good companion.

Part One

1

THE ARROW QUIVERED FOR an instant after the head embedded itself in the thick oak shutter, not an inch from Yan Tanafres's ear. Yan ducked back at once, having long ago learned not to stay where an enemy marksman had a clear shot. His heart raced and he gulped air.

"That was close."

"Not as close as the archer would have liked. You're lucky to be able to comment on it." Peyto Lennuick shook his head slowly, mouth pursed in rebuke. "I told you not to stick your head up, but since when have you listened to any counsel of caution from me?"

The clerk's unfounded complaint annoyed Yan; he had taken such advice more than once during their years of wandering together. Sometimes it had been good advice, other times Yan's lack of caution had saved their hides. There was no way to know the better path before walking it. Today Peyto had been right, but Yan knew better than to admit that directly.

"I thought they weren't in range of the keep," he said.

Peyto harrumphed. "Thought? You didn't think at all. You know as well as I that those bregil wild men are beastly strong. With such strength the bows they draw would have considerable range. As much as an Imperial arquebus, maybe more."

Certainly bregil were strong, but Yan felt sure that even

the most massively muscled bregil couldn't shoot an arrow as far as firepowder could hurl a ball from a gun; an arquebus would have had trouble reaching this side of the keep from beyond the walls. "They haven't shot at the keep before this. There was no evidence of their bows' capability to reach here."

"Well now you know what range they have," Peyto responded smugly. "Has it done you any good?"

"I wasn't interested in that. I wanted to see how the battle progressed."

"Badly enough that they're shooting at civilians now."

"Listen, though. You can still hear the sounds of the struggle."

"Probably going badly for Baron Yentillan's men," Peyto concluded sourly.

"How can you know?"

"The hillmen raiders shot at you, didn't they? As you said yourself, they hadn't shot at the tower before."

Yan couldn't deny that, yet he didn't understand the whys and wherefores of battle. If Teletha were here, she could tell him. War was her business as magic was Yan's. Like all magicians, he wanted to understand what was happening around him. "What has changed that our attackers now fire on the tower?"

"Them hill monkeys hain't shot afore because they hain't be ready to," said a gruff voice.

The new speaker was an old man, sitting among the score of village folk huddled around the massive table that dominated the tower room. His typical ruddy southerner's complexion was darkened by age to a deep copper hue, highlighting an array of scars. Likely he had been a soldier before the loss of his right hand had cost him his profession. Yan couldn't tell whether the man's bitter expression was prompted by their plight or the old soldier's inability to do anything about it.

"What makes you an expert?" Peyto asked in an annoyed tone.

Yan knew that Peyto hated interruptions in his conversations, especially by those the old clerk thought ill educated. Yan, however, found his curiosity piqued. Though the veteran's accent was obvious and his syntax poor, he was speaking the Empiric that Yan and Peyto had been using. That alone made him more interesting than the rest of the locals crowded into the chamber. So few of the folk they met hereabouts spoke more than the local Kolvinic, and most of those only knew one or two of the regional dialects. This man, if treated well, might be a source of information.

"You were a soldier once, weren't you?" Yan asked

"I was. Once."

"Well, Master Soldier, have you fought these bregil tribesmen before?"

The old veteran looked away for a moment. "Hain't a soldier now, so don't call me that. Name's Grembald."

"As you wish, Grembald. When you were a soldier, did you fight against the hill tribes?"

"Once or twice."

"Then perhaps you know what brought them howling out of their hills this morning," said Peyto.

"Depends."

When it was clear that Grembald was not going to speak more without prompting, Yan asked, "On what?"

"Whose coin they've taken."

"Are you saying that they are mercenaries?"

Grembald nodded. "They could be."

"Hired by one of Baron Yentillan's enemies?"

The old soldier shrugged. "Maybe they just took Baaliff's coin."

That was a phrase Yan had heard from Teletha. It meant soldiers fighting purely for the joy of it and the reward of loot. "Meaning they are here to plunder."

"Well, which is it?" Peyto snapped.

"Hain't no magician to read minds," the old soldier said with a hard stare at Yan. "And if I was, wouldn't want to read no monkey mind anyhow."

Peyto harrumphed. "If you were a magician, the Art would have come to a sorry state. But since you aren't an initiate, allow me to reveal to you something that is no secret to any person of education. Magicians do not read minds, bregil or otherwise. To do so would be unethical, and magicians are as limited by their ethics as they are by their abilities and skills. However, in your case there might not be any ethical dilemma since you are so clearly—"

"Enough, Master Lennuick!" Yan was thankful for the clerk's defense of the Art, but he didn't need Peyto antagonizing this man. "Pray excuse his words, Master Grembald. We are all put out of our humors by the straits in which we find ourselves. Not understanding the cause for this attack makes it even harder to deal with, wouldn't you agree?"

Grembald didn't respond, but he did stop glaring at Peyto and turn to Yan. Yan took that as encouragement and continued.

"As you know, we are newly come to Baron Yentillan's lands. Perhaps your knowledge of the area and those who live here can help me understand the situation. There are several hundred bregil attacking this fortress. That is a fair number of warriors. I thought the local tribes were small and that many held animosity toward each other."

"Clans hain't real big. Hain't friendly with each other neither."

Exactly. "The size of the force suggests that several tribes have combined to attack us. What lord could compel the tribes to put aside their own rivalries and attack this holding? Surely none of Baron Yentillan's rivals have such influence with the bregil of the hills."

"Lord's business hain't mine," Grembald said.

"Well, I've had some dealing with Lord Yentillan's correspondence and so know something of his friends and enemies," Peyto said. "I would venture that his rivals were no more prepared to arrange such an alliance with those wild men than he was, which is to say, it is unlikely that the hill tribes were united by a Kolviner lordling."

"What say you to that, Grembald?" Yan asked.

The veteran thought about the question for a while before whispering, "Could be *haggatan.*"

Several of the village folk looked up at the word. They had been ignoring the conversation in a language they could not understand, but they knew the strange word Grembald used. Knew it and feared it; Yan could see terror plain in their faces.

"*Haggatan?*" Peyto's brow furrowed. "Who's that?"

Grembald snorted in amusement. "It's a monkey word. Means a purging, a war the gods want."

Yan caught the scowl that suddenly darkened Peyto's expression. Before the clerk could explode, he asked, "Like a saü *jehavva*?"

"Hain't heard that word."

"A *jehavva* is a holy war in which the saü seek to drive unbelievers from their lands," Yan explained.

Nodding, the old soldier said, "Near enough."

A *jehavva* would mean real trouble. If the hill tribes of bregil had united in a holy war, the attack on Baron Yentillan's holding was only the start. If it *was* the start; the hillmen might have already attacked elsewhere, might be attacking elsewhere. Baron Yentillan's steading was very isolated. Who could know what was happening elsewhere?

"I'm worried about Teletha," Yan said.

Sighing, Peyto said, "She's probably safer than we are."

"How can you be sure? Her patrol didn't make it back before the attack."

Peyto nodded sagely. "So, at last we learn what really motivates you to stick your fool head out windows. If you are so worried about her whereabouts, why don't use some wizard's trick to look instead of risking that foolish head?"

"You know magic doesn't work well during a battle," Yan snapped back. Immediately he regretted the heat in his voice.

"Magic works for battle mages," Peyto said.

Yan didn't need to be reminded that there were gaps in his mastery of magic. "Sometimes. Just sometimes. Besides, I'm not a battle mage."

Grembald laughed bitterly. He rubbed the palm of his hand over his stump, saying, "Never the right kind of magic."

"Ignore the old man," Peyto advised. "I'm sure Teletha will be fine. She's had to arrange funeral rites before; she'll do just fine with ours."

"We're not going to die," Yan protested. "Baron Yentillan's men will hold."

The old veteran snorted. Disbelief rather than amusement

this time. Yan decided that he didn't believe it either, as the sounds of battle coming from outside increased.

From the lower levels of the keep, he heard shouting, urgent and strident. Some of the women in the chamber started to cry, joining their voices to the wails of their friends and relatives below. Outside the howls of bregil filled the air, while inside the clash of harness and stamp of feet echoed. Somewhere a horse screamed in fear or pain. A gun boomed, followed by a ragged volley of others. Yan took that as a bad sign. He had overheard Baron Yentillan order his men to save the guns as a last surprise should the raiders break the defense of the wall.

And that, Yan realized, was what must have happened.

More than ever, he wanted to know what was going on. Not daring to use the window, he started toward the stairwell. The soldiers below would know what was happening.

He reached the arch just as a score of Yentillan's archers barreled up the stairs. Yan barely threw himself out of their way in time, and they went past as though he wasn't there. The officer in charge sent one hand of five to each of the two small embrasures overlooking the keep's entrance before leading the rest up the ladder to the keep's upper reaches.

In the shelter of embrasures, the archers readied their crossbows. The two sergeants looked at each other and nodded. Each spun into the opening, sighted his weapon at something in the courtyard, and shot. Ducking back under cover, each sergeant handed off his discharged weapon, took a loaded weapon from one of his men, and sought another target while his man reloaded. Each of the other hand members stood ready to pass his crossbow to the sergeant when he was ready. Having the best marksman in a hand do the shooting was a common tactic in siege defense; the Kolviners showed themselves well versed in the drill.

More soldiers stumbled up the stairs and through the archway. The knight directed his four men-at-arms to take up a position blocking the arch. They stared anxiously downward. They looked tired, and most were wounded, but only lightly. Had they been seriously wounded, they would never have had the speed to outrace the more lightly armed hillmen in the dash across the courtyard.

Thunder echoed in the chamber below as gunners fired. Almost immediately after came the crash of the keep's doors slamming closed.

Outside, the bregil howled in frustration.

The knight heaved a sigh and ordered his men to stand down. They stumbled about the chamber seeking food and drink. Most of the villagers stayed huddled, staring anxiously at their defenders. Some few helped feed and water the weary men. Fewer still asked questions of the soldiers.

The knight waited alone on the landing until Baron Yentillan climbed up to join him. The baron's bloodied coat armor was torn, wool batting poking from the holes, and there were rents in the mail covering his arms, but he moved as a man uninjured as he strode across the floor. Ignoring the entreaties of his folk, he and the knight climbed the ladder to the upper chamber. Yan could hear them continue on to the roof. The baron remained there only briefly, but when he came down the ladder, he moved more slowly than he had going up. It was as though he had finally let his exhaustion take hold.

"Some stayed to beat on the doors, but the archers feathered the bastards well and good," Baron Yentillan announced. "The others have pulled back for the moment. Take what food and drink you will and send some up to the men on the roof."

No one moved until Grembald walked over to the table, poured a mug of ale, and brought it to the baron. Yentillan and the veteran exchanged glances before the baron reached out a hand and took the offered drink. Yentillan drained the mug at a draught.

"Their heavies still outside?" Grembald asked.

The baron nodded. "They'd have to shed their armor to scale the walls, and I don't think they'll do that."

"If the monkeys can't get in, they'll have to leave sooner or later," someone said.

"Some of the apes are already in," someone else pointed out.

"Hain't gonna be retreating," Grembald said. "They'll be starting on the gate soon."

"Can't they just open it now that they're inside?" Peyto asked incredulously.

The baron laughed a bitter laugh and patted the thonged keys at his belt. "Not with it locked."

"They could chop the locks out," Peyto pointed out.

"Not through the iron protecting them," the baron said.

Peyto's worried frown lessened. "Then surely they cannot force their way in without siege engines."

Grembald sneered at him. "For an educated man, you're not too bright. The woods are full of trees ready to be turned into rams."

Peyto's frown returned in full force. Baron Yentillan looked around at the remnants of his war band. His face plainly showed his frustration and anguish. "Once inside the wall . . ."

"But your archers chased them away before," Peyto said. "They can shoot down the tribesmen on the ram."

The baron sighed. "Those tailed apes are determined bastards. A ram will open the gate and then this keep, if they are willing to spend lives. And Vehr as my witness, they seem more than willing to do that."

"Then we're doomed," a woman wailed.

"Have you no allies to come to our aid?" Peyto asked the baron.

"Jost would, if he knew. We might hold out long enough. But he doesn't know, and we'll not get a courier out now. Our plight is known to none but the Beings Above. Unless . . ." Yentillan turned to Yan. "Master Tanafres, have you a spell to speak over the distance? Could you tell Baron Jost we need his help?"

Another reminder of a hole in Yan's mastery. "Alas, my lord, I have no such magic."

Grembald snorted. Yan didn't need the veteran's derisive condescension. He was very aware of what his deficiency might cost all of them. Shouts from the roof took everyone's attention from him. Baron Yentillan rushed to the left embrasure. He seemed barely to reach the window before he came reeling back.

A screeching beast like a nightmare bat arrowed through the opening. Its head was long, mostly a pointed beaklike maw studded with a fringe of teeth. Its broad wings were membranous and stretched from its hairy body along a single spar. Hot blood pulsed in the veins that showed through the translucent skin.

The creature dove on the baron. Leathery wings beat against the lord's armor for a frantic moment as the thing snapped with its jaws and clawed with its taloned feet. As suddenly as it had attacked, the beast fluttered away from him, flapping across the chamber apparently in search of less hard-shelled prey. The beast careened toward Peyto.

The clerk screamed as the animal's jaws fastened on his good arm. The lizard-bat folded back its wings, revealing clawed fingers at the midpoint of its wing. With these it gripped the clerk's arm, clinging tenaciously, as he tried to shake his arm free from the beast's grip. The creature swung up its hind legs and dug in with its foot claws as well. Then it began to chew.

More of the lizard-bats burst into the chamber, their high-pitched shrieks joining with the shouts and the screams of the villagers. The soldiers tried to swat the creatures down with their axes or spear them with their sword points, but the beasts dodged with a skill uncanny for their awkward flight.

In the confusion, no one moved to help Peyto but Yan. He struck the beast with his fist, skinning his knuckles against the hard bone under the creature's skin. The blow disturbed the animal. Removing its teeth from Peyto's shoulder, the lizard-bat shrieked in protest against Yan's blow. The creature twisted its head around and snapped at him. As the tooth-filled maw darted at him, Yan raised his arm to protect his face. He barely deflected the jaws. Hot lines of pain furrowed across his temple as the creature's teeth raked across the skin.

Fearful of the snapping jaws, Yan nevertheless struck again. This time he knocked one of the creature's feet free. Squalling, it released one of its finger grips and used the wing to beat at him. Yan snatched at the flailing pinion and grasped the bone that supported the membrane. The creature bucked and almost tore free of his grip, but Yan got his other hand onto the beast's wing and pulled. Squealing, the lizard-bat retained its tenacious hold on Peyto.

Yan leaned back, tugging hard. The wing stretched taut,

but still the creature refused to relinquish its grip on Peyto. The loose foot clawed at Yan, unable to reach him. The creature thrashed, its reptilian strength almost too much for Yan.

Yan's hands grew slick with sweat. He felt his grip slipping. The beast snapped at his arm, tearing his shirt and gouging bloody furrows in the flesh. One hand slipped from the wing. Just as Yan was about to lose his hold completely, one of the soldiers stepped up and ran the beast through with his sword. The creature's shrieks cut off abruptly, and, in a spasm of motion, it jerked itself free from Yan's grip. The beast fell, lifeless, to the floor.

"It's dead," the soldier said, staring down at it as though he was not really sure.

"You're safe," Yan said to Peyto.

"I wouldn't need to be saved from Horesh-forsaken lizard-headed bats if you hadn't brought us here. Your precious magical secrets won't do any of us any good if we're spitted and hung out to feed these scaly vultures by those wild men down there."

The clerk's tirade stung Yan; there was truth in Peyto's words. Yet, he'd never forced Peyto to follow him. Or Teletha either, for that matter, but follow him they had. For years now. Though he had learned much, there was so much more to learn. While it was true that Yan knew more of magic now and was a more accomplished magician, his accomplishments seemed to have little bearing on their current plight, and he was responsible for leading them to Kolvin.

He'd come to the frontiers of the Kingdom of Kolvin following rumors of an ancient city said to predate the dark times. He had hoped that finding such a place might offer him new clues toward understanding the old books that he had acquired from Laird Gornal's library, for he suspected that those books were at least as old as the long-vanished empire of the dark mages. So far, he'd found nothing to substantiate the rumors, and now Teletha was Einthof-knew-where, and he and Peyto were trapped in Baron Yentillan's keep with a ravening mob of hillmen baying for their blood. If not for Yan's thirst for knowledge, Teletha wouldn't be lost and Peyto wouldn't be injured. Yan had brought them here, brought his friends into lethal peril.

Something had to be done if any of them were to survive, but he didn't know what. He had no spells to attack the tribesmen or spirit the defenders away. Illusions he could produce, under normal circumstances, but such phantasms were almost impossible to conjure convincingly during a battle. If only he had spent more time trying to recapture lost battle magic instead of pursuing the secrets of the ancient books. Einthof's Mirror! Those books themselves might contain battle magic. But their secrets were secrets still, and he knew them not.

But there *was* something he could do. It was a last resort, an avenue open to the desperate. He could try to create a spell effect by direct manipulation of mana energy without the safeguards and restraints of a formulated spell. Such an attempt was risky at the best of times. The dangers of trying to harness the mana under the current circumstances, where so much psychic energy was already loose, were almost beyond contemplation. Yet he saw no other course. Not thinking about the dangers would be for the best. If he thought about them too much, he might lose his nerve.

He crossed the room to the left embrasure, the archers moving away as he approached. Just as well; he would be dangerous to be near. He didn't expose himself in the window; it was too early for that. There was no need to add the risk of making himself a target to the danger of what he was about to attempt.

Standing still, he closed his eyes and drew a deep breath. He shifted slightly, adjusting his stance until his weight balanced evenly and his center was stable. His mind still raced and his efforts to calm it met with little success. Reaching under his shirt, he drew forth his *claviarm*. The focus was warm from his body heat, comforting. He studied its form. Sliding his eyes along its curves and around the lines of engraving, he used the *claviarm* to guide himself into trance. Slowly, he succeeded in driving away the distraction of the fearful people huddled around him. Slowly, he calmed his own fears. Slowly, he readied himself to touch the magic. Normally, he could reach *prœha*, the state in which the magic was accessible, in a fraction of a moment. He had no idea how long it took him this time, but he knew it was far longer than it had since his first days as an apprentice. Finally, his awareness shifted.

In *præha*, magesight showed him the mana streaming around him. He reached out, and the first touch of the strands almost shocked him out of the *præha* state. The energy, so deceptively calm, actually surged like a wild sea, swelling in vast mountains and ebbing in chill troughs. The rapid shifting unnerved him. Cautiously, he reached out again, trying to shape it to his will. The magic slipped from his grasp, seeming to twist away of its own accord. He tried again, and failed again. Each time Yan tried to impose his desire on the energy it rushed away from him almost willfully.

This was not the way.

Clearly the ordinary methods of spell shaping couldn't be applied in a combat environment. Just as clearly, he knew what he would have to do. To succeed he would have to take the next step, the truly dangerous one.

He opened himself to the mana, pulling it into him to impose his will, his desire, his *self* upon it.

He gasped as the energy flooded him. It felt as though he had thrust his entire body into a fire. Painful, painful. But more than that. Invigorating and stimulating. Arousing.

His head spun as surges of emotion washed over him. Fear. Hate. Fear. Love. Anguish. And more fear. He thought he was crying, but he felt no tears on his cheeks. Then he knew he wasn't feeling his own tears and knew new fear: his own fear, this time.

A darkness swelled around him, deep, vast, and cavernous. He sensed a gulf within that darkness and was afraid. The abyss that had already taken so many others awaited him. He was too close to the edge of that gulf. He felt its pull. It would be so easy to drift in that direction.

Too close!

For a moment he sensed something else beyond that darkness: peace. A peace like none he had ever known. It called to him. Without knowing how, he turned his regard toward the source of that sensation. All he perceived was a distant light.

All he had to do was relax, and he would be on his way to that light.

On his way to peace.

Forever.

He rallied his will. This was no time to lose purpose. He could not abandon Peyto and the others. They needed him. He concentrated his effort, pulling more of the energy into himself, using it to fortify himself against the lure in the darkness. His blood sang, shrieked, howled, and moaned. He felt hot and grew hotter as he gathered in the mana. He would need a considerable amount to punch his will through the swirling energy. He gathered more in and grew hotter still.

He felt incandescent, more alive than he had ever been.

But around him he sensed the darkness, waiting.

He could not wait. He began shaping the energy. As he worked, he realized that there was little hope of achieving a sophisticated effect; the energy was just too hard to control. A fiery burst, a raging inferno in the physical world that mirrored the tumultuous energy of the mana plane, would do what needed to be done. It should have been an easy shaping, but the surging mana streams still fought his every effort.

"He's burning!" someone shouted from very far away. But not so far that Yan could not hear.

Was he burning?

He felt his control of the mana slip. He struggled with the energies, trying to hold them in check.

Something hit him. He wasn't sure if it was real or an effect of the swirling mana forces, but it staggered him and sent him stumbling into the embrasure. His knees buckled, and his chin struck the windowsill as he fell.

The mana roared, threatening to engulf him. He clung to the sill, vision dimming. The darkness was closer now.

He had to release the energy, or it would consume him.

The darkness beckoned. The light within it was closer, stronger. He tasted a hint of the sweet peace it offered.

Peace?

Not yet.

He gathered the mana, compressing it, forcing it to obey

him. It surged, nearly escaping his control. His head felt as if it were about to explode.

In the courtyard he could see the bregil gathering to swarm the keep. Yan tried to aim his spell at the largest group, but his vision was blurred. He could not be sure what he was looking at; there were so many images, real and unreal. His head ached from pain and overwhelming effort. Hoping he could hold the spell's shape, he released the energy.

As it left him, he knew he had not succeeded. Sparks flew as he felt the energy tear and claw at the stone around the window before bursting its way free from the tower. Wild and uncontrolled, the spell ripped its way howling into the courtyard. In Yan's magesight, the energy was a storm, swirling and chaotic. Flashes of energy gouted from its center. Several of those flashes combined into a massive bolt and struck the gates with a coruscant flare.

Slumped against the sill, Yan watched helplessly as the mana splashed against the gates, bathing the wood, stone, and iron in a glowing brilliance. Rivulets of magic ran over the surface of the wood and stone like water, pouring into the iron fittings in streams. Almost immediately, the iron fittings lightened, their dark protective patina flaking away. The iron turned an angry red, then dulled down to the harsh brown of old rust. For a moment that seemed to be all that was going to happen. Then hinges, nails, plates, and locks all lost their shape, sifting to the ground in a flurry of rust flakes.

All that held the wood together was gone.

Slowly one of the valves began to topple inward, separating into its component parts as it fell. In the space beyond the fallen door, Yan could see armored bregil.

He had failed.

He had done worse than that. He had opened the way for more of the raiders, dooming them all. Howling tribesmen poured into the courtyard. An arrow caromed off the stone, dropping sparks that stung his cheek. The pain was dull, far away.

Yan passed out.

2

THEY COULD HEAR THE SOUNDS of the fighting long before they came in sight of Baron Yentillan's holding, but the captain didn't order them to increase their pace. Teletha Schonnegon wondered why. If the village was under attack, there was little likelihood that an ambush was awaiting them. Finally, the captain ordered the patrol into line abreast, calling for his riders to keep a sharp lookout for ambushes. Captain Raff Janden was a scruffy sort, lacking in real military discipline, but he was a veteran of the fighting that had disrupted this part of Kolvin for the last few years. Maybe the possibility of an ambush was not so far-fetched.

They traversed the woods without incident, and Janden halted the patrol near the edge. Through the thinning trees, Teletha could see the fields that surrounded Baron Yentillan's holding. Unsurprisingly, they were empty.

The village and surrounding stockade lay out of sight just beyond those fields. Even the top of the lord's tower was screened by a low hill. Riders and horses fretted as the sounds of combat drifted across those vacant fields. Among those sounds she could hear the howls of battle-frenzied bregil, which meant that the attackers were hill raiders rather than the forces of a rival baron.

At Janden's order, two of the riders cut out of the line, heading cautiously along the edge of the woods. They skirted the hill, moving to get a better look at the situation. Teletha tried to sit her saddle without fidgeting. Yan and Peyto had been in the village when her patrol went out. Where were they now? She hoped they were safe within the stockade. A well-manned palisade was more than strong enough to withstand a hillman raiding party. But if they had been caught outside ... Neither Yan nor Peyto was what anyone would call a fighter.

The scouts came back at a canter, incautious considering the roughness of the forest floor.

"The gates are down! They're storming the keep!"

Their shout raised worried cries from the rest of the horsemen. Two of them, names of loved ones on their lips, started to spur their horses out of the woods. Having clearly anticipated such a reaction, Janden was already in front of them, heading off their impetuous rush.

"Hold!" he ordered, urging his mount into their paths.

Unable to pass, the riders reined up. They shouted angrily at him to get out of their way. Janden shouted right back, sweeping his gaze to take in all the riders.

"You're fools to go riding in blind. And fools are dead men looking for a place to fall down. You'll not help any of your families by being fools. You'll just get yourselves killed. Is that it? You want to die?"

No one answered.

"Thought not." He turned his mount toward the two who had raised the alarm. "Calmly now, Thom, just what did you see? Who's attacking? How many? I need a real report."

"Sorry, Captain," the scout gulped. "Bregil, sir. Scores of them."

Janden sat back in his saddle. "How many did you actually see?"

"A century's worth at least."

"No tribe's got that many warriors," the man next to Teletha said. That was Dantil, Janden's second and a veteran, too. He'd know.

"There's more than one tribe's warriors there," Martinn, the second scout said. "I saw Turtle, Obsidian, and Cragcat warriors."

"I saw one in Eagle harness," Thom added.

"Turtle and Eagle, hunh?" Janden's brow furrowed. "See any of our people?"

"No, sir," Martinn answered. "But the baron's banner was still flying from the tower."

The news of a mixed clan force raised mutters among the troop. Teletha understood that. From what she'd heard, most of the tribes in the hills hated each other. If they had buried those hatreds, it was bad news for the civilized settlers of the region. Very bad news, if it was *haggatan*.

She'd heard tales of the last *haggatan* from some of the older troopers. None of the hill bregil took kindly to the encroachment of civilization in these parts, and their independent harassment of the settlers was bad enough. When they joined in *haggatan*, harassment became a bloodbath. Under the direction of their hate-inspired leaders, the tribesmen would slaughter settlers indiscriminately, bregil or merin, whether farmer, hunter, soldier, spouse, or child.

Imperial troops would have settled the issue permanently; the emperor wouldn't tolerate such a suppurating wound. However, Kolvin was an independent kingdom and not a part of the Coronal Empire. She had to remind herself that they did things differently here. But differently didn't mean people didn't care about their families and homes.

"We've got to go in now," Jerr pleaded. She was the youngest trooper and recently married. Teletha remembered Jerr's young husband, a strapping lad of a farmer, but handsome enough for all that he was a ground grubber.

"And throw our lives away?" Janden asked with a deceptive calm.

"They need us," Thom protested.

"They don't need us dead."

"My woman's down there," Dantil said.

"There's nothing we can do," the captain snapped. "With the hill monkeys through the gates, everyone down there is as good as dead."

"Martinn said he saw the baron's banner." Dantil's eyes were wild. "That'd mean they're holed up in the keep."

"Yeah," Jerr agreed. "Everyone might still be alive."

Janden remained unmoved. "And they might already all

be dead. Or soon will be. What are you going to do about
that? Are you so high in Horesh's favor that you can call
back the dead?"

"We can kill us some hill apes," Jerr said.

"And get ourselves dead as well."

"What about our duty to Baron Yentillan, Captain?"
Teletha tugged on the black-and-white cord tied around her
sword arm, the sign of a guilded mercenary in hire. "You
wear this, as do I. Where's your honor?"

"Where it belongs, woman. None of us took a death oath.
If there are Turtle and Eagle warriors fighting together out
there, there's real trouble. Those fatherless monkeys will be
ravaging the whole countryside after they finish here. A few
more dead soldiers here won't make any difference in the
long run. But alive, we may do some good."

"We can do some good *now* by hitting those raiders,"
Martinn said.

"To what end?" Janden spat. "We'll do more good joining Baron Jost or Lord Kantrim than serving as the main
course at the apes' victory feast."

A gunshot sounded, distant and defiant.

"See? They're not dead yet. They need our help," Jerr
pleaded. "At least we might be able to distract the attackers
long enough for the survivors to make a break."

Several of the riders shouted their agreement. Janden
looked around at them. Teletha watched the cavalrymen
stiffen under his gaze. They were nervous and fearful and
very near rebellion against his authority. The captain's sour
frown showed that Janden saw what she did.

"All right," Janden said. "We'll try their temper. But
don't be foolish. Keep close and don't let yourself get cut
off. If you get caught up in a melee, you'll be easy meat for
them. If things are as bad as I fear, I'm going to give the
order to retreat. The other holdings will need soldiers.
They'll need us. Alive and able to fight. You stay, and you'll
be throwing your life away."

Janden led them out into the fields. They had only gone
a dozen yards when Teletha spotted the body of a farmer,
hoe still gripped in his hands. It had been an ineffectual
weapon against the raiders.

A few yards further on was another hoe, lying abandoned. A little bit further still, another body. This one lay sprawled on its belly. The tribesmen had not been so kind to this fellow; they had nearly hacked him to pieces. His head had been severed at the neck and placed, faceup, near the shoulders. Sightless eyes stared up at the sun. Teletha didn't recognize him, but curses from the other riders told her that some of them did. Janden brought them to a trot.

They got closer than Teletha thought they would without being spotted by the raiders. The hillmen seemed more mindful of other things than watching for a relief force. Too bad for them that they had thought it unnecessary to put out pickets.

There was a knot of the bregil tribesmen outside the gate, apparently intent on something occurring inside the palisade. Janden raised his hand in the signal to increase pace. Horses stretched their legs, hitting a canter. The line got a bit ragged, but the riders were still spaced effectively.

One hundred yards from the gate, one of the tribesmen noticed them. He tried to warn his fellows, but it was too late. Slowly the nearest bregil straggled out, forming a line to meet the riders. A line? Clearly they had too little experience with cavalry in open ground; they'd need more depth to resist a charge. Still, Teletha was relieved to see no pikemen among them. There were a few spears, but fortunately none of them were near her path.

At fifty yards Janden called the charge, and the horsemen thundered forward. A few arrows fell among them, but Teletha didn't see anyone take harm.

They made contact.

Teletha cut down at the first bregil that stood before her. Sword rang against sword, and she was past. The tribesmen were big and burly like all bregil, stout warriors, but the hillmen had little experience dealing with a mounted swordsman; they broke from fear of her sword and the hooves of her mount. She cut at the scrambling figures as she passed, feeling her sword strike home at least twice before she was through them.

She turned her animal and was surprised to see that none of the other riders had gone down. She set her spurs,

urging the animal forward for another pass. The other riders were doing the same. Move and strike. Keep moving,
keep striking. The cavalryman's way of life. Janden's troop
closed ranks for another charge through their enemies.

Two lengths before they hit, Thom's horse collided with
hers and threw her animal off stride. Slowed, she was left
behind as the others crashed into the bregil. Seeing good
fortune in a gap left in the ranks by the passage of the other
riders, she sent a quick prayer of thanks to Vehr. She
turned her horse's head in that direction, but before she
could spur the animal on its way, a bregil in an armor of
turtle shells rose up from nowhere.

She barely managed to touch steel against the Turtle
warrior's sword as he thrust. She felt the blade hit and
slither across her breastplate. So much for the troop's jokes
about her overly heavy armor; she would have been dead
without it.

Her return cut at the bregil's head glanced from his helmet. The warrior pressed his attack. They traded blows,
and with each parry Teletha felt the hammering strength of
the bregil as his weapon struck her sword. She didn't have
the raw strength to stand up to such punishment for long.

Hoping to break his control of the fight, she initiated a
flurry of cuts and urged her horse backward. Doggedly he
stayed close. She broke pattern for a beat and put her full
strength into an overhand cut. The bregil was quick; he
blocked and slid his blade down the length of hers. With a
twist of his wrist, he locked their hilts.

His first tug pulled Teletha halfway from her mount, and
she had to slap her free hand down on the saddle to retain
her seat. She had just managed to struggle upright when the
bregil's tail curled up and wrapped around her wrist. Teeth
bared in a savage grin, he started to haul her weapon hand
down, out of the way of his own sword. She lifted her other
hand clear of the saddle and watched the surprise blossom
in the bregil's eyes as he realized what she held. He hesitated.
She didn't dare give him time to recover. She shoved the
muzzle into his face and discharged the pistol.

He fell, dead, and still nearly dragged her from the saddle.
She gave the pistol a cursory wipe across her trousers

and replaced it in her saddle holster. There would be no time to reload it; the rest of the fight would be sword alone.

During her struggle with the Turtle warrior, the fight had mostly left her behind. She was relieved. Taking the moment to breathe, she looked around and considered her position. Though she could handle a horse well enough, she was no cavalry soldier. She had known it before the bregil had grappled with her, and his near unhorsing of her had driven home the fact that she lacked sufficient control of her beast. That lack deprived her of one of her most important assets in a fight: mobility. And she no longer had a charged pistol as a backup to close-quarter encounters. If she were to be unhorsed, she would likely be stunned long enough for at least one of the milling bregil to finish her. Besides, she was far more comfortable fighting on foot.

She slipped off her mount, slapping its rump to send it careening into a clump of four Eagle warriors headed in her direction. They tried to scatter out of the beast's way, and all but one succeeded. Staggered by the impact of the horse's shoulder, that one dropped to the ground, where the horse's hind hooves came down on his leg and snapped it like a rotten log. He howled, a high-pitched yelp totally unlike the war howls of his companions.

Teletha caught the nearest one with a quick thrust to the throat. The other two stopped their rush, suddenly wary of their opponent. Two against one was one too many for a safe fight. She sidestepped and struck at one, but the tribesman parried with his buckler, nearly catching her blade in the leather. She was more cautious after that, staying with thrusts for her serious attacks. It took two more attempts before she could maneuver one of her opponents behind the other and devote herself to the one. She slipped a thrust in on the low line and dug a furrow in his leading thigh. Parrying his tail-dagger thrust, she riposted and slipped her point in under his belt. He grunted and staggered away, vomiting blood as he fell.

The last one glared at her and feinted, apparently opening himself. She didn't fall for it, stepping back instead. She used her moment's respite to sweep her blade down and across the arm of the broken-legged bregil, who had been reaching to trip her. She took another step back and slit his throat.

Now alone, the last Eagle warrior backed away until he was far enough to turn safely. Over his fleeing shoulder, Teletha could see that the other bregil had been totally disconcerted by the riders' attack. The horsemen were having an effect all out of proportion to their numbers. Through the open gates, she could see that the bregil in the court were panicking. Several disappeared over the top of the wall on the side away from the gate, more milled in confusion inside the courtyard.

A half-armored warrior wearing an obsidian-studded helmet attacked, and for a moment she was too pressed to pay attention to more than her immediate survival. He was a poor swordsman, and only the threat of the blade gripped in his tail kept Teletha from immediately dispatching him. When he tried for a disemboweling thrust, she lopped off his tail. He screeched and threw himself at her. Sidestepping, she ran her sword into his unarmored back.

A flow of tribesmen poured from the courtyard, led by a bregil wearing a helmet festooned with plumes. The leader of the raid, no doubt. The plumed warrior stood in the gateway and urged his troops forward and, to Teletha's surprise, away from the riders. The rush was not a counterattack, but a breakout attempt.

After a moment, the plumed one stopped gesticulating and stared at the pitifully few horsemen harassing his troops. Teletha could see his bared teeth. For a moment he seemed to be looking beyond the melee toward the village, then the woods. He had to be wondering if the cavalry was the advance guard for a relief force or no more than the meager force they appeared to be. He made his decision, grabbing the next warrior passing through the gateway and shoving him toward the riders.

The sudden change in plan caused confusion in the hillmen's ranks. Those within pressed forward and tangled with those slowed in the gateway. Those already past their leader kept moving, scattering among the buildings of the village. The plumed bregil roared, but his shouts were drowned by the thunder of an arquebus volley from the keep. Merin war

cries filled the sudden silence; Yentillan's troops were sally-
ing. The sudden attack in their rear broke the tribesmen's
spirit and the war band dissolved into a mob. Heedless of
their leader's orders, they streamed away in disorder.

Baron Yentillan, at the head of his men, appeared in the
gateway and stopped; the baron halted his troops, apparently content to hold the gate. Janden rode in for a quick
conference while his riders regrouped. He led them in short
charges that broke any group of hillmen that tried to stand
their ground. Mercilessly, the horsemen rode down any
bregil they caught in the open. But there were too many
tribesmen, and both horses and riders were tired. Most of
the raiders escaped. Teletha, holding her place at the edge
of the village, killed the few that tried to escape past her.

The siege of Yentillan's tower was over.

Reining in his horse, Raff Janden sent his gaze roving
across the scattered bregil corpses. There were a lot of
them. The riders had been lucky, very lucky, that the hill
monkeys had panicked. There had been enough of the apes
to have done for all the riders had they stayed calm.

Raff mistrusted the timing of the bregil attack. He didn't
like seeing Eagles and Turtles fighting side by side. He
grew more worried when he saw from the corpses that
Thom and Martinn had been right: two other clans had
been involved in the attack as well. Four tribes in a single
war band! Very bad.

He especially didn't like not knowing how and why
this had come about. Despite his troop's fears, he didn't
think the clansmen were on *haggatan*. It didn't feel right.
Or look it either. None of the warriors he had seen had
painted their skin as *haggatan* warriors commonly did.
And where were the shamans? In a *haggatan* attack he
would have expected to see a mob of the flea-infested bastards jumping and capering around while their minions
butchered good folk. Still, there was *something* behind this
organized attack.

He had suspicions but no proof, and without proof there
wasn't much he could do. He wasn't about to go mouthing

off and be wrong; he'd seen too often what that did to careers. He wasn't going to get himself caught like that.

For the moment, caution was the best course.

Which meant he'd need all of the scouts. He didn't want them being foolish and getting themselves caught in ambushes and killed. He shouted until he got Dantil's attention and told him to blow the recall. The Kolviner scouts knew the woods round about well enough, but, flush with unearned victory, they weren't being cautious right now; they could ride into bregil ambushes too easily.

Raff cast a look at the stockade and shook his head at the mass of timbers in the gateway. With the gates down, the palisade was next to worthless. The only defensible structure left was the keep, and the tower wasn't big enough to house the whole population of Yentillan's steading. Given enough troops, the area might be held, but even with his riders back, Yentillan didn't command enough troops to secure the area. The hill monkeys might not have taken out Baron Yentillan's holding completely, but they had made it untenable.

Raff didn't like the situation.

He turned his horse's head in the direction of the stockade. He needed to talk to the baron.

No, he didn't like this situation at all.

Yan's welcoming hug was clearly heartfelt, for all of its brevity. He actually surprised Teletha by embracing her with uncharacteristic disregard for her bloodied armor. She returned his hug, glad he was still alive.

With her head crushed against Yan's chest she could see Peyto smiling indulgently to one side. So the clerk had survived as well. At the moment, she was glad of that, too. She was luckier than some of the other riders; all her friends had survived the attack hale and whole.

Perhaps not so hale. Yan trembled in her arms. When he finally released her, she got a good look at him, and she didn't like what she saw. He looked terrible, pale and dark-eyed, like a man with a wasting illness.

"What's wrong?"

"Nothing," he replied, shrugging out of her grasp. "Fra Bern needs some help with the wounded. We'll talk later."

"That we will."

He didn't react to her tone. He didn't even turn around. Teletha watched him shuffle over to the Einthofite priest. Teletha started after him, but Peyto took her arm. She turned on the clerk, ready to slap away his gnarled hand, but stopped when she saw his solemn face. There was real concern there, deep worry. Her anger fled.

"What happened to him?" she asked.

"He tried to be a hero."

Which meant he'd tried something magical. Yan was a stronger magician than he'd been when she'd met him, but he still lacked confidence in himself and his skills. There were times when he tried something foolish, and his lack of confidence was justified, usually when he pushed himself to try something out of his ordinary experience. She admired his bravery in trying such things; Vehr knew she wouldn't try a new pass for the first time during a real fight. So he had tried to be a hero. Just what had he done? "Battle magic?"

"I don't know what it was, but he had trouble with it. You saw the gates?"

She had seen them when she entered the stockade. She had thought the hillmen had used magic on them. "He did that?"

Peyto nodded.

Her mouth went dry. Such power. She had not thought Yan capable of such feats. Most of the time she was able to forget that he was a magician because he so rarely made a display of the power he had at his command. She didn't like being reminded about it, especially not like this. Most of the time his magical pursuits seemed no more than a scholarly curiosity, a bookish sort of interest. She liked it that way.

Looking back at the gates, her eyes were drawn to the scattered red dust that had once been good iron. She shivered, not knowing what bothered her more: that such magic might be, or that *Yan* might make such magic. Not that he was as untrustworthy as most magicians she had met over the years. He was . . . well . . . he was Yan.

Yan wasn't supposed to be able to do things like that.

It frightened her.

Raff Janden clattered into the gateway and reined in his horse. Teletha watched him study the fallen gates. She saw his gaze shift to the piles of rust. The captain stared at that damning red dirt for a long moment before spitting on the ground. The expression on his face was pure disgust. "Magic," she heard him mutter.

Few soldiers had a high opinion of magicians and their works.

Janden walked his horse over to her. "Where's the baron?"

"I don't know," she told him.

"Well, come along and let's find him," the captain said as he dismounted.

They found the baron in the stables, gore dripping from his right hand and the dagger in it. The horse at his feet would never again carry a warrior into battle.

"Baron Yentillan," Raff said softly.

"Those tailed bastards cut his hamstrings. Bastards! And left him."

"Baron."

The baron finally reacted to the presence of his soldiers. He dropped the dagger into the dirt. "Yes, Captain, what is it?"

"They're scattered, milord. We won't be seeing any more of them today."

The baron nodded wearily. "Good enough word for now, Captain. Better than I had been expecting before your timely arrival. I chose well when I hired you to captain my light horse."

Janden smiled at the compliment and sketched a bow. "All part of the service, milord."

Remembering Janden's reluctance to get involved, Teletha thought about saying something, but not for very long. She'd soldiered long enough to know she'd have to stand considerably higher in the baron's estimation to challenge the word of his captain. The word of a mercenary common soldier, even one of the guild, would hardly be taken to outweigh that of a seasoned captain, especially one who wore the token of the guild himself.

"No need to stand around in here." Baron Yentillan led them outside. His gaze roved the courtyard, taking in the damage to the people and buildings of his holding. He did not look happy. "They caught us napping. They were in the village before the alarm went out."

Janden nodded. "I thought so. We found some of the farmers."

"Dead, of course," Yentillan said grimly. "Mutilated?"

"One."

"See that he's buried before his family finds him." As the baron continued talking, Janden nodded to Teletha, and she nodded back her acceptance of the order. "There were hundreds of them. I've not seen such a gathering for twenty years. But we turned them back."

"Today," Janden said.

The baron stopped in his tracks. "How many got away?"

"Better than half, I'd say. As many as three out of four."

"Not good. Such a force is too dangerous. I saw the symbols of three clans. Eagles, Obsidian, and Cragcats."

"There were four, milord. There were Turtles, too."

"Four? Eagles *and* Turtles?" Yentillan asked bleakly.

"Aye, milord."

"This bears serious thought." Yentillan gave Teletha a brief glance and said to Janden, "We'd best talk in privacy."

"Aye, milord."

Teletha bowed courteously as they walked away. She was only a common soldier here and not privy to the councils of captains and nobles. Considering all the talk about *haggatan*, she was glad of that. It was time to think about moving on.

There was no point in acting on the order to bury the mutilated farmer's body. Several of the riders had recognized the dead man. Being locals, they'd take care of their own. They wouldn't want to have an outsider like her ordering them around in these sorts of matters.

She tugged loose the knot on her helmet's chin strap. Tipping her head forward, she let the pot roll off into her hands, threw back her head, and shook loose her hair. The air felt cool, good. She realized that she was thirsty.

While waiting her turn at the well, she watched Yan and

Fra Bern moving among the injured. The priest was deferring to Yan. No doubt Yan's knowledge of battle injuries was superior to the priest's. Not surprising, really. Fra Bern was an Einthofite, and priests of that scholarly order, even their doctors, rarely saw a battlefield so closely. Fine enough with theory but short on practical applications, those Einthofites. But Yan; Yan was eminently practical. At least when he wasn't chasing some fool detail of his magic.

Magic.

She shut that thought away.

The care Yan showed the wounded was as real as any doctor's, or priest's. She watched him bandage and dress wounds, using herbs and compounds from his own stock rather than those the priest offered. She listened to the murmur of his reassuring voice. Yan's attention to the wounded and their needs was absolute. For a moment, she wished she was injured herself. Then she remembered what he had done to the gates.

The water she splashed into her face was chill and made her shiver.

3

THE QUARRELING VOICES INTRUDED on Yan's awareness, forcing him out of the sleep he longed to retain. They were familiar voices: one he'd grown accustomed to over the years and the other newly known since their arrival in Baron Yentillan's lands. They'd wake Teletha as well if they were not quieter. No, they wouldn't, he remembered as he gathered his wits; she had stayed in the keep.

He forced his eyes open and closed them quickly. It was too bright to bear, near midday, he guessed. He'd be the only one still abed at this hour. Teletha would have been up and about long ago. Normally he would have risen earlier, too, but he still felt the debilitating effects of yesterday's disastrous attempt to use magic during the battle. Even after his sleep, his head still ached, and he hated starting a day with a pounding skull. Miserable, and aggravated by the disturbance, he threw back the covers and sat up, groaning at the ache in his skull. Still unable to open his eyes without pain, he groped for and found his shirt. Struggling into it, he crossed the loft to the ladder. Voices rose through the opening to the ground floor.

"Though I have taken the heavenly lord Einthof as my patron, I am a man of little learning," Fra Bern said with a voice that betrayed his pride in the professed humility.

"There's no doubt about that," Peyto agreed acidly.

"And there's no need for your rancor, Master Lennuick.

I am not your enemy. As Horesh rules the day, I am not. And I must say that I have no idea—"

"Exactly my point, priest. Like all your kind."

Yan didn't like where their exchange was heading. He eased himself down the ladder. "Peyto."

The clerk stopped in mid-tirade and gave Yan a withering look.

"I see my attempt to keep your rest undisturbed has come to nought, through the efforts of this good priest here," the clerk said stiffly. "That being the case, I will attend to business elsewhere." Peyto strode past Fra Bern and snatched his hat from the peg by the door. Taking up his document case and penner, he gave the Einthofite a surly smile. "Baron Yentillan has found an increased interest in matters literary now that he has access to a trained scribe and is no longer obliged to rely on men of little learning."

With that, Peyto stepped through the doorway and strode away, his empty left sleeve flapping like a wounded bird's wing. Yan sighed. As he finished his descent, he was pleased to note that the kettle steamed above the fire. He snagged a mug from the table on his way to the shelf where the kitchen herbs rested in their crocks. Remembering his manners, he looked about for another mug for his guest. "Tea, Fra Bern?"

"Your kindness will reap you reward," the priest replied.

"I will take that for a 'yes.'"

"Tea goes so well with honeyed crackers, don't you think?"

Yan's glance over his shoulder caught the priest's pudgy finger caressing the covered honey pot on the table. After Yan filled the pot and set the herbs, he got down the crock where they kept the crackers as well. The tea brewed, Yan joined Fra Bern at the table, where the priest had waited in polite silence. Yan imposed on Fra Bern's politeness long enough to let the steam from his mug rise and fill his nose with the fragrance of the herbs. They smelled good, especially the chamomile and mint. The priest maintained his pleasant bland expression while Yan took a long sip of his tea. Knowing he could not put matters off much longer without being as rude as the departed clerk, he put the mug down.

"I must apologize for Master Lennuick."

"That is unnecessary, Master Tanafres. I take no offense." Fra Bern's eyes were ringed with dark circles, a sign that he was also exhausted from his labors alongside Yan, but his smile held more energy than Yan felt remained in his entire body. "One of my Lord Einthof 'ss greatest teachings is that a man should know when he is ignorant and when he is knowledgeable, and that when a man is ignorant, he should seek out another who is knowledgeable, that light may come into the darkness and dispel the gloom of ignorance."

"Though I honor the gods, I've never been much for religious precepts, Fra Bern. I'm tired and in little mood for a sermon."

"My apologies, Master Tanafres. I did not mean to preach." The Einthofite hesitated, frowning slightly. "I am afraid I am feeling a bit awkward about this. You see, before you and your friends arrived, I was rather the authority around here."

And we don't need people like you around here. Yan had heard *this* speech before. He folded his hands around his mug so that the priest would not see them shake. Clearly Yan's work with the wounded was not enough to make up for his mistake, his irresponsible magic. So much for not taking offense.

The priest surprised him by continuing, "There is something about which I wish to ask your thoughts."

Fra Bern took Yan's lack of response as a signal to proceed. "You see, though my Lord Einthof is patron of arts magical as well as those scholarly, I am not versed in those arts. Though I would wish it otherwise, I have seen that my performance in the more formal arts of scholarship is less than it might be. However, in the Great Art, as I believe those of your calling name it, I am ignorant beyond the most basic theory."

Yan sighed inwardly. The *other* speech. This was not turning out to be a good day.

"I am not a teacher."

Fra Bern frowned. "Your pardon, sir. You seem to misunderstand me. I seek not teaching, but advice. You have far more experience in matters arcane than I, and I am disturbed by something that I think may be as much a matter for your sphere as mine. As I said, I am unversed in the arts magical."

"Not totally, Fra. I saw what you did with those for whom I had no medical help." The priest had healed some wounds that Yan had thought fatal. Some of the patients had subsequently died, but others had been alive when Yan could no longer stay awake; he had little doubt those same patients would be healthier today than they had been last night. Their survival was not due to anything Yan had done, but due to the healing that had come from the Einthofite's hands. If there was a greater magic than what the priest had done for those poor suffering souls, Yan didn't know what it was.

"The healing, you mean?"

"Yes, the healing."

The priest looked honestly abashed. "That was a matter of Faith, not Art. I was merely a vessel."

It certainly was a matter of power, and not a power to which Yan had access. "As you wish."

"As the Beings Above wish it."

There seemed little to gain in arguing the point. Yan's head reminded him that he was really in no shape for arguing anyway. "All right then, good priest. What is this matter in which you need the advice of a magician?"

For a moment Fra Bern said nothing, making Yan wonder what could have driven away the priest's jovial manner so thoroughly. Jowls trembling, Fra Bern seemed suddenly timid and ready to flee. His tongue appeared between his lips and quivered there for an instant before disappearing back into his mouth. He swallowed as his hand moved tentatively to the purse at his belt. He fumbled there for a moment, digging out something which he placed on the table beneath his cupped hand.

"Pray, Master Magician, what make you of this?"

The priest pulled back his hand, revealing a sparrow's egg–sized golden sphere of some smooth material—mineral?—held in a net of leather thongs. Why was this trinket so fearful to the priest? Yan poked at it with a finger and it rolled slightly, stopping when one of the thongs touched the table's surface. He could see no markings on the surface of the sphere. The thongs were knotted elaborately.

"It looks like a talisman," Yan observed.

"Indeed. I thought so as well. This is one of many found on the bodies of dead hillmen. None hereabouts recognize them as the sign of a known tribe. Most curious is that these trinkets have been found on the bodies of Turtle and Cragcat warriors alike. On warriors from all the clans, for that matter."

Yan's curiosity was piqued; the throbbing in his skull seemed to recede. "Are all the orbs like this?"

"Some of them are more elaborate, others less so, but in their essentials they are the same."

"Might it be a sign of the tribes' *haggatan*?"

"If it is so, it is a strange one, not known to the memories of any of the folk here around."

Yan poked the sphere again. It was clearly a symbol. But of what? Was it more than a symbol? These trinkets were, so far, the only thing the bregil tribesmen had in common beyond their thirst for blood. A puzzle. He realized he had been quiet for a while when the priest cleared his throat.

"So, Master Tanafres, what make you of it?"

The talk had restored some of Fra Bern's usual manner, but the priest was still hiding something. Yan stared at the trinket. "First, perhaps, you will tell me what you have already learned of it."

"Sir?"

"You have already examined this and the others and found something that bothered you, or you would not have brought it to me. What is it, Fra Bern? What about this bauble disturbs you so?"

Yan's assumption of the magician's all-knowing and commanding manner brought back Fra Bern's timidity in full. A fugitive smile flashed across the Einthofite's features. "Ah, I knew it was wise to bring the matter to you. Such perception. I am—"

"I was not asking for flattery, Fra Bern." Yan was sorry he'd spoken as he had. He liked Bern.

"My apologies," Fra Bern stammered. "I meant no offense."

Yan saw fear in the man's face. The priest was afraid of offending him. Considering what Yan had done to the gates, maybe he was justified. But Yan didn't like people being afraid of him. He tried not to sound threatening.

"Can we return to the matter to hand? Truly, it will help my understanding if you tell me what it is about these objects that bothers you?"

The priest looked uncomfortable as he struggled to select the right words. At last he blurted out, "They have an aura."

"An aura?" Yan felt nothing, but then he had not really opened his senses to the thing. "Are you sure?"

"I have felt it. It is faint but present."

"Linked to the gods?" That would be a magic not of Yan's ken, like the healing touch, but Fra Bern, a sanctified priest, would be sensitive to such ethereal vibrations.

Fra Bern hesitated for a moment, then said, "There is a sense of that." The priest shook his head, a worried frown of puzzlement overcoming his expression. "Yet it is like no holy talisman I have ever encountered."

Not holy? Could it be? "The Dark Ones?"

Fra Bern's eyes went wide. "Oh no! I would have sensed that taint."

Would you now? Yan wished he could be so certain of recognizing evil so easily. "Since you are sure this does not have the taint of evil, how do you account for the strangeness you sense?"

"I thought perhaps that the oddness might be some magical adulteration to the basic religious nature of the talisman."

An interesting thought, that. "Magic polluting the holy things?"

"I meant no offense, Master Tanafres," Fra Bern said quickly. He was sweating. Afraid again.

"Yes, yes. I know." Yan tried to sound reassuring. "No offense meant. Very well, then, I won't take any."

The priest looked relieved.

"At least not yet," Yan mumbled.

The priest's sudden, frightened look made Yan immediately feel guilty. His had been a thoughtless remark, born of tiredness and old memories that had no place in the present. He thought that he had better make amends for upsetting the man. No one liked bossy, *dangerous* magicians. He tapped a finger on the talisman. "You said there are others like this. May I see them as well? There may be something to be learned by seeing how they are different and how alike."

"Oh, of course. Of course. I will bring them to you at once."

The priest was as good as his word. Yan was still struggling with the laces on his jacket sleeve when Fra Bern returned. The priest didn't stay, pleading duties at the baron's chapel. Yan didn't mind; he preferred to be left alone to study the things; he didn't like people looking over his shoulder when he worked. But to simple observation, the collection of talismans offered nothing that the individual had not. Only when he tried to grasp their sense while in trance did anything become clear.

There *was* something to the Einthofite's fears after all. Each and every one of the stones had a sympathetic vibration indicating that they had once been linked magically in a single ritual. The strands of contact between them were clear. And beyond that, Yan had a sense of power clinging to the stones. It seemed familiar, in the way one remembers the taste of a half-forgotten but savory meal. Or the touch of half-forgotten magic.

Adain's *claviarm*.

Years ago Yan had encountered a magician who, apparently afflicted by a curse, had taken refuge in an inn near Yan's hometown. The mysterious man had died and left behind him some equally mysterious pronouncements and his *claviarm*, his magical focus. Yan, in turn, had left the talisman behind with his old master. It was a near-forgotten puzzle that he hadn't thought about in years.

But the years hadn't been the same for Yan as they had for other people. The timespell in the Scothic valley where he had met Teletha had made time strange for him. For everyone who had ventured into the hidden ruins beneath Gornal's tower, time had nearly stood still. Everywhere else, life had gone onward. Not realizing what had happened to them, they had escaped the spell, and only after they had returned to that nameless village where Larra and her father dwelt had Yan begun to understand the implications of the spell. People whom Yan had seen only a few weeks previously had lived years of their lives while Yan and the others had been under the timespell that had cloaked Gornal's valley.

Learning this, he had felt displaced from the world.

Fearful of how time had passed elsewhere, he had run away, throwing himself into his search for the secrets of Gornal's books and trying to forget a home and a family where he was sure he had been forgotten. Doubtless, having had no word of him, they thought him long dead. His mother and sister would think that; they were the only ones who had ever really cared.

It had taken time, years actually, before he came to believe that time was once again passing normally for him, and he came to feel in his bones that he was once again a part of the world. He realized then that he shouldn't have been afraid and became, instead, ashamed. The thought of how he had abandoned his family made him want to run some more. So he had. He, Teletha, and Peyto had taken to the road, ostensibly in search of secrets. Years of hunting and seeking, with little result; he had built his life around the search, to the exclusion of a normal life.

But what was a normal life for a magician? He hadn't had one back on Merom. Had he? He hadn't really worried about such things then. He had just wanted to be a magician, and wasn't that what he had been doing these last years? And now here he was, a magician, stuck in the middle of a foreign wilderness and facing what might be the beginning of a genocidal war. He was far from his old life. Far from his home and family. What did it matter that the time lost in that valley in Scothandir had robbed him of much of their lives?

What indeed? If he hadn't run away, he could have reclaimed that time. But he had run, and now he was here, in the middle of nowhere, looking down at a crudely fashioned talisman lying on the palm of his hand.

Another mystery? Another challenge to his intellect? Or just another waste of time?

For a moment he saw himself as the sphere, wrapped in a mesh of entangling circumstances beyond his ability to escape. Was that all he was?

Hot anger flared in him. Cursing, he hurled the talisman away. The sphere flew across the room, striking the center post and shattering in a cloud of amber shards. Yan was shocked to feel a ghostly burst of power. His anger evaporated.

What had he done?

4

"START PACKING," PEYTO SAID as he came through the door. The clerk slung his case on one of the pegs by the door and crossed the main room to the ladder. He continued talking as he climbed to the loft and started to rummage around in the bedchamber. "Baron Yentillan has decided that, given the lack of proper gates for the stockade, his holding is indefensible. With the population at risk, and his own hide as well, he has decided that the safest course is to move in with his good friend Baron Jost. Of course, we don't know how Baron Jost will take this turn of events. For that matter, we don't even know if Baron Jost is with us anymore, what with the *haggatan* and all. But such details are not bothering the good baron. He has decided on his course and we are all to set sail on it."

Through it all Yan stood staring down at the shattered remains of the yellow globe. Whatever he had sensed when it broke had been only a momentary fluctuation in the mana. Still, it had marked the end of the globe as a receptacle for . . . for whatever it had been a receptacle. The shards were now lifeless, showing no sign of aura that he could detect. He stamped down on them and ground them into the dirt floor just as Peyto climbed down the ladder.

"Why are you just standing there?" Peyto asked. "Weren't you listening? We're leaving this flea-infested place."

Yan didn't bother to look at him.

"Worried about losing your chance to find your precious lost city?"

"I—" Well, actually, he was. But there was more to it than that. "It's not that."

"Feeling guilty, are we?"

"Yes," Yan admitted.

"Rightfully so. I'm sure that if you hadn't messed around with magic you didn't understand, you'd still have your chance to go tromping around in the woods looking for old stones. Surely the cavalry would have seen the hill monkeys off, and the baron would be happy to stay, providing you with a nice, safe refuge in the middle of a war.

"Wake up, Yan. No matter what you'd done, we'd have had to leave. The hill tribes will be ravaging the countryside. You'd have had no chance to look for the city. Maybe after things have calmed down, we can come back."

If being unable to continue his search for the city was all that bothered Yan, things would be simpler. More immediate magic was on his mind, and he couldn't help wondering if what he had just done with the talisman might be as bad as what he had done to the gates. "People are dead because I couldn't handle the magic."

"And just as many, probably more, are alive because of what you did for them after the battle. Doubtless that bungling priest would have cost the good baron more of his subjects if he hadn't been able to rely on your medical knowledge."

"Some of those people wouldn't have needed medical help if I hadn't—"

"You can't blame yourself for everything that goes wrong. Although, Horesh as my witness, it seems that you would like to."

"That's not true. I can recognize responsibility. I know when I am the one at fault."

"About as well as you know battle magic. You made a mistake. That's all, a mistake."

Like whatever he had done with the talisman? "My magic let the bregil into the stockade."

"Some of them were already in. Came over the walls, as

I recall." Peyto rested his hand on Yan's shoulder, saying nothing more until Yan looked at him. The clerk's expression was one of sympathy. "Stop worrying over it. You're alive, aren't you? Fra Bern would tell you that Horesh is giving you the chance to correct any mistake you might have made. But you're not going to be able to do that yet." Peyto dropped his hand and gave Yan an encouraging smile. "Just now, you've got to pack."

"What's the hurry. The villagers will take time to get organized. They won't be leaving for at least half a day."

"I don't intend to be left behind."

"Then pack."

Peyto shook his head despairingly. "I won't pack those books of yours."

"Then don't."

"I won't."

"Fine."

"Fine," Peyto snapped back, turning away to return to his packing.

Yan went to the doorway and leaned against the frame. He was tired. The effort spent in studying the talismans had drawn on reserves depleted from yesterday's strenuous exertions. His head began to throb again. The doorway gave him a view of most of the courtyard. Looking about, he could see Yentillan's people working at putting things in order as though they did not yet know the steading was to be abandoned.

A man in Yentillan's livery emerged from the keep and walked to a small clump of workers. He talked, and they listened, the villagers' shoulders slumping and expressions growing grim. Yan guessed that the liveried man was the baron's messenger, the bearer of the tidings Yan had already heard. He watched the baron's man pass from building to building, talking to the crafters and servants, spreading the ill word to those who would soon have no home. In the messenger's wake people scurried, some busying themselves about their places, others hurrying off to some place outside the palisade. No doubt the latter would spread the word to the villagers and farmers. None of the people he saw looked happy. Why should they be? They had all worked hard to carve a place out of this wilderness. The thought of abandoning all they had built must be clawing their guts out.

"What's happening?" Teletha looked fresh, rested. The prawn-tail pot helm hanging from her hand and the corselet she wore shone with recent polishing. As a concession to the general unrest, she had a pistol tucked into her sword belt. She frowned slightly when she looked at him. "Has something come up, or are you still worrying about yesterday?"

Yan decided that he'd rather have her concern herself with the immediate problem. "The baron has decided to leave."

She gave a short laugh. "We soldiers are always the last to know. Still, it's probably a good decision, with the gate gone and all. That makeshift barricade won't hold a determined assault."

Did everybody have to remind him of what he'd done? "Would everybody be happier if I magicked up a new gate?"

"Easy, Yan. Even if you could, you know better than that. Haven't we seen enough of how people react to magic after it has done them a bad turn?"

She was right, of course. They'd had plenty of experience with the general dislike of magic and its repercussions. He'd known that all along, although he hadn't admitted it to himself. Was that why he hadn't done anything to strengthen the barricade? He wasn't really looking for an excuse to leave, to run away, was he? Teletha's touch on his arm brought him back from his worries.

"Maybe we should leave," he said.

She nodded, concerned. "If everyone else is going, count on it." Teletha started to say more, but a commotion at the barricade caused her to stop and turn. Yan looked, too, fearful of something, but he knew not what.

A runner, skin and clothes scarred by a rough passage through the wilderness, stumbled into the courtyard. Shrugging off worried questions and offers of help, the man staggered straight for the keep, shouting in a backwoods dialect for the baron. Yan recognized the cadences, but the man's accent was thick enough that he didn't understand more than Yentillan's name.

"What do you suppose that was all about?"

"Trouble," Teletha said simply.

"How can you tell?"

"Isn't it always trouble?" she asked cheerfully.

Yan didn't see the humor. They were in a bad situation. "Do you think it's the hillmen again?"

"Probably. We're a little far from the Nalat or Essarin for it to be saü, and there's a truce with the Rolesdakkans. The gods are not so unkind that it might be some kind of disaster."

It had to be the hill clans. Yan had a sudden vision of howling warriors descending on folk too busy packing to be on watch. "Is it an attack?"

"Not being prescient, I'll let you know when someone tells me. Meantime, let's wait and see."

"And do nothing?"

"That's right. Saves having to undo things."

Contrary to her words, however, she pulled her pistol and checked its readiness. Yan thought about going inside and digging out the one she had given him. He wasn't much of a shot; but he wasn't much of a battle magician, either, as he had so recently proven. Before Yan actually reached a decision, Raff Janden emerged from the keep, shouting for his riders.

"Boss is calling." Teletha put on her helmet and started tying the chin strap.

"Then it *is* serious trouble."

"Trouble, yes. Serious?" She shrugged. "I'll let you know."

One of Teletha's troop mates ran by the house, headed for the stables. She grabbed his arm, arresting him. "What's the fuss, Thom?"

"There's a dragon attacking the village at Homlat," the boy panted. As soon as Teletha released him, he took off again, calling back, "Captain wants us to horse right away. We're to leave soon as everyone is saddled."

"I'll be along presently," she called back.

"A dragon?" Yan couldn't believe he had heard the word correctly.

Teletha cocked her head and looked at him, a strange expression on her face. "That's what he said."

A *dragon*?

All of Yan's worries vanished in a surge of excitement. How could it be? He knew of no true report of a dragon within the memory of living man. Certainly there were travelers' tales of them in distant wild places, but they no longer existed in civilized lands. The Kingdom of Kolvin might be a backwater compared to lands of the Coronal Empire, as Peyto so frequently pointed out, but it was civilized after its own fashion. The country seemed far too tamed for such beasts to be roaming about.

Still, if it was a dragon, Yan wanted to see it.

"Just let me get my satchel."

Teletha's laugh followed him as he ducked back inside. Peyto was sorting scrolls on the table. Yan slapped him on the back as he rushed past and flung himself up the ladder.

"Come on, Peyto. Just grab what you need for a day or so."

"I'm not leaving my—"

"We'll come back for it," Yan said. In his rush he nearly tumbled to the floor as he came back down the ladder. "Come on. If you don't hurry, they'll leave without us."

"Why the sudden haste? You're the one who said that the villagers won't be moving out for another half day at least."

Yan stuffed a loaf of bread into his satchel. "Not the villagers." A half-eaten wedge of cheese followed the bread. "The horsemen." A couple of dried apples. "They're getting ready to ride."

"Horsemen? By any god who's bored enough to be listening, what are you talking about?"

"A dragon!"

Peyto stared at him. "Dragon? You're daft, boy. There aren't any more dragons. Who's the liar who said he saw one?"

Yan could hear horses in the courtyard. There wasn't time for this. "A man from Homlat. He said the village was being attacked."

"Homlat? That's half a day's ride at least. If there were a dragon, and if it were attacking, by now it would be long done with a miserable excuse for a village like Homlat.

You're wasting time better spent getting ready to leave this place."

"Captain Janden doesn't think it's a waste of time."

"Janden's an adventurer looking to make a name for himself. This messenger from Homlat is probably one of Janden's flunkies telling tall tales. The good captain has probably got a big lizard hide planted out there that he's going to bring back to the baron for a reward."

"Must you be so suspicious of everyone?"

"I must," Peyto said simply.

Yan was in no mood for Peyto's misanthropy.

"Well, Teletha's going with the cavalry, and she won't let him fool the baron. Besides, we're not leaving here without her, so we'll have to wait until they come back anyway. Come on. How can you pass up this chance?"

"Because I'm an old man and no longer a young fool."

Peyto turned back to his scroll sorting. Exasperated, Yan stared at his back for a few hammering heartbeats. Voices called back and forth in the courtyard, Janden chivvying his riders. A glance out the door showed him that Teletha was already mounted. No more time for argument. Yan ran out the door.

The tree was splintered about a foot from the ground. Captain Janden rode his horse up to it, stared at it for a moment, then backed his mount up to make room for his second. Dantil slid off his horse and moved up to crouch by the shattered tree. Yan wanted to examine it, too, but thought it best not to press himself forward.

"What do you make of it?" the captain asked quietly.

Dantil knelt by the stump, pulled loose a splinter, and sniffed at it. "Recent."

"Storm damage?"

Yan remembered last week's storm and the farmers' concern over its strength, but he didn't think its fury had been sufficient to do such damage this deep in the woods.

Spitting, Dantil shook his head. "Not lightning. Tree was healthy. There are others hereabouts that would've been broken were this a storm's doing."

Janden turned in his saddle to face Yan. His expression was sour, much as it had been when he saw Yan leading his horse out of the stable to join the riders. "Magic?"

"I sense nothing," Yan said.

The captain's mouth quirked to one side. He turned away.

"Lots of broken brush this way," Dantil called from just out of sight.

"Any sign of tracks?"

"None that I recognize," Dantil said as he came back into view. "Ground's too soft for clear track, but something went that way."

"Or came from that direction." Yan leaned forward in his saddle. "A beast?"

Dantil nodded. "A bloody big one."

"And a bloody strong one, if it split that tree," someone said.

"Could it be a dragon?" Yan asked.

Dantil looked uncomfortable and glanced at Janden. The captain sat his horse, still and grim. The scout looked back at Yan. "There're a lot of strange things in these woods, Master Magician, but I hain't seen a dragon in years of working them."

At Dantil's suggestion, they rode on.

Toward noon they came upon an isolated farmstead. There was no one about, and no dog barked as they rode into the small cluster of huts. From the condition of the place, the departure of the inhabitants must have been fairly recent, but there were no obvious signs of devastation. Janden ordered the riders to spread out and look around.

After a few minutes, Teletha called out.

"Tracks over here!"

One by one, the riders joined her by the tree line. Some swore, some gasped, but no one said much of anything after his or her first reaction to the tracks Teletha had found. The prints were extraordinary. The firm ground held a clear impression of three toes, broad and padded. In front of each toe print was a furrow, such as might be made by a dagger pressed into the dirt. Claw marks? There was something odd about the number and placement of the prints, but Yan couldn't quite say what.

Teletha placed her foot beside one of the clearest prints. Even in boots her feet were not large, but the foot of this beast dwarfed hers. Yan estimated the distance from the claw mark to the impression of the hind pad to be three times the length of Teletha's foot.

Squatting by the edge of the trees, Dantil sighted along the trackway. "It walks like a bird."

"What?" Yan walked behind the scout and bent over to sight along the path as Dantil was doing.

The veteran pointed. "See how the toes turn inward to the center of the track. Like a pigeon's."

Yan saw that it was so. He understood now what seemed so odd about the trackway. There weren't enough prints to account for the passage of a four-legged beast like a dragon. These tracks were indeed like a bird's, although their enormous size had kept him from realizing that at first. Having put aside the issue of size, he saw that this beast did walk like a bird—a bit like a pigeon at that. But a pigeon that left tracks with so great a stride would be the size of a house.

"How long ago did it pass?" Janden asked.

"Hain't sure." Dantil's brow furrowed with thought. "A while. Maybe a day."

"Can you track it?" Yan asked.

Dantil eyed Yan as if wondering what rock he had crawled out from under.

"Tracks go back into the woods, Captain," Teletha said. "The beast seems to like it there better than the open. It'll be more at home there than the horses."

Some of the men started to grumble, but Janden spoke loudly. "I don't like going in there either, but following it is the fastest way of catching up. So, mount up and get your crossbows out. Keep your eyes open."

There was more grumbling, but no one disobeyed.

They traveled for more than an hour without incident until a resonant bellow cut the still air. The sound reminded Yan of the steam horn of the bregil mining operation near his hometown. The horses reacted to the sound. Some bucked, some reared, all rolled their eyes and whinnied with fear. Yan barely kept his seat as his mount fought to run; he managed to rein it back. Teletha had more trouble;

her horse backed her into a low-branched tree. A stout limb thwacked her helmet. The gonging sound affrighted the animal further, and it reared, dancing in a circle. Teletha was thrown, but before Yan could calm his own horse enough to dismount, she was back on her feet, swearing and grabbing for her animal's reins. None of the other riders were spilled, although several had to drop their crossbows to manage their mounts.

Fortunately for them all, the beast made no appearance.

With the horses calmed, they recovered their weapons and rode on. The woods thinned, and they found themselves among rolling hills dotted with scattered steadings and copses of trees. The ground here was too stony for farming, but Dantil pointed away to the west, toward the mountains, and said, "Homlat hain't more'n another hour's ride that way." The riders turned their horses toward the village.

That hour was nearly up when Yan reined in. His mount Shean was normally a stolid beast, but something was causing her to twitch her ears nervously. The riders had just emerged from a small wood. Across the open space of a planted field there was another grove. Something, a hint of motion, in the shadow of those trees caught Yan's attention. The bright afternoon light made it hard to see anything in the darkness under the leafy canopy. Squinting, he strained to discern what, if anything, he had seen.

There was nothing moving there now.

Shean whickered uneasily.

The other riders were slowing, spreading out across the field. They seemed relieved to be out from under the shadows of the woods and were making jokes about each other's nervousness. Yan could understand the relief that motivated such humor, but his unease about the copse ahead kept him from sharing their laughter. He stared at the tree line, trying to convince himself that he was overreacting. But then he saw it: a huge shadow among the tree trunks. The shape wasn't what he would have guessed.

The beast?

"There's something in the trees ahead," he called out.

Janden signaled a halt. Heads craned in the direction Yan indicated, but no one pointed out the beast.

With difficulty, Yan re-located the beast; its striped hide blended very well with the dappled shadow under the leaves. The beast stood on hind legs like a bird's but thick and strongly muscled and near big around as a small tree. The creature's body was held horizontally, in line with its long tail. Its forelimbs dangled, clawed fingers clear of the ground. Those limbs looked small, but now having some appreciation for the beast's size, Yan estimated them to be larger than a man's. The claws on the fingers were as long as daggers; they would be as sharp. But those claws were not the most terrible thing about the creature—its head was. The head was in profile, and Yan could see a knobby ridge adorning a skull the size of a man's torso. Short horns projected above its glittering eye and yellowed teeth jutted down from the upper jaw, lying exposed along the lower. Those jaws seemed to stretch almost the whole length of the creature's head, and they were curved in a devilish grin.

There was a rustle in the brush near the beast, but the monster paid the motion no heed. Instead, it turned its snout toward the riders. Under the regard of those tiny, sparkling orbs, Yan felt like a mouse under the glare of a hawk.

In two strides, the monster cleared the trees that had sheltered it. Shean stirred restively beneath Yan. His was not the only animal to react to the appearance of the beast; in the field the horsemen were having difficulty controlling their mounts. Janden shouted to his men to spread out, to get clear of each other so they could shoot. The beast charged toward them, bellowing once with an awful, hissing roar. Its horned head seemed to disappear behind a maw filled with enormous teeth. The riders, disordered already, were thrown into chaos as the horses were panicked by the creature's threatening bellow.

To Yan's horror, Teletha's horse, bucking madly, careened into the monster's path. With the beast less than a dozen yards away, the horse reared, tossing Teletha from its back. Screaming in terror, the animal began to run; even free of a rider's weight it could not escape. In three strides the monster was by its side. The great head snapped down and the jaws closed on the horse's neck. With a hideous crunching, the teeth scythed through flesh and bone as the jaws closed. The horse's decapitated body ran a further three paces before stumbling forward to collapse. The monster drew back from its strike, head cocked to one side, staring at its victim.

For an instant, everything was still.

A pistol shot shattered the silence and Yan saw a gout of flesh and blood erupt from the beast's thigh. Its head whipped around, and it snapped at the air by its side. Then it looked up, directly at Janden, who was exchanging pistols. The captain fired again, but his shot went wide. His action inspired the horsemen. Bolts flew. More missed than hit, but at least half a dozen buried themselves in the creature's flesh. One caromed off the monster's snout, leaving behind a bloody furrow. The wounds only seemed to enrage the creature. Roaring, it charged. The horses, barely held in check by their riders, went berserk.

The beast was among them.

With its first bite the monster decapitated another horse, while a sweep of its tail bowled over two more. Riders sprawled, scrambling away as the beast moved after them. Dismounted riders and panic-maddened horses fled from the beast ravening among them. Janden had dismounted and was using his crossbow to put bolts into the creature, but the missiles only seemed to encourage the beast to attack more fiercely. Men and horses died, and the monster's jaws dripped with gore. Someone, Yan couldn't tell who, was struck a glancing blow by one of the beast's feet. He went tumbling to the ground. With its next step, the beast planted its foot on the man's legs, crushing them into the ground. His scream was high-pitched and piercing. He went on screaming as the beast strode after other prey.

Yan's heart went cold when he saw for whom the creature headed: Teletha, slowing rising from ground.

Yan spurred his horse, urging it toward her, but the animal balked, too frightened by the beast to respond to Yan's unfeeling use of the spurs. Made helpless by his rebellious animal, Yan shouted for Teletha to run.

She did, but toward her fallen horse. She dove behind the corpse, and the monster halted its pursuit when she disappeared from its sight. She appeared a moment later and the creature started forward again. Crouched by her dead mount, she awaited the beast's charge. It obliged her, mouth gaping wide. As it closed, she rose, pistol in either hand.

She fired one, smoke gouting toward the beast. It came on. She fired her second pistol, and this time the discharge smoke was scattered by the bulk of the charging beast. Teletha tried to throw herself aside from the creature's charge and almost succeeded. One pistoning leg struck her, upending her and sending her crashing to the ground.

The beast planted its foot on the corpse of Teletha's horse and started to swing its tail around in a turn. Its body responded to the motion, turning back toward Teletha. But as the beast twisted around, the horse's body slid beneath it. Unbalanced, the monster started to topple, jaws still reaching for Teletha.

The ground trembled as the beast crashed into it.

It lay there, sides heaving and forelimbs twitching. It might have been stunned.

Shean refused to approach the monster. Jumping to the ground, Yan abandoned his horse and ran toward Teletha. She was struggling to rise, clearly disoriented. She was only a few yards from the beast and, to Yan's horror, she started crawling toward it. Yan ran faster. His breath burned in his chest as he tried to reach her before she came within range of those terrible teeth. He launched himself at her and knocked her down only a yard from the beast's head. His nose full of the creature's stench of gore and rotted meat, he watched as its eyelid slowly opened and the eye swiveled to stare at them.

Yan felt himself suspended in time, hung upon an eternal moment. Still, his heart hammered, his lungs labored. He saw as he rarely saw. The air sparkled and he saw the beast outlined in a sputtering aura of glory, its life linked to his and Teletha's by the mana strings of possibility. Predator and prey, they hovered on the brink of consummating the eternal ritual of life and death.

Janden rushed up to them and raised his crossbow to his shoulder. Yan put all his strength into wishing that the captain's shot would be good as Janden put his bolt into the beast's eye. Its head whipped up, jaws snapping. The monster's head crashed down again and its teeth gouged into the earth.

The eternal moment faded and time was again as it was. Returned to his mundane senses, Yan helped Teletha rise. She was unsteady, but seemed to be coming back to herself.

"Tough bastard," she said.

"Deadly," Janden agreed.

She looked the creature over. "Could such a beast be anything but a dragon? The old descriptions must be wrong."

"Perhaps they might be wrong with regard to a physical description; there is some discrepancy among them," Yan said. "But they are clear and unanimous in one matter: dragons are magical. This beast used no magical abilities. Whatever it is, it is not a dragon."

Teletha frowned. "I don't know. The hide looks like something I saw once exhibited in Sharhumrin as a dragon hide."

"I have seen a similar hide myself, and it, too, was said to be that of a dragon." Yan had been very young and the memory wasn't clear. "Wherever such hides came from, I doubt they came from a beast like this one."

It was not the dragon he had come seeking, but it was a strange and wondrous beast. In an odd way, it reminded him of the great mountain lizards of his home island of Merom. But none of those were so massive, and certainly none ever strode about on their hinder limbs. And none had ever shown themselves to be so dangerous.

He approached the corpse more closely.

"Careful, it's still twitching," Teletha warned.

"But dead enough." He was confident of that. "For all that it strode about like a bird, its skin is a reptile's, and they are notorious for the length of time they move after death. There is no volition in such movement. I shall be safe enough."

"I'd rather you didn't go near it till it stopped twitching."

"Unnecessary caution. You sound like Peyto."

Yan ran his hand along the bumpy ridges above the beast's snout. The aura he had sensed as the beast lay dying was unusual. As with all living things, the aura faded with the fading of life; but sometimes one could learn things from studying even a dissipating aura. He awakened his arcane senses in the hope that, now that his mind was calmer, he could discern more than he had before.

He grunted in surprise at what he felt.

"What is it?" Teletha asked. She stood at his shoulder, and her sword was in her hand.

He didn't understand. Perplexed, he mumbled, "I sense something."

"Magic? Is this beast a dragon after all?"

"It's not magic exactly. It's more like the echo of magic."

"What in the demon hells do you mean an *echo* of magic?" Janden demanded.

Lost in the puzzle, Yan barely noticed the captain's attitude. "I don't really know what I mean. I've never felt anything like it before."

As he said the words Yan knew they weren't true. There was something familiar about what he was feeling. Something cold and distant. Something different from the magic he knew. When he tried to reach for understanding, it slipped away. He was confused, his thoughts unclear; he didn't have words to put to them.

Even as he tried to make sense of the magic's faint taste, the feeling faded. There was an aftersense, an odd sort of echo. Had he been dealing with a magic that he knew, he would have said it was the sort of personal mark a magician left on the mana he used. He sensed another sort of familiarity as well, but one that he recognized more clearly and remembered from a more recent encounter.

The hand that had united the talismans taken from the bregil had taken part in whatever magic was involved in this beast!

"There is a connection between this beast and the orb talismans," he announced.

"The ones the hillmen were wearing?" Janden asked.

"Yes, those."

"Is this beast theirs, then?" Teletha asked.

"I don't know. The correspondence is tenuous."

"Are you sure that you're not just confused?"

Reluctantly Yan admitted, "No."

"Mount up!" Janden's shouted order came as a surprise. "We're moving out."

"But I want to study the beast's remains," Yan complained.

"I said we're leaving," Janden snapped. "You've got as long as it takes to gather the horses."

"What about the wounded? They'll not be ready to move."

"Haven't you looked around? The beast left no *wounded.*"

Was that true? The silence in the field suggested that it was so. Such a terror, this beast. All the more reason to learn about it. "Why should we be in such a hurry? The danger is over."

Janden's eyes narrowed. "Listen, Master Magician. I didn't invite you on this trip. You want to stay, it's your business. When the hill monkeys come whooping through here maybe you can talk them into helping you study the beast's remains. I'll waste no more good soldiers on it."

"Don't you understand the opportunity here? Why—"

"I understand you're a troublemaker." Janden stalked away, shouting orders to gather the horses. Teletha remained by Yan while he poked and prodded at the beast. Before he had begun any serious study of the creature, Janden was back. The six surviving riders were with him.

"I gave the order to mount, Schonnegon," Janden said.

"My horse is dead, Captain."

"Martinn doesn't need his anymore."

Teletha looked from the captain to Yan. "I have to go."

Soldiers did have to take orders, but Yan wasn't a soldier. "All right."

"Yan, the captain's right. It's dangerous here."

"But the beast . . . "

"Is dead. And it's too heavy to haul back. Forget it and come back with us."

"But—"

"But nothing. You can't stay out here alone. The baron's still planning on leaving the area. There'll be no one to protect you. And no one to keep Peyto in check."

As if she couldn't accomplish that last task herself. Still, there were wild hill bregil somewhere around, and it was dangerous out here. And the beast, while intriguing, wasn't a dragon after all. In deference to the worry he saw in her eyes, he agreed.

They rode back to Yentillan's stronghold.

5

"HORESH SHALL SHINE IN GLORY on you for your compassion, Master Tanafres."

"As He will, Fra Bern." Yan settled himself awkwardly on the seat, barely finding room for his lanky frame in the space left by the rotund priest. He spent a moment to make sure his horse's reins were securely tied to the wagon. "I am only doing what is fit and proper for any man with my skills, poor though they are. What man with the ability to lessen suffering could ignore the unfortunates in your wagon, and then find himself able to gaze in contentment upon his own reflection?"

"Far too many men, I fear." The folds of flesh in Fra Bern's face bunched into a frown, but only for a moment. "I give thanks to all the gods that you are not one of them. Your patients praise your skill, at least those conscious enough to do so. Why, Baron Yentillan himself has nothing but praise for your work on behalf of his subjects. Though I know you think little of my opinion, I must say that I have learned much simply by watching you. Your knowledge of salves and ointments far exceeds my own. And your deft manner with—"

"Fra Bern."

"Yes, Master Tanafres?"

"You did not ask me to ride with you to discuss my medical technique."

For a moment, it seemed that the priest might dispute Yan's conclusion, then he said, "No, I did not."

They rode along in silence for several minutes. Since the priest did not yet appear ready to broach the real subject, Yan was willing to wait. But it would be a long, boring ride to Baron Jost's domain if Fra Bern never found the courage to say what was on his mind. Yan wondered what could still the tongue of the voluble priest so thoroughly.

When Fra Bern did speak, he used Nitallan rather than the Kolvinic in which they had been speaking. Formal Nitallan at that, which immediately lent an air of gravity.

"I continue to worry over the matter of the orb talismans, Master Tanafres. I find them a puzzle beyond my ability, and, though I pray daily to my Lord Einthof, I have yet to be graced with enlightenment on the subject."

"Though Lord Einthof is the patron of scholars, He is chary with His enlightenment. I have heard it said that He cherishes the task of seeking out the hidden better than the result."

Fra Bern chuckled, his solemnity gone on the light breeze. "Sometimes it does seem so, does it not?"

"So, good priest, what is it about the talismans that causes you to ask your god for answers?"

The priest's answer was delayed as he needed to encourage the mules up a hill. "I have looked into the chronicles. Many are the accounts of the hill clans sweeping down from their chill and barren haunts? This is nothing new to Kolviners. We have dealt with such raids in the past.

"Fewer are the accounts of *haggatan*. But we have dealt with the wars inspired by the bregil's spiritual mentors, and always, as Great Lord Horesh and His court are superior to the debased spirits guiding those poor folk of the hills, so are we Kolviners superior to the hill folk. We have always broken the confederations of tribes.

"Yet, nowhere in the chronicles have I found mention of the hill bregil following a single spirit. Nowhere have I encountered mention of the warriors of the *haggatan* bearing a sign common to them all."

"A sign like the orbs?"

"Exactly." Driving the wagon took Fra Bern's attention

for a while. "The soldiers say that the hill tribes are being particularly aggressive."

Yan had heard the same from Teletha.

"They fight almost as if inspired," the priest added.

"Good war chiefs are always inspirational to their warriors."

"That is true. Yet I find myself thinking that the tribes may be inspired by more than a strong military leader. I wonder, could these orbs, so strangely like the orb of our Great Lord Horesh Himself, be a sign that the hill bregil have been adopted by a deity spirit of some consequence, one arrogant enough to mock the Sun Lord by mimicking His sign?"

"Didn't you say that you would know if the talismans were touched with the power of the Dark Ones?"

"I believe so."

Yan wanted to believe so also. "So the Under Court and their Great One are not involved."

"That is both my belief and my most fervent hope, Master Magician. No sane man would wish for a return of the Dark Ones."

No *sane* man had ever been involved with the entities of the Under Court. If neither of the supernatural Courts were involved, just what was Fra Bern suggesting? An unknown deity? "I am a magician, Fra Bern, not a religious philosopher, but if you are postulating what it would appear you are, you tread on dangerous grounds.

The priest was sweating, nervous. "Master Tanafres, can I trust you to consider a postulation simply as a postulation, and to attach no certainty that the proposer holds to each and every aspect of the postulation?"

"I am no inquisitor."

Fra Bern's eyes darted to Yan, confirming Yan's suspicions of where the conversation was headed.

"I place myself in your hands, in the faith that you are a man of honor as well as one of knowledge," Fra Bern rushed on, whispering. "The unknown power I sense in the talismans can only spring from one source: the divine. Yet I am sure that there is nothing of the Celestial Court about them, and have no reason to believe they are tools of the

Under Court either. Logic demands another source, yet dogma allows only the existence of the Lords of Light and Darkness. I fear that these talismans have a source other than the divine Lords we know."

Yan was impressed that the priest had the courage to express that thought. Men, even clerics, had been burned in Horesh's purifying fires for suggesting such heresy.

"Such thoughts are far afield from the Triadic Church's view of the world. Are you really prepared to walk such a path?"

"Prepared?" Fra Bern shook his head sadly. "No, I am not. I am a minor priest of my Lord Einthof, Lord of Mysteries and a Prince of the Great Lord Horesh's Celestial Court. I have spent my life believing in the unity of the Court, its opposition to the Under Court, and the eternal duality of the Great Beings. Each day my prayers are formed in those beliefs. All my life I have risen to face the day armored in those beliefs, comforted by them. I understood the world in that light, as much as an ignorant man may. This day has dawned differently. What we are seeing here is strange and beyond my understanding. As a servant of my Lord Einthof, I vowed to seek truth. In my probing for truth, I have uncovered fear."

"I think you see too much in this matter," Yan said soothingly. "I see no need to seek the divine as an explanation when all may be explained as a strange form of magic, one unknown to me. For there is magic in those talismans, of that I am sure. Magic is a natural force, as much a part of the world as the elements and the turning of the seasons. It seems likely that you are sensing the magic, that in some way it stirs a reaction in you. Perhaps you are a sensitive. Lacking experience in the Art, you could easily misinterpret the unfamiliar sensations in a more familiar light, mistaking a manifestation of the Art for some ill-defined divinity."

The priest seemed unconvinced. "And if it is not so? What if it is truly Other?"

"There seems little to justify such conclusions."

"It is not man's place to justify the divine."

"Nor is it his place to create the divine out of vague misunderstandings."

Shocked, Fra Bern stammered, "Do you suggest that I seek to raise a false god?"

"Nothing of the kind, good priest. I merely suggest that you are misinterpreting what you sense."

"I wish I could believe your interpretation," Fra Bern said with a sigh. "Do you recall the largest of the talismans?"

"The carved one?"

"Yes. That one exactly."

Yan recalled it clearly. Of all of the orbs, it was the one which disturbed him the most, although not from any sense of otherworldly power. For all its size and its richer appearance and silver wire setting, that particular talisman was no different from the others in its essence. At least as far as he could tell. Did the priest know otherwise?

He recalled the talisman's image to his mind, puzzling as he had before over the sinuous shapes writhing across its surface. Those shapes tugged at his memory, evoking a sense of familiarity that he could not quite place.

"I have seen signs such as those on the surface of the orb before," Fra Bern announced.

Yan knew that he had as well. Somewhere.

"Where was that?"

Fra Bern looked nervously around. The villagers trudging along beside the wagon continued to ignore those aboard the vehicle. The Nitallan spoken by Yan and the priest was the language of the Church and of international commerce, but a tongue little spoken in this distant corner of Kolvin. The nobles spoke it, priests, merchants, and some soldiers as well, but the farmers and crafters had little need of it. Unable to understand what they heard, the local folk were paying no attention to the riders. Nevertheless, Fra Bern continued in a whisper.

"In the forest, in a certain place, there are stones, ancient and overgrown, and upon those stones are shapes, symbols of meaning I believe, like unto those carved upon the orb."

"Are these stones standing stones?" It might be a ritual place such as dotted the coastal kingdoms, a relic of the ancient empires. "Like the circle at Lentorach?"

"No. They are like nothing else I have ever seen."

"Except the carving on the orb."

"Except that. Yes."

"Perhaps the hillmen know the place as well," Yan suggested. "Perhaps they copied the designs on the orb from those on the stones."

"That could be so. Yet even in that I find cause for concern."

"Because . . . "

Fra Bern hesitated, clearly struggling with what to say next. Finally he set his jaw and drew a deep breath. "My Lord is Einthof, Master Tanafres. Perhaps I am not the best of His followers, but I pray not the worst. I can say without fear of contradiction that my Lord finds some worth in me. You have seen that He lets me aid those in dire physical need from time to time. Also from time to time, He has shown me in other ways that I have some small favor in His eyes."

"What exactly do you mean?"

"I have dreams, Master Tanafres." Quickly, the priest added, "Not often, mind you. But I have learned that I must trust such dreams, for my Lord chooses them to convey to me some of His infinite knowledge."

"I thought you said that you hadn't received any enlightenment."

"Enlightenment entails understanding, Master Tanafres. In that I am lacking."

"So what have you dreamed about?"

"I have dreamed of the place of the stones." The priest closed his eyes. His chins quivered. When he spoke, his voice seemed to come from far away. "I see the stones in my dream, shining under the light of a single moon, but that moon is not any of the Ladies. It is larger even than V'delma's orb. It is something else, and it owns the night sky.

"Under the light of that strange moon I see the ghosts of towers and halls unlike any built by man. The towers are tall, slender spires of a strange beauty, and the halls all are broad and strong with walls of odd curves. I walk among them in my dreams, and no soul do I meet. I do not find this strange, for I know that the stones of those buildings fell to the earth long before the first king of Kolvin was crowned, before even the woefully fallacious worshipers of the Dark Ones ruled the land.

"All of the buildings have carving on them. Sinuous glyphs that twist, almost writhing with a life of their own. In the carvings that adorn many of the buildings, I see a symbol repeated. I know only that the sign represents a name. I sense that I am on the verge of understanding the symbol, of recognizing the name, but something prevents me. I raise my eyes to the heavens to beseech the Celestial Beings for Their aid, but the only thing in the sky is the lone moon. A golden orb. Not a plain orb, but one with a dark stripe, narrow at either end and wider in the center. It is an eye, watching me."

The priest's voice trailed off.

"And?" Yan asked anxiously.

"And it is then that I awake," the priest said in his normal voice. He shrugged apologetically. "I have had this dream each night since the day that word came of the dragon at Homlat."

The same day that Yan had broken one of the orbs. Did that have any connection with the priest's dreams? Yan was too afraid to ask.

"What do you think of my dream, Master Tanafres?"

"I am not an interpreter of dreams," Yan said. He didn't like significant dreams; they defied understanding. Such dreams disturbed him. He liked them even less when they touched upon something involving him.

"I had hoped you could help me understand what I see in the dream. Look here. I have made a sketch of what I can recall of the symbols." The priest tugged a folded piece of smudged paper from within his gown and passed it across to Yan. Fra Bern looked around to see if anyone had seen, but as before, they were being ignored.

Yan unfolded the paper. Sketches were scattered across the page. Some Yan had never seen before, but others were familiar from years of study; he had been puzzling over them in Gornal's books. One symbol drew his gaze. That one was little more than a squiggle that curved back on itself once then once again, like a sidewinding serpent. Three zigzag lines crossed the middle of the curve. The shape nagged, at once alien and familiar. In a flash of memory, Yan saw another, less complete, version of the symbol superimposed over the crude drawing in his hand. In memory, he held a *claviarm* into which that symbol was engraved. Adain's *claviarm*. What possible connection could that old mage have had with the ancient city of Fra Bern's dream? And what with the orb talismans? This was a mystery that needed attention.

Fra Bern cleared his throat and meekly offered, "I could show you the place."

The thought of doing so clearly terrified the priest. Yan was intrigued by the man's reaction. "Why?"

For a while, the priest didn't answer. Finally, he said, "I must know what the orbs have to do with those stones."

And know whether they are connected to your Other? Yan thought it unwise to ask the question aloud; he was confident he knew the answer, and the asking would only disturb the priest. Whatever the priest's reasons, Yan was more than ready to accept Fra Bern's offer to show him the place of the stones.

The fields they passed were ripe with unharvested crops, emerald and golden in the late summer sun. The farmers trudging along with the column rarely looked at the fields, and when they did, Teletha heard them mutter curses under their breath. Those curses were followed by prayers to V'delma, begging the Mistress of the Fields not to mistake the farmer's rancor toward the circumstances keeping them from the fields for a rejection of that Bright Lady's bounty. Teletha didn't understand why the farm folk were so angry; she thought they should be relieved to be free of the work of harvest. As refugees they would be facing difficulties, but difficulties were a person's lot in any case. Why begrudge a lost opportunity for backbreaking labor? She knew no soldier who would curse so when relieved of a chore.

Taking advantage of her new position as sergeant of a troop of light horse, Teletha rode back along the column. If anyone asked, she would have said that she was checking on her troopers, but it wasn't her troopers she wanted to see. She found Peyto astride his nag and leading their pack-horse. Yan wasn't with him. Peyto gave her a sour look as she turned her horse and fell in beside him.

Nodding his head toward her mount, Peyto asked, "How much of your pay was assessed against the worth of that beast?"

She shrugged. With the baron retreating to the safety of his neighbor's holdings, there wouldn't be much in the way of pay. "Won't matter. My contract is as good as over. I'm grateful enough that I'm getting to ride to Baron Jost's place instead of walking." Remembering her encounter with the monster reptile that had killed her previous horse, she shivered briefly in the afternoon sun. "By Vehr's sword, I'm lucky to be here at all. I'll not fret about a few plaques of silver."

"We'll need all the money we can get to travel back to the empire."

"Do you really think he's ready for that?"

Peyto didn't need to ask to whom she referred. "It is the wisest course. He will see that once we have reached Baron Jost's holding."

"He'll see we haven't the money to live a week in Sharhumrin."

"We need not go directly to the capital. Perhaps not even to Sessandir at all. There are other islands, other opportunities. For Baron Yentillan, I have corresponded with a merchant on Omsess, and I believe that there might be positions with that gentleman's business that would suit all three of us."

She was surprised that he had included her in his plans. Still, he was missing the sticking point. "Yan has always insisted that Sharhumrin is the only place in the empire worth living in. Why should his mind have moved on this issue?"

"Have you not noticed how unsettled he has been since the attack on the stockade?"

"I've noticed he's been a bit distracted."

"A mild description. He is clearly vexed; and I believe that he may be coming to see the futility of this quest to unravel the secrets of these pox-ridden books we have hauled all over the coastal kingdoms. This, I believe, is the first step to reason. He will listen, you'll see." Peyto smiled at her. "He will especially listen if you speak to him about it, Mistress Schonnegon."

"Sergeant," she said stiffly, just to see how he'd react.

The smile vanished. "Beg pardon, Sergeant. I meant no slight to your military rank."

Teletha laughed. "I'm sure you would have used it had you thought it would have disposed me to favor your scheme. No, don't protest. We've traveled far together, Master Lennuick, and I have come to know you somewhat. I understand you better than you think."

"I do not believe that I care to be understood by you," Peyto said, scowling.

Teletha pretended to scratch her cheek, trusting her gauntlet cuff to hide her grin. "Well, in any case. I would be glad to return to the empire, and I believe that your intent to stay away from Sharhumrin may be a course of wisdom. At least for the time being. But working for a merchant? I don't know. It sounds awfully sedentary."

"Traveling may be fine for you young folk, but I am much too old to vagabond about the countryside."

"Then why have you been doing it these last few years?"

Peyto said nothing, just snapped his head forward and stared ahead. Teletha saw him shift his left shoulder slightly. The motion caused the empty sleeve of his coat to slip from his lap and dangle by his side. Absently, he returned it to its former position, tucking the cuff between him and the saddle bow.

The clerk had lost his left arm to a shark and, had it not been for Yan's actions, Peyto would have died that day. Teletha understood that sort of debt, but she was surprised that the scrawny old clerk would feel the weight of it. Perhaps she didn't understand him so well after all. She'd worry about it some other time since she had not come back to talk to Peyto. She decided to let the clerk off the hook if he would direct her to Yan.

"Where has our mutual friend gotten off to now, Master Lennuick?"

"He said he was going back to check on the wagon with the wounded. More likely he's in conference with that backwoods scholar, Fra Bern."

"Shall I find out for you?"

"Do as you please." Under his breath he added, "You always do."

Teletha turned her horse around, wondering if he had meant her to hear or if age had withered his hearing enough that he did not realize how loudly he spoke. The clerk's packhorse had barely passed when she spotted a troop of cavalry cutting across the fields at a gallop, headed for the front of the column. She made out Raff Janden at their head. She urged her mount on; there might not be much time to talk to Yan.

Yan was indeed with the priest, though any tending of the wounded was apparently concluded. The two of them were perched on the seat of the ambulance wagon. As Teletha rode up, Yan stuffed something into his doublet. It looked like a scrap of paper.

"Good day," she greeted them. "What passes?"

The sweating priest looked sideways at Yan. Yan himself hesitated. Clearly they had been speaking of something that they thought of import, and that they thought might not be her business.

"We were pondering the plight of Yentillan's people," Yan said.

"And have you solved all their problems?" she asked.

"All of this morning's. We have yet to take on this afternoon's."

She let herself be led into light banter. She'd do better at finding out what was going on once she got Yan alone. She was content to wait. The faltering conversation was stuttering to a halt when she noticed cavalry headed in their direction. She was interested to see that they were not just Janden's light horse; Sir Bryyan and a half dozen heavily armored men-at-arms were clattering back along the column as well.

"Now what?" Yan asked. He sounded annoyed.

Teletha shrugged. She hadn't been told.

"Form up," Janden called as he passed.

"Duty calls," she said to Yan. She turned her horse to follow along. "I'll see you in camp tonight."

"I thought we were to reach Baron Jost's town tonight?" Fra Bern asked with a plaintive note in his voice. The fat priest wouldn't have a good time sleeping out in the elements.

"Not at the rate the column's moving," she pointed out. She urged her mount to catch up to the other riders.

The armored cavalry reined in at the back of the column, but Janden's riders kept on. Her troop formed up around her as they headed off toward the hills. All her troop asked questions, wondering what was going on.

"I'll tell you when I know," she said.

As usual, dear Captain Janden was keeping his plans to himself.

"How can you want to go haring off into the wilderness with that priest?" Peyto's expression was sullen, not at all what Yan had expected.

"Surely you understand the opportunity here. This is the first real hint that what I've been looking for is actually out there." Yan waved his arm in a broad arc, taking in half the forest. "It might be the end of the quest. The gates to Ul-Schuttariat might be in the next valley over. Fra Bern has seen the stones carved in arcane fashion."

"Ul-Schuttariat?" Peyto's tone was skeptical.

Yan nodded. "It might be."

"More likely a bregil sacrificial ring. That's a wilderness out there, full of hills and trees and rocks and wild animals. If there was a city out there, don't you think that someone, just *one* of the locals, would have heard of it?"

"Fra Bern has. He has seen the stones." Peyto usually scorned clerical mysticism, so Yan didn't think it wise to mention the priest's dreams.

"What makes you think that, in the course of randomly stumbling around in the woods, this priest has found something that has been lost for centuries? Something that, I might point out, you yourself have been seeking, without success, for several years?"

"He's been here, and I haven't until recently. I told you

it was out here somewhere. I think he's found it. The carvings he describes are much like some of the symbols in Gornal's books."

"The symbols that the charlatan in Yareffi described were 'much like the ones in Gornal's books,' but they weren't what you were looking for either. The priest saw a few carved chunks of rock, not a city."

"Ul-Schuttariat was built before the time of Casorn, and the city he built is in ruins. There would not be much of Ul-Schuttariat left standing. The people about here would not recognize what lay before them; they are an unlettered folk."

"And you are an unthinking fool."

Yan didn't say anything. He just t ok up his satchel.

"What about your precious patien̩s?" Peyto asked.

"They'll be fine. There's little enough that I'm doing for them anyway. We can be back before dark. At worst, tomorrow. The column is moving slowly, we'll have no trouble catching up."

"There are wild bregil out there, and they're getting closer. They might attack the column at any time."

"It's not that bad." Yan hoped he was correct. "Teletha would have said something if it was."

"She wouldn't have gone off to reinforce Janden's scruffy crew if it wasn't bad. Nor would Sir Bryyan be lurking about at the rear, staring at every quivering bush."

"The riders are just doing some more scouting. Bryyan's rear guard is just a precaution." Yan didn't understand Peyto's reluctance. Usually the clerk was as curious as himself.

"What about the beasts like that—what did you call it?"

"*Terriserpens.*"

"And from what the soldiers said, it *was* a most terrible reptile. There might be others like it out there."

Yan refused to be intimidated. "There might."

"Or is that it? You were annoyed that Janden didn't let you stay and take that beast apart. You want to see another one of those *terriserpens.* These rocks are just an excuse to go into the forest and look for one."

"I saw the beast, and you didn't. Were I to go seeking one, I'd want more that an old clerk and a fat priest by my

side. By preference, a company of Imperial arquebusiers."
Seeing Peyto's sneer, Yan decided to switch tactics. "Look,
this is just a scouting trip, a chance to look around. We
won't be staying out there. We can't abandon Teletha.
She's bound to accompany Baron Yentillan all the way to
Jost's domain. After we get there, she'll be free, and things
will be different. The three of us can come back if we've
found anything important." Yan decided to try a gentler
tack. "I would really like your opinion on the stones."

Peyto ignored the offering. "You haven't even seen these
lumps of rock, and already you're planning a return trip.
You listen to that backwoods priest prattle on and take it all
in, but you won't listen to a sensible argument. I don't
understand, I truly don't. Are a few carved rocks worth the
risk of traveling out there?"

"Be reasonable, Yan. Back in the empire there are scholars who could probably read to you from the books. What
need have you of burrowing through the mud in the woods
when we could sail to Sharhumrin and find someone who
probably already knows everything in those moldering
tomes?"

Find someone who would take the secrets in Gornal's
books for his own, more likely. Yan had long ago abandoned that course, and Peyto should have known better.
"Then you won't come."

"You shouldn't go."

Yan bridled at the old man's tone. "You're not my
father, to give me leave or deny it."

"If I were your father, I'd surely deny it," Peyto snapped
back.

"You're *not* him, and I don't need to listen to you? If you
won't come, at least lend us your horse. Your nag is faster
than the fra's donkey, and we'll be back sooner with it. You
can ride on the ambulance wagon, if you don't want to
walk."

"Take the swaybacked beast if it pleases you. It was
bought with money you earned. You needn't ask me. It's
plain that you don't hear my words."

Peyto said more, but Yan gave up listening.

6

RAFF DIDN'T LIKE WHAT he was seeing. Didn't like it at all.

All the clans that had attacked Yentillan's stronghold were represented in the column winding through the valley. Such an alliance was bad enough, but he also saw the totem signs of at least half a dozen more. The new clans were small ones, true, but his last information had been that at least two of those tribes were feuding with the Cragcats.

The bregil warriors below were in greater numbers than they had been for the attack on Yentillan. Raff estimated at least five hundred warriors. There could no longer be any doubt that what was happening was more than simple raiding. Still, he had seen no signs of a true *haggatan*. No shamans. No screaming, painted fanatics. And if it wasn't *haggatan* . . .

The beast at Homlat had frightened him. Its appearance hinted at what might be behind the gathering of the clans. Yet Raff had seen no sign other than the beast itself. The monster might have been a rogue, its appearance simple coincidence. He wanted to believe it was so, but was afraid the situation would not be so simple. Still, he had a responsibility to determine the truth, no matter how unpalatable that truth might be. It was why he was here in this gods-forsaken wilderness.

The tribesmen in the valley were moving at a leisurely pace, but even so, they covered ground faster than ambling civilians and lumbering oxcarts. Something had to be done or the tribesmen would overtake Yentillan and his people before they reached the relative safety of Baron Jost's domain. Without walls to hide behind, the Kolviners would be overwhelmed by the swarming hill monkeys.

Raff 's options were limited. All he had were three troops of light cavalry. Thirty soldiers. Nowhere near enough to halt this horde. Even had he command of all of Yentillan's soldiers, he doubted he could put the bregil to rout. The baron's knights would take their toll certainly enough, but while those knights in their heavy armor were nigh invulnerable against one or even two hill warriors, they would be facing too many of the apes at once. And where knights would be destroyed, what chance did lightly armed and armored troops stand?

But fighting monkeys was what they were being paid for, wasn't it? They knew the risks. Though outnumbered, they would have to engage the hillmen.

Mounted, the cavalry troopers were more mobile than the tribesmen as long as they stayed away from the thickets and dense trees. With their leather and light mail, the riders were only light cavalry by Kolviner standards, but they were better armored than most of the hill monkeys. Another advantage. Only by using their every advantage could they hope to come away from the fight.

Raff Janden was one man who intended to come away from this fight. He was not going to die in a pointless skirmish. That did not fit his plans.

He called Dantil the Scout and Teletha Schonnegon, his troop commanders, and explained his plan. They would lead their troops in aborted charges, halting to give fire until the bregil responded. Once the apes came after them, they would withdraw. If some of the hill monkeys were stupid enough to get themselves separated from the main body, Raff's troop would cut them off. With luck, such harrying tactics would slow the bregil column. With greater luck, halt it.

The first few attacks went surpassingly well. Raff felt sure that the bregil had not suspected the presence of the riders; the turmoil in their ranks was too great. The crossbows took their toll, and the riders escaped unscathed. Raff observed that the hill monkeys did not charge out with their usual impetuosity; he and his troop remained idle. That situation couldn't last long; the tribesmen were not known for their stolidity while under attack. Eventually the harassing sting of the other two troops would draw the tailed apes out.

Schonnegon's troop was moving well, riding in to take their shots and pulling away again before the hillmen could reach them. Raff was relieved. She had been the weak link, the unknown factor in his plan. The newly made sergeant's timing and gauge of the enemy's temper were good. Too good for someone with no experience commanding troops. He guessed that she'd had Imperial experience, but not in the cavalry; her horsemanship wasn't strong enough for a cavalry leader, and she was proving that she was no stranger to leading troops. Whatever rank she had held before joining the Guild of the Sword, it had been higher than that of a common soldier. He had made a good decision in promoting her; he needed experienced people under him.

Still, he'd have to keep an eye on her; he just didn't know enough about her.

Dantil's troop was in, firing at the monkeys. Schonnegon's troop circled wide to hit a fresh part of the column. A bellowing roar momentarily drowned out the noise of combat. Raff savagely reined his mount down and scanned for the source of that awful, familiar sound.

He saw it: another great two-legged horror such as they had fought near Homlat. The beast was moving through the trees beyond the massed bregil and coming closer. But for whom? In moments Raff's fear was realized when the monster didn't charge the damned tailed apes. Ignoring them, it moved around the head of their column and started toward Dantil's troop.

A second roar boomed out from somewhere back in the trees.

Raff's throat went dry, his mouth suddenly soured with the taste of bile.

One of the monsters his soldiers might have handled,

with losses of course. They might have drawn it away from the hill monkeys, encircled it. But not two. Two were too great a threat, even without the danger of the hill monkeys' catching them while they battled the creatures. What they had done so far would have to be enough. Either they had bought time for Yentillan or they hadn't.

He sent a rider to Dantil; the scout had the trumpeter with his troop. Raff didn't like ordering the recall, but there was no other prudent choice.

As the call rang out, he saw the beast lengthen its stride and head straight for nearest of Dantil's riders. Dantil's troop turned their horses and set spur to them.

Now we'll find out how well it can run.

He turned his horse and applied spurs, leading his men away from the battle. His troop didn't hesitate; they were the survivors of the battle with the first monster. Dantil's troop thundered behind them as the beast gave chase.

Behind them, the beast roared.

Teletha and her troop cut in, joining them as they pounded through the trees. The horses strained, terrified of the fanged horror chasing them. Hooves cut the ground, kicking up the debris of the forest floor. Branches swatted at riders as they sought the most open paths. A horse screamed and Raff looked back. Groson, Dantil's second, was down, his horse screaming and thrashing with what looked like a broken leg.

No time to stop.

The monster gave a short bellow, and, a second later, the wounded horse's cries were cut off. Over the pounding of their flight, Raff thought he heard the snapping of bones behind him.

Dantil would need a replacement for Groson.

Raff urged his mount to greater speed.

7

"THIS IS THE VALLEY."

"How can you tell?" The valley was wooded, and Yan could see nothing but the wildness of it. No stones. Certainly no spires or strangely humped halls.

Fra Bern looked ashen. "I *know*."

Yan nodded.

They urged the horses downslope and though the trees. The valley's woods were old growth, large-boled trees with great limbs that shaded the ground beneath them and held the cool of the morning air though it was near noon. Even so, the sheltered vale was warmer here than the hills that surrounded it, and the trees here still held their leaves, verdant in the deep rich green of summer foliage and without the slightest hint of the coming autumn. Birds called, distant and lonely, like forlorn sentinels. Late summer insects droned. It might have been any of the dozens of small valleys they had traversed on their way here. Yet there was a strangeness to this valley that seemed to discomfort the horses.

When Fra Bern halted his mount, Yan did likewise. The priest pointed through a gap in the trees to a clearing a few yards distant. Warm sunlight shone down on mounded earth covered with tightly grown vegetation. Here and there, Yan could see the glint of a dark stone beneath the layers of leaves and coats of moss and lichens.

Yan dismounted and led his horse forward. At the edge of the open space, he tossed the reins over a bush and forced his way forward. Fra Bern remained under the shelter of the trees, still mounted.

Stopping at the nearest mound, Yan surveyed it. The green, encrusted shape was taller than he was and about as broad at its base as it was tall. It was narrow, a yard at most, in depth. Clearly this was no natural formation. Selecting a place where the vines were thinnest, he pulled some free, then scrubbed at the moss on the face of the stone, brushing at it until some of the rock's surface was visible. The stone was dark and glossy, pitted with the scars of clinging rootlets and the acids of the plants sheathing it. At the first hint of indentations on the stone's surface, he increased his efforts. In a few minutes he had cleared the obscuring foliage from an area about a foot across and could see what lay beneath.

He stared at the carvings his efforts had revealed.

They were as Fra Bern had said. In sketching the signs he had seen in his dream, the priest had missed some of the subtleties of the symbols, but he had rendered them accurately enough for Yan to recognize them. Now, here with the carving before him, Yan had no doubt that these symbols were from the same language as that in which Gornal's books were written. Surely these stones must date from that ancient time.

Had the priest unwittingly found what Yan was seeking? Was this Ul-Schuttariat? Yan needed to see more.

They spent the afternoon wandering from clearing to clearing, from mound to mound. While Yan dislodged vegetation from the stones to see the symbols, Fra Bern stood anxiously at his side, curious, enthralled even, but unwilling to put his hands to the stones. Mindful of his promise to Peyto that they would return soon, Yan made rubbings of some of the more intriguing surfaces.

By midafternoon, he concluded that the stones were a remnant of something, but whatever had been built in this valley was no city. It was too small. The Ul-Schuttariat of which he had read would have been bigger, of that he felt sure. Still, there was much to be learned here.

Perhaps it had been a temple complex. That might fit with Fra Bern's fears of a strange deity. The few remaining stones gave no real sense of how one clump of ruins might relate to another. The buildings that had stood here might have served any purpose. He was certain that there was some clue in the carvings.

These carvings were similar to those Yan had seen under the tower in the Scothic valley. The composition of the stones seemed similar as well, but the symbols were what hung in Yan's mind. The shapes, their orientations, and their progressions were like the symbols in Gornal's books. If they were not the same language, they were a very similar one. Did they hold hints that would enable him to decipher the books? What other secrets did they hold?

Yan wanted to know.

As they sat eating a belated midday meal, Fra Bern asked, "Now you have seen the stones. What say you?"

"I say they are of great interest."

"Can you read them?" the priest asked eagerly.

"No."

Fra Bern's face fell in disappointment. He sat silent for a while, chewing on his bread. Yan pulled out one of his rubbings and fell to studying it. He was deep in thought when the priest spoke again.

"You have seen the like of these symbols before."

"That is true," Yan admitted cautiously. He was unsure how much to reveal to the priest. Were Fra Bern firmly to decide that the carvings were linked to heresy, he might bring the matter before his superiors, and that could bring an inquisitorial investigation. The books in Yan's possession were clearly related to these ancient stones, and some would find such a connection to be damning evidence that Yan harbored heresy. He could do without the Church's attention.

"Why will you not tell me what you know?" Fra Bern asked.

Yan liked the priest too much to explain his suspicions. Or add the burden—or temptation—that knowledge of Gornal's books would bring. "I know little."

Fra Bern eyed him shrewdly. "But you suspect much."

"Suspicion without proof is nothing," he replied circumspectly. "It is not a scholar's meat."

"We have nought but bones here."

"The shamans of the Nalat see the future in bones."

"We are not pagan idolaters," Fra Bern said huffily.

"Saü-Yali calls the Triadic Church idolaters."

"The saü faith is a misguided approach to the fullness of the universe. Their priests are narrow-minded in their view of our world."

"Narrow-mindedness is not the exclusive prerogative of the saü. All around us is evidence that we are not the only beings to know this world we call Aelwyn. In ancient days, strange folk lived where we now sit. Might they not have worshiped strange gods?"

"There are only the Deities of the Courts."

"As the Church teaches. But consider. Those elder beings may have worshiped the gods we know. Being different from us, however, might they not have seen the deities in strange guises?"

"The gods are the gods."

"But were They always revealed as we know Them?"

Fra Bern considered Yan's suggestion. His expression made it clear that the thought was bothersome in some way. When he spoke, his voice trembled with uncertainty.

"The olden folk are all gone now. Even their children have passed from the world. We cannot know what they thought."

"We have these stones."

"Which you cannot read."

"That may change."

"How? Where will you find a teacher? The olden folk are gone."

"So it is said." But Yan was not so sure that it was so. He remembered the wizards under Gornal's tower. "But we still can see some of their works. Perhaps in such works we may find answers."

Fra Bern's question rankled Yan. A teacher would have made his struggle so much easier. In years of solitary work he had learned little, and the result of that work was still speculative. He just could not be sure he understood what he thought he understood. So much effort, so little result. What he would give for a teacher, someone to offer the insight into the minds of the writers of the books. To avoid wallowing in his own disappointment, he decided to shift the conversation. "Have you ever wondered what they were like?"

"Not really. I have had little cause, until lately. When I was a novice, I read the ancient chronicles as do all novice students of my Lord Einthof. There are accounts of many olden folk, and strange beings they were. Some so strange that I think they could not have been real."

"Some were real enough to have carved these stones."

"A mute and unique survival of those ancient times."

"Not so. Well, with regard to their singularity. I have seen such stones before."

"I thought so," Fra Bern said. He grinned with vindication.

Yan returned the smile. Speaking of stones was safer than speaking of books. "In the place where I saw the stones, I learned things. In that place I came to know that the olden folk were beings quite unlike us in form, yet in some ways they were similar."

"How so?" Fra Bern was clearly intrigued.

"The olden folk were wielders of the Art, for one. Some say the ability to touch the Art is the defining characteristic of humanity. That a race with magicians is a true race, one set apart from animals. The scholar Armiacodi would tell you that the Art is what sets merin, saü, and bregil apart from the animals and makes us alike despite our clear physical differences."

The priest shook his head. "It is the spark of the divine that sets us apart from the animals."

"And what is that spark, good priest? Can you define it? Measure it? Test for its presence?"

"'By his works, you shall know him.'"

"Might that spark be the ability to understand the Art?"

"Not all men are magicians."

"And not all men are priests."

"Point taken, Master Tanafres." Fra Bern chuckled. "What more did you learn in that other place?"

"The olden folk were builders in stone like us. The evidence is all around us in this valley, and you know it from other sources as well. In your dream you've seen their spires. You have told me you have great faith in your dreams. Do you deny what you have seen there?"

"Why did they build this place, do you think?"

"Who can say for certain that they did? This place is old, perhaps old enough to be made by their hands. How can you tell the age of a stone?"

"You are being argumentative," Fra Bern accused. "Who else could have built it?"

"You were the one who said the chronicles speak of many elder folk."

"Yet you speak as though from a certain knowledge. Do you know which of the elder folk carved these stones? Have you seen their form? Statues, perhaps, in that other place?"

"As you learn from your dreams, I learn from magic. There was, in that other place, a spell of great power that had preserved some of those folk."

"Alive?" The priest's excitement was plain in his voice, but Yan couldn't tell if it was born of enthusiasm or terror. "Did you speak with them?"

"We had no speech," Yan said. "As you said, the olden folk are all gone now." Yan saw no reason to describe his part in the deaths of those beings. He carried enough guilt without having this priest reproach him.

"So the spell was a form of preservation. I have heard that the ancestors of the saü placed their departed rulers in great constructs of stone as part of a ritual of preservation. Was this spell a magical form of some such ritual?"

"Something like that."

"A pity." Fra Bern shook his head sadly. "Had they been living, so much could have been learned from them. But that would have been a magic greater than man can achieve. Only the Sun Lord has the power over death." His expression brightened. "Could this place be a burial place, do you think?"

"I don't know. It is unlike that other place, though."

Fra Bern sighed. "I had thought it would be a wonder to

look upon the face of one of the olden folk, to behold their strangeness firsthand."

"Strange they were. And yet, however strange they were in form and thought, I think that they must have been human, and, being human, they must have had thoughts, desires, and needs."

"I had not thought of that." The priest looked disturbed by the concept.

"But in what strange forms? Would the essence of their hearts be knowable to us?"

"Who could say?"

It was Yan's turn to sigh. "Sometimes I think I could understand their writing if I knew the answers to some of these questions."

The priest's sharp look told Yan that he might have said too much. For all his lack of serious education, Fra Bern was bright and quick to pick up a nuance. He was saved from the awkwardness of the moment by a shout. Both men looked about, searching for the source, but the trees hid all. The birds and insects left off their chorus. Sounds drifted through the leaves: hoofbeats and harness.

"Not bregil," Fra Bern observed.

"But who?" Yan countered.

The sounds drew closer.

"Horses, Captain," a voice said.

"Keep moving. We've no time. We've got to warn Yentillan."

The sound of the horses passing diminished. Some had stopped.

"We can't leave these people to the hillmen and their monsters," said the very familiar voice of Teletha.

"Captain Janden," Fra Bern called out. "We're over here."

Sweaty riders on lathered horses emerged from the screen of trees and brush. Janden walked his horse over to them and looked down at them, disgusted.

"What in Baaliff's name are you doing out here? Having a picnic?" He didn't seem to be expecting an answer. "Don't you know it's dangerous out here? You should be with the rest of the civilians. Are there just the two of you?"

"Well, indeed, we, ah—" Fra Bern sputtered.

"Never mind. I don't want to know. Get yourselves mounted up. You're coming along with us."

"We have matters of interest here, Captain," Yan said.

Janden glared at him. "It seems to me that you're always wanting to stay where the damned hill monkeys will find you."

"And it seems to me that you're always trying to drag me away from something interesting."

"For all I care, you can stay here. But there are half a thousand apes behind us, and they're hungry."

"Oh, dear. We cannot stay here, Master Tanafres," Fra Bern said.

"Why is everyone always telling me that?" Yan complained.

"Because it's always true," Teletha said. "This is no place for scholars. Do what the captain says. Get your horses and get mounted."

The urgency in Teletha's voice touched Yan. Without further argument, he and Fra Bern gathered up Yan's rubbings and stowed them in his satchel. They mounted and joined the cavalry column. But he knew he'd be back to pry some of the secrets from the valley.

8

WHEN JANDEN LED THE EXHAUSTED riders to the crest of the last hill, they saw that they had come too late to give warning. A battle was already in progress, raging across the cleared land around Baron Jost's town. On the road west, a band of armed men struggling toward the town were engaged with a swirling mob of tribesmen. Another mob flowed and eddied around the town gate. From their vantage point miles to the south of the town, the struggling figures might have been toys. But the battle was all too real; on the road and in the fields, merin and bregil were fighting and dying.

"Horesh shine in mercy upon us," Fra Bern prayed aloud. "The king is beset on the road."

Janden pulled his spyglass from a saddle sheath and set it to his eye. "It is the royal Kolvin banner. And the king himself beneath it."

Yan squinted in the direction Janden was looking. He could see a large red-and-white banner waving. The quarterly division was plain enough, and he could tell that there was something in three of the quarters. The upper white quarter would be the twin swords, but whether the smears of yellow on the red quarters were royal crowns, he couldn't make out. Janden sounded sure of his identification.

The captain turned his glass toward the town. "Jost is holding the town gate open for the king's party."

"And not doing too good a job of it," Teletha commented.

"He doesn't seem to have the strength for a sally to reach the king."

"Maybe he doesn't have the will," Janden said.

"Baron Jost is an honorable man," Fra Bern objected. "He will do all he can to save the king."

"Are we going in, Captain?" Dantil asked quietly.

"Are you crazy? Our horses are blown. Half of you would be down before we crossed the fields and half of the rest in the first shock."

"We broke the hill monkeys from Baron Yentillan's gate and we were fewer than we are now," said one of the riders.

"There are more apes here," Janden replied. "We had fresher horses then as well."

That same rider objected, "A Kolviner is worth any two hill monkeys and a mounted Kolviner is worth twice that! Even with a blown horse."

The general grumbling made it clear that most of the riders disliked watching the battle. Janden insisted that he held them out for their welfare. Teletha gave Yan a look and a shrug, mouthing the words, "He is right."

A single trumpet sounded from the east, brazen and defiant.

Yan squinted at a previously unseen knot of horsemen that were trotting up the slope of a ridge. He saw that this small group had a banner, but it was too far away for him to make out the details.

"Yentillan," Janden said.

Baron Yentillan, at the head of his three knights and their half score of men-at-arms, was headed for the mob of bregil attacking the king's party. A force half the size of Janden's was headed directly for the battle. The Kolviner light horsemen murmured and grumbled.

"What's that further east of Yentillan?" Yan asked since he could not make out more than dark specks moving across the green fields and hills.

Fra Bern looked that way and said, "The baron's folk."

Dantil took a long look at the column of refugees, then cast a glance at Yentillan's small group. He urged his horse forward, placing himself in front of Janden and blocking the view of the spyglass. When the captain lowered his instrument,

Dantil said levelly, "If the soldiers are defeated, our people will be helpless. Baron Jost won't hold the gates open for them."

"We've got to do something," someone said, and several riders nodded or shouted in agreement.

Janden scowled, raking his troops with a steely glare. "This is madness! We're in no shape for combat."

"Who else'll save the baron?"

"Or the king?"

"We can at least threaten them," Teletha pointed out. "The tribesmen won't know our horses have no strength."

Janden muttered something under his breath, then spat. "All right! All right! Forward then, but at a walk. You'll need your horses' strength if it comes to a fight. No one charges without my direct order!"

They moved forward. Their own noise drowned out the distant surflike roar of the battle, but gradually, as they drew nearer the struggle, the sound reasserted itself. While they were screened from the fighting by one of the rolling hills, that noise changed its character. Shouts of alarm arose. Nervously, the riders approached the next crest.

Once there, they saw that Yentillan and his men were among the hillmen assaulting the king's party. As before, the bregil had been oblivious to the approach of the cavalry force until it was upon them. Dead and wounded tribesmen lay behind the knights like a wake of sea-foam. The surviving bregil were breaking up, losing cohesion under the impact of their mounted foes. The king's men fought on with renewed vigor.

"They see us!" Fra Bern called out.

"They" must have been the bregil, for the tribesmen began to break from the battle, a few stragglers at first, then whole groups. None headed toward the riders.

Yan saw the two banners come together briefly. When they separated, they began to move toward the town. The last of the hillmen facing them broke. Cavalrymen beginning a pursuit were called back. The king and Yentillan's combined force moved at speed toward the town.

At Janden's command, the riders changed course, angling across the fields.

A flurry of bolts and arrows flew from the town walls,

finding targets in the massed bregil. Tribesmen fell. Disrupted by the sudden casualties, the hillmen were in disorder when the knights reached them. Kolviner war cries and shouts dominated the air, driving down the bregil howls as the Kolviners drove the tribesmen from the walls and gate. This time men-at-arms were let to harry the retreating bregil.

By the time the riders reached the soldiers outside the gate, there was a conference under way beneath the king's banner. The king, a tall man in full armor of a style antique in the empire, stood by Baron Yentillan. A golden crown set upon the king's helm glinted in the late afternoon sunlight when he threw back his head and laughed. His voice echoed a little hollowly from within the helm.

"And did you see them run? I had thought to see forty lances of knights coming to my rescue, but instead only my good Baron Yentillan and his household. I knew I chose wisely in giving you some of this wild land to tame."

"Perhaps not so wisely, your Grace," the baron said. "I am here because I could not hold what you gave me."

"No?" The king's good mood weathered the news without a change. "A temporary setback. I will see you restored. These hill apes have not the stomach for real battle. It takes little to set them to running. This small fray has given them but a taste of the banquet I intend to feed them."

"You'll get your chance soon," Janden said without announcing himself. "There's more poxy hill monkeys coming."

The castle's hall was still chill with the night's cold when Yan found his way there. Most of the people already gathered there were clumped around the fireplace, but a few had taken station at the windows, preferring the morning sun's warmth to that of the fire. A handful of folk sat or stood away from such sources of heat in islands of privacy.

One such was seated in a chair near the head of the long table dominating the length of the hall. Beneath the man's fur-lined cloak, Yan could see a surcoat bearing the same arms as those on the banners flying from every turret. The stocky man was, therefore, Baron Jost. Without the heraldry,

Yan would not have recognized the baron outside the armor he had been wearing yesterday. Baron Jost's lank dark hair hung down onto his collar, and he played idly with a lock as he sat, a bored expression on his bearded face.

Baron Yentillan's banner hung on the wall near one of the windows. Since Yan had been requested to attend by Baron Yentillan, that was where he should be. As he crossed the chamber, he did not see the baron, but others of the baron's affinity were already gathered there. Sir Bryyan sat glumly on a stool near the banner, and the other two knights, whose names Yan did not know, stood nearby discussing yesterday's fighting. Yan crossed to where Peyto sat on the window seat.

"What's toward?" he asked after greeting the clerk.

Peyto fussed with ordering a stack of note tablets while he whispered to Yan.

"Baron Jost had already learned of the depredations of the hill tribes before Baron Yentillan's message arrived. Two villages under his protection had been attacked, their people killed or scattered. When the bregil came screaming out of the woods, Baron Jost's men were escorting the farmers and nearby villagers to the safety of the walls.

"The baron immediately sent a messenger west to the king, informing His Grace of the rising of the clans. By report, the road south was unsafe for travel, and it was not known if the messenger got through. The last band to try heading for more civilized parts, a group of merchants, returned to Jost's town a frightened, ragtag mob without arms or wagons. They had lost a quarter of their number to a bregil ambush."

"You sound as if you've been here all along, and not only just arrived."

"*I* have made good use of *my* time." Peyto smiled at the wizened gray-hair who approached him, and handed over a set of the tablets. The man opened the first panel, tilted the stack to see better the writing in the wax, and nodded in satisfaction before returning Peyto's smile. Tucking the tablets into his belt, the man shuffled away.

Peyto said, "Unless I miss my guess, we'll be spending some time here. Which is not as bad as it might be; Baron Jost's town is larger and better defended than Baron Yentillan's holding."

"The fields have no walls. The crops—"

"Are being gathered under the watchful eyes of armed guards. The harvest will be smaller than usual, but should be adequate to provide through the winter, even with the addition of Yentillan's people, and us, to the town's population."

Motion by the door caught Yan's attention. A tall, bearded man entered the hall. He wore an old, quilted pourpoint of faded red silk and carried a scabbarded sword. His hair was bound with a golden fillet, but he wore no other sign of rank. Yan took him for one of the knights until he noticed the deference paid him by the others accompanying him, including Baron Yentillan.

"Is that the king?" Yan whispered.

"Shain, seventh of that name," said Peyto. "That scar on his cheek is legendary and marks him immediately. I told you to pay more attention to the politics here."

It hadn't seemed important. Yan was just a scholar seeking old, dusty information. What need had he to know of the king?

King Shain seated himself at the head of the table. "Good morning to you, Jost."

"Your Grace." The dark-haired baron inclined his head.

"It seems your concern was well founded. Your neighbors had quite the reception for me. I am glad that they didn't know I was coming."

"I did not know either," Jost said.

"My messenger did not arrive then." Shain grunted. "I am not surprised; the road is perilous. 'Tis why I came on ahead." He grinned widely. "And well that I did. We gave them good strokes yesterday, did we not?"

"Good enough."

"We scattered them thoroughly, mostly thanks to Yentillan's timely arrival, and I am well pleased. It bodes well for the campaign. As soon as my troops arrive, we will seek out the tribesmen in their greatest concentration and slay enough of them to send them all home to their hills, thinking of the days when they were wise enough to war among themselves and leave us alone."

Jost folded his arms across his chest and leaned back in his chair. "Has your Grace brought any wizards?"

"There was no time to gather them from their towers. They will come on apace with the baggage train."

Jost frowned, but bit off a reply as others joined him and the king at the table. The conference began. Discussion of the town's situation and supplies preceded hours of speculation concerning the reasons for the bregil confederation and the whereabouts of its leaders. Speakers droned on and Yan soon found himself bored. Everyone seemed to have something long-winded to say on every subject. Yan was never asked to speak, and he wondered why Yentillan had asked him to attend. He dozed off, waking up as the conference broke up.

He wondered what he had missed and resolved to ask Peyto for a summary over the evening meal. Having wasted most of the day at this fruitless conference, he wanted to get in some study on the rubbings from the stones before the light went away.

Attending battle conferences was one thing, but attending the battles themselves was something else. In the previous few days Yan had often wondered why he had agreed to come along with the Kolviner army. Now, as he saw how badly the fighting was going, he especially wondered at the wisdom of following the army.

The moans and screams of the wounded gave him his answer. Unfortunately, there was little he could do until the fighting stopped. Little? Nothing. If he attempted to go down to the field he could easily become one of the wounded. Or one of the dead. He would have to wait until the battle was finished before he could offer the wounded any solace. That end, it seemed, might not be far away.

The first charge of the knights had gone well, but then the great beasts had appeared. A trio of *terriserpens* had emerged from the Prynlam Woods, before which the bregil had drawn up. The monsters had ravaged the cavalry, driving the horses mad with fear and slaying rider and mount with equal ease. With the knights scattered, the tribesmen had fallen on the Kolviner infantry, and the battle had broken into scattered small melees.

The behavior of the *terriserpens* held a terrible fascination for Yan. The beasts acted with far greater intelligence than he would have expected from mere animals, especially reptiles. They attacked cavalry in preference to infantry, seeming to exploit the terror of the horses to their favor. The great beasts retreated when it looked likely that they would be overwhelmed.

He watched a melee between one of the beasts and a handful of knights and men-at-arms. Surrounded and isolated, the beast suffered grievous wounds. Finally it fell, its left leg hacked clear of muscle below the knee. The Kolviners moved on, satisfied to have taken down their foe and unwilling to spend more time on it while others remained and their cause lay in jeopardy.

The *terriserpens* lay twitching on the field, its good leg clawing at the air. Yan stared in amazement as a creature like a tiny shadow of the great beast emerged from the trees at the edge of the field. It sprinted, body leaning forward and tail extended behind it.

The small figure stopped by the head of the *terriserpens*, ducking its own head down to touch muzzle to muzzle. A young *terriserpens*? The size disparity was great, but it could be so. The creature stepped back and took something from a sheath hanging by its haunch. Sheath? This was no young *terriserpens*. It wore harness and carried . . . what? Tools? Weapons? This was a thinking being! Yan watched as the small black creature stepped behind the writhing *terriserpens*'s head and plunged what it held in its hand into the back of the *terriserpens*'s skull. The great beast spasmed. The small creature leapt back, clear of the thrashing. The *terriserpens* died. In a moment, the black being was gone, a shadow vanished back into the woods.

Yan was left to wonder at its form. The dark being reminded him of the strange saurian magicians he had encountered in the time-haunted Scothic valley. But this creature walked. It was shocking to see such a creature alive and active.

And exciting as well.

Such creatures had written the books Yan so desperately wanted to read. He had thought all chance to speak with one gone forever down the well of time. Yet here before him was evidence that he was wrong. He had to learn more about the black saurian.

But it was not to be this day.

The Kolviners had regrouped, a smaller, more tattered force than had started the day. The hillmen held back, allowing the Kolviners to withdraw. Yan moved to join them.

As he tended the wounded, Yan saw King Shain moving among the disheartened troops. The king had removed his helmet, letting his sweaty and grime-streaked face show that he had not been idle. His expression was grim, but his voice strong.

"They have beaten us on the field this day, my brave friends. Yet this has been but one battle. It is not the last battle.

"Their great beasts caught us unawares, but we showed them our mettle. One of the monsters lies dead, and we have driven the others from the field.

"Take heart, warriors. We will yet prevail. Not today, but we *will* prevail. We will harry them from Jost's town. Those walls are too strong for the hill apes, and their beasts cannot pass such stout barriers.

"Time will be our ally. The weather is turning. The hill monkeys will not stay in the field."

"How can you know that?" someone called from the crowd.

"It will be as it has always been. The clansmen will disperse and retreat before the colder weather. There are enough supplies here to hold us through till spring. Their chiefs were foolish to start a campaign so late in the year. When the weather turns again, we will be ready for them. We will smash them and send them howling back to the hills."

There were a few cheers, but the sound was ragged. Still, the men took some heart from the king's resolve. They brought the remnant of the army, and all the wounded who could walk or be carried, safely back to Jost's town.

The cold winter wind slipped into the tavern when the door opened. Men bawled for the newcomer to shut it, and quickly. He did so and made his way across the room, dripping from the rain. Steam soon started to rise from his cloak and hat as he sat by the fire. Yan recognized the bedraggled man as Captain Janden. As he did so, the man caught his eye and abandoned his place by the fire, taking the seat by Yan without invitation.

"Let me buy you cider," Janden said. "Hot drink warms the body well on a cold winter night."

Yan contemplated refusing. Cider was costly in Jost's town, but not so dear as it would become. For while King Shain had ordered rationing of many basic commodities, cider was not yet on his list. The merchants-with-no-stalls were not yet interested in it. The current high prices were due to so-called honest merchants seeking to profit from the misfortunate times. While Yan hesitated, the captain ordered a round for everyone at the table.

Fra Bern thanked him at once, but Teletha just nodded to her superior. With the continued presence of bregil war parties, her contract had been extended by the king; not an entirely legal proceeding, as Peyto had pointed out, but hardly one to be disputed at the moment.

When the servingman brought the steaming mugs, Janden appropriated one, holding it between his hands. "I hear that you saw something the day of the battle at Prynlam Woods."

"I saw many things, things I'd rather not see again," Yan told him. "Battles are terrible things."

"Especially when you lose them," Teletha added.

The captain ignored her. "I was talking about something else. I've heard tell that you saw a creature. Like the great beasts, but smaller."

Fra Bern turned on Yan. "Is that true? You said nothing of it."

Yan shrugged. "I have no reason to deny what I saw, but I saw no reason to speak of it either."

"You should have told me," Janden said.

"And why is that?"

"I'm head of the scouts. I need to know what everyone sees."

"It was not a warrior. What matter of yours was it?"

"Then it really is true." Fra Bern's face was paler than its wont. "You saw one of them. If the ancient enemy has come upon us again, the weight of our sins must be heavy upon us."

"What are you talking about?" Teletha asked. "What is he talking about, Yan?"

"I don't know."

"Drakkenree," Janden said. "Good Fra Bern is talking about drakkenree. And you, Master Magician, seem to be the only person to have spotted one."

"Perhaps I have, Captain, but I don't recognize the name you speak. And I certainly don't know if it applies to what I saw."

Janden gave Yan a hard stare. "You're from the Iron League, right? No reason you should know the name. It's not used much in the empire these days. But if you've seen one, a lot of people are going to get familiar with the name soon."

"But the drakkenree have been gone for generations," Fra Bern objected. "They are long vanished from Horesh's world. No man in living memory has seen one."

"Except our friend the magician, here." Janden turned an unpleasantly avid eye on Yan. "You did see it, didn't you?"

"Look. I saw a creature, but I don't know if it was one of these drakkenree. If they haven't been seen by a living man, how would you know what they look like?"

"The chronicles, Master Tanafres," said Fra Bern. "Remember the chronicles?"

"There are drawings in the chronicles?" Yan asked. He hadn't yet had time to study the Kolvinic chronicles.

"No," Fra Bern admitted. "But there are descriptions in some."

"Perhaps I had best read these chronicles." He hoped he didn't sound too anxious; Captain Janden would surely misunderstand.

"And you will then tell me if what you saw was a drakkenree?" Janden asked.

"If I can," Yan answered.

"Good." Janden drained off his cider. "I will arrange for you to use Baron Jost's library. There's a copy of the chronicles there."

"Thank you, Captain. I think."

"Don't thank me. Just read, and read quick."

"Why the hurry?" Teletha asked. "The king has said there will be no more campaigning till the weather breaks."

"I don't care about the king. *I'm* the one asking the question, and I want an answer quickly."

Teletha was not put off by the captain's surly response. "You think these drakkenree are behind this invasion?"

Janden snorted in derision, but the captain's reaction had a false air to it. "Invasion? A big word for an uprising of hill monkeys."

"What else would you call it? They have not retreated back to their hills with the coming of the rains."

"They are acting most strangely," Fra Bern added. "I have heard that bregil occupy Baron Yentillan's stronghold. It is said that they den on farms hereabout and have set up villages of huts in some of the more sheltered valleys. Is it true, Captain Janden?"

Janden's eyes flashed over each person at the table, then around the room. Softly, he said, "It's true."

Fra Bern exhaled slowly. "Never have I heard of the hillmen trying to hold anything they have despoiled."

"They're doing it all right, and not just here. Scouts report camps scattered throughout the east. There are even some west of the Daige River."

"Have they cut the road to the capital?" Teletha asked.

"Yes, Schonnegon, they've cut the road." Janden stood up. "Look, I didn't come here for idle gossip, nor am I going to discuss strategy in the hearing of a bunch of civilians with wagging tongues. I just want to know what the magician saw, and I want to know soon. We haven't got all winter."

"But King Shain said—"

Janden cut the priest off. "*I* said soon. Clear enough?"

"Clear as mud," Teletha said in Scothic.

Yan repressed a smile. "I will look at the chronicles, Captain. Then we will speak again."

Janden gave him a hard smile. "I know where to find you, magician. Yentillan's your friend now, but he *needs* me. Remember that."

"I'll remember, Captain."

Janden returned to the storm outside, but he remained at the table, dominating the conversation of the three still sitting there. All their talk, however, threw little light on the scout captain and his motives.

Part Two

9

YAN NIBBLED ON THE DRIED APPLE, the last of the bunch that Teletha had brought in from her most recent foray in the countryside. Any pangs of conscience over eating food undeclared to the general stores were overridden by the pangs of hunger from his stomach.

Peyto's predictions of sufficient food for the winter had proven optimistic. As they came into early spring, most of the population had been reduced to starvation rations because the addition of the king's soldiers to the population of Jost's town had proven too taxing to the larders. None of the people within the walls were well fed; all had taken on a gaunt appearance. Even Fra Bern had lost his sleekness and his extra poundage to take on a leaner, hungrier look.

The afternoon light slanted in through the western windows of the chamber that served as Baron Jost's library. It was the best illumination of the day and, as usual, Yan and Fra Bern were taking advantage of it, pursuing their studies in the Kolvinic chronicles. Captain Janden's offer to open the library to Yan was more welcome than he wanted to let the captain know; the man's attitude put Yan off. Yan disliked being indebted to the captain, but he couldn't pass up a chance to use resources that would have been closed to him otherwise. Any information that he could gather on these elder beings, these drakkenree, could only help in his effort to translate their books.

Fra Bern had become Yan's enthusiastic guide through the library's musty tomes, proving invaluable in helping Yan through passages of archaic Kolvinic. Still, much remained vague, for the chronicles were written in an elaborate style and details were often recorded in a florid, ornate way that made any specific information suspect. What appeared to be a fact could as easily be an artifact of the chronicler's imagination, chosen for the poetry it evoked to the writer.

Though tidbits concerning the drakkenree were rare, there was much of interest in the chronicles. Yan often found himself wandering through the volumes for hours with no goal in mind other than learning something new. It was almost like being back in Gan Tidoni's library, where he had spent many long afternoons during his apprenticeship. Then, too, he had been avoiding the issues at hand, though cleaning glassware and pots was less momentous than an enemy invasion.

Fra Bern was a fine companion on such scholarly odysseys, but in matters of interpreting the passages concerning the drakkenree, their relationship proved to be a quarrelsome one. The chronicles were quite clear that Kolviners had long ago warred against another race. The priest saw a difference between the oldest accounts and those of more recent vintage, and he refused to equate the saurian that Yan had seen with those ancient enemies. Yan found the vague descriptions sufficiently clear, having seen the slumbering saurian mages in Gornal's valley. True, those ancient mages were slightly different from the creature Yan had seen at Prynlam Wood, but then so is a saü different from a merin. Yan thought the differences were minor. Fra Bern disagreed.

Though Fra Bern never mentioned it, Yan suspected that the priest's true basis for disagreement lay in something more profound than physical form. Since their visit to the place of the stones, Fra Bern had not spoken openly of his fears of the Other. Yet the tenor of his arguments suggested that the heretical concept was never far from his mind. The priest worked hard to perceive a difference between the enemy fought by the Kolviners so long ago and their most recent saurian enemies, as though by doing so he could separate the motivations of the ancient from the modern. The oldest of the chronicles called the enemy "god-ridden" and "servants of the serpent" and other suggestive terms, and those same chronicles made it clear that the ancient enemy did not worship the Celestial Court; there was no mention of the Under Court deities. Fra Bern seemed to wish to prove that whatever the ancient enemy had worshiped was theirs alone and existed no longer. The end of a deity was something Triadic theology could accept.

Yan didn't see how such a philosophical construct could eliminate the priest's fears that the confederation of the hillmen was based on worship of some strange and unknown deity. If the power behind the orb talismans was truly supernatural and not merely esoteric magic, it was real, no matter what the Triadic Church thought. Reality was reality. But without bringing the subject out into the open and discussing it, there was little Yan could do to help his friend with the dilemma.

He understood Fra Bern's reluctance to speak, even here in the library, where they were so often alone. Such caution was wise, as Yan had learned with his winter's exposure to the gossip that flowed through the castle. In a way the castle community was much like the village where he had grown up—you never knew when someone was watching, or listening. A whispered conversation held in privacy might be overheard, and were the matter of the talk heretical, it would be titillating. Nothing would stop it from becoming grist for the gossipmongers' mill. Soon or late, word of such a conversation would reach the ears of Fra Bern's superiors. Yan was unwilling to put his friend at such risk just to ease his own mind.

The scuff of footfalls beyond the door roused Yan from his musings. Guiltily, he tucked the gnawed apple core into his pouch. Just in time, for the library door creaked open to admit a page in King Shain's livery. A second, in Baron Jost's colors, followed; Jost was the master of the castle and all activity was, technically, at his pleasure. A week ago there would have been a third, wearing Baron Yentillan's livery, but Yentillan was no longer a part of this particular peculiarity of protocol. The relations between Kolviner lords were a tangled web of protocols, confusing to a foreigner, but probably less so than the corresponding tangle of privileges, rights, duties, and honors in the empire. The whole thing was a lot like bulls maintaining their pride of place in the herd.

Yan guessed the message before the pages delivered their summons. The king wanted to see them. Since being given the command to learn more about the drakkenree—would that all commands were so onerous—Yan and Fra Bern had been left undisturbed. It had only been a matter of time until the king wanted his answers.

Had it been only a week since Baron Yentillan had led a small army out to harass the hillmen? Briefly, Yan wondered how Yentillan was faring. Everyone said that there were thousands of tribesmen out there, and Yentillan had only three hundred men, too small a force to be decisive. But the expedition had set out as much to harry the invaders as to relieve some of the pressure on the dwindling larders of the town. Three hundred fewer mouths should have meant more for all, but the king was holding to his strict rationing orders. Wisely, Yan thought, for relief was not yet in sight.

Yentillan's force was composed mostly of the king's men, one company each of spearmen and crossbowmen and three troops of men-at-arms. Such a grant of military force was a grace, more than the usual honor bestowed on a dispossessed lord.

By the standards of Kolvin, Baron Yentillan, having been given an honor, was obliged to return one. His choice had been to transfer his noncombatants to King Shain's affinity; the baron didn't need scholars, clerks, butlers, and pantlers in the field, but the king needed a presence here in Jost's town.

King Shain's entourage, never large to begin with, had been reduced by the debacle at Prynlam Wood. Though he had his military officers, his baggage train with his own servants and staff had never made it to Jost's town. A king needed a presence both on and off the field, especially when times were difficult. Retainers were important in con-

veying the king's worth, but borrowing them from Baron
Jost while relying on Jost's hospitality was not good manners for a Kolviner king. The addition of Yentillan's people
to King Shain's affinity increased the king's dignity. Peyto
claimed that Yentillan had bought his army with the deal.

Yan was, obliquely, part of the deal. While he had aided
and supported Baron Yentillan and received recompense
by way of food and lodging, he was not truly of the baron's
affinity, never having sworn to the man. King Shain
ignored the distinction; hence the order to research the
drakkenree. Since the king's purse now supported Yan,
Yan worked for him.

King Shain's short, curt interviews made it clear that the
king would have been happier to have his own wizards
doing the work, but neither of those eminent personages
had reached Jost's town. One of them never would; her
body had been found among the debris of the baggage
train. Whether the other had been traveling with her, and
was now missing or captured, was unknown.

The task of doing the king's research had devolved upon
Yan and Fra Bern; and now they were called to present the
fruits of that labor. Reluctantly, Yan and Fra Bern closed up
the volumes spread out on the table and returned them to
their places. A king's summons was no reason to show dis-
respect for these venerable tomes. At least not this summons. The liveried pages and their calm demeanor
indicated that the summons was not an emergency; emer-
gencies left little time for the niceties of protocol.

The pages vanished discreetly, or perhaps prudently,
upon escorting Yan and Fra Bern to the door of the king's
day chamber. Proper protocol required them to deliver
their charges in person. Wondering what motivated the
breach, Yan reached out to turn the handle for himself, but
it moved away from his hand. Opened from within, the
door swung back, and Teletha bustled through, nearly
bowling Yan over in her rush.

"Sorry," she said as she helped him catch his balance.

Yan had seen too little of Teletha throughout the winter.
True, he had been preoccupied with his researches, but he
would have found time for her. Hadn't he always done so?

She'd chosen to barrack with the cavalry, ignoring her bedroom in the town house Yentillan had arranged for her, Yan, and Peyto. She had said bunking with the troops was part of her contract, but that was no excuse. Worse than none: Yan had checked and found that it was not part of the contract.

He hadn't confronted her with the fact that he knew. Every time he tried to bring the subject up, she cut him off by insisting that her choice of place to bed down was not personal before changing the subject. In the past week, he had hardly seen her at all, even though he'd known she was in the town. She didn't have the excuse of being out on patrol, either seeking foodstuffs for the town or checking on the tribesmen's winter encampments. She seemed more and more to prefer the company of soldiers to his.

"Got to run," she said.

Yet when she hurried off, he found himself holding a small pouch from which wafted the aroma of spiced food. A gift? An apology? He frowned at Fra Bern's smirk, deciding that he would track her down and ask. He tucked the sack into his belt and led the priest into the chamber. Their feet crunched on shattered pottery.

A bad sign.

King Shain had fretted the entire winter, his temper continually shortening. He had cheered up briefly when a break in the weather had enabled him to lead his knights in a foray against one of the bregil encampments, but the Kolviners had not fared well, and the king's temper had grown worse. Yan could tell from the broken pottery littered about the door that this was not one of King Shain's better days.

Baron Jost and a handful of knights were with the king. Captain Janden, now chief of scouts, was there as well. The warriors and their leaders were gathered around a small table covered in maps. They all looked up as Yan and Fra Bern entered the room.

"Yentillan's magician and the Einthofite. Good." The king's tongue was slurred slightly, and he spoke in his native Kolvinic rather than the cultured Nitallan he usually used for converse with Yan. "Have you found me a way to stem this scourge of my land?"

"I had not understood that to be your wish of us, your Grace," Yan said.

Shain scowled. "You're looking into the books about the lizards, aren't you?"

"We study the chronicles, your Grace," Fra Bern said.

"That's right." Shain turned to Captain Janden. "Didn't you say the magician told you there were lizards behind this?"

Janden's voice was patient, making Yan glad that the captain was answering the question; Yan had answered it too often for his liking. "Master Tanafres identified a creature he saw as a drakkenree, your Grace. My scouts have reported others among the hill apes. Your conclusion that the drakkenree are coercing the monkeys into this invasion seems sound."

Invasion? So, the captain had finally come around to that point of view. Teletha had reached that conclusion in the fall. Why else would the clansmen be settling in? Invasion was the only reasonable conclusion. But deciding that drakkenree were behind the hill tribes, however, was an unwarranted assumption; the one Yan had seen acted more like a groom for the *terriserpens* than a war leader. Yet Janden had said that more of the drakkenree had been seen. Were these others any different from the one he'd seen? That saurian had not participated in the battle, and it had certainly not led any attacks by the hillmen. Had these others? If so, perhaps Janden had a case. Whatever the situation, it was obvious that the presence of drakkenree among the hillmen was not news to the king.

"See you, magician, priest. I know the lizards are out there. With Mistress Goremengar dead and Master Publicandiam gods know where, I have to rely on you two to burrow into those books. My ancestors fought the lizards, but all they left for me are songs of great deeds. Damned little tactical information, and I have no experience fighting creatures that can make hill monkeys stand up to trained warriors. What can you tell me of how they wage war?"

Yan sighed. The king's old songs sounded no more specific than the chronicles. Shain would not like the answer Yan had to give.

"While the drakkenree I saw had some similarities to the drakkenree of old—"

Fra Bern interrupted. "To name the creature Master Tanafres saw a drakkenree is inaccurate. It and these others cannot be the ancient enemy. They can only be the children of the ancient enemy."

"A point of distinction that hardly merits the king's concern," Yan said to him.

"Not so," Fra Bern stated. "The chronicles speak of—"

"Enough," the king snapped. "I want answers, not arguments. What can I expect from these lizards and their monkeys come the good weather?"

As Yan started to explain why he could not tell the king what he wanted to know, a clamor rose from the watch tower: shouting and the alarum bell. Immediately King Shain threw himself upright and made a wobbly rush to the window, where he shouted for the sentries to give a report.

"Horses on the road!" came the answer.

"Banners?" The king's tone was anxious. "Soldiers?"

"It's an army!"

10

BY THE TIME YAN REACHED THE WALL, the parapet was crowded with soldiers and citizens, anxiously staring down the road. There was a distant rumble, drums and marching feet, but the army was not yet visible from the wall. The sentries on the tower could see it; he could tell by the way they gazed anxiously in the direction of the road.

The arrival of this force was unheralded. Could it be a relief column from the capital? Yan doubted that it was an Elsinarossian force, as some about him whispered. It was as yet too early in the year for those enemies of the Kolviners to have marched down from the north. These soldiers had to be more Kolviners. Didn't they? Perhaps they were an army led by the prince, come to rescue his father.

The first soldiers to come into view were cavalrymen. The setting sun glinted redly from their helms and breast-plates. Yan squinted, trying to make out details. Something about the cavalrymen seemed different from ordinary Kolviners.

The soldiers carried several banners. The largest had a red field with a white saltire cross and a canton bearing other arms. Yan was frustratingly unable to make out the details of the arms used by those to whom the unit owed allegiance. People started to point at the flag excitedly.

"Imperials!" the cry went up.

As the soldiers drew nearer, Yan saw that it was true.

The banner's canton bore the black Imperial rapenar surrounded by twelve stars. Now that they were closer, he saw why the cavalrymen didn't look like typical Kolviners. They wore breastplates over coats of good buff leather, and prawntail helmets protected their heads. Such modern designs were common in the empire, a far cry from the older styles of mail and plate armor worn by the bulk of the Kolviner troops.

In the courtyard below, King Shain burst out of the keep and ran across the courtyard toward the gatehouse, shouting all the while for his armor and his horse. Baron Jost stood at the keep's entrance and bawled similar orders. Servants ran helter-skelter.

Fra Bern tugged on Yan's arm. "We'll see more at the town gate."

That was where the nobles would meet the army. Yan and the priest forced their way through the townsfolk crowding the parapet. By the time they arrived, the king, the baron, and a small knot of soldiers were armed, mounted, and waiting outside the gate. The first of the Imperial soldiers arrived, a trio of armored cavalrymen. They conferred briefly with the Kolviners, then one of them galloped back along the column, disappearing over the crest of the hill. Captain Janden exchanged a few words with King Shain and, receiving a nod from the king, rode after the cavalryman.

The army continued to march toward Jost's town. After that first unit of cavalry came the foot. Yan counted a dozen companies of pikemen and four of shot. Three of the companies of shot were arquebusiers, marching with their arquebuses sloped butt-end high on their shoulders. The soldiers of the fourth and smallest company carried the great Cheddan longbow. Each contingent carried banners marking its allegiance and its subformations. The dazzle of colors made a brave show. Each unit marched past the gate, dipping its banners to the king as it passed. Block by block, they formed up outside the town walls.

Another section of cavalry led the second group of the army. Yan recognized the sword-over-sun insignia of the Order of Vehr and the black chalice of the Order of Baaliff, rival sects of martial clerics. Both units were armed and armored in their traditional way; the Vehrites in full mail and the Baaliffites in armors of mail and overlapping plates. The martial priests were fully armored and wore surcoats in the color of their order and each was attended by a pair of less well armored men-at-arms whose status as brothers of their order was marked with waist sash and baldric. Yan noted with slight amusement that each order appeared to have a score of knights. He counted to be sure.

"Twenty Vehrites and twenty Baaliffites," he said.

"Politics as always," Fra Bern commented.

The martial priests preceded a group of several men in fine armor. The quality of their harness, the flash of metal on their horse trappings, and the brightness of their clothing and pennons proclaimed these men the leaders of the force. A carriage drawn by four black horses was next in the column. No doubt it carried an important passenger, possibly the ambassador responsible for presenting this force to King Shain.

Teletha joined them on the wall as the last of the army cleared the ridge. Yan was surprised at the rear guard unit. The glance they exchanged showed that Teletha was as puzzled as he. The last soldiers were a mixed unit of pikemen and archers, less well clad than most of the troops. Truth to be told, they looked scruffy, more like a bunch of bandits than like Imperial soldiers. Their banner bore a spiked wheel in red on a yellow field. Unlike the other units, the banner's canton did not bear the Imperial rapenar. The sign of their allegiance was a vivid golden dnove's head engorged of a crown, all set upon a blue field.

"What is that symbol?" Fra Bern asked

"That is the badge of the king of the Scoths," Teletha answered.

"Scoths marching with Imperial troops?" Fra Bern's voice held the puzzlement that Yan felt.

"Scothandir *is* a part of the empire," Teletha said.

Yan knew many Scoths who thought otherwise. They seemed to offer a rebellion as a coronation gift for each new emperor.

Below them at the gate, the officers of the Imperial army

reached the king's party. Janden, riding with them, bowed like a courtier and swept one hand out to indicate one of the newcomers, a man in shiny three-quarter armor.

"Your Grace, may I present General Estem Honistonti, leader of this force." Honistonti swept off his hat, revealing a shock of graying curls and a weathered face at odds with his courtly waxed mustache and Vandyke beard. The general bowed to the king as Janden continued the introduction, "General, you stand before Shain the Seventh, King of Kolvin and Protector of the South."

"You are well and timely come, General Honistonti," said the king. "I am pleased to see the old alliance is not so old that it is forgotten."

"The empire never forgets its friends, your Grace," Honistonti replied.

"Nor its enemies." Shain laughed. "We've much to talk about, General."

"Indeed we do, your Grace."

Janden introduced the rest of the officers, but Yan was too busy staring at the arms painted on the door of the carriage. He had seen them before, and he had not forgotten them. They belonged to the Renumas family, powerful and influential Imperial nobles. Almost as powerful as the Imperial family, considering that their patriarch was Vornor Renumas, chancellor of the empire and Sorigir of Sessandir. The presence of the carriage spoke of the importance of the person inside, and of the mission entrusted to this Imperial force. Clearly the emperor, or at least his chancellor, took the Old Alliance seriously. But if there was a member of the Renumas family involved, why had Janden said that the general was in charge?

A hook-nosed heron of a man emerged from the carriage. He was dressed in a fashionable doublet and coat of the same shade of gray as his beard. Instead of the ordinary wide-brimmed hat, he wore a broad-crowned scholar's cap. Gold glinted from his shoulders, a collar of linked R's from which hung an elaborate amulet. The collar marked the man as a high-ranking member of the Renumas affinity, a notable distinction, but the amulet hanging from him marked him as a member of an even more elite circle. The amulet was a *claviarm*. The ambassador, if ambassador he was, was a magician.

"Gan Fasolt, magician, if it please your Grace," General Honistonti said by way of introduction.

The king eye's measured the magician, lingering on the sword scabbarded to his side. "A battle wizard?"

"I have so served and will so again, as needs be." Fasolt's voice was thin and sharp as a razor. "Your Grace's hospitality will be most welcome after so long and uncomfortable a journey."

"You shall have the best I can offer. Places will be made for you and all your officers in the castle."

"I am not in charge here," Fasolt said, cutting off the king's hospitality speech. "I serve. Honistonti will have to answer for his officers, but for my part, I will be most glad to stay in better surroundings than a mildew-clotted tent."

Fasolt turned back to his carriage, but Janden whispered something to him. The magician and the chief of scouts moved away from the gathering of Imperials and Kolviners for a private conversation. Honistonti gave the magician a hard glance, but schooled his expression to neutrality before speaking to King Shain.

"Tents are good enough for soldiers, your Grace."

"You will, of course, stay in the keep," Shain said

"My officers will stay with their men. I will, too," Honistonti said. "Now, these troops have marched far, and they need billeting. I'll see to that before we talk."

Shain sat straighter in his saddle, saying stiffly, "I will be in the hall, attending business."

Yan hoped the Imperial officer had not offended the king too badly with his refusal of hospitality. Kolvin was not a part of the empire, and they had a different expectation of manners and propriety.

Fra Bern again tugged on Yan's arm. "We had best attend his Grace. Surely he will want to impress the Imperials when they have their conference. He will want us there."

"As ornaments."

Fra Bern shrugged. "He may need our counsel."

Yan turned to Teletha. "You'll come with us, won't you? There will surely be a meeting of the officers."

"Surely," she said abstractedly.

Satisfied for the moment, he started down. Ignored by the great lords, they might find time to talk. On the third step, he realized that she was still on the parapet.

"I'll be along," Teletha said.

Yan looked back at her, surprised at the slight tremor in her voice. She was staring intensely at something. He followed the line of her fixed gaze down to the group of Imperial officers. What was disturbing her? She had once been an Imperial officer herself. Did the presence of these men remind her of that? Or was something else at work?

"Teletha?"

"Go on."

"Teleth—"

"Go on!"

Yan didn't like her peremptory tone, but this was not the place to discuss it. Nor the time. He yielded to Fra Bern's insistent tugging.

Teletha heard the guard announce her as a scout reporting in. She also heard another voice as well, a stranger's voice, and decided she had been wise not to use her name to gain entrance to the tent. The stranger's deep voice didn't sound pleased, but *his* voice, more even, prevailed over the stranger's objections to leaving. The guard returned and told her she was to go in.

A monster of a man followed the guard out of the tent. Yan was tall, but this man was taller by a double hand and more massive than the lean magician would ever be. More dangerous, too. The fellow had the demeanor of the dnove that his physique recalled. The giant's eye swept over her in quick evaluation, lingering for a moment on the black-and-white band around her sword arm.

"Who's your master, mercenary?"

"I've no answer for a man with no manners."

"Spunky. I like that." He grinned, scratching at the stubble on one cheek. "I'm Jax Vorsan, colonel of His Majesty's Third Regiment of Foot."

"Jax the Butcher?"

"You've heard of me." He smiled wider. "Still don't want to answer my question?"

"My contract is currently held in fee transfer by the King of Kolvin," she said, ducking her head and entering the tent before he could hold her longer in conversation. She heard his bass chuckle as he walked away, and the sound was reminiscent of a growl, making him seem more than ever a human dnove.

The man in the tent was seated on a camp stool, studying tablets. He didn't look up right away, but that was fine by her; it gave her a chance to look him over, closer now.

He looked older. Of course he looked older! He *was* older. Everyone she knew before that damned valley was older, grown so without her. She'd come here believing that it was better to face him, here, now, rather than have their meeting come unexpectedly, but her resolve faltered. How would he receive her? She could still slip back outside.

But the lines of his face held her, the remembered hunch of his shoulders, the familiar furrow on his brow. That brow had more wrinkles now. Not surprising, he had a general's worries. General? When had that happened? He'd been an aide to Colonel Jessidern when last she'd seen him.

"What is it, scout?"

He sounded annoyed at the disturbance. Well, he had reason to be. He was a general, with a general's concerns. What general had time to spend with a sergeant of the local forces?

"Come along now. I've business to . . ." His voice trailed away as he looked up at her face. He blinked, as if he doubted what he saw. "Teletha?"

"Hello, Estem," she said, suddenly shy.

His tablets went tumbling as he exploded up from his stool. His arms enveloped her and pulled her tight against his chest. She felt the hard, corded muscles beneath his shirt. Making general hadn't softened him. She was pleased but, she discovered, in an oddly detached way. Something was different between them, and it wasn't rank.

"Bert Smyth reported you dead," he mumbled into her hair. If she hadn't taken off her helmet before entering the tent, he would have mashed his nose and been bleeding all over her. She wondered what had happened to the helmet—she couldn't remember letting go of it, and both her hands were clasping his back.

"Prematurely," she mumbled back into his shoulder.

He broke the embrace, holding her at arm's length while he looked her up and down. "By Great Horesh, it's good to see you. You haven't changed a bit."

"Oh, yes I have." *We* have. "It just doesn't show much, I guess." Confused, but not wanting it to show, she changed the subject. "How is old Bert? He come along with you?"

Suddenly sober, he replied, "He died last summer on Montu."

"Oh."

"It was a good death. A soldier's death."

That didn't make him any less dead. Bert had been one of her crew in her last command. He'd been a good soldier. Now Estem said that he had died a good soldier. Bert was no longer a member of her crew, and she wasn't his captain any more. That command, and her captaincy in the Imperial forces, suddenly seemed far away and a lifetime ago.

"Estem, you don't mind my lying to get in to see you, do you?"

"Why would I mind? You saved me from embarrassing myself in front of Vorsan, for which I'm grateful. It's hard enough to hold the man's respect, I didn't need him seeing me dump my work and throw my arms around the first scout to report to my tent."

"I—I just had to come tonight. I wanted to see if it was really you. I mean, I saw you from the wall and heard Janden say your name, but I didn't believe it, I guess. It seemed so strange to see you here. I couldn't understand why you were here."

"Because the emperor ordered that we honor the Old Alliance."

"No. I mean why *you.*"

"Why not me? I'm a soldier, taking orders from my superiors. The Teletha I remember understood that well enough."

Was that a hint of reproach in his voice? He didn't understand, but why should he? He hadn't been trapped in a gods-forsaken tower and had the world go spinning on while he was unable to do a damned thing. He hadn't been roaming the coastal kingdoms behind a book-obsessed, gangly, inattentive, frustrating magician for months on end. He hadn't left his past behind and found it turning up unlooked for on his doorstep. He hadn't—he hadn't asked for her to turn up on his doorstep, either.

She felt a damned stupid tear crawl out of her eye and flee down her cheek.

Had she done the right thing in coming to see him? He might never have noticed her among the other scouts. She could have kept her face turned, her helmet pulled low. Who was she kidding? He would have recognized her at the first council meeting. He wasn't stupid. She was the one being stupid.

"You didn't really come here with a scouting report."

Not a question. Well, it must be pretty obvious, mustn't it? His statement was a nudge to get her around to talking about what was obviously troubling her. It had worked between them before. "I guess I—I wanted to talk to you, I suppose."

"About where you've been?" He plucked at the black-and-white armband. "Why you're wearing this instead of Imperial colors?"

She took a step away from him. "Are you handing out justice tonight, General?"

"I can if you want me to." His voice was gentle, promising understanding. But she knew Estem Honistonti, knew his sense of honor. Did she want justice of him? Or did she want something else? Unable to decide, she tried to put him off.

"What about your reports?"

He shrugged. "I can read them later. How often does a man get a lost lover back from the dead? Besides, that withered old curse-mumbler has assured me that the weather won't break for at least a week. We won't be doing much of anything till then. I'll have plenty of time to deal with those reports."

He reached out and touched her on the arm. His hand might have been fire for the heat she felt from it. Slowly she covered it with her own.

"Tell me about how you made general."

"And then?"

"Tell me. Then we'll see."

So he told her. Then they talked about a lot of unimportant things, then about more important things. Eventually, they did more than talk.

She never did get around to answering his questions about what she had done in the years they'd been apart. Leaving him peacefully asleep, she slipped out of the tent as Horesh began to lighten the sky and before His all-seeing eye had opened on the new day.

Iaf counted the buildings from the corner for the third time. The one he watched was still number three. He hadn't miscounted. He hadn't gotten the street wrong. Maybe he had come too late to catch him today?

The door of the third house opened and a tall, lean man wrapped in a long cloak emerged. Iaf couldn't see the man's face beneath the shadow of his broad-brimmed hat, but the satchel he carried tugged at Iaf's memories. Iaf hurried after him, catching up quickly only because the man was strolling. He knew how those long legs could cover distance.

"Master Magician?"

The man turned. "Yes?"

The face was just as he remembered it. Those eyes, so incongruously light in a merin face, as penetrating as ever. Iaf grinned, waiting for the recognition to rise in the magician's eyes. The fellow just looked expectantly at him. Iaf turned his weathered hat in his hands, further mangling the already-bedraggled feather.

"What is it you require of me, Sir Soldier?"

Iaf blinked. Maybe it was the coat and trousers. The magician's memories would have Iaf in the traditional tunic and hose of Scothandir.

"I cannot pluck your desire from your mind, to know why you are seeking a magician. You must tell me, or leave me to go about my business. I know you have a tongue, for you have already spoken." The magician paused before adding in Scothic, "We may speak in Scothic if you find that more comfortable. Your accent suggests that this is your native language."

"Aye," Iaf replied automatically. Maybe he was wrong. Maybe he had just made this man be the man he'd hoped to see. The magician he remembered was taller. "Are you Master Tanafres, the magician?"

"I am." Again the expectant look. "What is it you wish of me?"

He hadn't been wrong. He straightened and threw his shoulders back, coming to attention as he had been taught. "I am Iaf Smyth, sir."

The name seemed to make no impression on Master Tanafres. "Have we met before, Sir Soldier?"

"Have we—" Iaf groaned with exasperation over his own stupidity. "Of course. You wouldn't know me by Smyth. I was just Iaf then."

"Just Iaf. When? Iaf is a common Scothic name, but I don't recall any soldiers by that name. Your height is unusual in a Scoth, surely I would have remembered you for that alone. Perhaps you have me confused with someone else?"

Could he have made a mistake? Iaf shook his head in disbelief. "But you look just the same."

"Sir Soldier, you begin to be an annoyance. I have business elsewhere and I really—"

Iaf cut him off. "But it has to be you. They said you had a one-armed man as a friend. And the woman soldier. Aren't you the magician old Gormen brought home from the sea?"

"Gormen?" Now Master Tanafres looked confused. "What do you know of Gormen?"

"Only what everyone in the village knew. I was a kid, so they didn't tell me much. I remember when he brought you and the old man from the sea. A gift of the domarag, everyone said. I thought it was wonderful."

The magician interrupted his babbling. "What was the name of Gormen's daughter?"

"Larra."

"And the headman?"

"Sednal, of course."

"You are Iaf," Master Tanafres said. He sounded amazed.

Iaf felt his smile stretch wide his face. "You *do* remember me."

"The Iaf I remember was a boy barely on the edge of becoming a man."

"It has been some years, sir."

"Some indeed," the magician agreed, giving a rueful chuckle. "But I am pleased to make your acquaintance again. You've grown into a fine-looking man, but aren't you a little young to be a soldier."

"I'm not so young as all that. I've served the emperor since Bert brought me back from Gornal's valley. Young or not, I've served and served well." He had nothing to be ashamed of there. "I am the youngest of Colonel Kensie's aides."

"Kensie? The commander of the Scothic regiment?"

"None other," Iaf replied proudly.

"You have done well for yourself. So what is it you require of an itinerant magician?" Master Tanafres's question was asked in a friendlier tone than his earlier attempts to ascertain Iaf's business, and even though the magician now knew who he was, Iaf was a little confused.

"Require?" He hadn't thought to require anything. "I wanted to see you again, sir. I have always remembered your concern for a poor Scothic boy when we were jumped by the Imperial airmen."

"But they were no danger to us."

"We didn't know that at the time. We were fearing killers and brigands at the time."

"And spirits," said the magician with a raised eyebrow.

Iaf felt his ears start to burn. "I've seen a lot more of the world now, sir, and I've grown out of such superstitions."

"Have you? I'm glad to hear it."

Master Tanafres asked him about what had happened after he and the others had disappeared into Laird Gornal's tower. Iaf told him, trying to keep the story as short as he could; his life would be of little interest to such a wise and learned man. He was flattered at the way the magician listened so carefully to him. Becoming involved in his tale, he forgot about the people passing them in the street until he heard a voice speaking from behind him.

"The morning's a bit old to be lazing in the street, Master Tanafres. And with a soldier? I thought you didn't like the company of soldiers."

Could it be? Could it *possibly* be? He was almost afraid to turn around and see. He could feel his heart hammering against his lungs. Slowly he turned.

It was she.

Air Captain Schonnegon.

She was as beautiful as he remembered. He let go the breath he had held. He'd been afraid that the image he cherished was the nonsense of a boy. Her hair was cut differently from what he remembered, but her face was the one that haunted his dreams. *Air Captain Schonnegon.*

"He's not a new friend, but rather an old one," Master Tanafres said to her.

She raised a curious eyebrow. "Not one of mine. I'd have remembered such a handsome lad."

Handsome? She thought him *handsome.* But like an idiot, he didn't know what to say. Growing up around soldiers hadn't given him an education in polite conversation. Old Bert always said Air Captain Schonnegon knew how to be polite.

The magician stepped into the awkward silence. "Allow me to reintroduce Iaf Smyth, late of Scothandir."

"Scothandir?" She searched Iaf's face. He almost trembled with fear that she would find something wrong. "This is the boy who was your Scothic guide?"

"The very one," Master Tanafres said.

She glanced at the magician, a strange expression on her face. "He looks to be of an age with you."

He nodded. "So it would appear, but a calendar would not agree with your evaluation. Iaf's had a busy life, while others stood still." The air captain and the magician exchanged a conspiratorial look. "He's an aide to Colonel Kensie now."

She looked at Iaf with sudden respect. He felt his ears burning again, but the emotion fueling that fire was different this time. She stuck her hand out for him to grip. "A lieutenant now. You've done well for yourself."

He took her hand. Even gloved, it felt wonderful. Most

wonderful because his hand was a man's hand and not a child's. His hand enveloped hers now. At last, he found his voice. "It is my pleasure to see you again, Air Captain."

"No." She dropped her grip. The vehemence in her voice shocked him. "No longer. Do not speak of it."

He didn't know why she would want to hide her past, but he would not argue. This was Air Captain Schonnegon. She did what she did for a reason, and no sane soldier questioned her. Old Bert had taught him well. Her wishes were his orders.

"Yes, sir!"

She frowned more deeply.

Damn, *damn*, *DAMN*, DAMN! This was not turning out the way he dreamed. He was screwing it up.

"Don't salute me," she ordered. "You're the lieutenant. I'm just a sergeant, and a merc at that."

"But you're Air Cap—" He regretted it before she cut him off.

"I told you not to call me that."

"Teletha." The magician's voice held a note of reproof.

"Don't take his side, Tanafres."

She brushed between them and stalked away. The magician watched her go, shaking his head.

"She's not in a good mood," said Master Tanafres.

The magician's tentative tone suggested that he meant his words as an apologetic explanation. Iaf barely heard them as he stared after the departing Air Captain Schonnegon. She was somewhat different in person than she was in old Bert's stories. "She's not always like that, is she?"

"No. Sometimes she's worse." The magician reacted to something in Iaf's face and added, "But not too often. Something about your arrival has upset her."

"My arrival?" It was hopeless! His dreams were dust.

"Sorry," the magician said. "I didn't mean to make it personal. I meant the arrival of the Imperial force."

Not personal? Maybe it wasn't hopeless. "Does her humor have something to do with her not wanting to be called air captain?"

"Ask the gods. I don't know."

"Will she ever speak to me again?"

"You're a lieutenant. You could order her to."

Iaf shook his head. "I could never order her to do anything."

The magician said nothing, and the silence stretched out. Finally, Iaf turned and found Master Tanafres regarding him strangely.

"I really do have to attend to business," the magician said. "And I'm sure you have things to do as well. I would wish you luck in your endeavors, but you must be beyond such superstitions now, being a man and a soldier. Good day, Lieutenant Smyth."

The magician walked away, leaving Iaf standing by himself in the street.

11

THE BREEZE THROUGH THE OPEN window was warm and carried the scent of magnolia blossoms. Spring had finally come. The trees were returning to life, the small creatures were emerging from their burrows, birds unseen since autumn were again flitting about, and the bregil were on the move. Soon the army of King Shain and his Imperial allies would be, too. Yan, his role as royal adviser taken over by the Imperial magician Fasolt, would be going along with the army, but more as an adjunct to the priests and surgeons than as adviser, and definitely not as a battle magician.

In an odd way Yan was happy that the war leaders had focused their attention on Fasolt; he still had nightmares about what he had done to Yentillan's gates. Yet, though he was glad that he no longer had to deal with Shain's badgering, he felt twinges of jealousy whenever the liveried messengers came to them as they were in conference and asked only for Fasolt. Today, as he closed the town house's door on the messengers' departing backs, he felt none of that envy-tainted relief. Today's message had been for both of them: the army was to leave at dawn.

Yan returned to the hall to find that Fasolt had been in the aumbry and hauled out Yan's rubbings of the drakkenree stones Fra Bern had shown him. Fasolt's gray-haired head was bent over the pages, his expression set in his habitual sour frown. One hand, long, bony fingers extended, traced along the rows of symbols. The other held spectacles to the magician's hooked nose.

Yan stopped in the hall, frowning. Most people would have had the courtesy to ask before pulling out someone else's property. But most people weren't Imperial wizards or clients of the emperor's chancellor. Fasolt was both and had a fine sense for his own importance. Yan was glad he kept no more than the rubbings in the cabinet. He was trying to decide what sort of tart remark was appropriate when Fasolt looked up and spoke.

"These stones you saw, Tanafres. Will we be passing near them?"

"I wouldn't know. I'm not privy to the king's counsel. Haven't they told you the route?"

"By the maps, I know that well enough, but the maps do not show where these stones lie."

They wouldn't. The stones were ruins in a wilderness. Farmers opening a forest had no time for ruins. "Finally found something you need me for?"

Fasolt's eyes narrowed. "All men know something that others do not, and you are no different in that regard. I know for a fact that you have knowledge that I do not. Your skill in the arts of medicine, for example. I have never had much interest in such things, save for certain specific applications." Yan didn't want to think about what those applications might be. "Likewise, there are always things beyond a man's ken. Magic, for example, is a demanding Art and can sorely tax any practitioner's attempt to master its many facets. Most magicians find that they must specialize in order to excel. Don't you find that to be the case? You must neglect something in order to give attention to another. A most distressing situation, yes?"

"Some men are satisfied to have one thing they do well."

"Indeed. But most men are not magicians as we are. I believe that it takes a certain kind of curiosity to follow the Art, a dedication to knowing the unknown and seeking out the answers to riddles." Hand resting possessively on the rubbings, Fasolt looked sideways at him. "I have heard that you have books with symbols such as these."

And *where* had he heard that? Yan hadn't told him. Peyto

wouldn't have told; he disliked Fasolt even more than Yan did. Was Teletha the source? Yan didn't want to think so.

"How do you know about the books?"

Fasolt's face split with a raptorial smile. "Then you do have some. Most interesting."

Yan clenched his teeth to hold in a scream. He had walked into that verbal trap like a fawn taking a mountain lizard game trail, straight in the maw of the predator. But then he'd been pretty stupid about a lot of things lately.

He'd thought stupid things and, worse, said them.

Like the things he'd said to Teletha the last time he'd seen her. Why he had said anything at all still puzzled him. He'd never given a thought to the way she acted around men until the boy started visiting the town house whenever she stopped by. Her distancing herself over the winter still gnawed at him, and that had been part of it. No one liked being ignored. Still, something had set him off. Maybe it was the way the boy looked at Teletha, or the way he jumped to get anything she wanted. Yan had seen puppies less eager to please their masters. But Iaf wasn't a puppy anymore; he was a man, and a soldier, and Teletha liked the company of soldiers. Iaf was not of an age with Yan, in a natural sense, for their dates of birth were still as widely separated as ever, but the time spent in Gornal's valley had allowed the boy to grow into a man, a man whose attentions Teletha seemed to encourage. She was just being polite, though. She was. He knew she was. Still, he'd been stupid and said—he didn't even remember exactly what he had said—but he remembered Teletha's reaction well enough; he'd never seen her so angry. He'd been stupid.

Fasolt's voice dragged him out of his stupid reverie.

"You say you studied under Tidoni?"

Yan nodded, trying to get his mind back on the present conversation. "Gan Tidoni was my master."

"Private tutoring only? No university training?"

"I have never been to Sharhumrin."

"Ah, well. A pity, that."

What did Fasolt mean by *that?* Even when the Imperial magician was in a good mood, Yan found the man irritating.

Colored by his other feelings, Yan's distaste for Fasolt's demeanor was turning to positive dislike.

Fasolt hummed to himself as he riffled through the stack of rubbings as though they were his own. "Yes. I would say that these are definitely drakkenree symbols. I've seen their like before."

Where, Yan wondered, but he didn't ask. "We'll have to see to our packing if we leave at dawn," he said, temporizing as he started to roll up the rubbings. He wanted them away and out of Fasolt's sight. Still, he couldn't resist asking, "Can you read them?"

The Imperial mage snorted. It was a strangled sound, but Yan had come to recognize it as the way Fasolt expressed amusement. "No one reads them."

"No one?"

"No one human."

"Then you have no idea what the symbols mean."

Fasolt made an airy gesture. "Some of the shapes are suggestive, and some of the juxtapositions reminiscent of certain ancient scripts. I believe that I see some tentative correspondences, but I have found no certain affinities. Have you?" Fasolt's eyes gleamed. Yan swallowed, feeling the man's hot gaze burning into him. "Perhaps you would care to enlighten a poor, ignorant man who has not had the benefits you have had?"

Yan wished Fra Bern were present; Fasolt never mentioned the drakkenree stones in the priest's presence. But Bern was off readying his ambulance wagon, and the armor of his presence was unavailable. If the priest were here, Yan wouldn't be facing this dilemma.

Yan's struggle to unlock the secrets of the books had for so long been a lonely, solitary one. Fasolt was a scholar and a magician, and Yan had wanted to discuss his theories with another magician for so long. Being able to speak about his researches to someone who could understand and sympathize with him would lighten his burdens and might open his eyes to things he was overlooking. A thoughtful and empathic ear could be of immense and immeasurable help; another's perceptive eye might be the answer. Yan didn't like the Imperial magician, but Fasolt was better educated than he, and a battle mage. The section of the books that Yan felt closest to understanding dealt with battle magic, but Yan knew too little about that arcane specialty to be confident that he was understanding the symbols correctly. An expert would know so much more. Once those symbols were clear, so much more would be clear as well. One secret could unlock another, and so on until he understood it all.

Fasolt pressed again. "My studies in the Imperial archives have led me to think I am very close to understanding, but it is as though I am missing something. Sometimes the patterns of the symbols seem to follow rules, other times not. I feel as though I stare at a puzzle with pieces missing. The fragments in the archives are so frustrating. Had I more complete manuscripts, as you have, I might understand more. Surely you have come to understand something of their writing?"

He had already admitted the existence of the books. Only a fool would believe he had not studied them, and Fasolt was no fool. "Well, I don't know for sure."

"But you have some ideas."

"Some," Yan admitted.

"Anything would help."

Yan had often felt that way. "The previous owner seems to have had a greater knowledge of the symbols than either of us, but I don't think he understood them completely. In fact, I'm quite sure he didn't. He did leave some glosses concerning some of the passages. But even his notes are cryptic, for he kept them in some sort of personal code. I think I have worked out a little bit of his code, which lets me make guesses at some of the symbology, but I cannot be confident of the fidelity of my translations."

"I have some experience with ciphers. Perhaps I can be of help."

Fasolt was smiling, but the avidity in his voice was clear, making Yan wonder if he had not already said too much. Much as Yan wanted someone to confirm his work, he found himself unwilling to let Fasolt see the books or even his notebooks. What if he stole them? What if he was lying about being unable to read the drakkenree script, and left Yan the books while stealing the secrets? The secrets in those books were to be Yan's entrée into the magical community of Sharhumrin. With such knowledge at his command he could impress the dons at the university, perhaps even the emperor's own wizards, when he finally reached the capital. Those secrets would make him a comfortable life, mark him as a scholar and a magician of note. That was the dream he had followed since he left Gornal's tower. To hand it over to Fasolt now . . .

"Normally I'd be more than pleased to sit down with you and the books, Gan Fasolt, but with matters standing as they do, I fear there is no more time for scholarship this day." Yan tugged the last of the rubbings to his side of the table and started to roll them. "With the army leaving at dawn, I am sure you have much to do before then. I know I do."

Hiding the books, for instance.

Fasolt eyed him narrowly for a moment. "There is indeed much to do." He stood and gathered his satchel and hat.

"We will speak more of this as we journey," he said stiffly.

The frozen mask of Fasolt's expression revealed nothing, but its very rigidity suggested much. Yan concluded that hiding the books was the best course. There would be no time for serious study on the campaign, and taking them with him would make them too easy a target for acquisitive hands.

"I look forward to our conversations," Yan said politely as he showed Fasolt to the door.

That night, he put all his strength into the cloaking spell he used to hide himself when he stole away to secrete the books in what he hoped would be a safe place.

Iaf was out of breath when he reached the Imperial command group atop Dobbin's Knob. It had been a long distance to run in armor, even just the breastplate and tassets he was wearing. Climbing the knoll at the end of his run nearly did him in. He panted for a moment, catching his breath. As an aide handed him a waterskin, General Honistonti acknowledged his presence with a nod, the giant Colonel Vorsan with a sneer. The martial order commanders and the other officers gave him a glance and returned their eyes to the battle in progress. Iaf wet his throat so that he would speak clearly.

"General Honistonti, Colonel Kensie asks aid. The tribesmen press us harshly."

"Aid, is it?" Colonel Vorsan thundered. "You Scoths are here to prove your loyalty to the emperor. You'll do it by fighting like men. Dying if necessary."

"Save your anger, Colonel," Fra Ystram advised. "We are here to smite the enemy and not to squander the emperor's resources."

Iaf thought the Vehrite's words wise and, much as he wanted to, Iaf didn't lash back at Vorsan. The man's hatred of Scoths was well-known, a bitter joke in Kensie's regiment. Bluster didn't impress Vorsan, only action, and Iaf was determined to see the colonel impressed. Still, dying needlessly wasn't a good way to impress anyone, and dying needlessly was what the soldiers of his regiment were doing right now. He tried to keep his tone polite when he spoke.

"Begging the colonel's pardon, but I believe his responsibility is command of the left flank not the right."

"Why have you not gone to Baron Jost then?" Fra Ystram asked before Vorsan could respond.

"I have, Eminence. The baron has no men to spare."

"Go see Shain then," Vorsan suggested. "He's got men he isn't using."

"The center must remain in place," said Fra Zephem, the Baaliffite commander.

Fra Ystram addressed Honistonti. "With the general's permission, I shall lead my brothers to the Scoths' aid."

Honistonti, his attention on another part of the field, nodded absently. The left wing of the army was heavily involved, but unlike the right, where Iaf's regiment was fighting, they were having some success in pushing back the bregil warriors. A quick look told Iaf that Vorsan's command wasn't facing as many tribesmen as the Scoths, either.

Taking the general's nod as an order, the Vehrite commander lifted his barbutte from his saddlebow and settled it on his head. The leader of the Baaliffites moved his horse forward to stand between Iaf and Fra Ystram. Fra Zephem complained, "My lord General, 'tis too soon to move a reserve force. We've seen none of the great beasts."

Honistonti's head came up slightly, but his eyes remained on the battle. He raised a hand. Ystram's voice echoed from within his helm. "My lord General, do not listen to this ill counsel. The beasts have not been seen everywhere the tribesmen roam. Surely, if they were here, they would have been unleashed ere now. Vehr offers us the day, to be settled with steel and between men. I think that we shall see none of the monsters today."

"You don't know that, Ystram," said the Baaliffite.

"I know your temper, Zephem. Had I not spoken before you, you would be claiming the right to succor the Scoths. Your jealousy does not serve us here."

"And your arrogance serves us less. You'll cost us the battle by moving prematurely."

"Losing the flank will cost us the battle," Ystram countered.

"That flank will not decide the battle. The Scoths will hold," said Zephem. Colonel Vorsan snorted in derision, but Fra Zephem continued his tirade. "The Scoths are doing their job. Their blood, spilled in fulfillment of their duty, will please Baaliff. We all know that the Reaper must be paid in every battle. Today the Scoths pay. By His will we will triumph."

"You overestimate your Master's influence here," said Ystram.

"And you overestimate the need for your interference."

Those two could go on forever, and General Honistonti showed no sign of stopping them. Colonel Kensie had sent Iaf for help; it was a trust he could not betray. "My lords, this is pointless bickering. Men die while you argue."

"Stop whining, boy," Colonel Vorsan ordered. "Men die in battle. That's what they do. Scoths do it better than most."

Iaf almost broke his resolution not to provoke Vorsan's legendary anger, but Ystram spoke before him. "The young lieutenant rightly points out our fault, Colonel Vorsan."

"If the reserve is to be committed, send both our troops," Zephem said.

"If you fear the great beasts, you should understand the

need for retaining some reserve. Or has your desire to see
blood shed masked your wisdom?" Ystram turned in his
saddle. "General Honistonti, what is to be the reply? May I
lead my brothers to the aid of the Scoths?"

"Yes, Ystram. Go."

Iaf raced along beside the Vehrite commander as he
rode to his troops. Fra Ystram questioned him about the
disposition and condition of the regiment and deployment
of tribesmen assaulting them. Iaf panted out answers as best
he could.

Seeing their commander approach, the Vehrite cavalry
had started donning helms and readying their arms. Their
horses were shifting restlessly by the time Ystram arrived
and started shouting his orders. The horsemen moved out.
No one offered Iaf a mount or even a place behind them.
Almost instantly, he was left behind, choking on the dust
they raised. He ran on.

He saw the Vehrites ride along behind Kensie's regiment, using a stand of trees to screen their approach from
the hillmen swarming around the Scothic pike block that
held the right flank. The Vehrites paused only for the
briefest of moments to dress their ranks before charging
into the flank of the attacking warriors. The impact of the
mailed knights was impressive, shattering to the tribesmen.

The bregil recoiled in disorder, leaving dead and
wounded behind them. The Vehrites re-formed and
charged again. Heartened by the support, the Scoths raised
a mighty cheer. The regiment's bowmen fired in a volley,
and the pikes charged forward, thrusting steel into gaps
torn by iron-tipped beech. The tribesmen wilted under the
pressure. Their flanking maneuver had gone from near success to failure.

It was too much for the hillmen. They fled.

The retreat of the bregil left flank led to a general collapse of their force. General Honistonti, no doubt fearing to
have his cavalry scattered in the woods, forbade pursuit.
Being a foot regiment, Colonel Kensie's troops would not
have been involved anyway; but since the bregil force they
had fought today was not the largest the scouts had
reported, Iaf approved of the general's caution. Still, he was

a little disappointed. A decisive victory could have ended the campaign before it had rightly begun, leaving them with mere mopping-up operations. Too bad the tribesmen hadn't cooperated. Still, the expeditionary force's first encounter with the bregil ravagers had gone well. As Iaf reached Colonel Kensie's position, he saw that the Vehrites had even captured some of the tribesmen.

Iaf gladly accepted the backslapping from Kensie's other aides. Someone thrust a skin at him and he took a pull from it, swallowing before he realized it was wine rather than water. He let his second swig stay in his mouth long enough to taste it. It was sweet.

The screams and moans of the dying and wounded mingled with the shouts of victory. Though he was tired, his fatigue was from running, not fighting. He had come through alive and unwounded; he offered a prayer of thanks to Vehr and to Horesh. He had survived his first major battle. He might not have fought in the front rank as others had done, but he had done his job.

"Men die in battle. That's what they do," Colonel Vorsan had said. Many had done just that. Scoth, Islander, and Kolviner alike. Yet it seemed to Iaf that the Scoths had borne the brunt of the fighting. Seeing the cost of the battle spread on the field before him, Iaf resolved to be more insistent the next time he sought aid from the command staff. Men fighting for their lives had no time for the vain pretensions of their commanders.

Already the ambulance wagons were moving down from the hill behind their lines. Iaf could see the blue and yellow of the robed priests among the attendants. Surely the magician's friend Fra Bern was among them. Possibly Master Tanafres himself was there. Master Tanafres had a clear head. Perhaps the magician could help Iaf sort out what he was feeling about his superiors.

12

YAN REMINDED HIMSELF TO COUNT it as a blessing that
Fasolt was their only passenger in the ambulance. Each
time one of the wheels hit a bump, which given the parlous
state of the trails was quite often, Fasolt grunted and complained. At first Yan and Bern had shared surreptitious
smiles at the Imperial magician's discomfort, but as the
grumpiness became constant, the humor wore off.

The battle at Dobbin's Knob had not been the complete
success that everyone had hoped for. The tribesmen, contrary to their traditional pattern, had not dissolved into
chaos and fled back to their hills. But neither had they
faced the combined Kolviner-Imperial army in full battle
again. The bright hope of an early end to conflict that came
with the setting sun on Dobbin's Knob had faded as the
campaign had dragged on into the summer.

Fasolt's carriage had been lost in a river crossing less
than a sennight after the Solstice. The magician had
demanded alternative transport and been told to ride with
the wagons. To Yan's annoyance, but not to his surprise,
Fasolt had grumpily ordered his gear to be loaded into the
ambulance wagon crewed by Yan and Fra Bern.

The arrangement made it harder to avoid the Imperial
magician. Fortunately, Fasolt did not mention the books, or
anything else related to the drakkenree, in the presence of
Fra Bern. Yan found himself keeping company with the

priest more than he would have otherwise. Not to say that he disliked Bern's company, but Yan was spending the campaign functioning more as a doctor than as a magician, spending much time with Bern attending the wounded. There were moments when getting away from the man who stood by his side through so much dying was what he needed most. But those moments when he sought solitude were the very ones Fasolt chose to badger him.

The army was trekking across the undulating hills of Gremaire Forest in pursuit of another concentration of tribesmen. Honistonti continued to try to bring the hillmen to a decisive battle, but so far all the army had achieved were glorified skirmishes. Not glorified for the wounded, of course, but not big enough to decide anything beyond the fate of individuals. Still, the army pressed on.

The column of troops and wagons was strung out along the trail that wound through the hills. Trees pressed them closely on all sides, offering a confining tightness that reinforced the uncomfortable narrowness of the track. The light dappling through the trees made a patchwork of shadow confusing to the eye. The soldiers of their escort glanced warily from side to side. But for all their vigilance, they failed to detect the ambush before it was sprung.

Bregil warriors came howling out of the trees, leaping through the brush and waving their weapons. The timing couldn't have been worse for the army; confined by the trees, the cavalry could not deploy. The tribesmen were soon among them, hacking at man and mount alike. From the sounds erupting before and behind them, Yan guessed that the hillmen were striking up and down the column.

But this time there were more then just bregil. Yan's mouth opened in amazement as he saw a wedge of six armored drakkenree emerge from a blind of brush. They ran forward with frightening speed. Their three toes spread to give them a sure grip on the uneven ground, and they moved with birdlike quickness, smashing into the arquebusiers guarding the wagons before the soldiers realized their peril. The warrior saurians stood little taller than a man but were more massive. They bore enormous, two-handed swords and wielded them with frightening efficiency and horrific strength, splitting men open with the force of their blows. The carnage was awesome.

One drakkenree, grappled by three soldiers, showed how much more dangerous than a man its kind were in close combat. Its jaws snapped closed on one man's arm. The soldier screamed and let go of his hold. The drakkenree tossed its head to one side, spitting out a chunk of bloody flesh and gleaming bone. Yan watched horrified as the man's arm folded at a new joint. The saurian snapped at another of its attackers. Having seen what had happened to his comrade, that man recoiled. The drakkenree raked his face with the talons of its hand. The third soldier was no match for the saurian's elemental strength; with a shrug, the drakkenree tossed him to the ground. It slew him and then his companions with wide sweeping blows from its blade.

Captain Janden galloped through the melee, pulling up alongside the wagon. His fist hammered on the canvas cover.

"Fasolt!" The Imperial magician crawled up to the driver's seat and stuck his head out. Janden screamed at him. "You see? They *are* here!"

Eyes narrowed, the mage coldly replied, "I see."

A deep, terrifyingly familiar roar split the air. Janden's horse reared and the trace horses panicked, almost wrenching the wagon from the road. Fra Bern fought them, barely managing to restrain them from careering into the confused tangle of soldiers and saurians on the trail in front of them.

A *terriserpens* rose from concealment in the ravine at the edge of the road. Its head towered over them. A beam of sunlight glanced off its yellowed fangs as its charnel breath gusted over them. The horses went wild, rocking the wagon with their struggles to escape their harness and bolt from the monster.

Fasolt threw himself forward, climbing onto the driver's bench with unexpected agility. He thrust forward a hand, fingers extended in a commanding gesture. The air crackled as Yan's skin tingled with the gathering of the mana. Blue fire flashed around Fasolt's hand and leapt toward the monster. The blast missed the beast, splintering a tree behind the *terriserpens*.

The beast hauled back its head, as if surprised. It cocked

its snout to one side then the other, entirely too much like a bird searching for a worm.

Fasolt mumbled a chant, gathering the energy for another blast.

The *terriserpens* tilted its head several times in rapid succession, each shift bringing one of its glittering eyes to focus on the wagon. Claws digging furrows in the hillside, it charged up the slope.

Yan saw that they had to leap clear before the beast hit the wagon. He reached past Fasolt to tug at Fra Bern, trying to pull him from the seat. Struggling with the reins, Bern refused to budge. Yan cast a glance over his shoulder and saw that it was too late.

The *terriserpens* crashed into the wagon. Yan tumbled, falling from the seat. Visions of himself sprawling on the ground near the beast's clawed feet flashed before him, but instead of the earth and debris of the forest floor, he hit the wooden bed of the wagon. He slid across the interior, pummeled by baggage as the wagon tilted. Wood splintered, canvas tore. A talon gouged through the cover, snapping framework as it passed.

There was a flash of blue light from the front of the wagon. Horses screamed above the chaos of noise. Then for a moment all was still. The wagon teetered, then crashed over on its side. Something massive slammed against it. The monster's tail bashed against the framework, shattering the structure and nearly tearing it all away. Canvas, wood, and baggage collapsed onto Yan as he sprawled helplessly. The wagon started to slide down the slope.

Bundles of baggage and cases of supplies battered against Yan as the wagon crashed and bounced down the side of the ravine. The shredded canvas that enveloped him threatened to cut off his air. He fought back against the tangling mass until something struck him in the head and everything went gray. Sometime later, he realized that he had stopped moving.

Yan shook his head to clear it and immediately regretted the action. The pounding in his skull intensified as he struggled to free himself from the debris. As he finally managed to drag the last fold of canvas from his face, his stomach heaved rebelliously. Screwing his eyes shut, he hugged his stomach, hoping to restrain himself from vomiting. When the urge passed, he lay still and gulped in the air he had finally managed to reach. Cautiously he felt his scalp and found a lump just above his left ear. His hand came away bloody. That explained the fuzziness of his vision and the nausea.

The ravine in which he lay was quiet. From elsewhere in the forest, he could hear the sounds of battle: shouts and howls and screams, the clashing of weapons, gunshots, and the roar of a *terriserpens*.

Belatedly, he recollected his peril. The beast could make a meal of a disoriented magician in a single bite. He crawled to the back end of the wagon—the front was a crushed mess of splintered wood and offered no exit. Before crawling outside, he looked about for the beast that had attacked the wagon.

He saw it lying on the slope. A cavalry horse lay next to it, as still as the *terriserpens*. There was no obvious wound on the horse, but the great beast's head was a splintered mass of bloody bone and shredded muscle. Fasolt's magic must have done that.

Since the Imperial magician had slain the beast, he was likely still around somewhere; nothing less than a *terriserpens* could threaten a wizard with that kind of power. Yan spotted him a dozen yards upslope, sitting on the ground. Fasolt was slumped against a tree, his head in his hands. The man's lean frame sagged with exhaustion. Knowing what effort ordinary magic took, Yan supposed Fasolt had good reason to be tired; the man had executed two powerful battle magic spells in an extremely short space of time and without any preparation. And an impressive display of battle magic it had been. The effectiveness of Fasolt's second spell was undeniable, as undeniable as the fact that Fasolt had saved all their lives.

Or had he? Yan did not see Fra Bern.

He scanned the slope leading up to the road. He did not see the priest there, nor was there any sign of him in any part of the ravine that Yan could see from the back of the wagon. Yan clambered out, wincing at the pain. Nothing seriously wrong, or he wouldn't be moving as well as he was. He found Fra Bern under one of the dead horses, unconscious but alive. Well aware of his own depleted strength, Yan climbed up the slope to get Fasolt.

"Come help me with Bern," he said.

Fasolt looked up at him. "He isn't dead?"

"Not yet."

The Imperial wizard looked back up toward the trail. Nothing moved. The sounds of unseen fighting grew fainter, as if the battle were moving away.

"All right," Fasolt said. "We may need him before this is over."

He hauled himself unsteadily to his feet. Supporting each other, they staggered back down to the wagon. Together they managed to free the priest from the burden of the dead animal and drag him away from the wreckage. Upon examining Bern, Yan found the priest's left arm was broken. He suspected the priest's ribs were cracked as well.

Yan listened again for the sounds of combat. They were fainter still.

Good. No one was likely to disturb them while he tended Fra Bern. Taking advantage of his friend's unconscious state to save him the pain, Yan got to work. Yan had the bone set and splinted before Bern made any sound other than a moan of pain.

"Yan?" Fra Bern's voice was weak.

"Quiet," Yan told him.

Fra Bern looked at the rough splint and frowned. "It hurts. Is it broken?"

Yan nodded. "Can you mend it?"

The priest forced a strained smile. "The gift is rarely granted for one's own benefit."

"You can try, can't you? Ask after the ribs, too. We can't move quickly with you in this shape."

Bern offered a weak smile. "I shall pray."

Yan left him to it and walked over to where Fasolt had retreated. The Imperial magician looked up from his seat on a fallen tree. His face was haggard and worn as though he had not slept in days. A heavy toll from the battle magic, clearly more taxing than benign sorcery.

"Are you all right?" Yan asked.

"The weariness will pass." Fasolt waved a dismissive hand. The hand shook.

"That was impressive magic you used on the *terriserpens.*"

"Serviceable."

Clearly the man was not in the mood for a conversation. Yan abandoned his effort to talk to the mage and returned to see how Fra Bern fared. The priest was breathing more easily. Yan was relieved.

"Some small favor has been granted me," said the priest, struggling to rise. Yan helped him stand. "I believe that I can walk."

"Good." Fasolt's comment caught Yan off guard; he hadn't heard the man approach. Fasolt said, "We must rejoin General Honistonti."

"We don't know where he is," Yan pointed out. The forest around them was quiet now; the sounds of battle completely gone.

"Then we must find him."

"I think it would be better if we tried to get back to Jost's town," Yan said. The temple priests would be better able to care for Fra Bern.

"I agree," Fra Bern said weakly. "If the army suffers as I fear, they will return there as well. It is the nearest fortified place."

Fasolt shook his head. "General Honistonti will not be put off by so small a setback."

"Small?" They had only seen a portion of the fighting. "How can you say that?"

Fasolt looked insulted. "I have had some experience with battles."

"Have you any, ah—*knowledge* of the results of the battle or General Honistonti's plans?" Bern asked.

"I do not need any," Fasolt said sharply. "If the drakkenree and their servants had been of sufficient strength to destroy our forces, you would still hear the battle. This ambush was simply an attempt to reduce the army, to wear it away. I do not believe the damage to be very great."

There were dead men on the road above; the damage to them was great enough. Yan looked around at the injured

Bern, the destroyed wagon, and the dead horses. "Great enough for us."

"If the attackers were not numerous, why didn't the general stay and fight them?" Fra Bern asked.

"The woods are no place for a battle. He will try to find more open ground. The tribesmen will not continue to attack there unless they have mustered more numbers than they have yet assembled. Honistonti will camp and regroup." Fasolt sounded confident.

"The woods are no place for us either," Yan pointed out.

"Agreed," his companions said together.

While they debated whether to try to find the army or head for Jost's town, he searched the debris of the wagon for anything usable.

The wounded were Teletha's first clue that something had gone wrong. Clearly the army had been attacked. All the banners were flying, though, so things could not be too bad. She left her second to make the report and headed her horse toward the wagon lääger. There were fewer vehicles than there had been in the morning. She searched among them for one in particular and failed to find it. A Manarite priest, her robe spattered with dried and drying blood, told Teletha that Yan and Bern's wagon had not been seen since the attack. They had been near the rear of the column, where the *terriserpens* had attacked. Someone had told the priest that he had seen the wagon go off the trail into a ravine.

Teletha's gut knotted. Her ears rang with the last angry words she had exchanged with Yan before they left Jost's town. She'd regretted them almost immediately, but there had been no opportunity to tell him so. With all the activity in the campaign, she hadn't seen him since the scouts had pulled out the day before the army did.

Was he dead? Or lying injured in the forest?

She hated not knowing.

She thought about going to Estem, but knew he'd have enough worries now. Besides, how would she explain that she wanted to know about another man? Estem would draw the wrong conclusions.

Or maybe they wouldn't be wrong conclusions. She'd abandoned her career in the Imperial military and trailed Yan across the coastal kingdoms. For what? For a man whose abilities terrified her? For a man who spent more time thinking about his books than about his next meal? If they had been lovers, she'd understand better. Estem would understand better, at least he would think so. But it just wasn't so. She and Yan hadn't even made pledge to each other.

Maybe Yan was just an excuse for her. The thought was not a new one, and now that he was missing, she wondered about it again. If he was just an excuse, why was her stomach so tight? He confused her, the situation confused her, and she didn't like it. Her great plan to hide out in the communal barracks all winter and figure things out hadn't worked. A whole winter of worrying at the problem hadn't solved anything. Then Estem had shown up, and that hadn't solved anything either, only added to the confusion.

Fortunately, Yan didn't know about Estem; the fuss he was making about Iaf was bad enough. In an ordinary man, she would have taken such a fuss as a sign of interest at least, but Yan was so damned inconsistent. One minute he'd be complaining about her encouraging the boy, and the next he'd be babbling about Fasolt prying into his secrets and trying to see those precious books of his.

Damn Yan's secrets! Damn his books! Damn him!

Damn him for doing this to her!

She was a *soldier,* damn it! Not some simpering court lady or moonstruck farm lass.

Her second hailed her and she nearly took his head off with her snarling reply. After she apologized, he told her that the scouts were being ordered out to screen for the army. Duty called; there was a lot more at stake here than one man. Still angry, she mounted up.

Fasolt was even more helpless in the woods than Yan, and Fra Bern was barely managing to keep himself from walking into trees, which meant that if anyone kept them out of trouble, it was going to be Yan. He stayed out in front of the others and tried to remember everything he'd seen

Teletha do in similar circumstances. This forest wasn't the bog woods of the Megeed, and avoiding the bregil tribesmen didn't pose the same problems as dodging Megeed warlords, but he hoped that if he were alert enough, he might spot trouble before they stumbled into it. He became acutely aware of how much he had relied on Teletha.

It didn't take him long to realize that they were lost. Since they had no idea of where they were or in what direction they should be traveling, their choice of destination had become irrevelant. Darkness was coming and it was now obvious that they were going to be benighted in the forest. They'd need a safe place to rest for the night.

As he crossed a creek, Yan saw an exposed rock face gleaming in the light of the sunset. It was only a few hundred yards away. He headed for it, hoping that a dark shadow on its surface indicated a cave. He always felt safer with walls around him. It wasn't until he was facing the dark opening that he thought about the possibility that the cave might already have inhabitants. He sniffed the air, but could only detect the scent of the trees and other forest vegetation from the surrounding landscape. The cave didn't smell like the lair of some man-eating beast; he saw no litter of gnawed bones or piles of dung. Still, he cautioned the others to wait while he explored. His magesight was next to useless in the darkness within the rock, and so it was only when he called magelight to banish the darkness that he saw the carvings.

Ready to call the others, he looked back over his shoulder. The light of his spell caught in something, raising a flickering reflection to his right. There he saw a tall, slender plinth and upon it a rough polished sphere of some metal, glimmering redly in the light. No natural formation, that.

Outside in the pale moonlight, he could see the silhouettes of his companions. Beyond them, scattered among the trees, he saw mounds that he had missed as they passed among them. The humped shapes were overgrown with vegetation. They were like those in the valley Fra Bern had taken him to. They had come upon another ancient drakkenree place. The region seemed full of them, once you knew how to spot them.

"What is it, Yan?" Fra Bern called.

What indeed. "Seems empty." Now.

Leaving Fasolt standing at the opening, Fra Bern joined Yan. Upon seeing the carvings flickering in Yan's magelight, he swallowed. His head turned, eyes slipping along the rows of symbols. "Drakkenree carving," he whispered.

"Eh?" Fasolt abandoned his nervous scanning of the woods and shuffled in. The exhausted sag in his shoulders vanished as he saw what the others were looking at. He called his own magelight and bent to study the nearest symbols.

"This is an ill place," Fra Bern said.

"Safer here than outside tonight, I think," Yan told him.

"As may be. I like it not."

Fra Bern returned to the entrance. Yan left the Imperial magician tracing symbols with his fingers and moved deeper into the cave. The passage twisted away to the left after a dozen or so yards, and began to slope downward. The wall on the left curved away, but the path grew no wider; it hugged the right-hand wall, its left edging dropping away into darkness. Yan's magelight didn't penetrate into the abyss. He tossed a pebble out into the darkness and waited to hear the sound of it striking. He waited a long time; and when the sound came, it was that of stone striking water. There was much more to this cavern. What lay sleeping in that darkness?

"Yan?" The priest's call was soft; Yan almost didn't hear him.

"What is it?" he called back, only to get a shushing sound in return. Puzzled, he joined Bern at the entrance.

"What is it?" he whispered.

"I heard something moving in the brush."

"Animals?"

"It could be, but I don't think so."

There seemed plenty of reason for caution. Hastily, Yan cast a cloaking spell to mask the entrance to the cave and hide the people in it.

Less than a minute later, a drakkenree stalked from among the trees to stand in the moonlit clearing at the foot of the rock face. The creature was like the ones that had attacked the column. It was taller and longer but of slighter build than those saurian warriors, but not so slight as the

slumbering mages Yan remembered. The creature's scaly
hide was as black as the bottom of a covered well. The
drakkenree wore a harness of straps, from which depended
a number of pouches and bits of metal. A large, circular
plate of gleaming bronze, bisected by a black line, protected its chest. Something about that chestplate tugged at
Yan's memory. The saurian's head turned as it scanned the
area, and the moonslight glinted from its fierce yellow eyes.

More drakkenree emerged from the gloom among the
trees to join it. Two were mottled gray and black and the
other four were a dull green. The green drakkenree carried
the great two-handed swords. They fanned out across the
clear area while the others stood together, bobbing heads,
and hissing and growling at each other.

Two more green saurians and some thirty bregil emerged
into the clearing. The bregil all wore the sign of the *haggatan*,
although only some of them were armed as warriors. Most
carried leather-wrapped bundles strapped to their backs.
One of the green drakkenree hissed at the tribesmen; the
bregil warriors fanned out to follow the drakkenree soldiers,
while the porters lay down their burdens.

"What are you two—"

Yan hushed Fasolt with an anxiously waved hand. The
Imperial magician joined them at the entrance of the cave,
and, when his eyes fell on the drakkenree, he gasped. Yan
turned to find Fasolt with an expression of shock on his face.

"They wear the sign of the serpent's eye," Fasolt said in
an awestruck voice.

The wizard started to push forward, and Yan grabbed
his arm. If the fool stepped outside the protection of Yan's
spell, they would surely be spotted. Fasolt resisted the tug.

"They don't know we're here," Yan told him.

"They will." Fasolt hunkered down and clasped his
hands. He stared at the drakkenree over his interlocked fingers. Leaning over to Fra Bern, he started whispering
urgently to the priest. Yan couldn't hear what Fasolt was
saying, but he decided that not hearing was all right. If he
couldn't hear it while squatting next to them, the drakkenree wouldn't be hearing it down in the clearing.

Below them, the warrior saurians returned. One of them

approached the black one, bobbed once, and hissed. The black one, clearly the leader, inclined its head. The warrior bobbed again and backed away. Under the direction of the warrior drakkenree, the porters took up their burdens and started back into the woods. Soon all but the leader had left the clearing. Yan watched as it took two steps, then stopped and cocked its head to the side. Seeing a human do that same thing, he would have said the man was listening. The saurian's neck twisted around and it faced in their direction, snout pointed toward their hiding place.

"He's seen us." Fra Bern's voice was forlorn.

Yan was not so sure that the drakkenree had seen them. He might just have noted a flaw in Yan's magical cloak and be wondering what was out of place. "No, it would be calling its warriors if he had."

"Now or later, we will be found," said Fasolt, fumbling in his satchel. "We must strike while we can."

"Let's wait it out. The creature's not sure." At least Yan hoped that was the case. He continued to watch the drakkenree, hoping it would decide that whatever had caught its attention was unimportant. Unfortunately, the saurian continued to stare at their hiding place. Behind Yan, Fasolt was mumbling to Fra Bern again. He almost shushed them, sure that the talk would provide what the drakkenree needed to penetrate the spell, but feared that his own noise would only contribute. He just wished them quiet.

The drakkenree remained as still as stone.

Fasolt moved up beside Yan.

Yan knew it was a risk to say anything, but restraining Fasolt from foolishness was worth it. Yan whispered, "It's still not sure. We may get out of this yet."

Fasolt nodded.

"We'll get out," he said. "I will teach it the folly of meddling here."

Holding a wire-wrapped rod in his left hand and a crystalline cube in his right, Fasolt stood. He started to step clear of the cloaking spell. Yan grabbed at his coat and missed. The wizard cleared the boundaries of the spell. Raising his hands, Fasolt began to chant.

Thanks to the mage's foolishness, they were undone.

Yan felt the tingle of gathering mana. The air around Fasolt began to glow faintly. Shocked, Yan saw that the black drakkenree hadn't run or called its warriors. It stood, its body facing them now as well—and that body was glowing.

The saurian was a magician!

Fasolt's whining chant rose to a high-pitched wail. The man's voice stopped, but the noise went on, ripping up to the edge of audibility. He lifted the cube aloft and it transformed into a globe of crackling, blue light. The black drakkenree inclined its torso as though it were bowing and bobbed its head. An azure bolt of magical energy cracked from the cube in Fasolt's hand only to splash on the air before the saurian. The mana energy scattered to harmlessness.

The drakkenree tilted its body upright, arms widespread. The air at the mouth of the cave whipped into an instant frenzy. Brush, dirt, and small stones leapt up into the air. Larger debris scampered around the ground, more and more of it becoming airborne. Fasolt stood in the midst of the sudden whirlwind, unharmed. The storm grew, battered the cave mouth. Dragging Bern, Yan ducked deeper inside to avoid the debris carried by the wind. A chunk of granite spun out of the storm and struck the base of the plinth, cracking the slender spire. It toppled and shattered. The metal sphere fractured, a large piece rocked and wobbled its way to fetch up against the prone priest.

Through the dust of the storm, Yan could see movement among the trees. The other drakkenree were returning. Yan could see their chance of escape evaporating.

"We've got to get out of here," he said.

Eyes wide with fear, Fra Bern nodded. "We can't abandon Fasolt."

"He's chosen his own course."

Yan pulled the priest out of the cave, trying to keep his concentration focused and pull the cloaking spell onto them. Movement usually destroyed the illusion, but he hoped the warrior drakkenree would be too busy watching the dueling mages. If the drakkenree mage turned its attention to them, they would be spotted in a heartbeat, but the creature was very busy just now.

The moaning wind began to die down. Fasolt was mastering the spell, beating it down. Yan risked a glance back. Yes, the dust devil was faltering. He could see the Imperial mage making laying gestures with his right hand. Fasolt's left hand and the rod in it glowed with a ready spell.

He never got the chance to use it.

The drakkenree unleashed its own spell before Fasolt finished with the whirlwind.

A ghostly image formed around the black drakkenree, a shape like unto itself. The saurian pointed a taloned figure at Fasolt and the image separated from it, stalking forward toward Fasolt. The mage jerked, his bared teeth showing that the movement was against his will, and suddenly he, too, was overlain with a duplicate image.

Yan gasped when he understood what was happening. The drakkenree mage was forcing a spirit duel, a raw contest of will and mana control. Yan had read about such things but had never seen one, although Gan Tidoni had taught him tricks to resist such a spell. Such duels were nearly always lethal engagements.

The physical forms of the contesting magicians were rigidly still. To any but the magesighted, the battle of the spirit forms was invisible. What were the other drakkenree making of the sudden stillness of the two duelists?

The ghost images met midway between the contesting magicians. Fasolt manifested a sword, but the drakkenree relied on its natural armament. At first Fasolt's swings kept his opponent at bay, but Yan feared that the drakkenree was only testing the Imperial magician. When Fasolt lunged, Yan was sure. The drakkenree skipped aside and its neck pistoned forward. Spirit jaws clamped on Fasolt's forearm. The ghost sword and the hand holding it vanished. Fasolt's body staggered back as his hand, severed at the wrist, fell to the ground. The stump started to spout blood.

The battle would not last much longer.

Yan tore his eyes away and shoved Fra Bern into a stumbling run. They had to get as far away as they could before Fasolt fell.

Screams cut through the night behind them.

To Yan's astonishment, and immense relief, the drakkenree did not pursue them.

13

STANDING AWAY FROM THE TABLE in the center of the king's tent, Teletha didn't feel like she was a part of the discussions among the war leaders. She was just a scout troop leader and not a king or a baron or an Imperial officer. But she had been out in the wilderness and she had been an officer and she had seen the enemy. She had her opinions of what had been done and what was being talked about. Maybe it was just as well no one asked her opinion, because she didn't like the way the war council was headed at all.

The ambush in Gremaire Forest had established one thing that two months of campaigning had failed to do: there were drakkenree with the bregil. The presence of the so-called ancient enemy had spooked the commanders all out of proportion to the few drakkenree actually seen. Both the king and Estem seemed convinced that the drakkenree were the masterminds behind this whole invasion. How they'd reached that conclusion, she didn't know. There wasn't any evidence to suggest anything more than an alliance between the saurians and the hill monkeys. For all they knew, the lizards could be mercenaries.

Though the ambush had clearly been bad for morale, Teletha didn't think it justified the timidity it inspired in the leaders. Now, it seemed, the nearly intact army was to retreat to Jost's town and await reinforcements. Directly. There would be no skirmishing. There would be no searches for stragglers. She listened as the leaders settled the details of the order of march. She couldn't believe that they really would abandon those unaccounted for in the ambush. Yan was among the missing. So were Fra Bern and Gan Fasolt. She stepped forward to speak.

"Your Grace, I'd like to take my troop out to search for survivors."

Janden threw her a blazing look for violating the chain of command. She didn't care, because she'd gotten the king's attention. Shain looked at her, puzzled at first, but then enlightenment lit his face. "Schonnegon, isn't it?"

"Aye, your Grace."

"I've heard you're a good troop leader."

"I do my best to serve you, your Grace."

"I've need of good troop leaders. More so now that we have unmasked the enemy behind this invasion." The king motioned for a servant to fill his wine cup. "Leaders of your gender are rare in the empire, rarer still in Kolvin."

"About my request, your Grace," she said stiffly.

Janden spoke up before the king could answer. "Your Grace, this woman came to the kingdom in the company of the magician Tanafres. That is who she wants to search for."

"Your husband?" asked the king.

"A friend," she answered. "Fra Bern the Einthofite is missing, too."

"There are many unaccounted for," Janden said. "Including Gan Fasolt. Were we to risk searchers for any, we should for him. Are the men she seeks worth the risk? As your Grace knows, Tanafres has been of little use in our struggle against the ancient enemy. Admittedly, the priest's healing gift would be a benefit, but I don't believe the risk justifies sending anyone out. Their wagon was the one that the *terriserpens* attacked. We have no proof that any of them survived that attack."

"We have no proof that they didn't survive, either," Teletha pointed out.

"We cannot afford to lose more troops in those woods. We've lost enough to the lizards already," Shain said.

"What about Gan Fasolt?" Teletha objected. "The emperor will not take kindly to our losing his magician."

"We did not *lose* him," Janden said indignantly. "All reports indicate that he was killed in battle with a *terriserpens*. Gan Fasolt was directly in the path of the beast, and his magic failed to stop it. No one could have reached him in time; no one could have helped. I do not believe that the emperor will hold us responsible for the life of a wizard who could not protect himself."

Shain nodded at Janden's words. "The loss of the estimable gan is indeed regrettable."

"His Imperial Majesty will understand, your Grace," Janden assured him. "We must proceed with this war against the drakkenree as best we can. If we must do so without the aid of the wizard, that must be the gods' wish; and since we must rely on soldiers, we must have reinforcements. Once the levy has reached Jost's town we can march forth again and bring the enemy to battle, where we will break their forces."

"A day to which I look forward," Shain said. He stood, and those around him bowed. The meeting was over. "For now, we must away to Jost's town. I'd sooner sleep in the castle than a tent."

Teletha stepped in front of the king. "What about Tanafres and Fra Bern, your Grace? Is this the reward they receive for service to you?"

King Shain glowered at her. "You are impertinent, Sergeant. You clearly do not understand your place here. There are more important duties for the scouts than searching the woods for the dead. The army must return safely to Jost's town."

"Sergeant Schonnegon has brought up a legitimate point of concern, your Grace," Estem said.

Trust Estem to take her part, even if she didn't want to involve him. "I'm not in your command, General Honistonti."

Irritation in his expression, Shain looked at Estem. "As I myself was about to say."

Estem didn't flinch. "Gan Fasolt's safety was entrusted to my command. Perhaps we *should* consider a search party. Your scouts are swift, and they know the woods better than my men."

"There will be no searches," the king said. "I have more

important uses for *my* forces. Before risking your own, consider what other charges your emperor has laid on you."

"I never forget my orders, your Grace." Estem smiled at the king, making politeness his shield against Shain's ill humor. "If your Grace does not trust my judgment, he should ask the emperor for a replacement commander for this expeditionary force. I am sure one can arrive before next spring."

The king's face was hard. "General, I am leaving for Jost's town. I charge you, by your orders, to accompany me with your forces. You will support my efforts against the enemy, and you will not question how I choose to use my forces." The king strode away, leaving Estem to glare after him.

Teletha's attempt to get permission to search had failed. As a contracted mercenary she was bound to obey the orders she was given, so long as they were not suicidal. If anything touched on suicide here, it was her suggestion to ride into enemy territory in search of the lost.

"We'll do something yet, Tel," Estem whispered.

"I didn't ask for your help."

Estem clearly thought about saying something, but changed his mind. He took his leave of her and joined the rest of the Imperial officers and their aides at one end of the tent; the king's men had followed him out. Teletha stood alone near the table. All around, the king's clerks were tidying up and preparing to leave, but one clerk remained seated on his stool in the corner, Peyto. Janden was standing over him, seemingly waiting for a response. The clerk was ignoring the captain and continuing to scratch at the tablet in his lap. Janden snatched Peyto's stylus away and slammed it to the floor. She decided to intercede; this, at least, was a here-and-now problem.

"You know where they are, clerk, and I want them," Janden was saying as she arrived. Peyto caught her eye and shook his head slightly, warning her off. She stopped a few steps away, out of Janden's sight. The captain leaned over Peyto. "We need the information in them."

"I know he hid them, but I don't know where," Peyto said to Janden. "He doesn't confide everything to me, you know."

"I think you're lying."

"Had I a higher opinion of your mentation, I would be insulted." Peyto picked up his stylus and frowned at the crack in the ivory. "Even were I to tell you where the books were, presuming I knew, you would not be able to take them in your hands."

"How so?"

"Master Tanafres is a magician. Do you think he would not protect his goods? Though he is by your word not very useful, he has, in my estimation, more than a small capability in the Great Art. Were I he, I would surely have placed a protective spell on the chest, sealing it to anyone without magic. Alas for you that he is probably dead. Since magically protected books need a magician to open them, you will need a magician to see what is inside. Presuming you get your hands on them.

"Your relationship with Gan Fasolt was rather friendlier than with Master Tanafres. How unfortunate that Gan Fasolt was with Master Tanafres when the column was attacked. Doubly unfortunate that he is presumed as dead as Master Tanafres. Were one or the other of them alive, you would be in a better position. Gan Fasolt could unlock a spell at your suggestion, regardless of the propriety of the matter. Then again, he might not choose to let you see the books either. I trust you know how he would have reacted better than I. However, were Master Tanafres to be found alive, you could proceed as a gentlemen should, and ask the owner for permission to view his goods."

Teletha wanted to laugh at the feisty old clerk's response. So much for her rescuing him. He had his own ways of prodding people to the actions he wanted. They didn't work with Yan and Teletha, much, but they did work. They certainly seemed to be working on Janden. The captain did not find the matter amusing, and his face darkened steadily during the clerk's speech.

"What are these books, Captain Janden?" Estem asked as he joined Teletha.

Janden started at the question. "General?"

"The books of which you speak, Captain. What are they?"

"Drakkenree books, sir. I believe they may shed some light on the enemy."

"Anything would help. If Tanafres is the only one who knows where they are, perhaps we should make some effort to find him."

"He must be dead," Janden said.

"You don't *know* that," Teletha said.

"They would have rejoined the column," Janden countered.

"They might have been captured," said Fra Ystram. The argument had attracted the attention of the rest of the Imperial officers, and they had gathered around.

"That would be bad if they were," said Colonel Vorsan as he joined the conversation. "If the lizards caught Fasolt, we could be in trouble."

"Perhaps the sergeant is right. Perhaps there should be a search," Janden said. "If Gan Fasolt survived the great beast's attack, he might still be alive. Since he has not returned, we must consider the possibility that he has been captured. If that is so, then the emperor will surely be wroth."

"I thought you said the emperor wouldn't hold you responsible for the loss of the wizard," Teletha said sweetly.

"Not for his death." Janden appealed to Estem. "If either of the magicians has been captured, he must be rescued. The drakkenree cannot be allowed to hold any magician. A search party has become imperative."

You bastard! "Why didn't you say that in front of Shain."

"The sergeant asks a good question," Estem said.

Vorsan made a rumbling noise that sounded like a bear growling. "All this talk is getting us nowhere. Janden says we need one or both of these magicians, and we don't even know if either of them is still breathing. Seems to me we ought to find out one way or another."

"Exactly," Teletha said. "That's what I was—"

"I didn't ask you, mercenary," Vorsan snapped. "I'll go."

"I know the land better," Teletha protested.

"I marched out there, and I marched back. I know the land well enough. My regiment can scour the place. We'll turn up the wizards, or their bodies."

"Impossible," Estem stated. "You know the orders. Shain has commanded me to go with him. Besides, we can't risk a whole regiment on detached service. There are enough hill-men out there to surround and annihilate a regiment."

"Not *my* regiment."

Estem sighed briefly. "Colonel Vorsan, while I respect and honor your regiment's prowess, I'm concerned about weakening our forces overall. The ambush made a hash of things as it was. If your regiment were ambushed as well . . . "

"Then I won't take a whole regiment. A battalion, then."

"A company would be too much to lose for nothing," Janden said.

"So I'll take a hand," Vorsan said.

"You would be courting death for all who accompanied you, Colonel Vorsan," Estem warned.

"Jax Vorsan ain't afraid of hill monkeys or big lizards."

"We still have Shain's command to accompany him," Estem pointed out.

"The king ordered you and your forces to go with him, General," Teletha said. "As long as each banner is flying and men march behind it, who will count heads? A small patrol would not be missed, and a small party would find it easier to avoid contact with the tribesmen."

"Well said." Vorsan leered at her. "Bright for a woman. How'd you find her, Janden?"

"Colonel Vorsan," Estem snapped, "I'll thank you to keep your talk confined to military matters." Vorsan saluted, but retained his grin, despite Estem's frown. "If you are determined to attempt this adventure, I think it advisable that you take only volunteers."

Vorsan replied jauntily, "If that's the way you want it. I've no shortage of brave men in my regiment."

"Cavalry would be faster. They could cover more ground." Teletha didn't want to trust the mission to this lumbering giant.

"Sergeant Schonnegon, the king has already forbidden you to go on a search," Estem said.

"Infantry's better for scouring the woods anyway," Vorsan said.

"I will volunteer to go with Colonel Vorsan." Iaf's voice brought all heads around to stare at him. Teletha could see that the young Scoth was watching her more closely than he was any of the officers. Was he trying to impress her? Probably.

Vorsan wasn't impressed at all. He snarled, "Go away! I'll rot on Fisean's Gibbet before I have a Scoth at my side."

Colonel Kensie's face hardened at Vorsan's announcement, and the Scoths around him bristled. More than one hand drifted toward a dagger hilt. Vorsan's aides seemed eager for the fight.

"We have more than enough foes hiding in the woods and among the hills," Estem said, stepping between the two groups. "Colonel Kensie, I'll want your regiment with the king's bodyguard. Colonel Vorsan, pass the word quietly and select among whatever volunteers you get. No more than a company, less if you think it wise. I'd prefer that you not go yourself."

"And miss all the fun?"

"At least leave me one of your lieutenants. I trust you will put his Majesty's concerns above the needs of anyone's personal honor. Don't look for trouble. I expect we will all have more than enough opportunities for glorious encounters with the enemy before this campaign is finished."

Teletha doubted that Vorsan understood all of what Estem was trying to tell him, but the giant colonel saluted and departed, grinning. His aides were a raucous flock around him. Colonel Kensie and the Scoths departed with more dignity for all their rural demeanor. Estem excused himself, citing the need to prepare for the march back to Jost's town.

She asked Janden if he needed her, careful to phrase it exactly that way, and was relieved when he said "No." That was the answer she'd wanted. Her not being needed by her immediate superior was a slim thing to hang her plans upon, but it was all she had. She left the tent and gathered her gear.

Iaf caught her as she led her horse out of the corral. He had to have been waiting at the entrance to pounce so quickly.

"Air Cap—I mean, Sergeant Schonnegon, do you think they will find Master Tanafres?"

If she did, would she be sneaking out of camp to do the

job herself. Vorsan wouldn't look very hard for anyone other than Fasolt, and once he found the wizard—*if* he found the wizard—the big man would head back without a thought to Yan or Fra Bern. Vorsan couldn't be trusted to bring either of them back.

"They will do what they can," she said.

Iaf seemed to notice her horse for the first time, taking in the stuffed bags and the travel cloak rolled up behind the saddle with a knowing nod. "You're going out there after them."

It wasn't a question, so she didn't bother answering.

"I want to come with you," he said earnestly.

"I'm hardly the one to be telling you this, but going out there is not very bright. A lone searcher will be meat for any tribesmen she can't outrun."

"You won't be alone."

"Iaf, I'll be blunt. I don't want you along. You're a foot soldier, and you don't know the territory. You won't be doing yourself any good."

"I'm not worried about myself. I want to do some good for Master Tanafres. And Fra Bern. Besides, I can ride. Don't you remember?"

She hadn't wanted to. "You don't have a horse."

"I'll get one. I've done that before, too."

The brave young lieutenant had been a horse thief, eh? Interesting. She'd not have thought it of him. Well, if he could do that . . . What was she thinking? He still had a career in front of him. Should he accompany her, he would catch enough trouble with having horse theft as an additional charge. "I said I don't want you along."

"I'm going to go. It would be better if we went together."

She thought about knocking him on his fool head, tying him up, and going on without him; but if he was really serious about this, he'd probably head out as soon as he got loose. If Yan was right about the boy's infatuation for her, he'd definitely follow. The practicality of his suggestion nagged at her. He was right about one thing; together they might have a better chance. A companion would allow her to get some sleep on the trip; one could watch while the other slept. Rested eyes saw more than tired eyes.

Running out on her contract was something she'd have to square with her own conscience, but the boy would be deserting from Imperial service. If they survived this little adventure, he'd not have an easy time explaining what he'd done. And if Vorsan was on the court, he'd not get away with his life. Still, if Iaf had won himself a slot on Colonel Kensie's staff, he'd know the danger he faced. He was making his own decision, wasn't he? She had made up *her* mind for herself; she supposed he had the right to do the same. She hoped he was doing this for some better reason than to impress her.

He seemed to sense she had given in, and said, "You'll wait here until I get a mount?"

"Half hour. No more." She tried to sound like she meant it.

"Right!" He grinned, teeth flashing in the torchlight. Then he was off and running toward where the cavalrymen camped.

When he was out of sight, she thought again about leaving without him. That grin had been more than simple excitement. If she was gone when he got back, he'd follow. And get lost. And get killed. He wouldn't have a chance out there alone. While she might never know what actually had become of him, she would know that she had contributed to his death. Remembering the boy she had met in Scothandir, she realized that he was still there, inside this young man. She had liked that boy. For that matter, she liked the man he had become.

She waited.

He was back in twenty minutes, leading a big bay horse that looked suspiciously like Colonel Vorsan's own mount. She would have to ask him about that once they were clear of the camp.

14

ANY LINGERING HOPES IAF held for a romantic interlude on the ride into the wilds of Kolvin were laid to rest by the brutal pace that Teletha set. Even avoiding the main trails, they reached the attack site in less than two days, well before Colonel Vorsan's party could hope to get there. She was woodswise for a cavalry soldier, and Iaf was impressed. But then everything about her was impressive.

The site was identifiable from a distance by the smell of rotting meat. That was a little curious. Most battlefields would have lost something of that odor in the time since the fighting, especially in a forest full of hungry scavengers. Iaf understood the lingering of death's perfume when he saw the carcass of the *terriserpens*. There was far too much meat on that giant corpse for scavengers to dispose of. It would have been different in Scothandir, but there were no dnoves in this part of the world; it was too hot for those great beasts here in the south. The result was a smelly pile of decaying meat and massive, raw bones. They had to tie wine-soaked cloths over their mouths to avoid gagging.

The *terriserpens* had to be the one that had attacked Master Tanafres's wagon. It would have taken magic, or cannon, to have blasted the beast's head to splinters. The expeditionary force had brought no cannon and the tribesmen had none, so the death wound had to have come from magic. Since the beast was dead by magic, it had to have been slain by a magician. And didn't that mean the magician was alive? So one of the wizards had survived the attack, but whether the magician had been Master Tanafres or Gan Fasolt, there was no way of knowing. But the dead *terriserpens* didn't mean both magicians had survived, nor did it mean that either still lived. Teletha pointed out the wreckage of a wagon in the ravine below.

"Let's check it out," she said.

Iaf let her pick a route down that the horses could handle. While he was a rider, most of his experience was in Scothandir, a place as wild as these tightly entwined cuts and hills but of a different character. The soils here were moister, thicker, and more treacherous. She'd been riding this wilderness for some time now; he was happy to rely on her experience.

The wagon was fit for no more than firewood, but clearly someone had disturbed the debris. Survivors or captors? After a few minutes of searching, Teletha found Fasolt's hat. The ground proved too disturbed for any reliable estimation of who had been poking around. They found no bodies, and the only definite prints were those of merin.

Had the magicians and priest walked away? Had they been captured? He discovered a patch of dirt that was stained darker than the soil around it. Blood would do that. Might they have been . . . eaten? He didn't want to suggest that grisly possibility to Teletha. Another possibility suggested itself when he found a small pot nearby; there were smears of something sticky inside, and a sniff revealed the pungency of a medicinal ointment.

"Sergeant Schonnegon, over here."

By the time she arrived, he had found some scraps of bloodstained linen. He showed them to her, along with the pot. She sniffed at the ointment and nodded. "Someone attended a wound here."

"Master Tanafres?"

"It's one of his jars, but anyone could have used it."

"Would the tribesmen tend a wounded captive?" he asked, thinking it unlikely.

"Not that I've heard."

"There are no other jars, so it's not just debris. It must

have been used by Master Tanafres, and he must have taken the rest of the kit with him."

"Let's hope so."

Further search revealed no more signs of those they sought. Seeking ground that was not too trampled for tracking, they started to circle the site in ever widening arcs. They found a track, but not what they had hoped for. Iaf dismounted and bent to study the trail.

"Drakkenree?" she asked

The three-toed prints were distinctive; there could be no doubt. He nodded. "A dozen, I think. Bregil too. Laden."

"Any merin?"

"Not that I can tell."

"Those bregil, might they be carrying captives?"

"They were carrying something heavy."

They exchanged glances and began following the trail. The general trend seemed to be back toward Jost's town. Iaf hoped that it didn't mean that the tribesmen and drakkenree were gathering for an attack on the settlement.

"The trail looks to lead to the town," he said. "It might be that the enemy is planning an attack. Maybe one of us should ride back with a warning."

"We don't know anything definite."

"Can we take the chance? If you ride back, I can follow the trail."

"You ride back," she said.

"I'm the better tracker. It makes more sense for me to stay on the trail."

"I'm not going back till we find something definite."

She wouldn't consider any more of his arguments, insisting on devoting her attention to the trail. Was there something between her and Master Tanafres that kept her to this search? He hoped not. How could a simple, ignorant soldier compete with a wise magician for a woman's heart?

They had followed the trail for the better part of a day before he spotted another set of tracks. Without getting off his horse, Iaf could see that the party was mixed drakkenree and bregil. These tracks were very fresh; their makers might not be far away.

Dismounting, they hid the horses by one of the many

streams that cut through the hills. The noise of the water would help disguise the restless shifting and small sounds of the nervous animals. They returned to the trail, and Iaf examined the sign.

"How many?" Teletha whispered. Her sword was in her hand.

"Three drakkenree and many bregil, more than a company's worth."

"Too many for us to deal with. Maybe you're right. Maybe they are heading for Jost's town."

"If so, they're not taking a direct route."

"Having second thoughts about your theory?"

"Just reading the sign. Reading it wrong is as bad as missing it."

A sudden clamor arose to the east, the direction in which the drakkenree and bregil prints led. Gunfire sounded. They had seen no guns among the tribesmen or the drakkenree, and there were very few among the Kolviners. Imperials were likely engaged. Iaf drew his sword. Without a word they moved cautiously in that direction.

They found a melee in progress. The giant form of Colonel Vorsan was immediately recognizable. The Imperials had encountered the drakkenree and bregil. Who had attacked whom was unclear; what was clear was that both parties seemed inclined to annihilate the other. The battle was undecided, but the Imperials outnumbered their foes.

If it had been anyone other than Vorsan . . .

Colonel Vorsan was engaged with one of the drakkenree. The two foes traded blows. The giant colonel grunted with effort whenever he stopped his opponent's blows, but stop them he did. The drakkenree hissed when it parried the colonel's blows. Its attacks became more tentative. Perhaps it had never faced anyone who stood up to it before. Certainly, its fellows were smashing through the defenses of the soldiers they fought.

The colonel thrust at the saurian's head, and the creature reared back to save its snout from his point. He took the moment to duck in under its weapon's sweep. Vorsan's shoulder hit the drakkenree hard in the chest; the creature gave a strangled grunt. Vorsan hammered a fist into its belly as he shoved hard with his shoulder. The drakkenree teetered up on one leg. It pounded on the colonel's back-plate with its sword pommel, and the claws of its free hand raked across his sword arm, ripping through the buff coat, shredding the shirt beneath, and coming away bloody.

Vorsan screamed with the pain, but shoved harder, knocking the creature completely off its feet. It hissed and lashed its tail. Clawed feet raked at Vorsan, but he avoided the frantic blows. He struck with a lunge, thrusting his sword point into the drakkenree's throat. The creature stiff-ened from the shock as a man might, then went limp.

Vorsan had killed it unaided, a notable feat. The colonel stood over his fallen foe, gasping for breath. Iaf spotted a second drakkenree turned toward the colonel. The creature was behind Vorsan and well out of the man's line of sight. The drakkenree raised its sword and charged him.

Vorsan might be a bastard, but he was a warrior.

"Behind you!" Iaf shouted.

Vorsan started to turn, but he was too slow. The drakken-ree swept its two-handed sword down and across, catching the colonel hard on the side of the head. His sword dropped from limp fingers, and he went down. The drakkenree paused, head cocked back. Waiting to see if the man was finished, no doubt.

Vorsan fumbled for his sword. The drakkenree swept up its own blade for the killing stroke. Iaf threw off Teletha's grip on his arm. The colonel had fought too well to be butchered in such a way.

Iaf ran, screaming to draw the drakkenree's attention. He could hear Teletha calling him back, but ignored her. If he was fast enough, he could engage the drakkenree before it completed the death stroke. His effort had an effect; the drakkenree hesitated. It was looking at him now. He heard Teletha behind him, crashing through the brush. He had no breath to forbid her.

Rather than using his weapon, he dove for the drakken-ree. His maneuver caught it by surprise, and it was unable to change the course of its downward-sweeping weapon. The blade buried itself in the earth mere inches from Vorsan's head. Iaf bounced off the creature and fell sprawling to the ground. The drakkenree shifted its stance, barely discomfited by Iaf's assault.

For a moment, Iaf's eyes met Vorsan's as the colonel struggled to rise. There was surprise there.

The drakkenree knew which of the two was its more dangerous opponent. The creature kicked with its taloned foot, catching Vorsan in the head. Iaf heard the thud of impact and shivered in sympathy.

Time seemed to move with startling slowness. Every detail was etched in Iaf's sight: the gleaming darkness of Vorsan's forge-blued helmet; the mud-spattered toes of the drakkenree's feet, forest leaves impaled on its black claws; a tiny Teletha, framed between the saurian's legs and the extended body of the colonel.

As the saurian dragged back its foot, Iaf could see the dent in Vorsan's helmet. Those black talons scraped on metal with the sound of a dying man's scream. The colonel rolled away from the blow, blood spraying from his nose, to sprawl bonelessly on the forest floor.

A pistol shot brought Iaf back to the true flow of time.

Blood sprayed from the drakkenree, spattering him with hot droplets. Its right elbow was shattered by the shot, and the great sword sagged. Iaf glimpsed smoke in front of Teletha, but he had no time to think about that. The drakkenree raised its intact arm. The motion was a little awkward, but the creature clearly had the strength to wield its weapon with a single hand. Iaf dodged its first blow and tried to cut its sword arm as the blade passed him. The saurian skipped back, giving Iaf time to scramble to his feet. He didn't have Vorsan's strength, and he knew better than to pit his small sword directly against the creature's weapon. Alone, even with the drakkenree wounded, he would have little chance. His best hope was to draw out the fight until blood loss weakened the saurian.

He faced the creature alone for but a moment. Then Teletha stood at his side, adding her blade to his. Together they forced the wounded saurian onto the defensive. Iaf thrust himself forward, seeking to focus the creature's attention on him. The drakkenree's blows tended to rip Teletha's blade far out of line. The only things that saved her from being sliced open were Iaf's continual attacks and the saurian's own weakness.

Taking the brunt of the fight was not something he did out of bravery. He feared that Teletha would be injured. It was a foolish concern, he knew; she was a soldier and a good swordsman, but she was also a woman and weaker even than he was. The drakkenree made a cut that forced her sword down; the creature's blade screeched on her breastplate. Iaf pressed harder, offering himself as a target for the drakkenree's weapon. He didn't want to see her killed. Not now. Not when he had just found her again.

The weakened saurian threw a sweeping cut intended to force them back, but the blade tip dipped too low and caught against a fallen tribesman's body. Teletha nicked in, slamming her blade against the drakkenree's in an attempt to immobilize it. With both hands on her sword hilt, she tried to lever the drakkenree's weapon down. Iaf drove in with his point. He felt his blade slide along rib bone before rising up and embedding itself in the creature's chest. The creature tried to bite him, teeth crunching against the iron of his helmet. He withdrew his sword and thrust again, and again. The creature abandoned its weapon, attacking him with rakes of its taloned hand and snaps of its fang-filled mouth. Iaf defended himself wildly. At least he had finally drawn it away from Teletha. Slowly, slowly, the vitality drained from the drakkenree. Its attacks faltered, and Iaf was able to put a thrust into its throat as he had seen Vorsan do to its fellow. It was enough; the drakkenree folded into death.

"Well fought," Teletha said as she helped steady him on his feet.

He looked around, fearful that they were not yet done. The glade was quiet, the melee over. The tribesmen were in retreat. The Imperial survivors stood, too weary to do more than watch the enemy retreat. For the moment they could afford a rest.

"You fought well, too, but that is no surprise. Old Bert always said you were a bonny fighter."

"Old Bert was a liar," she panted. "In most things. He knew bladework, though. Taught you well enough."

He flushed at her praise.

Around them the Imperials were taking stock of their situation, finishing wounded enemies, and tending their wounded. A man wearing the gorget of a sergeant was looking in their direction. The man eyes fell on Vorsan's fallen form.

"Colonel!" he shouted, and ran to the giant's side. The soldier laid down his sword and went to work on Vorsan's helmet. He got the pot off the colonel's head; the lining was stained with blood. The sergeant pulled off his own recognition sash to stuff under the colonel's gore-smeared head. Vorsan stirred, surprising Iaf; the man should be dead.

"What are we going to do, Colonel?" the sergeant asked.

"The Scoth," Vorsan mumbled.

"We'll take care of him for you, Colonel."

Vorsan mumbled something unintelligible. Teletha, however, spoke clearly and loudly, though she never seemed to take her eyes from her task of reloading her pistol.

"I don't think fighting among ourselves is very bright," she said.

"This is no business of yours, mercenary," Vorsan's sergeant said.

This wasn't the time or place for foolish quarrels. Iaf put his foot down on the man's sword before he could raise it. "She's right, soldier. We saw tracks for several bands of tribesmen. One of those groups might have been close enough to hear this fight. The sound of gunfire may not travel far in the woods, but it's not quiet either. There could be tribesmen headed here right now."

The soldier had enough sense to look worried at the prospect.

He glanced around at his fellows, then down at the colonel. "What are we going to do?"

The inarticulate sounds coming from Vorsan were no answer. Teletha turned to Iaf and said quietly, "You're one of Kensie's lieutenants. That gives you the highest rank here."

Iaf looked over the survivors. The sergeant who had come to the colonel was the only one wearing a sign of rank. She was right; no one of his rank or higher was among those standing about them. Not exactly the way he wanted to achieve command, but so be it.

Iaf drew himself up. "I don't see any other officers, so guess I'm in charge here."

"Not of us, you bloody Scoth," the sergeant said. Several voices among the gathering soldiers echoed the sentiment.

"His rank is Imperial just like yours, Sergeant," Teletha pointed out.

"I told you to stay out of this, mercenary."

"Whether you like it or not, Lieutenant Smyth outranks you. You'd not complain if he was an Islander."

"But he's not," the sergeant said. Someone else added, "Even if he was, who'd follow someone who hides behind a woman?"

Trust Vorsan to gather men like him around himself. "I am not hiding behind a woman. We both fought, just as all of you have. The colonel's down and there are no other officers. I *am* taking command here."

"Not of us."

"Vehr's sword strike me down if I'm not! I am a commissioned lieutenant in his Imperial Majesty's expeditionary force. You defy my orders, you're defying the emperor's orders. Since we're in enemy territory, that's treason. You can be hanged."

"They chop heads in the empire," Teletha whispered.

"I'll chop heads *here* if I have to." Iaf swept the soldiers with what he hoped was a withering glare. Half these soldiers were older than he was. He supposed they were more experienced, but if they'd had the flair for command, they would have earned it by now. He beat down his doubts, knowing that if he showed any, they'd seize upon such weakness to undermine his authority. He had to get them doing something, something they'd approve of, and quickly. Once they started listening to him, he hoped they'd stay listening to him.

"The first thing we do is make a litter for Colonel Vorsan and the other wounded," he said.

"They'll slow us down," Teletha pointed out.

Did she think he'd abandon the wounded? No. *She* didn't, but some of those Islanders probably did. They thought him a bloody Scothic barbarian. Idiots! He had sworn the same oath of allegiance that they had. "We're not leaving without our wounded."

Still no one moved.

Gritting his teeth, Iaf drew his belt knife. He saw several of the soldiers flinch, and a couple raised their weapons. Turning his back on them, he strode over to the nearest sapling and started to hack it down. Once it was cut, he started stripping the branches from it. Still no one moved to help him.

"You," he said, pointing at a soldier. "We left our horses over that way about a quarter mile. Take someone with you and go get them."

"Gonna ride off?" someone asked.

Iaf didn't bother to look to see who had spoken. "They can pull the litters."

He went back to work on the sapling. After a while he noticed the sound of another blade against wood. He glanced out of the corner of his eye. It was the sergeant, working on another sapling. When the man finished cleaning his piece, Iaf used his own recognition sash to tie the two together. Before long, several pairs of hands were hard at work.

15

THANKFUL FOR THE FARMER'S OFFER to drive them to Jost's town, Yan loaded Fra Bern into the cart. He was even more thankful for the farmer's word that they were no more than a few hours' ride from the town. The priest was at the end of his strength—beyond it, really. Bern had been moving by sheer willpower for the last six days, stumbling on as Yan tried to lead them back toward safety.

The priest had developed a cough that grew in intensity along with his tremors and fever, but Bern had refused Yan's every suggestion that they stop and rest for more than a few hours. Yan himself was near exhaustion, and he could only imagine how tired Bern must be.

Once Yan got Bern into the farmer's cart, the priest lay still. His panting slowed and steadied into a regular rhythm. Yan saw that he had finally surrendered to sleep, as though the assurance that they were near the end of their journey was enough for his peace of mind. The priest slept through most of the bumpy but uneventful ride to Jost's town. It saved him from the farmer's lengthy tale of his troubles since the invasion. Bern was asleep when the walls of the town came into view and stayed asleep as the cart rumbled up to the gate. The gates were guarded by men in Shain's livery, and the king's banner flew from the castle. Yan was relieved to know that the king's army not only had not been destroyed, but had returned here. The sergeant at the gate recognized him despite his bedraggled condition.

"The king'll be glad to see you," the soldier said. "Best you go right to the castle."

"All right," Yan said, just to get past the man. He had more important things to think about than the king's peace of mind; Bern needed immediate attention. Once his condition improved, he would need care of a kind he was unlikely to get in the king's house. As the cart rattled through the gate and onto the streets of Jost's town, Yan laid a hand on the farmer's sleeve and whispered, "Take us straight to the temple."

The farmer raised an eyebrow, but did as Yan directed.

The priests at the temple got Fra Bern settled in one of the dormitory cells while Yan made arrangements with the high priest to see the farmer rewarded. That done, he went to the cell. Lying on the bed, Bern looked relaxed, better than he had in days. Yan supposed that he should go see the king, but he didn't want to leave Bern. They had been through so much together; he wanted to be sure that the priest was going to make it.

An acolyte brought him a stool and Yan sank gratefully onto it. He leaned back against the wall, content to let the temple's physician, a Manarite, attend to his friend. Normally Yan had little use for the mystic trappings priests put on their medicine, but he'd seen the supernatural healing they could sometimes command, and Bern had spoken highly of this woman. If the Manarite's prayers invoked the gods' favor for Yan's friend, that would be good. He watched her as she worked and decided that, whether or not she had a mystical healing touch, she was a good doctor. She also had access to the temple's supply of herbs and powders to treat Bern's cough and fever; Yan agreed with what she asked the acolyte to bring her from those stores. It seemed that the nightmarish trek through the forest had come to a safe end.

Yan jerked awake, not knowing when he had fallen asleep. The drakkenree, magic flashing around it, faded from his mind's eye. He shivered, more from memory than from the chill darkness of the room. He told himself that he had left that saurian far behind, that it couldn't possibly be here. Still, something was changed. In the close darkness of the small room, his magesight was not at its best, but he surveyed the room as well as he could. Bern lay on the bed, covered in blankets to ward off the cold. The door to the cell was now closed; light from the torches outside seeped through under its edge and showed the presence of two booted feet. Inside the room? Yan's eyes ran up the dark, cloaked figure into the shadowed, angular face of Peyto Lennuick. The clerk looked worried. Seeing Yan's eyes open, Peyto spoke softly.

"They said you'd come back."

"Disappointed?" Yan immediately regretted his gibe: it was unfair. "You did say we'd come to grief going with the army."

"From the looks of you, I'd say you had a fair share of grief."

"At least we're still alive."

Peyto looked at the sleeping priest. "Just the two of you?"

Yan closed his eyes. In his mind's eye a spirit form snapped its jaws together and a hand fell to the ground.

"Fasolt is dead?"

Yan nodded in confirmation, unwilling to trust his voice. The image of a handless wrist pumping blood pulsed beneath his eyelids. Hoping to force the image away, he reopened his eyes.

"The king will be upset," Peyto said.

One less military asset. A true tragedy. Of course the king would be upset. What about Fasolt's family? If he had a family. Yan realized that Fasolt had never spoken of a family, and now never would. What had Fasolt sacrificed himself for? Surely not simply to let Yan and Fra Bern escape; Fasolt had made it clear more than once that he held them in little regard. Maybe he had been thinking that he could defeat the drakkenree wizard? Maybe he had been thinking that—who knew what the mage had been thinking? Who knew anything about the mage, other than his name? And now he was just a name. Another dead man.

This is what it meant to be a mage, Yan thought giddily. To learn and strive, to master the magic, and then to be a tool of others, used until broken, then thrown away.

A damned dark thought, that.

He was tired. That was it. Just too tired.

"I thought you ought to know Janden's looking for you," Peyto said.

And why not? Lose one tool, pick up another. Yan almost laughed, but held it in. Even Peyto, who had traveled with him for years, would not understand. He felt a tear roll down his cheek. Such a mighty wizard! Crying like a baby.

Peyto, in an uncharacteristic show of compassion, pretended not to notice. Instead, the clerk recounted the council meeting and the debate over rescuing the wayward magicians and the priest. So much foolishness. From Peyto's account, no one had actually called them tools, but the council had talked about the missing men with no more warmth than a farmer would have for his plow, and less than an honest farmer would have for his mules.

Peyto told Yan of Janden's interest in the books, and the captain's attempt to get Peyto to turn them over. That shook Yan out of his melancholy.

"And how did the captain come to know of them?" he asked.

"Don't look at me like that. I didn't tell him. I don't like the son of a serpent. He's got too many people giving him an ear."

"What do you mean?"

"Haven't you noticed? People who shouldn't be listening to a mercenary woodrunner like Janden nod sagely when he speaks. What has he got to say that a king would have any interest in? Beyond the scouting reports, of course. It's not as though there are palace revolutions being plotted in the woods."

"Janden *is* the captain of the scouts."

"Indeed he is. And I can understand him having *some* access to the king because of it. However, in a reasonable operation, a scout's reports are made to the war leaders, right? *All* the war leaders? So why does Janden have private conferences with good King Shain whenever he stops by the castle?"

Why indeed. "Perhaps it is at the king's order."

"And was it at the king's order that Janden had the first chat with the Imperial wizard?"

Now that Peyto mentioned it, Yan recalled Janden pulling Fasolt aside soon after the expeditionary force had arrived. What gave a mercenary scout captain a higher precedence than a king with regard to conferences with wizards? "I don't think it was at the king's order."

"Exactly my point," Peyto said in a self-satisfied tone.

So much had been happening around Yan that he hadn't seen. Or, if he had seen it, had ignored. "You seem to know a lot more of what's going on around here than I do."

Peyto snorted. "No more than you would if you paid atten- tion. If you can't survive out here, in this miserable backwoods excuse for a court, they'll eat you alive in Sharhumrin."

Sharhumrin was a distant, fading dream. "I've more important things to worry about than courtly politics."

"Don't believe it, boy."

"I'm a magician, not a courtier. I've no need to pay attention to politics." Good tools do whatever they're told.

"You need to pay attention precisely *because* you are a magician."

"That's why I keep *you* around."

Peyto huffed indignantly. "Firstly, you don't keep me around. I stay around. Gods know why.

"Secondly, I've yet to meet a magician who did not spend some time as a courtier, or one who survived at court by hiding in his books and researches.

"And thirdly, I'm an old man. Even assuming I had the interest and the energy to look after you, I won't be around forever. You need to learn, boy, if you're going to survive."

Bern stirred, prompting Yan to shush Peyto. "If you're going to get excited, we'll have to talk later. The good priest needs his rest."

Peyto scowled, but he didn't go away. At least he low- ered his voice when he asked. "Is he all right?"

There was actually concern in the clerk's voice. "I thought you didn't like him."

"I don't have to like him to be polite."

"You don't sound polite."

"Pretend I never asked, then," Peyto said brusquely.

"We got thrown around a lot when the *terriserpens* attacked the wagon. He cracked some ribs. He might have injured something inside. He's picked up a cough, and I'm worried."

Nodding knowingly, Peyto asked, "What can you do for him?"

"Not much, and I've done that already. There's a Manarite here who is more experienced with this sort of thing than I am; she has taken over his care. I just want to stay and make sure he's not going to spit up the broths and medicines they've fed him."

"You seem to have changed your mind about him."

Had he? "He's not a stupid man, just poorly educated. When given facts, he draws good conclusions. Most of the time. He's still a little blinded by his faith."

"He *is* a priest," Peyto said.

"An Einthofite," Yan pointed out in Fra Bern's favor.

"Best of a bad lot," Peyto agreed. "But why the defense? The two of you were arguing in front of the king the last time I saw you."

They had been, hadn't they? It seemed a long time ago. "We talked a lot out there. About what we saw."

"And what did you see?"

Yan told him about the drakkenree wizard and its party, and about the death of Fasolt. He described the old drakkenree cave. He considered explaining Fra Bern's conviction that there was a religious motivation behind the invasion, and decided to remain silent on that. To speak of it, he would have had to explain Fra Bern's theory of the Other; Bern's heretical theory had been shared in confidence. In all honor, Yan couldn't speak of that without Bern's permission. So instead he said, "Fra Bern has a theory about the drakkenree we have been seeing."

"Ah, the 'children of the ancient enemy.' "

"No, he's given up on that."

"I see. No doubt he yielded to your excellent logic while you wandered the woods."

"I don't think it was anything I said." In fact, he was sure of it. "The credit goes to Fasolt. That fellow knew more about what was going on than he confided to me. How much more we'll never know, but consider this: he was not surprised to meet a saurian mage."

"But you and the priest were."

Yan nodded. "They are only mentioned in the oldest of the chronicles."

"You said those things in Scothandir were magicians."

Ah, Peyto. Always quick on the scent of an issue. "Yes, I did."

"So why were you surprised to see one here?"

"The more recent chronicles recount years of struggle without the least hint of magic being involved, despite earlier accounts of its use in battles. The logical conclusion is that the drakkenree lost the ability to field battle magicians."

"If that was so, where did this one come from? Not from Gornal's valley. Those creatures all died."

"Fra Bern has a theory."

"Which you do not quite believe."

"I don't know what to believe. There's so little information."

"But you have some different thoughts on the matter?"

Yan tried to decide if he could tell the tale without bringing up Bern's idea that the talismans were signs of an ancient deity unknown to the Celestial Court. Though important, the issue of the Other was a sidelight to the explanations he currently considered most likely.

"You and I have some experience that time is not as simple as most people think. I told Bern something about our experience in Scothandir. He didn't understand it, which is not surprising, but he saw at once that these drakkenree we face might not be the children of the ancient enemy. He thinks it possible that they may be those elder beings themselves. He thinks that the enemy here have awakened an ancient battle mage."

"Preserved, as those in Scothandir were?" Peyto looked duly appalled at the idea.

"It is possible that these drakkenree are remnants of a once-mighty race, but there is another possibility." Mercifully, Peyto waited quietly while Yan groped for the courage to say aloud what he feared, to someone who had not seen the drakkenree mage and felt the tingle from the power it wielded. "The presence of this mage could mean something else. With the merest touch of their ancient magic, we were separated from time. Time slid past us. We were, in essence, transported to what would have been our future, and we experienced none of the time between."

"I remember," Peyto said softly. "Are you suggesting that one of the ancient mages has been transported to our time?"

"That would be no different in effect from awakening a slumbering wizard."

"No different in effect, but vastly different in possibilities. If one came forward, more could."

"But this wizard was not like the others."

"Making you believe that it has not come through time." Peyto frowned at Yan's affirmative nod. "If they are different, why bring up the magic that altered time for us? What is the connection?"

"Do you recall my speaking of an ancient presence that I felt when the Scothic drakkenree died? Do you recall that I thought it spoke to me?"

Peyto nodded slowly, apprehension on his face.

"What if these drakkenree we face have a way to speak with their ancestors? What if they have found a way to communicate with the ancient wizards, to learn those awesome, ancient magics?"

Peyto, of course, had no answer. Yan didn't have one either, just the gnawing fear that the hypothesis might be true.

Sure that the acolytes were lying, Raff bulled his way past them. The magician had brought the priest here, and no one had seen him leave, so he had to be here still.

The latch snagged as he worked it, and the door did not open as he expected. His speed caused him to slam into the door. The force of contact forced the latch free and the wooden panel swung wide, its hinges complaining. The torches behind him threw his shadow across the small cell and up the wall on the other side. A sun disk glittered on the wall over an empty stool. The Einthofite priest was struggling to sit up on the bed; Raff's loud entrance had roused him.

The priest was alone.

Raff wanted the magician, not the priest. He turned to leave.

"Please," the priest croaked. "Captain Janden. A moment of your time?"

Baaliff's blood! The man was almost ready for a shroud. Raff could hardly hear the reedy voice, but something in the tone caught his attention. A man reaching out from near death might have a good reason for wanting to talk.

"A moment only, Fra."

The priest nodded slowly. "Gan Fasolt said I should speak to you. He said you would understand."

Fasolt? The gate guards had said that only Tanafres and the priest had returned. Raff snagged the stool and set it near the head of the bed. He sat and leaned close. "Where is he?"

The priest's throat worked as if he were trying to drag the words out. At length he whispered, "Gone to attend the Court."

With the slowness of wood wearing under the tread of booted feet, the priest recounted the story of Fasolt's death. The first mention of drakkenree ruins riveted Raff's attention. The revelation of a drakkenree wizard chilled him. Raff listened carefully to everything the priest said, no longer worried about letting the sick man speak at his own pace. Occasionally he asked a question. His patience was rewarded.

A lot became clearer, clearer and more worrying.

While he pondered how this new information changed the situation, the priest told him of a conversation between the magician Tanafres and one of the king's clerks, the irritating Lennuick fellow. The two of them must have thought Bern was asleep when they spoke, or they would not have spoken so freely. Raff was not surprised to learn that Tanafres had been withholding information.

Without Fasolt's help, the struggle was going to be harder.

To compensate, all resources had to be brought into play. With Fasolt dead, Tanafres was the only magician within a reasonable distance. The only *human* wizard, he reminded himself. Still, Tanafres's protests to the contrary, the man was a magician of some power; Raff remembered what he had done to the gates of Yentillan's palisade. Raff also remembered that Tanafres claimed to be an Imperial citizen, which might give him an angle to make the man more pliable.

"Thank you, Fra Bern," Raff said with real gratitude. "You are a true servant of the empire."

"I am a servant of my Lord Einthof first and a Kolviner second, Captain," the priest croaked.

Did the priest sound indignant? What did it matter if he was? Raff didn't care about offending the man's sensibilities, but he knew better than to make a show of his feelings. The priest might be dying, or he might not. If he didn't die, he might still be useful. If he did die, it would be a small enough matter; Raff had already gotten something useful from him. "I'm sorry, Fra. I meant to say that you are a blessing to the Old Alliance."

The priest's eyes glittered with feverish intensity. "You will tell the king what I told you?"

Raff smiled reassuringly. "Of course. Of course I will." When the time's ripe.

The priest seemed to take comfort from Raff's words. He tilted his head back and blinked slowly. "I feared I would not live to carry the word."

"You've done your duty, Fra. Rest. Get well."

"Pray for me, Captain."

"Of course." He stood. "Now, I must be going. There's a lot to do."

And a lot to think about.

16

THE RETURN OF THE ILL-FATED rescue expedition brought a call for an immediate council session in the great hall of Baron Jost's castle. Teletha had been on the verge of heading back out to look for Yan when she overheard some of the soldiers say that Janden was searching for him within the town. A few quick inquiries revealed that Yan had returned safely the previous day and that the king had called him to attend the council. Relieved, she obeyed the summons to the council.

Once in the hall, she skirted the crowd to take her place behind Janden. Janden stood in his usual spot between and behind King Shain and Baron Jost, a step back from their seats as befitted the chief of scouts.

The captain turned around as she arrived, a disapproving glare on his face. She would hear about her unauthorized departure later. She gave him a smile. Let him make what he would of that. He had already made a statement of sorts by not having her thrown into irons for desertion as soon as he saw her.

King Shain, Estem Honistonti, and all the other war leaders, Kolviner and Imperial alike, were in their places—all save Vorsan. Aides and chosen advisers stood behind the leaders or scurried about in last-minute preparation. The hall quieted as Yan entered the room. He looked more gaunt than she remembered, and there were dark rings of exhaustion around his eyes, but he seemed unwounded.

Yan bowed to the king and, walking to the corner of the room where a stool stood vacant, seated himself without a word. Yan leaned against the wall and folded his arms across his chest; he sagged, like a tired man finally getting a chance to rest.

Janden had started when Yan arrived, and the captain stared stonily at him until he sat. Teletha guessed that Yan had managed to avoid the captain until now. King Shain's lack of reaction suggested that Yan's appearance was no surprise to the king. Curious. She'd get the story from Yan later.

"Proceed with the business at hand," the king ordered.

A clerk summoned forward Iaf and Vorsan's sergeant.

Estem called on the sergeant, Neshoran, to speak first. Neshoran gave his account of the attack, surprising Teletha with its accuracy. The man left out any mention of her, which was fine, but otherwise told the tale honestly. Iaf's account differed little, and he surprised her more by leaving her out as well. She knew he hadn't forgotten her part; on the way back he'd thanked her often enough for the shot that had wounded the drakkenree he'd killed. Iaf avoided looking in her direction, an exclusion she thought no one would notice until she caught Janden staring at her again. The captain knew she had been out there, as did the men testifying before the council; this conspiracy of silence denied her disobedience to the king's orders by the simple expedient of never mentioning her participation in the events under review. She wondered what the price would be, and to whom she would have to pay it.

There were questions directed at the two men, but no one, neither the questioners nor the two men, made mention of Vorsan's refusal to include Iaf in the expedition. Another conspiracy to preserve appearances.

"How many men did you lose?" Estem asked.

"A dozen, sir," Iaf answered.

"Nine of those in the first attack, General," the sergeant volunteered. "Two of the others died on the road."

"You lost only one in the second attack?" Baron Jost sounded as though he didn't believe it.

"They were just hill monkeys, sir. The lieutenant figured

where they'd hit, and he was right. We were ready for them."

"But they outnumbered you by that point," the king said.

"They had no stomach for Imperial steel and shot, your Grace."

The king turned to Estem. "It seems that your lieutenants do a better job than your colonels."

"The colonel was caught unawares," Iaf protested.

Shain looked at him out of the corner of his eyes. "Though they are just as outspoken."

"We wouldn't have made it back without the lieutenant," the sergeant said in his defense.

"Unproved," said Bachem, Vorsan's chief lieutenant.

"We wouldn't have," the sergeant insisted. "Even if we had, we would've had to leave the colonel behind."

"Maybe you should have," Colonel Kensie said. "The doctors say his wits are addled. He may not be fit to feed himself, let alone command a regiment."

"Even with half a brain, he's a better strategist than any Scoth ever born," Bachem exclaimed.

"A Scoth saved his hide," Kensie responded calmly.

Bachem was about to say something else, something intemperate by the redness of his face and the way he dropped his left hand to his scabbard, but Estem didn't give him the chance.

"I will tolerate no more division in the ranks. We will discuss this matter later, gentlemen." His stern expression made it clear that he would countenance no further contention. "Bachem, you will take command of the Third Regiment. Colonel Kensie, your lieutenant did a fine, if unauthorized, job."

"I shall write a letter to the emperor conveying your words," Kensie said.

Estem put on his polite smile. "I'll sign it if you like. He brought back some important people."

Iaf and Neshoran retired, separating to take their places at the sides of their respective regimental commanders. Janden asked for recognition, at the same time as Baron Jost and Fra Ystram. The king indicated with a nod that Janden should speak.

"My lords, the adventures of a few soldiers, however valiant, will not save us from the threat we face." Janden stepped forward as he spoke. "Drakkenree are appearing in greater numbers among the bregil. We have fought them, but they are not here as warriors."

Several voices raised objection to that remark, forcing Janden to amend his statement.

"All right. Let me say, rather, that the drakkenree are here as *more* than soldiers. There is a strangeness to their behavior. From all quarters our scouts now report that the lizards are behaving oddly. They seem more interested in seeing the sights than in battle, which they leave to their hill ape minions.

"Before he died, Gan Fasolt learned that these drakkenree are connected to the bregil tribesmen in a deadly and insidious way. You all have seen the talismans worn by the monkeys, those golden orbs. You have all seen that some of those talismans have a black stripe on them. The tribal chiefs wear those striped signs. Have you wondered why that is? I did. Fasolt did. There is significance to these talismans and the way they are worn, my lords.

"In the forest Gan Fasolt saw drakkenree wearing this same sign." Yan's head came up at the statement, but his expression was schooled. Teletha couldn't tell if the remark was news to him, or if he was surprised to hear it from Janden. The latter, probably, since if the gossips were to be believed, Yan had been out there with Fasolt when the Imperial magician saw the drakkenree. Yan watched Janden closely as he continued. "Gan Fasolt called that symbol the sign of the Serpent's Eye. The emperor's best scholars believe the Serpent's Eye to be something of vast importance to the drakkenree, something akin to a holy relic. It is said that long ago, the drakkenree used this Eye to subjugate the world. They kept the Eye in a great city. No one knows the location of that city; all records of it have been lost. I believe that the drakkenree infesting this land are seeking that city in order to recover the Serpent's Eye. I fear, as Gan Fasolt feared, that once they have it, we will face a far more terrible menace than any heretofore."

When Janden stopped speaking, a babble of questions

erupted. Some, by dint of louder voices, came through clearly. "Tell us of this relic," Fra Zephem demanded, while Sir Bryyan asked, "How can you know there is such a thing? Who has seen this Eye?"

"No one," Janden replied. "Yet. And that is the matter we must address."

"How can you say that the lizards have come to look for this Eye?" Baron Jost asked suspiciously.

"They are here in these lands. They are searching for something. It must be that they seek the Eye."

"What matter if they find their relic?" Fra Ystram asked. "The Celestial Court wards us from the deceits of the false deities worshiped by the evil and unenlightened."

"Were it a relic of an unfounded faith, that would be so. But Gan Fasolt believed that the Serpent's Eye was actually an arcane artifact, born of magical arts such as the world has not seen for centuries."

"Captain Janden, you try to frighten us with goblin tales." Fra Zephem sounded contemptuous of the whole idea.

"I try to warn you of a danger that may be averted," Janden said in response. "The Eye is real. We must be ready to answer its threat. We must take action. If we can destroy the Eye before the drakkenree find it—"

"Destroy it!" Baron Jost barked a derisive laugh. "We have only just learned that it *may* exist. Even were we certain that it is real, we know no more than they do where it is."

"But we do have some idea of where it might be. There is a place where the sign of the Serpent's Eye marks the ruins. It is where Fasolt battled the lizard mage." Janden spun to face Yan. "Isn't that so, Master Tanafres?"

Yan was silent, staring coldly at Janden.

"Say nothing, then, magician. I don't need you to confirm the existence of this place. I know that it does exist. What you must tell us, Tanafres, is whether you can find that place again."

Yan stood and wet his lips before speaking. "We were lost."

"But you walked out and came to Jost's town," said Janden in an accusing tone.

"We were lucky. I do not think I could navigate through those woods again."

He sounded unconvincing to Teletha; she hoped that it was because she knew him better than did the others present. She glanced at Peyto; the clerk had a worried expression. Was Yan lying?

"Besides," Yan added, "the place is in territory controlled by the tribesmen."

"That can change," Janden said.

"It hasn't so far. You threaten us with a goblin tale, suggesting that some mythical artifact might change the course of history. What proof do you offer that this Serpent's Eye exists?" Yan glanced around the room, raising his voice. "Gan Fasolt told me that no one alive can read the drakkenree script. How did he learn of this Serpent's Eye? How could he know what it could do, or where it was kept?"

Into the silence following Yan's question, Janden said, "He was a wizard."

"Wizard?" Yan's voice mocked the captain. "Are we to take that as an explanation for unsupported pronouncements? Do you think that being a magician means a man can do anything? Magicians are *men*! Men who study the Great Art. The Art gives them skills, but it doesn't make them all-powerful. It doesn't give them prescience. And it doesn't let them pluck ancient knowledge from thin air. Where did Fasolt get his information, Janden? Did he make it up? Or are you making it up for him?"

"Master Tanafres, restrain yourself," Estem said.

Yan gathered his composure and stood up straight. He still glared at Janden.

"The emperor's scholars know of the Serpent's Eye," Janden said. "The Imperial archives have ancient documents that a provincial hedge wizard would never see and could not be expected to understand.

"My lords, do not be misled by this man. The Serpent's Eye is real, and the drakkenree must not be allowed to regain it."

"But how can we prevent them from doing so?" King Shain asked. "My good lords, I wish your counsel."

"We could keep them busy while we look for it," Fra Zephem suggested.

"Even should we succeed in distracting them, we remain at a disadvantage; we know not what we seek," Fra Ystram pointed out.

"We shall have to find it anyway," Estem said.

The leaders fell to discussing strategies for disrupting the drakkenree plans. Taking advantage of the shift in his questioners' attention, Yan slipped toward the door. Peyto folded shut the tablets on his lap and handed them to one of the other clerks before heading for the door himself. Teletha checked to make sure Janden was involved in the discussion, and followed.

"I see what you mean about Janden," Yan was saying to Peyto when she caught up to them.

Peyto nodded. "You see only the smallest bit."

"He has some kind of strange hold on the king and the general; they agree with everything he says. I don't trust him."

"You talk about him the way most people do about a magician," she said.

Yan's brow furrowed. He was too taken by her comment to be surprised that she had joined them. Finally, he said slowly, "Janden is no magician."

"Are you sure?" Peyto asked.

"Allow me *some* intelligence. I'd know."

"If you say so," Peyto said.

Yan was still frowning, so Teletha tried to make light of the situation. "I would think that it would take a magician to make Es—General Honistonti listen to such nonsense."

Expression still troubled, Yan said, "I have things to take care of."

Yan was thankful that Peyto thought it wise to return to the wrangling discussion in the great hall. He was even more grateful that the clerk pointed out that Teletha would be missed as well. But Yan was most grateful that neither suggested that he return. They all knew that eventually the leaders would be looking for him again. They wouldn't like finding that he had left.

Yan turned the problem over in his head all the way back to the town house. The commanders were following Raff Janden's lead, and Yan hadn't liked where the captain's questions seemed to have been heading. If Yan had stayed, there would surely have been attempts to coerce him, to prevail upon him to use the Art to their ends. A magician always had to be wary of such men.

The Serpent's Eye was another problem. If Fasolt had told Janden that the Eye existed, it probably did, although a magical artifact of such power as Janden had hinted at was beyond anything known in the world. However, Fasolt was not the sort to tell the whole truth to anyone. The crafty old magician might not have told Janden much of the truth at all. The Eye might not be what Janden believed it to be.

Janden had referred to the Serpent's Eye as a holy relic. Janden had also suggested a connection among the Eye, the talismanic orbs, and the drakkenree symbols. Yan recalled Fra Bern's fear of the Other, the strange, non-Triadic deity. Was it all connected? Religion had motivated wars among men; were the drakkenree different in that regard? Belief in sacred things had changed the world as much as magic ever had.

Whatever the Eye might be, its existence gave a reason for what was happening in Kolvin. The behavior of the drakkenree supported Janden's allegations that they sought *something*. Yan had made the same marches Janden had; he'd seen the battlefields. Now that Janden had suggested a connection, Yan realized that he had seen signs of drakkenree ruins near each of the battle sites. The implications seemed obvious: the invaders fought to control such places.

Could this whole area have once been a single great city? Were the armies actually traversing back and forth across what had once been Ul-Schuttariat? Ul-Schuttariat was supposed to have existed before the dark empire's time. Could it have been built by the ancient drakkenree? Did the Serpent's Eye lie hidden in one of the city's ancient vaults?

Could it be that the drakkenree sought Ul-Schuttariat? Rumors of ruins that might belong to that ancient city had brought Yan to the Kolvinic wilderness in the first place. Had similar rumors brought the drakkenree?

If Ul-Schuttariat, or the ruins of it, were the drakkenree's goal, why did they not contest again for any place from which they were driven? They could not have had sufficient time for a thorough search of any of the ruins. Perhaps the ruins meant nothing to them, and there was some other explanation for their actions. Could they be operating from some completely different motive?

Fasolt had died trying to stop the drakkenree wizard. Gan Fasolt was not the sort of man to throw his life away over something inconsequential, which implied that the drakkenree mage was a key element in the puzzle and heavily involved in whatever was behind the invasion. How much had Fasolt *not* told Janden? Might the drakkenree wizard have been close to its goal? Was that why Fasolt was willing to fight it? That would make sense.

But there were still pieces missing from the puzzle.

By the time Yan reached the town house, Fasolt's sacrifice had taken on a larger significance in his mind. He retrieved the metal fragment he'd taken from the cave. Laying it on the table, he sat and contemplated it. The shard had been part of the golden sphere that had nested on a pylon near the cave's entrance; there was no power in the sphere that he could detect. Was it a secular symbol, a mark that the vault of the Eye was nearby? Or was it a religious object, a symbol proclaiming the site as sacred to a cult dedicated to the Other? Or was it something else entirely? Whatever it was, Yan had found it in a place where an Imperial wizard had thought to make a stand, a place that had drawn the drakkenree magician's interest. There had to be something of importance nearby.

If Yan told the war leaders of his deductions, they would want to act, to send the army there. Armies were destructive things; soldiers searching for the Eye could easily destroy precious information. Yan thought about the secrets that the ancient city must hold. What would be lost as the army tramped around, wrecking everything in their attempt to find and destroy the Eye? Janden wouldn't care. The man had no use for scholarship, except where it gave him a better way to kill something.

Like too many military men, Janden's answer to a threat

was to respond with force and destroy what he didn't like. In this situation such a response might do more harm than good. It seemed inevitable that moving the army into the area would bring the saurians down on them in force

And if the drakkenree knew of the site's significance, if it held what they sought, they would respond even sooner and in greater numbers. They would not be content to retreat before the allies' forces, and they had at least one wizard capable of battle magic. There would be carnage and destruction greater than any yet seen in this campaign.

Yan reached out and laid a finger on the shard. He could use it to find the place again. He knew spells to conceal himself. Hadn't he used one to hide from the drakkenree wizard? And one man was far easier to conceal than an army. One man could move more quickly and with less notice.

Once he satisfied himself about the nature of the place, he could tell the Kolviners and General Honistonti what lay there. If the place was no more than another empty drakkenree ruin, there would be no need to send a destructive expedition. If the Eye was there, then an expedition would be justified. But without solid information, action was foolhardy and possibly self-defeating. With information, reasonable and judicious action could be taken.

He saw only one way to get the necessary information.

Peyto returned as Yan was sorting through his magical supplies. The clerk looked at the pile by the door: bulging satchel, bedroll, pair of bottles, hat, and cloak. Pursing his lips, he shook his head. "Were you going to leave a note, or did you expect *me* to explain your disappearance to the lords?"

"I am not obligated to explain my comings and goings to anyone."

"No note, then." Peyto sighed. "It is a fool's plan."

"Do you have a better plan?"

"Yes. Forget these lizards and their books. The road to the west is open now. Leave these miserable lands, and go to the empire."

Yan couldn't do that. "There is too much unsettled. It's not yet time to go back to the empire."

"Not time? It is the best time. We've got to get out of this war before it claims us all."

"Ul-Schuttariat is out there."

"Not *that* again. There is a *war* going on around here? This is neither the time nor the place for scholarly pursuits."

"Some things need to be done here. Now."

Peyto regarded Yan solemnly for a moment. "You are determined?"

"I see no other course."

"You won't *let* yourself see any other course. I don't know why I bother." Peyto raised his eyes to the ceiling. "If you won't listen to me, maybe you'll listen to her."

Peyto left before Yan could object. "Her" was undoubtedly Teletha. Of course, Yan would listen to her. He might even agree with her, if she objected to his plan. More likely, she would suggest that she accompany him. He heard the rumors about how she had deserted to go into the forest to rescue him. It was unlikely she'd be willing to let him go back out there alone. She'd try to talk him out of it, convince him that it was a fool's plan, as Peyto had called it. It might be a fool's plan, but it was *his* plan. Someone had to investigate Ul-Schuttariat, and who was better qualified than he?

But was he really qualified?

Or just a fool?

He selected a few jars, stuffing them into his second satchel rather than refilling the smaller containers already within. If he didn't see her, he wouldn't have to risk letting her talk him out of it. If he did see her, she might change his mind. She was sensible. Her practicality was something he admired about her. Her evaluation of the situation might offer another alternative, one he hadn't seen. It wouldn't be the first time.

He took down another jar, but instead of tucking it away in the bag, he held it, staring sightlessly at the label.

Was he being a fool?

The courier bringing news of fresh incursions to the west had been most unwelcome in the general's tent. Iaf had listened to the impromptu conference between General Honistonti and King Shain, simply because he had been carrying a message from Colonel Kensie to the general when the messenger had arrived. The preoccupied general had failed to dismiss Iaf, allowing him to listen in. The news upset King Shain, but the king rightfully argued against any thrusts to the east or south.

"Honor compels us to defend good Baron Jost's lands," King Shain asserted.

Honor and a certain practicality, Iaf thought; the baron's holdings were the most populous in the area.

"The withdrawal of the royal contingents from offensive operations will be telling," General Honistonti predicted. "The situation hereabouts will soon return to what it was before we arrived. Jost's town will slowly but surely become isolated again. The stronghold will become a frontier outpost within a territory largely held by the drakkenree and their bregil minions."

"That will change when the levy arrives," the king said.

"In the meanwhile, what would you have me do? We cannot afford to stop all operations."

"What about Captain Janden's proposal?"

"You know as well as I that Janden's proposal to sweep Gremaire Forest looking for some magical thing is foolhardy; it begs for ambush."

The king shrugged. "Then remain here. When the levy arrives, we will march and clear the whole forest."

"Whether my force stays here in the town or goes after the enemy, one thing is clear. We need a significant victory—soon—or the war will spread."

To Iaf, it almost seemed as though the drakkenree were trying to draw the king's forces away from something in the east. If Janden was right about this matter of the Serpent's Eye, the invaders' timing might be significant.

And Master Tanafres had tried to steer away from talk of the Serpent's Eye. Why? Iaf didn't want to think that the magician was hiding something, but his behavior at the council meeting had been suspicious. Iaf was uncomfortable having such thoughts about a man he had admired for so long. Was he letting his feelings for Teletha get in the way, looking for flaws in a rival? It was odd to think of himself as jealous of Master Tanafres.

But jealousy had no place in a soldier's thoughts; military operations had pride of place there. Master Tanafres was an important resource in this campaign, and one in danger of being squandered. Gan Fasolt was the source of the information about the Eye, but he was dead, and there would be no more information from that source. That left Master Tanafres their only expert on arcane matters. Captain Janden's interrogation had clearly upset the magician with its hostile tone. What might the magician have to say if he were approached in a more friendly manner?

Iaf resolved to find out.

As he approached Master Tanafres's town house, Iaf spotted Master Lennuick and Teletha hurrying toward it. He hailed them, attaching himself to their party despite the clerk's disapproving glower. Teletha's matter-of-fact acceptance of his presence countered the clerk's annoyance. As they walked, Master Lennuick and Teletha returned to their interrupted conversation. He gathered from what they said that Master Tanafres was contemplating a trip into the forest.

An interesting twist.

"Damnation!" Master Lennuick said upon entering the house. He sounded upset, but not surprised.

Iaf could see that someone had gone through the magician's work area. Jars and boxes were disordered, and there seemed to be fewer of them than when he had last been here. It was not violently disarrayed, though, so likely the disorder was due to Master Tanafres himself. A man in a hurry might leave such a mess behind him.

Master Tanafres was proving to be both more and less than the man Iaf had held in memory. Men had died trying to haul him back from the wilderness. Teletha had risked her life to do so. Iaf, too. Now Master Tanafres was going back out there, voluntarily placing himself in danger. Though he commanded arcane powers as few men did and was a master of obscure and natural lore, Master Tanafres sometimes seemed to lack common sense.

"We ought to go after him," Teletha said.

"And compound the idiocy?" Master Lennuick asked. His

tone made it clear what he thought of the idea. "If Yan was foolish enough to go off by himself, he deserves what he gets."

"You don't mean that," Teletha said.

The clerk sniffed disdainfully, but said nothing. Teletha waited a moment for him to reply, and when he didn't, she started poking about the room.

"If he had wanted us along, he would have asked," Master Lennuick said at last. "Waited for us to get here, at least. He knew I was going to get you."

"Janden's expecting me for a conference in an hour," Teletha said. "I won't be missed before then."

She was thinking of trailing after Master Tanafres again. Something inside Iaf tightened. Why did the magician hold so much of her attention and not he?

"Leaving wouldn't be wise," he said. He told her what the courier had said, and what the general and the king had decided. "Master Lennuick is correct. Master Tanafres has chosen his own course. We have our duties here."

"He'll get himself killed out there," she said.

"He came back by himself before," Iaf said

"Without your help, Teletha," Master Lennuick pointed out.

Iaf was relieved to have an ally in the fight. He pressed harder. "Master Tanafres will be able to rely on magic to protect himself, skills that neither you nor I have. He will be safe. He was before." Teletha looked confused. She appeared to be accepting the argument, so he pressed on. "We didn't do so well rescuing him the last time. Now such a task would be far more difficult. We have no idea where he's gone."

"We could track him." She didn't quite sound as though she believed it.

"As Master Lennuick said, if he'd wanted you along, he would have waited. He wanted to go alone. He knows you might try to follow him, and he'll have taken care to hide his track."

She ran her hand through her hair, a distracting gesture. She wore it no longer than a man might, and Iaf noticed once again that she was no man.

"He would," she said ruefully. "Vehr as my judge, the man would."

"So there really isn't anything we can do about him. We still have our own duties. Things we *can* do. The king and General Honistonti will not be able to overlook a second desertion as easily."

"Estem would understand."

Estem? She called the general by his first name. Honistonti had served in Scothandir when she was an air captain in the Imperial forces. Did Iaf have another rival? Was he fighting on one flank only to find the real battle on another? Whatever her relationship with the general, he was not the only one to whom she was answerable. "The king wouldn't understand, and you are in service to him."

"Mercenary service," she said.

Iaf didn't see how that changed anything. "Meaning he wouldn't invoke military justice against you?"

"Don't fool yourself, Teletha," Master Lennuick said.

Iaf nodded quickly. "The penalty for desertion in battle is death."

"This isn't a battle," she said.

"With hillmen and drakkenree raiding throughout the kingdom, a commander cannot but see it otherwise."

"I think it likely that Shain would take an extreme view," Master Lennuick added.

Teletha looked at the clerk, then turned bleak eyes on Iaf. His chest constricted. He hated to see her torn like that. He wanted to comfort her, but refrained from reaching out to her. He ached as she did, but for different reasons. He tried to put comfort in his words.

"Master Tanafres will be all right. He is a magician and a scholar. A good man. V'zurna, Einthof, and Theur will guard him. And should They be too busy, he has his magic. He can take care of himself."

She nodded slowly, won over at last.

Master Tanafres would have to take care of himself.

Still, Iaf hoped he hadn't betrayed Master Tanafres by convincing Teletha to remain. He didn't want to see the magician hurt; but then, he didn't want him around distracting Teletha, either. And they really did have obligations beyond chasing a man who clearly didn't want their help.

Part Three

Part Three

17

ONCE FREE OF JOST'S TOWN, Yan had found a secluded spot
and constructed a spell centered on the shard he had taken
from the drakkenree cave. Using the fragment's affinity for
the rest of the sphere, he had set up a resonance, an echo-
ing trace in the mana, that he had followed for four days
now. The spell's guidance offered a straight-line path, and
he'd had to abandon the roads to travel across the untracked
wilderness in as direct a route as possible. Fortunately,
Yan's horse had been up to the effort. Shean was a sturdy,
stolid beast, little bothered by the wildness around them; so
when she began to show signs of unease, Yan took notice.

Reining her to a stop, he looked around. The forest surrounding them was quiet, but his own passage would
account for that. To his mundane senses, nothing seemed
out of place among the trees. He dismounted and patted
Shean's neck, whispering reassurances in her ear and wishing he had someone to do the same for him. Though Shean
quieted, her ears continued to flick nervously.

He decided that it would be wise to dismount before trying what he had in mind, and did so. His *claviarm* lay
against his chest, warmed by his own body heat so that he
felt no more of the amulet than its weight and hardness.
Reaching through the *claviarm*, he focused his sensitivities
and opened his inner eye to the mana stream.

He immediately noticed the change in the affinity bond

he had placed on the shard. The sense of wholeness was strong, which meant the cave that he sought was near. He took the shard from his pouch and held it up, studying the aura that surrounded the fragment. The glow was more evident than before, stretching out toward the sphere's sundered parts. The tongue of energy was longer, too, tapering to a thin line that passed through the trees to the east. By every indication he could read, he was near to his destination.

As he looked along the spell's manifestation, he caught an ordered swirl in the free-flowing mana. Someone was making magic. To Yan's knowledge, no edifice lay in that direction other than the old drakkenree ruins. Who could be doing magic there?

Who, other than the drakkenree mage?

Yan knew that he could discover who was making magic, could see with his own inner eye who the magician was. All he had to do was to send his spirit form forth along the spell's line. But in doing so, he would likely come to the attention of the unknown magician. The drakkenree mage would not take Yan's disembodied spying kindly. Yan had seen what the saurian wizard had done to Fasolt, and knew that he couldn't win in a duel with the drakkenree. He dropped back into mundane awareness, knowing that he would be safer doing his spying where trees could hide his body and the wind carry away his scent.

The impression he'd gotten from the spell was one of nearness. He should be able to reach the cave without too long a walk, which was good, because riding closer would increase the chance that he would be spotted. Of course, that assumed that there were watchers who could spot him. He didn't dare not assume so, especially having sensed the activity of another magician. It was possible that the magician was not at the cave at all, but somewhere farther away and just coincidentally in the same direction. Yan didn't really believe that to be the case and intended to take whatever precautions he could. He might not be as good as Teletha at skulking about in the woods, but neither was he a novice.

He unbuckled his satchels from Shean's harness and rigged them into a rude backpack, taking care that all buckles were filled with leather and snugged down, lest they rattle. The contents of the bags were already padded against the jostling of travel, and so would give no sound likely to betray his passage.

He looked into the forest toward the cave. Nothing had changed that he could see. He had no reason to delay, but he felt reluctant to set forth. Was he ready for this? What if the drakkenree had occupied the cave? He'd seen no sign of saurians or tribesmen during the trip, but that didn't mean they weren't nearby; there had been no warning before they attacked the army's column either.

Whispering in Shean's ear, he asked her to wait for him. She stretched her neck and bounced her head in a horsey sort of nod. His word wouldn't hold her forever, just past the first, or perhaps even the second, pang of hunger; certainly she would not stay should she catch the scent of a predator. Tying her would do neither of them any good should unfortunate circumstances befall either of them, and so he left her on trust and set off.

The terrain did not offer easy passage along the line he wanted. A steep banked stream forced a wide detour, until he found a place to cross. The broken ground soon left him uncertain about direction. He pressed on, and, half an hour later, he was sure he had gotten off course.

He took out the shard to confirm his direction. Touching the spell again was chancy if the other magician was watching, but the alternative was stumbling around lost in the woods. That could be even more dangerous if the drakkenree or their minions really were nearby. He touched the spell.

When he had set the spell days ago, he had built it on the strength of the relationship between the shard he carried and the other pieces that had once comprised the globe. Such spells were subject to the length of separation and the distance between the parts of the object; varying either affected the reading of the spell. Like all correspondences, such relationships decayed over time as well, adding more uncertainty to an interpretation. Comparing the sense he now got from the shard to that of the last time, he knew that he had misjudged. He must have misunderstood the strength of the affinity among the parts of the sphere, fooling himself into thinking the physical proximity was greater than it was. The broken orb must have been nestled in its place in the cave for a very long time to have such a strong associative aura. The new reading gave him a better understanding of distance and reoriented him.

As he restored the shard to his pouch, he also knew that he was no longer alone. While he had been concentrating on his spell, someone had crept near.

Friend or enemy?

Out here there seemed only one likely answer.

A shift in the shadows among the nearby bushes betrayed the newcomer's position, but Yan had no time to take advantage. A drakkenree, jaws agape, burst from the foliage and raced toward him. Its arms were spread wide, taloned fingers stretched ready to grasp. Yan didn't know whether or not to be relieved that the saurian had not drawn the sword that flapped against its hip.

Unsure of what he could do against this green terror charging him, Yan reached into his shirt for his *claviarm.* He had no weapon other than his magic, if that was a weapon. But the drakkenree gave him no time for magic; it covered the ground between them at a frightening pace. It reached for him. He ducked under the outstretched arm, but was caught in the ribs by the saurian's pumping leg.

It was like being struck by a ram. The violence of the stroke wrenched Yan's arm away from his body. His hand was still clasped on the amulet. The *claviarm*'s chain bit into his neck and parted. He felt the amulet slip from his numbing fingers, saw it arc away from him. He hit the ground and rolled.

The drakkenree stopped and regarded him, apparently confused by his response to its attack.

Yan looked frantically for where the *claviarm* had landed. A gleam in the forest loam caught his eye, and he scrambled in that direction. Without the access to the magic that it provided, he would be utterly helpless against the reptilian fury of the drakkenree. Even with his magic, he feared the saurian would kill him.

The drakkenree rushed him again before he could

recover the amulet. Desperately, Yan again threw himself to the side, trying to get out of its way. It anticipated him. A clawed hand swept out, raking him down his right arm. Fire burning along his arm, he fell to the ground, and the impact knocked the wind from him. Swinging its tail to the left, the drakkenree pivoted on one leg with frightening speed. Yan lay sprawled on his back, arms spread; he was helpless. The drakkenree stood over him, poised for the kill.

It looked as large as a *terriserpens*.

For a moment of excruciating sharpness, he could see every detail about the creature above him. Its form was similar to the *terriserpens*, but no more than a merin resembled one of the tailless apes of Omsess. The drakkenree's mottled green hide was rough, scaled and studded with rows of bony scutes along its flank and spine; its hide was rubbed raw in several places by the straps holding its weapons and pouches. The wedge-shaped head drew back, ready to strike from its sinuously curved neck. The forward-facing eyes were proportionally larger than those of a *terriserpens* and had wide, oval pupils that were fixed upon him. The gaping jaws were studded with a single row of sharp teeth; one near the front of the lower jaw was much shorter than the rest but gleamed whiter. The three fingers of its hand were tipped with black, curved talons, ready to claw or grasp. The drakkenree held its body parallel to the ground, tail thrust out in a shallow curve, tip pointing to the sky. The creature stood on one heavily muscled leg, holding the other leg raised, its clawed foot ready to lash out and gut Yan. A brown leaf was already impaled on the outermost of the three toes.

How strange to be studying one's own killer so calmly.

18

"DON'T MOVE, IF YOU WISH TO LIVE."

The words were spoken in accented Rolesdakkan, but the voice did not come from the drakkenree; the speaker was somewhere off to Yan's left. The saurian remained still, poised to murder him, so Yan dared to take his eyes from the drakkenree's claws and glance toward the speaker. A half dozen bregil stood in the bushes; they were dressed in a miscellany of cloth and leather and bore burdens rather than weapons. The speaker must have been one of them, though none showed any expression of concern that Yan could recognize. Most of the bregil were obviously hillmen, but one wore what looked to be the remnants of a civilized outfit. That one nodded slightly at Yan.

At a hissing, growling sound from the drakkenree, Yan's eyes snapped back to it. There was an urgency to the noise; it might have been a demand, an order, or a question. Not understanding, Yan didn't know what to do. The saurian repeated the noise, the toes of its raised foot extending briefly before returning to their curled readiness.

"He wants you to submit," the bregil said.

Turning his head to respond, Yan said, "It's obvious that I'm helpless."

The drakkenree hissed as Yan spoke. Its foot lashed out and clipped his temple. But the saurian kept its toes curled, and the claws did not rake bloody furrows in Yan's flesh.

Still, the pain of the blow was ample demonstration of the saurian's mastery of the situation. If it did not want Yan to turn his head, Yan would not turn his head.

The drakkenree returned to its foot-lifted, ready stance.

The saurian said something to the bregil, and the bregil answered. More exchanges followed. Finally the bregil spoke to Yan, "Khankemeh allows me to speak to you. He is a most generous lizard. He says he won't eat either of us if you submit to him. At least not right now."

"I don't seem to have a choice," Yan observed.

"No, you don't."

"All right. Tell it I submit."

"You must tell him yourself."

Yan looked up at the drakkenree. "I submit."

The drakkenree stared down at him, but didn't move.

"Khankemeh doesn't know this language," the bregil said. "You must tell him in his language. Or as close as you can come."

"But I don't know its language."

"That's why I'll tell you the words."

"You know their lang—"

The drakkenree's hiss and flexing claws cut Yan off.

"He's getting impatient. You'd better not say anything else except what he wants to hear."

Yan nodded.

"Wise," said the bregil. "Now tell me your name, merin."

"Yan."

"Whole name, stupid. And don't be even stupider and lie. He can smell it."

Yan wondered if the bregil's claim was true, but with black-clawed death standing over him, he didn't want to test it. "Yan Tanafres."

The bregil grunted in satisfaction. "All right, Yan Tanafres, this is what you have to say to him. You won't be able to get the inflections right, but nobody who isn't a lizard can. Say, '*Gifni* Yan Tanafres. *Gifni skess kedja'hreff. Shess Khankemeh.*'"

The words had a different ring from what the bregil and the drakkenree had spoken to each other. Clearly two languages. Was either the drakkenree tongue?

"What will I be saying?" Yan asked.

The drakkenree hissed softly, and the bregil said, "Does it matter? If you don't say it, you will die."

"*Gifni* Yan Tanafres. *Gifni* . . . "

"*Skess kedja'hreff,*" the bregil prompted. "*Shess Khankemeh.*"

Yan repeated the words, and the drakkenree seemed to relax slightly.

"*Gifni Khan'kmm'eh,*" it said. "*Gifni ss'jend kedja'k'krr che* Yan Tanafres."

The drakkenree struck postures to accompany the syllables "gif" and "ja," and growled and spat others, but it pronounced Yan's name in exact mimicry of his own pronunciation. When it finished the statement, the saurian lowered its foot to the ground. The drakkenree bent low, snapping its jaws closed in front of Yan's face. He could smell the fetid odor of rotting meat on its breath. Yan didn't know if the gesture was a threat or a promise, but he could not miss the potential violence that it implied.

Stepping away from him, the drakkenree turned its back as if to dismiss him as a danger. The saurian stalked away, but stopped suddenly and began examining the ground. As Yan got shakily to his feet, he saw what had attracted the drakkenree's attention. The saurian had found Yan's *claviarm* and was scooping it from the ground. Yan started to protest his claim to the amulet, but the drakkenree cuffed him and growl-hissed something at him.

"Khankemeh says no talking," the bregil translated.

The drakkenree cuffed the bregil; apparently the order not to speak applied to him as well. The man took the blow and bowed subserviently to the saurian, but Yan saw the glitter of hate in the bregil's eyes.

The drakkenree gave an order, and the bregil shouldered their loads. Unsure whether he should interfere, Yan watched as one of them slung Yan's satchels over his shoulder. The group moved out, Yan receiving a rough shove from the bregil spokesman to get him started. He made a point of keeping his eyes on the bregil with his satchels; but he had no opportunity to recover his goods, for they didn't have far to go, only a few tens of yards.

Their destination was what Yan had feared it would be:

the clearing near the ancient cave. Several wattle huts and a fragrant midden heap proclaimed that the drakkenree and their minions had been encamped here for some time— probably since Yan and Fra Bern had fled the place, leaving Fasolt to lose his duel with the drakkenree mage. Even if Yan had not been captured, he would have been disappointed; his hopes to visit the area and learn its secrets would have come to nothing. His plan had been doomed before he had conceived it.

Dejected, he watched the bregil unload their burdens, including Yan's satchels, into one of the huts. Their labor completed, they retired to the shade at the edge of the clearing. Some lay down: some sat, legs sprawled or backs to a tree. None showed much interest in anything around the camp; they acted like very tired men thankful for a rest. A nudge from Khankemeh's tail urged Yan to join them. Yan went and found a space next to a bregil lying on his belly and already snoring; the bregil's tail twitched, the grasping pad on the end curling and uncurling on nothing. Ignoring its bregil and token merin, Khankemeh walked to the other side of the clearing and struck up a conversation with another green-scaled saurian. Neither drakkenree seemed concerned that Yan might be contemplating escape.

Which, of course, he was. But he knew that he wouldn't get far, especially without his *claviarm*, and Khankemeh held that. For the moment all he could do was to stay watchful and learn what he could.

The bregil paid him no attention. Before long he realized that they paid little attention to each other, either. There was a general air of despondency about them, making Yan wonder if they all had submitted to Khankemeh as he had. Were they feeling the same sense of despair that was threatening to overwhelm him?

Or did they feel things differently? Yan didn't know very much about bregil; not about how they lived and thought, anyway. As far as he knew, their race lived everywhere merin did, but they were nowhere near as numerous. A settlement of them mined the hills above Yan's home-town on Merom, but they had rarely visited the town. Now and again he'd met a bregil in his days of wandering among the coastal kingdoms, but wherever he had seen bregil, they were always the minority in a crowd of merin. They were not the minority here, outnumbering the drakkenree by at least ten to one.

Yan was the minority here: a minority of one. Nowhere did he see another merin.

But in looking over his enforced companions, he began to suspect that he was not the only person who comprised a group of one here in the drakkenree camp. All of the bregil working about the camp wore some form or another of the orb talisman that he had once thought a sign of *haggatan*. Khankemeh's porters wore similar ornaments—all except the one who had spoken to him—but while that bregil's lack of a talisman might be happenstance, there were other things that set him apart. Most of the bregil wore only the rough-spun cloth and leathers of the hill tribes. Some had one piece or another of finer stuff; one even wore the sleeveless remnant of a buff coat such as the Imperial soldiers wore. Much of what the talker wore was rags, but his clothes appeared to have once made up a complete suit in the Islander style, suggesting that he might have come from the empire. He also showed a familiarity with the drakkenree language that even the learned Fasolt had lacked. So who was this bregil?

Yan checked to confirm that Khankemeh was still ignoring them; the saurian was nowhere in sight. All the other saurians seemed involved in a conversation, and the bregil were dozing or absorbed in their camp tasks. Satisfied that it was as safe as it was going to get, Yan moved over next to the talker and seated himself. The bregil didn't look around, but continued to stare across the camp. Yan gave a look in that direction, but didn't see anything worthy of intent study.

"I want to thank you," Yan said, using Rolesdakkan, which he knew the man could speak.

The bregil turned his head slowly to look at Yan. The man's dark eyes were unreadable. Raising the left side of his bifurcate upper lip, the bregil showed his strong yellow teeth. Yan was unsure whether the expression was a half smile or a snarl, and the bregil said nothing to clarify his attitude. The bregil looked away.

Yan tried again. "I am grateful, but I don't understand a lot of what happened. Why did you speak up back in the forest?"

"If I hadn't, the lizard would have killed you."

"What difference would that have made to you?" Yan asked.

The bregil turned his dark eyes on Yan, searching his face. Finally the man turned away and shrugged. He gave no other answer.

This was a most awkward conversation, but Yan was not ready to give up just yet. Yan made his next comment in Empiric, just to see what kind of response he'd get. "I see by your clothes that you are not from the hills."

"No, I'm not. Quite a ways from here, actually," the bregil said in the same language. "No more a local than you."

"You speak Empiric well."

"Well enough."

"Might I inquire your name and your profession?"

"Haven't you magicked up an answer?" the bregil asked scornfully.

"In truth, no."

"And your kind can't stand not knowing, eh, Yan Tanafres? Well, too bad; I'd prefer you not knowing. When the lizards call for Threok, I answer. You can use that name for me, too."

"And what profession do you follow, Threok?"

The bregil snorted. "Me? I'm a mule for a lizard."

"I meant before you—"

A frightened neighing from the other side of the camp interrupted Yan. He recognized the sound even before Khankemeh led Shean into the open area of the camp. The horse was terrified; Yan felt a little frightened himself.

Two green-scaled drakkenree rose from where they lay next to the camp's fire pit. They swiveled their heads to look. Jaws opened as their heads jutted forward, but they remained in place, wedge-shaped heads pointing at Shean as Khankemeh led the horse into the center of the clearing.

Stomping back and forth at Shean's side, Khankemeh made an announcement composed of hisses and growls. The horse fought against the hand that held her lead rein, but the drakkenree's grip was strong, and it held her head low, frustrating all of Shean's efforts to break free.

A half dozen drakkenree appeared from the trees around the clearing. All were mottled green and wore weapon straps like Khankemeh. Two wore armor and bore the long two-handed swords that had done such devastating butchery in the ambush weeks ago. Those two saurians planted their blades point-first in the ground and assumed postures mimicking the two who were in the clearing when Khankemeh brought in the horse. The rest of the newcomers turned toward Khankemeh and the horse and fell into open-jawed stillness. The camp took on an eerie hush, broken only by Shean's whinnies. For all his sympathy for Shean, Yan was glad that he wasn't the center of the saurians' attention as the horse was. The sight of a ring of drakkenree, mouths agape and teeth flashing in the light, chilled him, but not as much as the appearance of the next saurian to answer Khankemeh's call.

At the mouth of the cave a black-scaled drakkenree appeared. Yan was unsure if it was the same one that had dueled with Fasolt. That one had been black, and had worn straps with pouches and fetishes as this one did, but the arrangement of the harness was not what Yan remembered. Still, drakkenree were thinking beings, and thinking beings changed their clothes from time to time. Was it so far-fetched to imagine that a drakkenree might rearrange its harness? But if they were creatures of ingrained habit, the harness arrangement might never be changed, which would mean that this was another mage; a thought Yan found terrifying. Then he saw Fasolt's blackened *claviarm* hanging among the clutter of items on the harness. Though lacking his own *claviarm*, Yan remained sufficiently attuned to the mana to sense that the amulet decorating the drakkenree's belt was dead. Fasolt was dead. Yan felt regret, and some small relief; one mage among the drakkenree was bad enough. Who else but the Imperial wizard's conqueror would be wearing his *claviarm* as a trophy?

He nudged Threok and whispered, "What's that one's name?"

The bregil looked at the black drakkenree, and, grimacing, he spat. "Yellow Eye."

"What kind of a name is that? Why not more of those strange syllables like you used for the other one?"

"Yellow Eye is what the hillmen call it. That's good enough for me, since I don't belong to it."

Shean screamed. Yan turned his head in time to see Khankemeh sink its teeth into the horse's neck. Yan was appalled as the drakkenree tugged its head back and ripped open the animal's throat. Shean reared up and fell over backward, kicking. The other drakkenree spread out into a circle around the dying animal.

The drakkenree ringing the horse's body began making bobbing bows to Khankemeh. Khankemeh held itself rigid, body parallel to the ground, tail out stiff behind it. The eight saurians began to circle Khankemeh, who placed one foot on Shean's now still corpse. The bizarre scene was disturbed when Yellow Eye reached the circle. Most of the drakkenree backed away from the black one, who Yan could now see was larger than any of them. As they retreated, the saurians stopped their bobbing and stood more erect. Necks that had been coiled in tight curves straightened.

Khankemeh and one of the armored saurians reacted differently. Though both stood more erect, neither retreated, and each kept its neck drawn in a sinuous curve. Yellow Eye turned its head to regard the armored one, who seemed to shiver slightly before stretching its neck out like the others. Yellow Eye turned its gaze to Khankemeh, who did not react at once. Its body dipped slightly, freezing when Yellow Eye opened its jaws slightly. Slowly Khankemeh straightened, stretching its neck out like the others.

It was a display unlike anything Yan had ever seen. He guessed that the black one had just asserted its authority over the others, but nothing had been said; the strange postures of the drakkenree seemed to serve in place of the words or gestures a human would have used. It was utterly strange, but fascinating.

Pacing forward, Yellow Eye planted one foot on Shean's chest and bent down to rip a chunk from her belly. Muzzle bloody, Yellow Eye raised its head. Entrails and flesh hung from its jaws. With a flip of its snout, it repositioned the morsel before working the mouthful down its throat, like a Meromian great lizard swallowing prey. Yellow Eye removed its foot from the carcass and backed up three steps. At that signal the other drakkenree moved in to snatch their own bites. Yellow Eye turned away and returned to the cave.

Yan listened in misery to the thunks and cracks and slurps of the hideous feast. Had he so recently considered them thinking beings? These drakkenree were acting like beasts, gorging themselves like animals. It was disgusting.

It did not take long for the saurians to strip Shean's carcass down to the bone. One by one they moved away, walking more slowly now that they had eaten. Most found a place near the fire pit, stretched out, and closed their eyes. Khankemeh, last at the feast, came to Yan and motioned him forward with a crooked finger. The drakkenree led Yan to the remains of the horse. Threok and a couple of the other bregil followed, but most of Khankemeh's crew stayed in the shade and watched. Shean had little more than bloody bones left to her, and the smell of blood filled Yan's nose. Khankemeh placed a hand on Yan's shoulder and pressed down. Under that insistent pressure, Yan's knees buckled. Off-balance from the drakkenree's push, Yan fell to the ground. He felt the blood-soaked earth against his cheek and nearly vomited.

"*Che'rr'dent,*" the drakkenree said.

"Eat some," Threok translated.

"But it's raw," Yan complained.

Khankemeh hissed and kicked Yan. "*Che'rrrr'dent!*"

"Like this." Threok snatched up a loose rib bone and gnawed at it. Yan was revolted. Smirking, Threok suggested, "If you can't do it, pretend to."

"Why?" Yan moaned.

"For your life. If you don't eat, old Khan here will kill you."

Under Khankemeh's watchful stare, Yan reached out a hand a stripped a shred of muscle from Shean's hind leg.

He brought it toward his mouth, but using a sleight, palmed it instead of placing it in his mouth. He pretended to chew, then to swallow. Khankemeh seemed satisfied; the drakkenree walked away and joined the circle of saurians lying by the campfire.

The show over, Threok and the other bregil returned to their shady spot and their apparent indifference to the world around them. Two other bregil sauntered over and began to drag the carcass away. Feeling exposed sitting in the open space, Yan picked himself up. He dropped the shred of Shean's flesh in the dirt and joined Threok. Yan spotted a daub of blood near the corner of Threok's mouth and didn't feel like asking any more questions for the moment.

He sat sullenly watching camp activities until night came on. Shortly after sunset, the two bregil who had taken away Shean's bloody remains appeared again. They built up the fire in the pit, and when they had it roaring, hauled out a kettle and set it in the flames. They had to work around the drakkenree lying about. Eventually the two bregil dished up bowls of a gummy porridge and passed them out. The bregil with whom Yan sat took them eagerly.

"What's this?" Yan asked, poking at a dark mass that lay half-submerged in the smelly mess.

"Food," Threok answered. "Best not ask more questions about it."

Yan didn't ask any more questions, for his imagination was already supplying answers. He put the bowl down and turned away from it. He heard a rustling behind him and turned in time to see Threok dump the last of Yan's portion into his own bowl.

"No point wasting," the bregil said.

Yan didn't feel like complaining; he wasn't hungry anyway. Seeing Shean butchered had taken away his appetite. He turned to look at the forest and the darkness under the leaves. With his magesight, he would be able to run through the forest almost as well at night as during the day. But would it be enough of an advantage for him to escape his captors? How well did drakkenree see in the dark, anyway? One, at least, might be able to see as well as he.

Yan's inconclusive musings on escape were interrupted by a familiar tug; it was not so much a pull as an awareness, but it riveted his attention. He looked over at the fire and saw Khankemeh bring his *claviarm* from its pouch. Within a certain distance, a magician was always aware of his *claviarm*, an ability borne of the piece of his soul that was bonded to it. A *claviarm* was a magician's principal tool for the manipulation of magical energy; the best mages could do minor spells without it, but most, like Yan, needed to have their focus in close proximity. Unfortunately, the distance at which he could use the *claviarm* was less than that at which he could sense it.

The saurian displayed the amulet to the others like a trophy. They passed it around the circle. Seeing the *claviarm* made it harder to bear being parted from it. Leaving it behind would be difficult, but he didn't see how he could take it back from the saurian.

Without warning, the black drakkenree appeared out of the darkness on the far side of the fire like an apparition. In a half dozen strides it skirted the pit and stood behind Khankemeh. Yellow Eye's hand snapped out and snagged the *claviarm*'s cord, snatching the amulet away from the soldier returning it to Khankemeh.

Khankemeh hissed and scrambled to its feet. It bent low, neck coiled, ready to strike; its head pointed at the black one. Khankemeh's jaws opened wide and it hissed again. Yellow Eye bent low, too, but opened its jaws only a little. Khankemeh shut its jaws and rocked back at the hips. It took a step backward, neck relaxing out of readiness to strike. Yellow Eye opened its jaws a little wider, and Khankemeh backed farther away until it stood at the edge of the firelight.

The drakkenree mage relaxed its posture and held Yan's *claviarm* out so that the firelight reflected on the amulet. Holding the *claviarm* at arm's length, Yellow Eye stared at it. After several minutes of concentration, it snapped its jaws once and stared some more. Abruptly, it flipped the amulet up and caught it as it fell. The broken chain snaked down into its palm and taloned fingers closed over the *claviarm*, hiding it from view.

Yellow Eye pivoted on one foot and stalked toward Yan. The bregil near him shifted away. Yan wanted to run, but he didn't dare. The drakkenree stopped a pair of yards away. Yellow Eye folded its legs, lowering its body to the ground with the exaggerated slowness of an egret settling on a nest. The drakkenree said nothing, just looked at Yan. He couldn't meet that cold yellow stare.

Finally Yellow Eye said something in a guttural language to one of the bregil cowering behind Yan. The man got up and trotted over to the fire, and got himself cuffed by Khankemeh for his trouble. The bregil picked himself up and trotted to one of the huts. He emerged a moment later with Yan's satchels. The bregil returned and laid the bags by the side of the black drakkenree.

Yellow Eye began to sort through Yan's things. The mage separated several items from the rest, including Yan's case of working materials, the herbal jars, and all of the few handbooks Yan had brought with him. From among the last, the saurian selected Yan's travel-stained copy of Costigern's *Of Light and Air*. The drakkenree opened the book, turning pages with a deft claw.

"Your teacher is wrong, mammal. Light is not of air," the drakkenree said abruptly in Nital.

Yan was taken aback, as much by the statement as the voice the drakkenree used. Though each word was pronounced correctly, the words seemed unconnected, as if spoken by different persons.

"What say you, mammal?"

Yan didn't know what to say. "Costigern was not my teacher."

"You have the words of a magician other than your teacher?"

Should that be surprising? "Yes."

The drakkenree poked at the other books. "None of these are your teacher's words?"

"Not directly."

Yellow Eye raised its chin, cocking its head to stare at Yan with one eye. Yan dropped his eyes to the ground, unwilling to face that fierce glare.

Clearly this drakkenree mage didn't understand how

human magicians learned magic. Revealing the true process might be unwise; Yan sought for some way to deflect the conversation. Knowing so little about drakkenree, he could not be sure what was safe and what wasn't. Fearing that Yellow Eye would ask questions he wouldn't think it wise to answer, Yan asked the first question himself; the subject seemed safe enough.

"What happened to Fasolt?"

"Who is Fasolt?" Yellow Eye's pronunciation of the Imperial wizard's name matched Yan's with uncanny exactness.

"The mage you fought here a fortnight ago."

The drakkenree's jaws opened slightly. "You know of that?"

"I—" What was the right thing to say? "Yes, I know of that."

"How?"

"What happened to him?" Yan insisted, trying to deflect that line of questioning.

Yellow Eye clicked his jaws. "He is gone."

"Dead?"

"Dead, yes. He was foolish, mammal. He challenged me. Are you as foolish?"

"I have no wish to challenge you."

"A small wisdom. Why did you come, if not to challenge me?"

"I—I was looking for Fasolt," Yan mumbled.

"Fasolt was your master?"

"He was . . . an acquaintance."

The drakkenree nodded its head in an oddly human way. "You hunt, but not for an acquaintance." Yellow Eye mimicked the phrase "an acquaintance" perfectly.

"I was looking for Fasolt. We didn't know what had happened to him."

"You lie."

Yan stammered a denial, remembering Threok's assertion that Khankemeh could smell lies. Yellow Eye seemed oblivious to Yan's distress. "The hiding spell tasted different," the drakkenree said. "It was not his. It was yours, then."

Since it seemed that the saurians could smell lies, there was no point in telling untruths. "Yes."

"Better," Yellow Eye said. "Come here."

Yan did as he was told, squatting in front of the drakkenree. Yellow Eye unfolded one arm and reached its hand toward Yan's head. Yan wanted to flinch away but didn't dare, fear holding him still more solidly than courage ever could. The taloned hand disappeared out of Yan's vision, and he felt the rasp of scaled skin against his cheek. There was a sudden, sharp pain in his earlobe, then the drakkenree's hand came back into sight; the tip of one claw was beaded bright with blood. Yellow Eye licked the blood from his talon while it plucked something from one of its straps with its other hand. The saurian affixed the object, an earring, to Yan's ear. The slight pain in his punctured lobe faded as the drakkenree spelled the thing. Even without his *claviarm* Yan could detect that there was power in the charm.

"You no longer belong to *Khan'kmm'eh*," Yellow Eye said. Its pronunciation of Khankemeh's name was different from Threok's; the middle syllable was more of a growl. "You are mine now.

"*Gifni ss'jend kedja'k'krr che* Yan Tanafres."

19

"TELL THE GENERAL WHAT YOU told me," Raff ordered the priest.

"But Captain Janden—"

"Just tell him about Tanafres."

Fra Bern hesitated, his eyes asking for a reprieve. Did he think Raff was going to explain for him? Raff gestured toward the general, who was waiting patiently for the priest to speak; he wanted Honistonti to hear the priest's revelation from Bern himself.

Finally Bern turned his worried face to Honistonti. "This is not a matter with which I am comfortable, General."

"I've yet to confuse the message and the messenger, good priest. Put away your concern and say what you have to say. I have come to hear you, but there are many other things that I must attend to."

Bern nodded and swallowed. Having steeled himself to speak, he spoke in a rush of words. "Master Tanafres is in trouble with the drakkenree. There is magic. He is involved, and so is that dreadful drakkenree magician."

Honistonti showed neither surprise nor concern; his expression remained solemn attentiveness. Like a good courtier. Raff knew that the man had spent time in the capital; he would be schooled to unexpected and unexplained pronouncements.

"Could you be more specific, Fra Bern?" Honistonti asked quietly.

Bern looked down at the floor. "I do not exactly understand the situation myself."

Now Honistonti frowned. "What is the source of your information, Fra Bern?"

"My dreams, General," Bern said without looking up. "It is not widely known that I have these dreams, but I do. The gods, in Their wisdom, send me these dreams. His Eminence Myskell will tell you it is so. You need only ask him."

"We need not disturb the high priest, Fra Bern. Your word as a priest is sufficient. Are these dreams prophetic?"

"Sometimes. Other times I am gifted with knowledge of things that are happening in the present but at a distance. I never know which it is, until I learn by experience that I have had a true dream."

"And how have you learned that this new dream is a true one?" the general asked.

"I have not. I just feel that it is."

"A feeling?"

"A very strong one, sir. The dream has come more than once. The true dreams are like that."

"I see."

"I believe the priest," Raff said.

"Do you?" Honistonti did not look as though he believed Raff's statement. "On what basis?"

"Tell him the details of your dream, Fra Bern."

"Please do, good priest."

The priest cleared his throat. He looked even less comfortable than when he had related his dream to Raff earlier.

"In my dream, I stand in a strange place," Bern began hesitantly. "It is a place I have been before, but now it is different. It was different once before as well, when the drakkenree built their towers there. The towers are gone in my dream, but the drakkenree have returned to the place. They are building again. Building and digging.

"There is a great sense of dread. Of impending peril. I see Master Tanafres. There are drakkenree all around him, and he walks among them unmolested, yet he is unhappy. He is like a bird in a cage.

"Master Tanafres goes into a cave and, as he does, I see

that he is glowing. It is magic. I also see the great black drakkenree, and it glows as it enters the cave, too. I follow them, but it is dark. I stumble. I see Master Tanafres and the drakkenree mage, deeper in the darkness. They are searching for something. Sometimes the two seem to be one, but other times not. I don't understand this, and it frightens me. I run out of the cave.

"I try to leave the place where the drakkenree are raising their pointed towers and find my way barred by a river of blood. I cannot bear to try to cross the river, so I run along the bank. Drakkenree chase me. I run very hard, and they fall behind, but then there are more in front me, rising from the ground as though summoned by the dark magics." The priest's voice trembled from his very real terror. "I fear the ancient enemy is upon me, and I look to the heavens for succor, but the gods have forsaken me. In the heavens I see a great, bloated, yellow moon in the sky, looking down like an eye. It is powerful, and it is not of the Celestial Court. It is something else. I am filled with terror, and I scream," the priest finished, panting.

Raff could see that Honistonti was moved by Bern's recitation. Caught up in the priest's sincere terror, the general let his courtly discipline crack. He looked worried and a little afraid; he was reacting just as Raff had hoped he would. Just in case the general had missed the significance, Raff explained, "The moon is the Eye of the Serpent."

"I don't know that for truth," Bern said.

"You told me you suspected it," Raff said. "And didn't you say you don't always understand these dreams?"

Bern nodded. "That is true."

"It sounds like a nightmare to me," Honistonti said.

"It is," Bern agreed.

"A nightmare, yes, but one that must be ours as well," Raff added. "If Fra Bern's dream is prophetic, we face a great danger, the resurrection of the ancient enemy. We must act before it can become reality."

"If the dream is prophetic, mortal man cannot change it," Honistonti said.

"It might be only a warning," Raff pointed out. "A notice from the gods that we must act or suffer dire consequences."

Honistonti rubbed his chin with a finger. "Well, good priest, is it a warning or a prophecy?"

"I wish I could tell you, General." The priest looked dismayed. "I do not know. But I fear for the soul of Master Tanafres."

"Souls are your business, not mine. I deal in lives."

"I fear for his life as well, General."

"Fear for yourself, priest," Raff said. "Tanafres went out there of his own will. If he was captured, he brought it on his own head. Your dream suggests that the rest of us face a peril as great or greater."

The priest shook his head sorrowfully. "I fear that, too, may be so."

"Is there not some sort of scrying that you or the other priests can do to learn more about this dream?" Honistonti asked.

"That is not in the gift of any at the temple. We can only pray for enlightenment."

"Do so," the general ordered.

"In fact, why don't you return to the temple and start immediately," Raff said. "We can send for you if we have more questions. You will be at the temple, won't you?"

"I—Yes, of course."

When the priest had left, Raff turned to Honistonti. "So you see, General, we must do something about Tanafres's capture."

"Must?" Honistonti's expression soured, as it always did when someone else told him his course.

"Must," Raff insisted anyway.

The general clenched his jaw and Raff let him fume for a moment. He was pleased when Honistonti said, "The priest said that in his dream Tanafres and the drakkenree wizard were one. Do you think that means Tanafres is collaborating with the lizards?"

"A likely possibility. We must remove him from their power."

"If he's aiding them, they'll likely kill him before surrendering him."

"That would be preferable to having them use him against us."

Honistonti looked annoyed. "What man would help the lizards?"

"His collusion may be unintentional."

"You think that he went after the Eye."

"It is almost a certainty. He now knows that the Eye is a powerful artifact; he will want it, if only to see how it works. And Tanafres has shown himself to be a man more concerned with his Great Art than with people. He has a history of risking his life to gain knowledge that he thinks important. In taking it upon himself to seek out the Serpent's Eye, he risks all our lives. He might not even realize he is helping the enemy."

"How could he not?"

"Perhaps he thinks to outwit the lizards and gain the Eye for himself. He may even have hopes of turning the Eye against the lizards. But such a plan is born of arrogant pride and will come to nothing. Tanafres is too poor a magician, and far too foolish to succeed in such a scheme. At best he is being used by the drakkenree, and at worst he is a willing ally. Either way, he cannot be allowed to remain in the lizards' possession. We must act, and act swiftly."

Honistonti gave him a sour frown. "Why do I think that your 'we' is me?"

"You command the expeditionary force, General."

"You can't mean to send the entire force in an attempt to wrest this magician from the drakkenree? With the drakkenree and the hillmen ravaging the countryside, we need to reinforce King Shain's army. He has insufficient force to deal with the enemy."

"I'd send your force *and* the king's if I thought it would serve."

"Serve or not, the king's army is not subject to your whims." Honistonti's eyes narrowed. "Just what do you have in mind?"

"I think we must strike hard and fast for the place in the priest's dreams. It is no longer a matter of flailing about trying to destroy the artifact. We have a more definite path now. If a sufficient force hits the drakkenree—"

"Wait a moment. What 'definite path'? We don't even know where the lizards are."

"But we know where they can be found. The priest's dreams—"

"It's bad strategy to base military maneuvers on dreams."

"It's worse to let magic get the upper hand," said Raff. "Old soldiers like us know what happens when arcane things disturb military matters. If we can crush the lizards' mage before it uncovers the Eye, we can keep the issue strictly military. Surely you understand that, General? And by crushing the mage's guardian forces, we expose the wizard. It might flee, but that would still remove it from the campaign. It would be best to catch it and kill it."

"We'd be risking too much on such a throw of the die. It is too great a gamble."

"Every battle is a gamble."

"More a calculated risk," said the general.

"Little difference beyond the words."

Honistonti shifted the argument. "Even were I to agree that we should make the effort, how are we supposed to find this place? Fra Bern says he doesn't know where it is."

"Ah. He told me earlier that he recognized the place in his dream; it is where he and Tanafres abandoned Gan Fasolt. He does not know the exact location, but he knows the general area, and from his description, the place shouldn't be hard to find. If the army goes there, the drakkenree will come out to fight in order to protect their wizard and the hidden Eye. Once the lizards and their monkeys are beaten, you will have no one to stop you from searching the area and securing the Eye for the emperor."

"I still do not think this is wise."

Raff drew his *staliarm* from beneath his shirt, cupping it in the palm of his hand. He felt the warmth and knew from the look in Honistonti's eye that he saw the glow. There was no way to counterfeit the sign, and Honistonti knew what it meant almost as well as Raff himself.

"And if I mention the emperor's name?" he asked.

Honistonti sat back in his chair, back straight. "I know my oath."

"Of course you do, General. I thought no less of you."

Shaking his head, Honistonti said, "I never thought that

'all possible aid' would mean throwing away the emperor's troops in a foray with little hope of success."

"There is great hope of success. Success that will crush the lizards and extinguish their dreams forever."

Honistonti harrumphed. Shoving his chair back from the table, he stood. "When do you want this foray to start?"

"Yesterday would have been good."

"Tomorrow will have to do."

"Tomorrow it shall be." Raff smiled in satisfaction. "And, General, I think it wisest not to speak of the priest's dream to anyone."

"*You* think it wise?"

"I believe the emperor would think it wise as well."

"I see."

Honistonti departed to make his arrangements, leaving Raff to make arrangements of his own.

Teletha doffed her helmet and wiped the perspiration from her brow. It was too hot for the sweaty, grunty work of practice, and she had kept at it far longer than her troop would have liked. Removing her helmet had been the long-awaited signal for a break; they dispersed at once. She sighed. It wouldn't be easy to gather them again for another session. Maybe someone else would want to do some sword work. With Vehr's help, she'd find *someone* to work with. That way she wouldn't have to think about what kind of trouble Yan was getting himself into. Practice and drill helped her remember why she was still with the army.

Her duty.

Right. Her duty hadn't stopped her from going after Yan when she had thought him lost. That time, the army hadn't been ready to move out. And that time he hadn't left of his own will and given her no notice. And . . .

What was the point in beating it all to death? She was here, and Yan was Horesh-knew-where. If she couldn't find anyone willing to put on the padded gambesons and heft the practice swords, maybe a long ride would clear her head. Maybe the ride would be even better, since it wouldn't be so Vehr-forsaken hot; there was no breeze to cool her sweat in this courtyard. But there was a fountain, and its water would be some comfort. She turned around in that direction and saw Iaf sitting on the fountain edge. He smiled, splashing his hand in the water.

"You look like you could use some," he called.

She walked over, putting the helmet down before dunking her head into the water. She knew that it was warm, but it still felt cool to her. Soothing trickles ran down her neck and under the soggy padding to her torso. It felt good.

"Come by for a little practice?" she asked.

"Got mine in this morning when it was cooler."

"Always use a little more."

"Some other time."

It wasn't like him to refuse an opportunity to work out with her. Something must have brought him here. "What passes?"

Iaf didn't look at her as he said, "Word is we're moving out tomorrow."

"King Shain said the army wasn't to leave for another two days."

"Not the whole army. Just the expeditionary force. Captain Janden's getting his way."

"Estem knows better than to split the army and go chasing some mythical artifact."

Now he looked at her. "Colonel Kensie got the orders directly from the general."

"No." Estem wouldn't give such orders.

Iaf nodded. "The colonel said the general didn't sound happy about it."

"Then why is he doing it?" she asked.

"That's what I asked Colonel Kensie, and what the colonel asked General Honistonti. The general said he was following orders. The emperor's word."

Teletha was perplexed. "There haven't been any couriers in recently."

"True. Strange, isn't it? No couriers. No magicians. Yet we get the emperor's word here. You don't think the general has been—well—imagining things?"

She shook her head. Estem wasn't the type. So what was the reason for the change in plans? She resolved to ask him herself. "I assume the first elements will ride at dawn."

"Before it, actually," Iaf said.

"Guess we won't get much sleep."

"*I* won't. Why won't you? You don't have to get up."

Of course she did, didn't she? "What do you mean?"

"Your light horsemen are attached to King Shain's army, remember?"

She did, now. With so many Imperials around, she'd fallen into old habits of thinking. Things were different now. She wasn't a soldier of the emperor anymore; she was a mercenary, under contract and legally bound. Honor-bound as well, for she wore the black-and-white cord of the Sword Guild.

"Where are you going?" she asked.

"Into the wilderness. We're to kill the drakkenree wizard and recapture Master Tanafres."

"*Re*capture?"

Iaf nodded solemnly. "The general believes that the drakkenree have him."

"Then we know where he is."

Iaf looked uncomfortable. "Not exactly."

"Then the force will need scouts."

Iaf looked downright upset. "I know you want to go, but General Honistonti has specifically stated that none of the king's forces will be involved."

"We'll see about that."

Iaf turned his head away, apparently struggling with himself over what he should say next. He seemed to reach a conclusion, but instead of speaking to her, his eyes focused on something behind her. She looked over her shoulder and saw Jax Vorsan standing in the shadow of one of the buildings at the courtyard's edge. Was Iaf's business with an ex-Imperial mercenary scout so important that colonels needed to spy on it? Or was Jax the Butcher just out on his own to settle accounts with a Scothic kid?

Turning back to Iaf, she asked, "What's *he* doing here?"

Iaf gave an aggravated sigh. "Following me, I suppose."

"Following you? I thought he was still abed with his injuries."

"I thought so, too, but he was standing outside Colonel Kensie's headquarters when I came out after yesterday morning's meeting. Didn't say a word when I greeted him; he just stood there with a grim look on his face. I thought he was being his usual haughty self and went about my business. Then he turned up at the mess last night, and at the drill field this morning. I've spent most of the day running errands for the colonel, and every time I stopped, he's been there. He's following me. Everywhere I go, so does he. He hasn't said anything, just stands at a distance and watches. Always frowning. It's weird."

"At least he hasn't got any of his toadies with him."

"Funny thing about that. I went by their headquarters and that was the only time he didn't follow me. I talked to his Lieutenant Bachem—uncivilized bastard—and managed to find out that Vorsan had just up and walked out of the temple hospice yesterday at dawn. Surprised the priests completely. I think he surprised his men even more by not coming to them."

"What do you think he wants? Is he after you?"

"I don't know. But if he wanted to ambush me, I would think he's had plenty of chances."

A clatter of hooves sounded from the road beyond the arch where Vorsan stood. The giant colonel stepped back into the deeper shadows just before a trio of horsemen rode past him. They paid him no attention, but one of them called out to Iaf.

"Lieutenant Smyth, you're wanted at the general's tent."

Iaf looked at her apologetically. "I've got to go."

"Do your duty," she said.

20

YAN'S FIRST FEW DAYS AS Yellow Eye's property were filled with fear, confusion, fascination, and awe. Not since Yan's apprenticeship to Gan Tidoni had he found himself in a place where he was at once so terrified and so enthralled. Everything about the drakkenree engaged his interest, and the more he saw and heard, the more he wanted to know. The saurians did not teach Yan anything directly, but observation provided him with more than enough to ponder. Some things, such as their feeding habits, continued to repulse him; other aspects surprised and intrigued him.

Threok was the only one who showed any interest in talking with Yan, and so the bregil became his adviser, a reluctant interpreter of what was going on around them. Their conversations were rarely long, for the drakkenree seemed to dislike noise from their minions; Yan risked their displeasure nonetheless, since he was brimming with questions. Yan just couldn't stay away from the only person who'd speak to him.

But Threok was a limited resource. Though the bregil seemed to know much more than Yan about the drakkenree and the hill tribes, he would not answer all questions with equal candor. When it came to sharing what he knew of proper responses to the drakkenree and the customs and etiquette of the camp, Threok spoke freely. Yan was sure that without the bregil's advice, he would have made some sort of horrible mistake, transgressed the drakkenree customs sufficiently that the saurians would have killed him. But when asked how he had come by his knowledge, Threok responded, "By staying alive," and would say no more, leaving Yan in the dark regarding Threok's origin. And for all his knowledge of daily life in the camp, the bregil displayed little knowledge of the drakkenree's origin, less of their motivations, and still less of their magic, in short, all the areas in which Yan believed the most important answers lay.

Yan spent his days in the cave with Yellow Eye. It was an easier life than Threok and the other bregil endured; they faced hours of heavy labor on poor rations. Even with good meals, Yan would not have been able to keep up with the heavy work the bregil did; he was much better suited to the more scholarly pursuits that were his lot as Yellow Eye's property. Had he remained with Khankemeh, he would surely have been worked to death.

As it was, in an odd sort of way Yan found himself transported back in time. The saurian mage kept him nearby, using him like a new apprentice; Yan held what the drakkenree told him to hold, fetched what he was told to fetch, cleaned up any mess the mage's experiments made, and tidied Yellow Eye's instruments at the end of the day. For all that the surroundings were rude and his master alien, Yan fell into the pattern easily. He had served Gan Tidoni in these ways when he was young and ignorant. Gan Tidoni had rarely commented on the usefulness of anything Yan had done for him in those early days, and had never stopped to explain any of the procedures he had been performing; so having the drakkenree mage give unexplained orders seemed somehow suitable. But with Gan Tidoni, Yan had eventually learned. He would learn here, too.

As often as not, when Yellow Eye became engrossed in its studies, it seemed to forget Yan was there, much as Gan Tidoni had. Under the current circumstances, this was a pattern that Yan found congenial. It gave him a chance to observe the drakkenree mage close at hand.

Yellow Eye had a book to which it often referred as it

worked. Yan recognized the script immediately; it was the same as the writing in Gornal's books that had puzzled him for so long. Carefully Yan watched what Yellow Eye did before and after consulting the book and, whenever a magical operation was involved, Yan tried to commit to memory the symbols on the pages the drakkenree mage consulted. He hoped that a repetition of elements might suggest possible correspondences between magical actions he understood and written sequences he did not, giving him a key to understanding some of the symbols. It would have been easier if he could ask questions, but Yan's first few attempts had gotten him cuffed into silence.

Reduced to observation and deduction, Yan found that each viewing of the book suggested one or more magical experiments that could test his developing theories concerning the meanings of the sinuous script. Unfortunately, without his *claviarm*, he could do nothing about conducting such experiments, assuming the drakkenree would allow him to perform magic in their camp. Yellow Eye kept Yan's *claviarm* in a painted leather bag hung from one of the straps girdling the saurian's torso. Yan assumed the bag was enchanted, because he could not feel the *claviarm* even when he stood next to the drakkenree; he only knew that it was there because he had seen Yellow Eye place it in the bag. Knowing his *claviarm* was so near was almost unbearable; he gained new insight into the tale of the blind old mage Kalisham. Unlike Kalisham, Yan at least had the hope of making a new focus should he escape. Though being so near magic and unable to touch it gnawed at him, he vowed that he would not fall into despair and take Kalisham's way out. As long as he had all his faculties, he had a chance to recover what had been taken from him. As the old proverb said, "The patient egret is rewarded."

Though Yellow Eye worked in the cave at night, as Yan could tell from the glow of magelight escaping the entrance, it did not require its attendant for those sessions. Once Yan was released for the evening meal, he was free to wander the camp and mingle with the bregil. As the only merin in the camp, he was conspicuous, though by the third day

none of the drakkenree seemed to pay him any more attention than they gave to the bregil.

Except for Khankemeh. That saurian watched him con-
stantly whenever the two of them were in the camp. Yan
knew it was Khankemeh who watched him because the gap
in Khankemeh's dentition made it possible to distinguish it
from the other green-scaled saurians in camp; beyond the
gear they wore—and much of that was similar—there
seemed to be little by which to distinguish one from another.

Several times Khankemeh advanced toward Yan, but
each time Yan managed to reach the relative safety of the
cave or a group of bregil before Khankemeh reached him.
Such measures seemed to discourage the saurian, causing it
to abandon its attempt to reach Yan, for which Yan was
grateful. The constant attention from Khankemeh made
Yan wonder. Could it be harboring some sort of resentment about Yellow Eye's usurpation of its property?

Yan got his answer the next night when he was returning from the slit trench that the camp's bregil used for sani-
tation. That afternoon Yan had witnessed a discussion
between Yellow Eye and one of the soldiers; Yan had
finally decided that soldier was the best description for the
green-scaled drakkenree. The saurians' conversation had
involved much hissing and growling and a great deal of
posturing; Yan recognized little of what he heard and saw.
The drakkenree language frustrated Yan, who had always
found languages easy to learn. The saurians relied tremen-
dously on gestures, some broad, some subtle. Many of their
sounds were impossible for a person to duplicate, but Yan
was determined to puzzle out as much as he could; Threok
knew bits of the language. Yan had committed some of the
saurians' conversation to memory, intending to ask Threok
about it. Distracted by trying to figure out how to describe
some of the subtle body and tail angles the drakkenree had
used, Yan failed to see Khankemeh's approach until the
saurian soldier had gotten between Yan and the bregil
sleeping area.

Yan had no magic, no weapons, and no hope for help.
Yesterday he'd watched the bregil hoot and cheer as one of
their number was disciplined by a drakkenree soldier; they

certainly wouldn't risk the ire of their masters by coming to the aid of a merin. Glancing quickly around, Yan desperately searched for some alternate route, some obstacle to place between himself and the drakkenree striding purposefully toward him. One of the huts was only a few yards away, closer to him than to Khankemeh. Yan headed for it. Khankemeh shifted its course as well. Yan's fleeting hope that he was mistaken about Khankemeh's intentions faded.

A few quick steps put the hut between him and the approaching saurian. As soon as he could no longer see Khankemeh, Yan stopped. The drakkenree's course would have intercepted Yan's on the far side of the hut. How long was long enough and how long was too long? Too much time and the saurian would emerge from beyond the hut and see him, too little time and his ruse to increase the distance between him and his stalker would fail miserably. Judging the time right, Yan turned on his heels and ran. If this worked, he would have a chance to reach the protective knot of bregil before Khankemeh caught on and caught *him.*

Unfortunately for Yan, Khankemeh was too wise to the ways of thinking prey. The drakkenree had stopped near where Yan had last seen it, and positioned itself to watch both sides of the hut. It caught sight of Yan as he emerged and started after him.

Twenty yards to where the bregil clustered. Twenty yards to safety.

Yan ran as fast as he could. Much as he wanted to, he didn't look back; he was afraid it would slow him down.

Ten yards.

He could hear Khankemeh's footfalls growing louder behind him. The bregil noticed the racers, but none, not even Threok, did more than point or hoot.

Eight yards.

Khankemeh's snout appeared in Yan's peripheral vision. In the next moment Yan was tumbling off-balance and falling toward the ground. He hit, somersaulting once. It was hard to breathe, and the side of his head stung from the blow. Khankemeh hadn't used its claws, but the blow had been powerful. It had felt as though the soldier's fist had driven Yellow Eye's earring into Yan's cheek. The wire through his earlobe burned.

Khankemeh checked its rush after a pair of strides. It was between him and safety. Tail scything an arc through the air, the drakkenree pivoted on one foot. It almost stumbled as the earth yielded beneath its foot, but a twist of body and shift of tail restored its balance. Khankemeh opened its jaws, displaying its serrated teeth, and advanced on Yan. Its fingers were spread wide, talons flexed and ready to rend.

Yan tried to scramble out of its way. It was a worthless gesture; there was no way he could get around the drakkenree. His left ankle failed painfully, and he sprawled. Helpless to escape and unable to defend himself, Yan opened his arms in the submission gesture.

The skin near Khankemeh's eyes flushed darker. Threok said that was the way they laughed. The drakkenree spoke in a mixture of Kolvinic and its own language.

"Stupid, *maah'nn'kun'yee.* You *kedja'k'krr.* Property."

Khankemeh bent over him. The awful stench of the carnivore's breath filled Yan's nostrils. He twisted his head away. Khankemeh hooked one claw in Yan's cheek. Under the needle-sharp pressure of the talon, Yan turn his head back to face the drakkenree. Khankemeh's green eyes glittered within the dark folds of skin surrounding them like star emeralds on velvet.

"*Che'rr'dent'ni,*" it said.

Something about eating.

Khankemeh placed its other hand on Yan's chest for a moment. The four claws poked through his shirt and pierced his skin, just slightly. Khankemeh left its hand there for a moment, as though daring Yan to twitch. He remained still. The drakkenree removed its hand and hooked a claw into the neck of Yan's shirt. Yan could feel the coolness of the talon against his skin. Only the curve of the claw touched him this time. Khankemeh moved its hand down and Yan felt that claw run along his chest and belly and down toward his groin. He heard his clothes tear. Khankemeh slashed left and right, tugging the shredded fabric away and exposing Yan's torso to the cool evening air.

"*Che'rr'dent'ni,*" it said again.

Yan felt certain he knew now what Khankemeh intended to eat. He felt his bladder let go. The stream splashed against the drakkenree's flank. Khankemeh twisted its neck to look. When it returned its gaze to Yan's face, its eyes were ringed in darkness. Yan hated Khankemeh then, hated that it should be amused at his shame.

Khankemeh reached down and ran its claws through Yan's groin hair like a comb before touching the needle points to the skin just under his navel. The talons dug in slowly, three broad knives of hard fire. The drakkenree gave a slight tug and Yan cried out. But it wasn't the disemboweling stroke, just another tease. Khankemeh was playing with its food. Yan felt tears streaming down his cheeks. He would have pleaded if he'd thought the drakkenree would understand him.

A bellow reminiscent of a *terriserpens* war cry resounded through the camp. The claws jerked away from Yan's skin, and Khankemeh froze. Drops of Yan's blood dropped from the claws onto his belly. Slowly, Khankemeh turned its head toward the source of the bellow. It froze again, hissing softly.

Yan turned his head to see what Khankemeh was looking at. Yellow Eye was picking its way down the slope from the mouth of the cave. No other drakkenree in the camp moved. Most of the bregil huddled wherever they were, looking about fearfully. What had made the sound? Yan got his answer when Yellow Eye reached level ground and started toward them. The drakkenree mage lifted its head and repeated the sound.

Khankemeh hissed briefly. Turning back to Yan, it snapped at him. He managed to twist his head aside in time to avoid losing his nose, but the saurian's teeth scraped bloody furrows across his cheek. Then Khankemeh was off him and running toward the trees.

Yan lay on the ground, almost disbelieving his reprieve.

Yellow Eye stopped, watching the fleeing Khankemeh. Once Khankemeh disappeared into the trees, Yellow Eye just turned its back and returned to the cave. For all its apparent disregard for his condition, he felt sure that

Yellow Eye's timely interruption was all that had saved him from ending up like Shean. Had there been any feeling there, or was the drakkenree just protecting its property? Did it matter? Yellow Eye's actions had saved Yan's life.

Now that the drama was over, the camp began to return to its normal routine. The drakkenree and bregil went back to their own pursuits. Only Threok still watched him. Why? When Khankemeh had killed Yan's horse, the drakkenree had shared its meal with the other drakkenree. Would Khankemeh have done the same with Yan's body? And afterward, would the soldier have offered the leavings to its minions? Would Threok have partaken? Every day Threok had said he regretted advising Yan when Khankemeh had captured him; Yan had thought it a jest. Had it been? Was the bregil now regretting the missed opportunity for an extra meat ration?

Dismissing such dark thoughts, Yan picked himself up. He gathered his sundered clothes about himself as best he could. The shirt and pants were dreadfully rent but might be repaired; he could be repaired as well, with time and the right attention. His bruises ached already, but they were minor. The cuts would need care; drakkenree were predators, and foulness often entered wounds caused by predators. But as long as the wounds did not sour, they were minor, too. He had survived Khankemeh's attack.

He had "stayed alive whichever way," as Threok might say.

Yan accepted a thong and a bone needle from Threok and managed to contrive a lacing that kept his pants up. Once he could walk without tripping over his clothes, Yan went up to the cave, to the storage area where Yellow Eye had placed what it had taken from Yan's satchels. The drakkenree mage looked up when he entered but said nothing, and when it saw what he was gathering, returned to the book it was studying. Yan dressed his wounds there in the cave; Yellow Eye's magelight provided better illumination than the darkening sky. He used the cleanest scraps of his tattered shirt as bandages, further reducing his raiment. Had he been in a civilized place, he would have visited a temple and seen a healer priest as a precaution. But this was not a civilized place, and there was no temple here—save perhaps a ruined drakkenree one—and there were no healer priests. Did the drakkenree have such among them? Yan had seen no signs that they did. And if they had such, he doubted that they would deign to attend to mere property.

Yan hesitated at the mouth of the cave. He would be safer in the cave than anywhere else. He didn't know if Khankemeh had run off for good or might still be lurking around, awaiting a chance to make good its boast to eat Yan. The company of the bregil had kept him safe before, but who could know whether it would now? Yan looked over his shoulder at the drakkenree coiled on the floor. Its snout moved back and forth as it read. It was his protector, but it paid him no attention. If he slept here, out of the way, it probably wouldn't object. Horesh's light, it probably wouldn't even notice! Yan surveyed the lean shape, the clawed feet and hands, the deep, narrow snout lined with teeth. The sharp teeth of a meat eater. For all that it had saved his life, Yellow Eye looked too much like Khankemeh for Yan's comfort. Yan left the cave and spent the night with the bregil.

21

HIS INJURIES MADE SLEEP difficult, so Yan was not surprised when he was the first to wake in the morning. The camp was as quiet as it ever got and lay shrouded in the morning ground fog. He sat up and looked about. What he saw made him wonder whether surviving the night had been a blessing. A pair of *terriserpens* stood in the central open space of the camp. The great beasts simply stood there, necks craning about as they surveyed the camp. They did not seem ready to pounce, although they might have just been selecting the choicest morsels; Yan knew what havoc they were capable of causing. Other than the cave, the camp offered no refuge from them.

Moving stealthily to avoid attracting the attention of the beasts, Yan moved closer to Threok and poked him in the side. He had some vague idea that they might flee, although he knew that a man afoot couldn't outrun the monsters. The bregil finally stopped trying to bat away Yan's finger with his tail and opened his eyes. Sleepily, Threok sat up and looked where Yan pointed. The bregil nodded and lay down again.

"Go back to sleep until it's time to eat," he mumbled.

Yan shook him again. "We may be able to use the attack as cover to escape."

"What attack?"

"The beasts."

Surly, Threok said, "They're not going to attack anything here."

"How can you know that?"

"The lizards use those monsters for war the way merin use oxen for plowing or mules for hauling. If there was a battle going on, things would be a lot noisier."

"Use them? How?

Threok's tail slapped Yan's shoulder. "I can see that I'm done sleeping. Should have let old Khan eat you the first time." Threok rubbed his eyes. "How do they use them? How would you use such a hungry monster? The gray ones set them to eating people, which is real easy since eating is what those beasts do best. Too bad the gray ones don't take exception like I do to merin that are too noisy in the morning."

"What are the gray ones?"

"Are you sure you're not an Einthofite priest?"

"I'm not a priest," Yan snapped. "Tell me what you know about the beasts. And about the gray ones. What *are* they?"

"The lizards call the big bastards drakkenkain, or something like that. Anyway, that's as near as I can say it. The gray ones are their keepers. They've got a lizard name, too, but I don't know it."

"Drakkenkain. That sounds much like the name for their own kind."

"They do sort of look alike. If you ignore the size. What does it matter if the words are similar?"

"It may not mean anything, but then again it might. When I first saw one, I didn't know a name for it. No one I knew had seen one before or what to call it, so I dubbed it a *terriserpens.*" Yan remembered Fasolt raising an eyebrow the first time Yan had mentioned the beasts to him. "I wonder if Fasolt knew they were called drakkenkain."

"Horesh save me from magicians," Threok prayed to the sky.

A sudden change in the drakkenkain's attitude caught Yan's attention. Both beasts had stopped looking about and were concentrating on an area on the far side of the clearing. Two drakkenree emerged from the woods there; they were of a type Yan had not seen since the day of Fasolt's duel with Yellow Eye. Yan guessed that these were what Threok called gray ones, for their coloration was mostly greenish gray, with some black mixed in. Their scales were arranged in a mottled pattern like that of the soldier drakkenree, and like the soldiers they would be difficult to see in the dappled shadows of a forest. Unlike either Yellow Eye or the soldiers, each wore only a single strap around its torso from which depended an elaborately hilted dagger in an even more elaborately decorated sheath.

One of the drakkenkain took a hesitant step toward the gray drakkenree. The beast, apparently disliking to have its weight on the advanced foot, immediately brought its other foot up next to the first and stood with its weight on that one. The drakkenkain turned broadside to the new arrivals and folded its legs until its belly rested on the ground. Yan could see that the beast's thigh was injured, a ragged circular wound seeping blood.

One of the gray drakkenree approached the prone drakkenkain's head first and butted its head against the side of the great beast's muzzle. The beast made a rumbling sound, and the smaller saurian echoed it. Yan remembered seeing the first drakkenree he'd observed in Kolvin do a similar thing. Was it a greeting? Intrigued, Yan watched the other drakkenkain bend down until its head was near the second gray one and conduct the same exchange. The first gray one busied itself tending the wounded beast's leg. Fascinated by the rapport between the saurians, Yan missed the call to breakfast. He crouched, watching them and wondering at how the great beasts seemed to respond to the gray ones. Such a harmony between different beings was almost magical, and he could not help but wonder if it might actually *be* magical.

"Yan Tanafres," Yellow Eye called from the mouth of the cave, putting an end to his musings. That summons could not be ignored. Yan limped regretfully off to his duties. What he had seen in the morning stayed with him all day, nagging at him with hints of significance.

The drakkenree name for the great beasts, even allowing for the inability of humans to pronounce correctly the drakkenree language, was something close to drakkenkain.

The similarity of the sound to the word the drakkenree used for themselves intrigued him, suggesting a relationship as it did. There was certainly a similarity of physical forms, but there were differences, more than mere size.

When Yellow Eye finally released Yan for the day, the drakkenkain were gone from the camp, but still on Yan's mind. After eating Yan decided to try to sharpen his thoughts, using one of the techniques he had learned from Gan Tidoni. He found a place near enough to the bregil for safety from Khankemeh, yet not so near that the bregil would disturb him. He sat and regulated his breathing and tried to put his mind into the receptive frame.

Always before, he had used a focus to touch the magic and clarify any foggy images or thoughts, but today he was denied such a tool. He had to struggle to achieve the right frame of mind. He began to fear that without his *claviarm* the task was hopeless. Such thoughts were lethal to what he sought to accomplish, so he forced them away; and slowly, so very slowly, he began to achieve something akin to *præha*. He began to believe he could succeed in this small, internal magic. He might not be able to affect the outside world, but he could still rule his inner world. Like a cloud on a still summer day, the outer world drifted away, and he turned his eyes inward. A picture of the Scothic drakkenree came to his mind, and he learned that his conscious memory had betrayed him.

With the images of those ancient survivals floating before his mind's eye, he realized that they were almost as different from the drakkenree around him as they were alike. The ones he had seen under Gornal's tower in Scothandir were smaller and slighter than those that held him captive here. Their muzzles were narrower and their hides smoother. Their feet were different, too; the fourth toe of the Scothic drakkenree was larger and more distinctly clawed. Perhaps Fra Bern was right and the invading saurians were not the real ancient enemy after all. But same or not, they were surely related.

Yan realized now that all those Scothic saurians had been black like Yellow Eye. No green ones, or even gray

ones. What significance did that hold? Those drakkenree
had all been wizards, and so was Yellow Eye. Did that
mean that only black drakkenree were wizards, or that
drakkenree turned black when they became magicians? Or
did it have any significance at all? Yan had seen too few of
the saurians to know.

One thing seemed certain: he needn't fear that Yellow
Eye was a relic out of time. For all that it was black-scaled
and a mage, Yellow Eye was built more like its fellows here
than the saurians in Gornal's valley.

Yan opened his eyes and saw Yellow Eye standing
before him. For a moment, Yan thought that the drakkenree was a vision; he hadn't heard the sound of its approach.
Then it moved, stretching out its hand toward him. In that
hand it held something that hadn't been a part of Yan's
remembering. Yan's copy of *Of Light and Air*. Yellow Eye's
fingers held the book open, and Yan could see that the
mage had annotated the text in its own script. Tapping a
taloned finger against the page, Yellow Eye demanded,
"Explain this passage."

The passage that Yellow Eye had selected was one of the
more obscure sections of the book. Costigern's theory was
controversial, but Yan tried to explain it as best he could,
citing the support and objections he had come across in the
writings of other scholars. Yellow Eye listened closely.
Though the drakkenree knew none of the theorists Yan
named, Yellow Eye's questions showed that it was
acquainted with the subject matter, holding a view similar
to Costigern's on the essential nature of light as a medium
with some similarities to water. Yet Yellow Eye could not
or would not cite any other drakkenree mages in support of
its position. Yan pointed out what he thought was the most
significant objection to Costigern's theory, specifically the
differences in the metaphysical natures of Air and Water.
They talked for hours, exploring the possible ramifications
of Costigern's assertions.

The longer they talked, the more disturbed Yan became.
The drakkenree were totally inhuman in appearance and
had an unsavory, carnivorous nature. He had known that
they were intelligent; he'd seen their tools and weapons,

heard their language, and seen that they had a social order. It was not that he could not conceive of a civilization that was neither merin nor saü; bregil were neither merin nor saü, and they were civilized. But Yan had yet to meet a bregil interested in arcane philosophy. Neither had he ever met a bregil magician, although he knew that such existed. Yellow Eye was beyond doubt not just a magician but a wizard, and one of a scholarly bent, at that. It was a bit like discovering that a wolf wished to discuss poetry.

Yellow Eye's mind was quick and agile, easily a match for any theoretician with whom Yan had ever argued. Beyond the reptilian exterior there was an intelligence and a curiosity much like his own. Their conversation sparked a sense of kinship that Yan had rarely felt. As they talked Yan began to sense a change in Yellow Eye's attitude.

"I have watched you and smelled you," Yellow Eye said after a pause. "In some ways you and I are closer than the green ones and I. You have a mind that knows. You seek communion with the *ssess'trak'ka.*"

The drakkenree word was new to Yan. "Sestraka?" he said, trying to pronounce it properly.

"You do not understand?" Yellow Eye asked.

Yan shook his head. Yellow Eye reached out and hooked a claw in the earring. A heatless glow washed over Yan's cheek. His eyes opened wide as he recognized the sensation of what was being forced onto him; without his consent or will, he was being propelled to the edge of *præha.* His resentment vanished as he saw the mana flow again. He felt tears pooling in his eyes. As abruptly as his senses had opened, they shut again.

"*Ssess'trak'ka ,*" Yellow Eye said.

Still shaken by the experience, Yan said, "We call it mana."

"*Ssess'trak'ka* is the true name. It is the heart of magic. You are drawn to it as I am."

"All magicians are drawn to the magic." Even those stripped of their connection, rendered blind and powerless. Yan couldn't help himself; his eyes drifted to the bag on Yellow Eye's strap.

"Not all are true seekers," the drakkenree said. "You are a seeker."

Was he? Right now, all he sought was the ability to touch the magic again. He knew he couldn't snatch the bag from Yellow Eye's strap, but he wanted to try. He restrained himself, forcing himself listen to the drakkenree's words.

"You hid yourself and the other magician, so I know you have a strong way with *ssess'trak'ka*. You came here even before I did. You came here again, so I know that you know what is here."

What was Yellow Eye talking about? "I don't know anything about what's here."

Yellow Eye tapped the enameled disk on his breast. "You know what this symbol means."

"I have no idea," Yan said, though it reminded him of the orb talismans.

"The Serpent's Eye," the drakkenree said. "You know."

The Serpent's Eye? Could it be real? Would Yellow Eye tell him about it? "I've heard the name, but I don't know more than that."

"Would you like to see the Serpent's Eye?"

"You've found it?"

"Soon, I think." Yellow Eye opened its jaws slightly, then clicked them closed. It was a gesture similar to that which Threok had said they used to show contentment. "Sooner with a fellow seeker."

Suddenly Yan distrusted Yellow Eye's abrupt candor and interest in Yan as a thinking being. What motivated it? Why was the drakkenree suddenly offering to make Yan a partner in its search? Was it simply a ruse to make him a tool?

"We can find the Serpent's Eye together," Yellow Eye said. "It holds answers to the questions of a seeker."

It wanted his help, but why? If it needed him, he would have some leverage. He wished he knew more.

"Would you like to see the Serpent's Eye?" the drakkenree asked again.

Surely he would, but not in Yellow Eye's hands; however, *that* did not seem a politic thing to say. How desperate was Yellow Eye's need?

"I would be of no more help than a first-year apprentice, without my *claviarm*."

"Without *claviarm*?" Yellow Eye tapped the bag. "The amulet?"

Yan nodded.

"You can only touch *ssess'trak'ka* with this?"

Clearly, the drakkenree mage didn't know that merin magicians needed *claviarms* to cast spells. So how did the saurians touch the mana? Yan suddenly realized that for all his observation, he didn't know. He had always just assumed that Yellow Eye was using some sort of focus, as he would.

"Answer," the drakkenree prompted.

Yan wasn't sure he should answer. Should he confirm a magician's weakness to this creature? If he did, and Yellow Eye truly wanted his help, it would have to return his *claviarm*. If he didn't, he could do no magic. A middle course, a lie that confined the weakness to himself, might work. Or it might not; hadn't Threok said that drakkenree could smell lies?

Yellow Eye gestured, and pain burned in Yan's skull like a hot wire lancing in from his earlobe.

"Yes," he stammered. "I need it."

Yellow Eye clicked its jaws in satisfaction.

The drakkenree mage tugged open the pouch and spilled the *claviarm* into its hand. Cocking its head, it growl-hissed something over the talisman before touching the *claviarm* to the earring Yan wore. With his *claviarm* uncovered and nearby, Yan could feel the magic as it was shaped, even though he couldn't tell the intent or effect. The spell done, Yellow Eye dropped the *claviarm* into Yan's lap.

"I will know what you do," it said.

Yan didn't understand how that could be, but he did not dispute it; he knew that the drakkenree had magics unknown to him.

"Now we will seek together," it said.

What other choice did he have? If the Eye was here, the drakkenree would find it sooner or later. If the Eye wasn't here, what harm would be done by the search? Perhaps even some good could come of Yan's working with Yellow

Eye; he would gain insight into the drakkenree magic, a knowledge that could be useful in combating it. At the least, the search might buy him time to plan an escape. Now that he had his *claviarm* again, escape was a possibility.

Yan put the *claviarm* around his neck.

Yellow Eye clicked its jaws.

22

THE HORSE WAS SO TERRIFIED that it plunged right into the midst of the Scothic regiment. The horse's rider wore the crimson surcoat of a Baaliffite priest, and he reeled in the saddle from the shock of the impact. Clearly he could not control the frightened beast, and it trampled two men before a soldier managed to hamstring it. The beast went down screaming, and the Baaliffite was pitched headlong from the saddle. The soldier who had brought the horse down stopped its thrashing and screaming with a swift thrust.

Iaf ordered his company to close up ranks; they could not afford to leave the gap in their line. Nothing else emerged from the fog-shrouded woods. At least there were no enemy in close pursuit of the priest. Even so, Iaf was sure they were out there. Watching. Waiting. They would strike again when it suited them.

"Hey," someone shouted. "This fellow's still alive."

Which might mean that he could answer questions, such as: was he a courier? He certainly wasn't support from the main force; one knight would not change the regiment's situation at all. Iaf hurried in the direction of the shout. The Baaliffite was the first they'd seen of other Imperial soldiers in hours. Despite his precipitous arrival, Iaf was glad to see him; the warrior-priest just had to have a better idea of how the force was faring than the isolated Scoths.

The Baaliffite lay on the ground, clearly wounded and

exhausted. The rents in his armor bespoke the hard fighting he must have seen and said that this man was no fugitive coward. Not that Iaf would have expected cowardice from a priest of bloody Baaliff, but a lone man in a battle was more often fleeing than charging the enemy. Or he was a courier. The priest had seen hard fighting. He was no coward. He could only be a courier. Iaf dared to hope that he had come to call them to a rallying point.

Deep woods were no place for a battle, but it was where this battle had been forced on them; there was little option in this wilderness, for none of the clearings that they had passed through would have held more than a company or two. The Scothic regiment alone was five companies.

General Honistonti had been cautious in the advance, but all his precautions had been barely enough to keep them from being ambushed as they had been the first time they'd entered Gremaire Forest. When the first groups of hillmen had been spotted through the morning mist, Honistonti had ordered the Imperial troops into battle formations. Colonel Kensie's Scothic Regiment had been given the anchor position, holding the force's left flank against the river they had been following. The fog had grown thicker as they deployed, and men had tangled their pikes with the trees and with each other. When it seemed that confusion was at its greatest and visibility its least, the hillmen had attacked. There were a few drakkenree among the bregil, and Iaf had heard the bellows of *terriserpens* in the distance, though none of the great beasts had threatened the Scoths. It was just as well, for they had suffered terribly in the first melee. The regiment had held, but it was an expensive success. Most of the officers, including Colonel Kensie, had been wounded; many killed outright.

The regiment stood now as it had after reforming from the first attack, in company blocks of pikes, the archers gathered into two blocks in reserve. Calling the companies "pikemen" was no longer accurate. After the first attack, many of the men had cut their pikes down to a length more suitable to this closed terrain. Some had simply abandoned their pikes and were relying on their swords and Scothic bucklers. Both approaches harked back to more traditional ways for Scoths to go into battle. Iaf couldn't fault the men; their solution seemed suited to the situation.

The situation wasn't good. Since that wild early morning melee, the hillmen had done little more than harass the Scoths. The regiment's battle line had shortened as a result of casualties, drawing closer to their secure flank against the river. As a result of that, and the continuing fog, they had lost contact with the Third Regiment of Foot, their neighbors in the Imperial battle line. The colonel had sent men out to reestablish contact, but none of them had returned, and no runners had arrived from the rest of the Imperial force. Distant sounds of conflict, hard to place in the fog, told of continuing battle; the regiment held its place, doing its best to follow the last orders Colonel Kensie had received. But standing in place in the shrouding fog wasn't easy, and the constant sound of battle and the harassing attacks of the hillmen made it harder. Though they had beaten off each sortie with few casualties, the men were beginning to show signs of panic.

Iaf silently prayed to Vehr that the courier's news was good. Unslinging his water bottle, Iaf knelt by the priest and offered him a drink. Hand trembling, the man took the bottle and drained it.

"You," Iaf called to the nearest man. "Tell Colonel Kensie a rider has come in. Tell him there'll be news shortly."

"I'm not a courier," the priest croaked.

Iaf's hopes fell. "Then why have you come?"

"Horse went mad. Carried me away."

"Still, you must know more than we. Since the ambush we have not heard from the general. It's been more than an hour since we've seen anyone other than our own people and the enemy. None of our scouts or runners have come back. What is happening?"

"Do you know what grief you're asking for?" The priest's expression was grim.

"How bad?" Iaf asked apprehensively.

Speaking so only Iaf could hear, the priest said, "General Honistonti is dead. A *terriserpens.*"

Very bad. "The other officers?"

"Scattered. Or dead. Who knows? The beast caught them, too."

"Who's in command of the force now?"

"No one."

No one? How could that be? "What about your own commander?"

"He lies beneath his horse, crushed by the *terriserpens*."

"*Someone* must be in command."

The priest's voice was full of despair. "Why? There is nothing to command."

"That cannot be! What of the other regiments? They cannot all have been destroyed. Listen? Can't you hear the sounds? They still fight."

"Lost," the priest said. "All is lost."

Angrily, Iaf threw himself to his feet. "All is not lost. We can regroup."

"Too late for that." The priest shook his head. "Nothing to do now but die. We must take as many souls as we can with us to lay before the god."

His last words were nearly a mumble as his head sagged back. He was not dead; his chest still rose and fell. Iaf left him to lie there and sought out the slight knoll where the injured Colonel Kensie had been taken.

Captain Graint met him halfway. Graint had started the day as commander of the fourth company; since the hillmen's first attack he had stood in the line in place of Colonel Kensie as the senior surviving, unwounded officer. Graint looked ten years older than he had at the start of the day.

"Where's the courier?" Graint asked.

"He is no courier, but he brought news," Iaf told him.

"What news?"

"The colonel must know what the Baaliffite told me."

"The colonel is dead. I'm in command now. Tell me."

Iaf felt numb. "How? It wasn't that bad a wound."

"He had another from a bregil tail blade. He'd bled his life out before we knew."

Like the Baaliffite, Iaf had lost his commander. Without leadership, what hope did they have of escaping this disaster? For a moment, Iaf knew the despair that gripped the priest; then he knew, just as certainly, that they could not afford to believe that there was no hope. Baaliff might expect His devotees to give their lives in a hopeless battle, but Vehr was the martial deity who had Iaf's devotion. Vehr did not expect His warriors to die needlessly; He expected them to find the path to victory. Vehr understood that there would be other battles.

"What did the priest say?" Graint gripped Iaf's arm hard. "Are the others pushing the monkeys back?"

"General Honistonti is dead," Iaf told him. "The priest says all the commanders are dead."

Graint's eyes went bleak. "No. No. They've got to be winning. That's why the monkeys are not pushing. The others are beating them!"

"I pray to Vehr that it be so, but I doubt it." Iaf couldn't share Graint's unfounded hopes. "We must look to our own survival."

"Hillmen!" the cry went up.

Iaf spun and looked for the shouter. He followed the man's pointing hand and saw the stocky shapes of bregil in the fog between the trees. The flickering shades were hard to count.

"There must be a thousand of them," someone said in an awed voice.

"You can't even count to ten, Delph," Iaf snapped. "I don't even see half of your thousand. We still outnumber them."

Iaf's words got nods from some of the veterans, but he could see that he hadn't really had much steadying effect. Such words should have come from their commander, but Graint stood silent, apparently paralyzed by the sight of the approaching hillmen.

Iaf said, "Captain, we should extend the line to the right toward that outcrop. They're flanking us."

Graint just stared. Iaf spotted several of the terrible, hunched shapes of drakkenree among the bregil. Graint whimpered, tears rolling down his cheeks.

"Captain?"

No response.

Iaf gave the order himself.

The redeployed First Company clashed with the hillmen's flanking force. The attackers weren't pressing hard. Yet.

"Give me a weapon," said a voice behind Iaf. "Mine are useless."

It was the priest, gray-faced but standing. His shoulders sagged under the weight of his harness, but his expression was determined as he said, "My Lord Baaliff shows His aspect as the Reaper. I must do my part."

Each to his beliefs. Iaf drew his own sword and gave it to the man. He could get another from one of the dead.

The priest bowed in thanks as he took the weapon. He swung the sword a few times and nodded in satisfaction.

"I shall try to do it honor, warrior."

The Baaliffite saluted Iaf, then turned and limped downslope. He walked through the space between Third and Fourth Companies as one of the larger groups of hillmen was moving toward that position. Taking up a place a few yards in advance of the front line, he set himself to await the enemy.

He did not have to wait long.

The priest thrust at the first bregil that came within reach, gutting the hillman. He wounded the second, but took a cut to the arm before finishing his opponent. The soldiers cheered him as he took the third, and then he was lost to Iaf's sight as the tide of hillmen crashed onto the rocks of the Scoths.

The attack on their right flank intensified. Iaf saw drakkenree hacking their way into the front ranks of the Scoths. The First Company began to give ground, moving back toward the river. With the river at their backs and nowhere to run, they'd be massacred.

Iaf ordered the first block of archers into action, hoping to take the hillmen's flank as they exposed it in pressing the Scothic footmen back. He sent the other block to aid Third and Fourth Companies.

To his relief, the archers' missiles broke the attackers' impetus. The drakkenree withdrew into the depths of the fog, but the hillmen didn't flee as they had after their first attack had failed. They hovered in ominous clumps at the edge of Iaf's fog-restricted vision. They had seen that they could push the Scoths back, perhaps even sensed that the regiment was on the brink of disintegration.

If the regiment held its position, it would eventually be overwhelmed. Their only hope was to move, to rejoin the rest of the force. If no one else could see the necessity, Iaf could. And if no one else would give the orders, Iaf would.

"Form hedgehog!" he shouted.

Second and Fifth Companies obeyed as they got the word, shifting their formations until weapons were facing in all directions, spears pointed outward in a bristling array. First Company was slower, but moving; he left them to it. The battered Third and Fourth Companies only milled about in confusion. Iaf could see the hillmen concentrating opposite them again and feared what would happen to the companies—and the regiment—if they were caught unprepared. He ran to the wavering companies and, by dint of shouting and a few well-placed clouts, beat them into a ragged order. He had to combine both companies to make a decent defensive arrangement.

He succeeded just in time.

The wave of hillmen crashed down again, swirling around the hedgehog. The fighting was short and sharp, but the Scoths held. Someone with a brain brought up both blocks of archers and dropped a withering cloud of arrows onto the heaviest concentration of hillmen. The bregil lost their nerve and fled.

The respite wouldn't last long. Iaf ran from hedgehog to hedgehog, explaining to whatever officers and sergeants he could find his plan to link up with the rest of the Imperial forces. He split the archers up among the hedgehogs so that each would have some missile power. The arrangement also gave the lightly armored archers some protection; they would need protection when the hedgehogs moved, and only the spearpoints and swords of their fellows would offer it.

At Iaf's command the four hedgehogs began to move toward the last-known position of their Imperial neighbors. Keeping their protective formation made for slow going, but the formation was the only way they could move through the enemy-infested trees. It was slow, but it was better than being backed against the river and slaughtered.

Whoever commanded the local contingent of hillmen must have guessed Iaf's plan, or maybe he just wanted another go at his victims before they left the area. The bregil warriors attacked again, in more force than before. All the hedgehogs were engaged simultaneously. Iaf, within the combined companies' formation, soon lost track of how the others fared; the fighting around him was desperate.

A trio of huge bregil in turtle armor smashed their way through the outer edge of the hedgehog. Spearheads glanced from their bony armor as they bulled their way forward, slashing at anyone who opposed them. Iaf moved to block them before realizing that he had neglected to replace his sword. The lead hillman cut at him and he ducked back—or tried to. Someone was behind him and his motion was checked. The bregil's sword came down on his helmet. His head seemed to explode as the chin strap parted. The steel cheekpiece nearly took away his ear as the helmet was ripped from his head. Dazed, he collapsed to his knees. Someone stuck a spear into the bregil; Iaf saw the point slide in under the hillman's armor.

Iaf vomited. His vision darkened.

Had he taken his death wound?

All around him the fighting went on. No one noticed when he fell over on his side. It was getting darker. Around him, the Scoths were still fighting. Vehr bless them, they were fighting and not running.

"Keep moving," he tried to tell them.

He didn't know if they heard.

23

DAYS OF WORKING MINOR MAGICS with Yellow Eye had given Yan a more certain sense of the drakkenree mage's competency and confirmed Yan's earlier impression of his—Yan could no longer think of Yellow Eye or any of the other drakkenree as an "it"—superior grasp of the Art. The drakkenree displayed none of the sanctimonious attitude Gan Fasolt had so readily shown—at least with regard to the Art. When they were not actually discussing theory or performing a spell, Yellow Eye self-confidently assumed the role of master to Yan's servant.

When a soldier called from outside the cave, it was Yan who, as the inferior participant, backed out of the resonance spell he had constructed with Yellow Eye, leaving the drakkenree to continue studying the pottery fragment they had retrieved from the lower levels of the cave. Yan waited until he was sure that Yellow Eye had gathered in all of the mana strands before dropping out of *præha* and responding to the soldier.

Thus it was Yan who saw the newcomers first. They were the largest collection of drakkenree he'd ever seen; they and their bregil and beasts crowded the clearing to overflowing. Yan counted more than a score of soldiers and six of the gray drakkenree that Yellow Eye referred to as keepers. Unlike Yellow Eye's drakkenree, all of these saurians wore orb talismans.

The largest of the soldiers looked almost as big as Yellow Eye and was considerably more massive, his height enhanced by a curious headdress of feathers. Either the headdress or his very elaborate orb talisman might be taken as a mark of high rank, but more convincing was the way the other saurians behaved around him. When other drakkenree approached him, they never got very close, and they were always careful to stand erect so as to offer no challenge; unchallenged authority was the mark of an important personage. His entourage of soldiers was in keeping with high position, being more than twice the size of Yellow Eye's group.

The bregil warriors among the newcomers wore elaborate decorations of feathers and fur. Some wore bracelets and necklaces of silver and gold, proclaiming their high status in their clans. They, too, showed deference to the big drakkenree

Could this be the general of the invasion?

Though the soldiers had first commanded Yan's attention, his eyes drifted to the new keepers and their mud-colored beasts. Most of the gray ones were giving their attention to heavily laden beasts that, while bigger than a drakkenree, were significantly smaller than a *terriserpens*. These animals stood on their hind legs like the other saurians, but were built to a coarser standard, with none of the lean, dangerous look of their cousins. One gave a honking bellow, and Yan saw that its mouth was filled with flat teeth unlike those of the carnivorous drakkenree. An herbivore perhaps? These beasts were being treated as mules by the drakkenree; perhaps they were like mules in other ways as well. Were these also drakkenkain, or was there another name for them? They were certainly not *terriserpens*.

The saurian mules were intriguing, but they did not capture Yan's interest as completely as the beasts of the one keeper who held himself aloof from both the pack train and the soldiers. Yan had seen such creatures before. Lizard-bats. Three of the creatures perched on the keeper's back and a fourth sat upon his arm like a falcon. With a chill, Yan remembered the lizard-bat attack during the siege at Baron Yentillan's steading. If the drakkenree could train the *terriserpens* for war, why not the lizard-bats? Had it been a drakkenree keeper who sent the creatures against Baron Yentillan's keep?

But he had not come out here to study animals, as the soldier by the entrance reminded him with a poke. The drakkenree pointed down at the newcomers and hiss-growled something that included the syllables Yan had come to associate with Yellow Eye. The soldier pointed again, shoved Yan back into the cave, and repeated Yellow Eye's name. The message was clear enough: the general wanted to see Yellow Eye.

Yan braved the soldier's ire and stepped back into the sunlight. Pointing at the feathered drakkenree, he asked "*Ka'a*?" Who?

"*Ss'grm'lktn*," the soldier said, again shoving Yan back into the cave.

Yan repeated the name as best he could to Yellow Eye, being careful to begin with the honor hiss. The mage let out a low-toned hiss that was no honorific. Yan had heard Yellow Eye make that sound when a spell had fallen apart, but that wasn't the reason this time; Yan could still sense the active resonance spell until the mage carefully closed it down.

"Stay," Yellow Eye ordered as he stalked away from his work.

Yan waited a few seconds; then followed, finding himself a place near the mouth of the cave to watch.

Gremlekten—Yan's more pronounceable name for the feathered drakkenree—was waiting for Yellow Eye to finish climbing down. When the mage approached near enough, the two drakkenree started making bobbing bows to each other. Subordinate saurians edged away. To Yan's surprise, the greeting ended with Gremlekten standing more erect than Yellow Eye.

The two drakkenree spoke for some time. Yan was too far away to hear what they said, and wouldn't have understood it in any case. Watching their postures did little to enlighten him about the nature of their conversation. Finally the conference concluded and Yellow Eye turned back toward the cave. From the stiffness in the mage's gait, Yan could see that he was agitated.

Yan edged deeper into the shadows before turning and hurrying back to the work chamber. He was industriously occupied in rearranging one of the storage shelves when Yellow Eye entered. The drakkenree watched him for several minutes before speaking.

"*Ss'grm'lktn* says an army of your people approaches."

Did that mean rescue was at hand?

"Do not be hopeful," Yellow Eye said. "*Grm'lktn* says he will stop them."

Yan had many questions, but the drakkenree's demeanor seemed to forbid speech. Yan went back to sorting jars, but his mind wasn't on it. Yellow Eye stalked about the chamber, gathering things into a box. Most of the items were unknown to Yan, but several he knew to be magical artifacts. Yellow Eye closed and sealed the box.

"You will take this to the honorable *Grm'lktn* and return. Bow once, quickly, to him, then stand as tall as you can. Wait until he nods, then place the box on the ground and back away. If any molest you, show them the sign." Yellow Eye tapped a claw to the side of his head near his earhole and Yan felt a tingle in his right ear. "Return swiftly."

Yan delivered the box as he was told without incident, despite the evident hostility among the newcomers. Their attitude quenched his desire to stay and observe them; he immediately headed back to the cave. This was not a time to do anything other than follow the orders he was given. By the time he reached the work chamber, Yellow Eye had completed a chalked circle of protection and was starting a second. Yan recognized the symbols and configurations at once.

"I thought we needed more information to refine the circles."

"Time presses," was all Yellow Eye said by way of explanation. "Begin the outer circle."

"The correspondences are not complete."

"They will have to do."

Yan started to object to operating with improperly configured protections, and his ear began to burn. He stopped trying to complain and did as he was told.

It took nearly two hours to draw the circles, and by the

time they finished Yan was sweating in spite of the clammy chill of the cave air. Yellow Eye looked no more perturbed than a lizard sunning itself on a rock.

"Lay out the *shoitai*," Yellow Eye ordered.

Yellow Eye entered the tunnel to the outside and began to speak. Yan had heard Yellow Eye cast the warding and alarum spells once before, and he thought he recognized the rhythms. On the other hand, he might have been recognizing the charge that was gathering in the air. Yellow Eye returned, and, together, they sealed the circles, from outer to inner, with themselves inside.

The *shoitai* lay where Yan had placed it, centered in the innermost protective circle. It was a ritual tool that Yan had heard of only in theory until Yellow Eye had showed him how to make this one. The *shoitai* was a cord of braided traslen fiber, binding together small bits of significant or symbolic items. Half of the items had been chosen by Yellow Eye, the other half by Yan. The *shoitai* would bind them together in this magic and allow them to draw each upon the other for a strength greater than either would have separately. Should one falter, he might drag the other down with him as well. Yan didn't know why Yellow Eye trusted him in this. For his own part, he knew that he needed the drakkenree mage's strength and skill to conduct this ritual.

Yellow Eye believed that the artifact he sought could only be found through this method. Although the drakkenree knew more about the Serpent's Eye than did Yan, it was clear, from the probing and tentative nature of his search, that the artifact was at least a partial mystery to Yellow Eye. If Yellow Eye believed that he needed Yan's help in the ritual, Yan saw no reason to question his judgment. In fact, Yan was glad of it. Without knowing just what the Serpent's Eye was, Yan could not even guess at its real strength or significance. Here was his opportunity to see it and learn of its nature at the same time the drakkenree mage did. Here, too, might be an opportunity to deny the artifact to the drakkenree should it prove too dangerous; by sundering his end of the *shoitai* Yan could disrupt the spell. It was a dangerous course, but all too possibly a necessary one. If Yan had believed in provident gods, he might have believed that they had arranged his capture for just this end.

Yan bound his end of the *shoitai* around his waist. Yellow Eye moved into position across the circle from him and did the same. Yan being merin and Yellow Eye being drakken-ree, they couldn't match their physical rhythms exactly, but from their days of lesser rituals, they had found a complementary pattern that allowed them to work together. Bit by bit, as they dropped into *præha*, they slipped into that pattern. The shimmer of the circles became visible as their senses adjusted to the realities of the mana realm that encompassed and overlay the everyday world. In the mana realm, their spirits would be free from many of the limitations of their bodies and able to go where bodies could not.

This was the first time Yan had opened himself so fully to the mana realm within the cave, and so for the first time he felt the presence of the place. The painted symbols on the walls glowed with the eldritch light of witchmoss, the ground murmured beneath his feet, and the air moved in currents that felt warm but raised goose bumps on his skin. All around him he felt the echoes of strength like a sound of a favorite, departed aunt's voice recalled from youth. The feel of the place unsettled him.

"What kind of place is this?" he asked.

"Sacred."

To what? Yan wondered. He didn't voice his question, because he wasn't sure that he wanted to know the answer.

Yellow Eye led their spirit forms down into the cave. They traversed the sections they had explored and prospected for the bits and pieces the drakkenree mage had been using to construct the correspondences for the protective circles. They moved through dark galleries made more strange by *præha*-enhanced perceptions. Everywhere the presence of the ancient lay like a coiled but lethargic viper.

Yellow Eye tried paths they had not yet explored. Some led to natural chambers, others to dead ends where the path stopped or became too restricted for the passage of mortal bodies. A few provided entry to chambers that had been worked by intelligent hands and shaped into rooms beneath the earth. In these the dust of ages lay undisturbed. At last, while traveling a long, narrow chamber widened by tools, they came to an obstruction. Debris and blocks of rough stone filled the way, a tumble of rock born of a shift in the earth above. Yellow Eye stared at the obstacle for some time. Finally he said, "We must go on through the rock."

Moving through physical barriers was possible in the mana realm, but it was also possible to lose one's way and become lost. Yan saw many dangers, asking after the most obvious. "But how will we know what is passage and what is virgin rock?"

"Can you not smell it?"

Without waiting for an answer, Yellow Eye's spirit form passed into the rock and out of Yan's sight. Yan hesitated, watching the slack in the *shoitai* draw taut. He could let the cord draw tighter, tautening until it parted, but then he would never know what lay on the far side. Or he could go along, trusting Yellow Eye's ability to find a way through the darkness of the rock . . . assuming anything remained beyond the fallen rock; anything the builders had done might be utterly crushed and buried under the weight of the earth.

And if something *did* lie beyond the cave-in? What secrets might be there? What wonders would he never see?

Yan griped the *shoitai* and stepped into the stone.

Yan's blind stumbling through the stone went on for what seemed like hours—and it might have, for time did not always pass normally in the mana realm. The passage through the dark embrace of the rock was shorter than Yan feared, for it did come to an end. He emerged from the physical rock to join Yellow Eye in a chamber that was familiar to Yan despite its ruined condition. Fallen blocks marred the perfection of the arched walls and floor. Once the walls of the chamber had been globular, just like the ritual chamber he had discovered under Gornal's tower in Scothandir. In that chamber, six ancient drakkenree mages had slept their strange sleep. But here no dark shapes hung suspended in a sphere of exotic magic. Here, there were no mages save Yan and Yellow Eye; but he could feel the echoes of magic that dwelt in the stones.

"The chamber of the guardians," Yellow Eye announced.

"Is this important?"

"It means I was right."

Yellow Eye's spirit form drifted up and across the chamber toward an opening on the far side. Yan followed. Had they been present physically, they would have been denied passage to the opening; the smooth stones of the curved floor would have defeated their efforts to clamber up them. The opening proved to be the mouth of a natural tunnel leading deeper into the earth.

As they moved along the new tunnel, Yan began to get the dreadful feeling that something was watching them. He felt a pressure, a weight that meant something was pressing against the circles of protection and the magic that warded them. It wasn't a directed magic; that would have been distinctive. The feeling was more like the weight of water against one's chest when one dove deep into a pond.

"Can you feel it," he asked.

"Yes," Yellow Eye responded. "We must go on."

The tunnel widened and became a naturally domed chamber. Spikes of rock hung from the ceiling and thrust up from the floor. In places one strand melded with another to make a column that stretched from floor to ceiling. Cascades of stone icicles festooned the walls. Carpets of witchmoss gave the scene an eerie blue light.

After the first ten feet or so, the floor of the chamber dropped away, making the entry area a balcony for a lithic amphitheater beyond the first set of stone columns. The open space was bigger than the great theater in Talinfad; had they physically walked here, their footsteps would have come back to them in distant echoes. An intense aura filled the open space, radiating from something in the amphitheater. With no little trepidation, Yan edged forward so that he could see what lay below. In the center of the floor stood a reptilian creature, its long neck supporting a massive head whose snout pointed toward the magicians. The creature's scales glittered, but its eyes sparkled even more in the azure light of the witchmoss.

Could it be?

"A true dragon!"

Yellow Eye denied Yan's identification with a shake of his head, saying, "*B'ahn'ssu'uss.*"

The creature gave no sign that it noticed their presence, and Yan finally gathered enough presence of mind to see why. It was not a true animal, but a sculpture of surpassing skill. Its glittering scales were mineral, its eyes gemstones. The aura had misled him into believing that the statue was alive; he saw now that the power emanated from a dull amber orb situated in the center of the thing's brow ridge like the third eye Galenistians claimed allowed their greatest mystics to see into the realm of truth.

From the aura of slumbering, powerful magic around it, this orb could only be the Serpent's Eye.

Yellow Eye took a step onward.

The air began to howl around them, and the pressure against their protective circles instantly trebled. The first circle crumpled, delivering Yan an almost-physical blow that left his head ringing. Invisible claws raked against the second circle.

Yellow Eye growled spells and hissed charms, defiant against the power that sought to crush them. The mage by Yan's side pulled metaphysically on the *shoitai.* Yan gave of his strength to the drakkenree. What other choice did he have? What was happening was beyond his knowledge and skill. The drakkenree's spirit claw grasped Yan's arm, tugging him forward. Yan had to force his way forward, ducking his head as through a storm. Yellow Eye and Yan pressed ahead, out of the balcony area and into the amphitheater. Then, as suddenly as the assault had begun, it was over; they were through the defenses that protected the idol. Though Yan had shaped no magic himself, he felt as drained as if he had been casting spells all day. Yellow Eye sagged, his spirit form no longer as bright as it had been.

But they were through.

Yan could feel the latent power in the Serpent's Eye, more clearly now, almost as if it were calling him.

Yellow Eye floated toward the head of the idol. Without waiting for the *shoitai* to tighten, Yan followed. Together they hovered before the barbeled snout of the sculpture, staring in wonder at the prize they had sought. The jaws of this Baansuus curled up in an almost–drakkenree-like grin.

Yellow Eye stretched out a hand and laid a finger on the orb. Immediately he snatched it away, like a child discovering that fire burns. Yan, also like a child, needed to know for himself. He reached out and touched the orb. Before he could snatch his fingers away a shock ran up them, coursing through his arm and into his body. His heart skipped, losing a beat in its hammering.

The touch told him much and nothing, raising a thousand questions for every one that it answered. They had set out seeking an artifact of great power, but the Serpent's Eye was not an artifact, at least not in any sense that Yan understood. It felt solid to the touch; but if the Eye had physical substance, Yan's *præha* senses could not detect it. The Eye's whole fiber felt of magic, as if it were a thing made of spells, the very distillation of magic.

Yan had to learn more about it. What magician could pass by such an opportunity? The Eye's very nature was a siren call to the curiosity of a mage. Its construction was unknown and perhaps unknowable. Mastery of its secrets was essential—not for gain, or for any power that it might confer, but for the simple necessity of knowing how such a thing could be.

Yellow Eye reached out just before Yan could. The drakkenree closed his fingers on the part of the orb projecting from the idol's forehead. The stretch of Yellow Eye's fingers seemed to encompass the orb perfectly. Slowly he drew back his hand, removing the Eye from its resting place. As it came free, the Eye began to glow softly, casting a wan ocher light that lit golden fire in the drakkenree's eye.

Yellow Eye clicked his jaws in satisfaction.

24

IT WASN'T UNTIL YAN SAW his physical body that he had some idea how long their expedition had taken; his beard had grown until it covered his jaw and cheeks with dark fuzz. He understood then that the weakness he felt was more than just exhaustion from his magical exertions; it had been days since he'd eaten or slept.

But it had been worth it, hadn't it?

They *had* returned with the Serpent's Eye.

Rather, Yellow Eye had. The drakkenree laid the insubstantial Eye in the casket he had prepared for it, locking and warding the box before lowering the protective circles. The prize secured, Yellow Eye broke into his emergency stock of supplies, wolfing down several pieces of dried meat. Yan's first response to the demands of his body was to grab the water jug, heaving the heavy pottery up and balancing it awkwardly while he drank. Much of the soothing water spilled down his front, but enough entered his mouth to feel like salvation. He finished his first draught to find Yellow Eye offering him some meat. Yan had seen the strips dried over a fire and knew that they were from some sort of forest antelope; he took them gratefully. Chewing on a strip, he poured water into Yellow Eye's trough so that the drakkenree could drink as well.

Their immediate needs satisfied, they became aware of the sounds outside the cave. Two drakkenree were arguing.

Yan suspected each was suggesting that the other be the one
to disturb Yellow Eye; he had observed that none of the soldiers liked to be near Yellow Eye. Whatever brought them
to the cave did not seem to be compelling enough for them
to risk entering the restricted area.

"*Grm'lktn* has returned," Yellow Eye explained as he led
the way to the cave's entrance.

At the opening the messengers acknowledged Yellow
Eye's superior rank and immediately began babbling their
message. Yan didn't need a translation, he could see for
himself. Many drakkenree crowded the camp's open space,
and Gremlekten stood tall among them; his feathered headdress held more plumes and he looked more resplendent
than before. A clump of the camp's soldiers stood near the
drakkenree war leader, and Yellow Eye moved to join
them.

Yan spied Khankemeh among the soldiers and stuck
close to Yellow Eye; it would be too easy to lose track of
Khankemeh among so many drakkenree, and Yan didn't
think he could afford to be without Yellow Eye's protection.

Gremlekten and Yellow Eye went through their ritual
greeting, and Yan thought that this time the war leader conceded more slowly than he had before. Yellow Eye didn't
seem to mind. Gremlekten made a short speech that ended
in chuffs, foot stamps, and clicking jaws from the drakkenree of his immediate entourage. Yellow Eye simply clicked
his jaws once.

At the war leader's signal, a line of heavily burdened
bearers filed into the camp. Most were bregil, but a few
were Imperial soldiers. Yan searched their faces, but saw
none he recognized. The men looked exhausted, and the
few showing any energy had fear in their eyes. One of
those men caught sight of Yan, and his eyes narrowed with
hate.

Their drakkenree masters directed them to unload their
burdens into a pile between Gremlekten and Yellow Eye.
The bearers deposited load after load of spoils: breast-
plates, helmets, gauntlets, swords, daggers, bucklers, carefully wrapped firearms, and other martial debris
predominated, but Yan spotted smaller items of loot—both

the sort of precious things soldiers carried with them, and larger items such as might be carried in a baggage train. A second line of bearers appeared and angled toward the hut where the cooks worked. Yan overheard several of the camp's soldiers talking, and caught the drakkenree word for eating; they were looking at the bundles borne by the bregil. Yan hoped that the bearers were only burdened with horseflesh.

There were no merin in that line of bearers.

The last of the bearers deposited his load in the pile of loot and shuffled away. Yellow Eye surveyed the spoils impassively while Gremlekten made another speech. The war leader's words were met with approval by the drakkenree; even Yellow Eye stamped his foot.

"What has happened?" Yan whispered to the mage.

"*Grm'lktn* has fought a battle. Your people are broken. They flee like *hnk'kaln.*" Yellow Eye stretched out a foot and snagged a prawntail helmet from one of the piles, dragging it close enough that he could bend down and pick it up easily. He held it out to Yan. "You see, their shells and fire weapons did not save them."

Yan stared at the helmet. Once it had been a shiny example of solid Imperial craftsmanship, now it was a pitiful thing, battered and missing several of its rivets. Dried blood stained the leather lining. A tattered cord of braided hemp was tied to the plume holder with a fisherman's knot. That cord and the tooth marks on the brim told Yan who had owned this dented and abused helmet.

It was Iaf Smyth's helmet.

It seemed wrong that the boy should have died in a strange forest so far from home. But the boy had chosen the life of a soldier, and death in foreign lands was often a soldier's lot. Iaf certainly hadn't died alone.

Yan wondered whether Teletha had been with the army. If she had been, had she survived, or was her helmet lying among the booty as well? He was afraid to look. Had she died with the army? Or was she still alive somewhere? Yan found that he wanted to know the answer to that last question as much as any that he had concerning the Serpent's Eye.

Yellow Eye held the helmet aloft, displaying it to the assembled drakkenree.

"It is a good day," he said to Yan.

The mage hiss-growled something to his fellows. All around them, drakkenree jaws gaped open in a display of teeth and snapped shut with a sharp clicking sound.

Hillmen surrounded him, screaming and prancing. Their barbaric feathers, hides, and clan totems make them figures of nightmare. Swords, spears, and knives poked at him. Clubs and rocks pummeled him. Just beyond the ring of taunting, torturing bregil, he could see a drakkenree. The saurian was huge for its kind; its eyes glittered on high as it watched its minions ravage him. The lizard's face split in a wide, curving grin full of pointed teeth, and it breathed heavily in anticipation. The deep, sonorous rhythm of that breathing pounded against his head. He closed his eyes and prayed for relief, but the sound remained.

Was this his reward after death? To be tortured by his killers for eternity? Had he offended the gods so badly?

The breathing. The awful, threatening breathing. Did it have to surround him so, gathering him in this shroud of smothering closeness? It seemed so much more real than the capering bregil, more real than the vision of the drakkenree.

No, it *was* more real. There truly was something nearby, breathing with the same rhythm that he had heard in what he now knew as a dream.

The damage inflicted by the dream enemy resolved itself into real aches and pains. He was not dead but, against all odds, alive.

A captive?

Listening to that ominous breathing, he was almost afraid to open his eyes and see. But eyes open or not, the situation would be the same. Steadying himself with a prayer to Vehr for courage and another to Manar for mercy, he opened his eyes. Or rather one of them; the other didn't seem to respond.

He was lying in a makeshift shelter. A roof of crudely

lashed sticks supported a covering of leafy branches and brush. Small patches of early morning sunlight showed through the gaps. A slight breeze wafted the fresh, foresty smell of the vegetation to him. The unevenness beneath the blanket on which he lay told him his bed was of similar branch-and-cord construction.

The breathing had turned into something more like a growl.

Searching for the source of the sound, he tried to turn his head and found himself restricted. A pole retaining its sapling bark blocked both motion and vision. A similar pole lay on the other side of his head. Both canted away from the point above his head where they crossed; the distance between them widening toward his feet. Bands of pressure against his chest and hips suddenly made sense; he was bound to a litter. Someone had cared enough for him to build this and carry him away from the battle.

But he wasn't moving.

The battle! What had happened?

As if in answer to his question, a concerned face appeared in his vision. A merin face, with the wild red hair and light complexion of Scoth. A stranger.

"Lieutenant Smyth?"

Iaf tried to reply, but he found he had no voice.

"It's all right, Lieutenant. Stay quiet."

The face disappeared and he heard a voice shouting for Fra Ystram. How could that be? Wasn't the Vehrite commander dead, along with all the other commanders?

The shouting disturbed the breathing that had brought him back into the waking world. Something stirred behind him. He tried to lift his head and see around the poles. With his chest restrained, the task was difficult, but on his third attempt he managed to get his head high enough to glimpse the dnove of a man curled up on the ground near the head of the litter.

Jax Vorsan!

Where had *he* come from?

Iaf managed to get a hand up to the band tying his chest. His fingers fumbled at it, and he strained to get his head up to see the knot. His vision spun, darkening at the edges. He got his other hand up, but even together his hands could only fumble at the binding.

A gentle hand pushed his head back down.

"Easy, lad." Fra Ystram pulled Iaf's hands away from the knot. "I'll undo it if you promise to lie still. You had a nasty blow on the head."

"You're dead," Iaf croaked.

"Many an enemy of the gods has wished it so, but my Lord Vehr has not called me to His standard as yet. In truth, though, there were several times in this last fray when I thought I would not see Horesh rise again. We feared for you, lad. You've been communing with the other side for days."

"Days?"

In a sudden explosion Vorsan rolled to his feet, weapon in hand. He loomed over the litter, his eyes fixed on Fra Ystram. The Vehrite priest remained still.

"All is well, Colonel Vorsan," he said. "There is no need for alarm."

For a moment it seemed that Vorsan had not heard; he stared wild-eyed, and the sword quivered in his hand. The giant mastered whatever had impelled him and haltingly lowered his weapon. The great black-maned head swiveled until the dark eyes were looking at Iaf. Vorsan crouched, reaching out a hand to touch Iaf's chest. Vorsan's brow furrowed, then he turned a questioning look on the Vehrite.

Fra Ystram gave him a smile. "I think he will be well, Colonel Vorsan."

Vorsan nodded solemnly.

Iaf was confused. "Eminence, what is going on?"

"Colonel Vorsan seems to have taken your welfare for his own concern. You should be grateful. I believe that you owe your continued existence on this earth to him."

"Hunh? How? I don't remember . . . "

"Your soldiers say you were wounded when the enemy broke into one of your regiment's hedgehogs. Many thought you dead, or soon to be so. Then Vorsan appeared from nowhere and smashed his way through the bregil that were assaulting your regiment. They say he fought like a man possessed of the God. I did not see it, but that is what they said. Vorsan fought his way to you and killed all the enemy around you. God-possessed or not, it was a hero's feat."

It seemed impossible. Iaf looked at the colonel. "You did that? You saved me from the hillmen?"

"Hillmen." Vorsan nodded. Abruptly he straightened and disappeared from Iaf's sight, moving around behind the head of the travois. He was back in a moment, laying a cluster of thick, dark cords on Iaf's chest. "Many," Vorsan said proudly.

Iaf realized that the cords were not cords at all. Each was lightly furred and had a handspan of leathery pad near one end. They were bregil tails, trophies. Iaf looked to Fra Ystram.

"His mind is no longer what it was, but his strength and prowess are undiminished."

Undiminished prowess, indeed. Iaf didn't know what Islander custom was, but only the Scoth who killed an opponent was allowed the right to take trophies. There had to be at least a dozen tails. Why Vorsan had done what he had done was as much a mystery as how, and Iaf suspected the reason would remain locked in the simpleton's skull. While reasons are always invisible, actions are not; but a clear head was needed to make sense of any battle and a controlled tongue to tell the tale.

"How could he have reached us, Eminence?" Iaf asked the Vehrite. "We were surrounded."

Fra Ystram gave a slight shrug. "The touch of the gods? Luck? I believe he acted according to Vehr's will. One instrument of my Lord Vehr acting to save another."

"To save an—" Was the priest saying what Iaf thought he was saying? "I'm not an instrument of Vehr."

"You wear His sign."

Iaf felt the weight of the talisman he wore against his chest. The little sword trinket was common among those who followed the soldier's way, a new one bought for luck in each campaign. The one he wore he'd gotten at the temple in Brandespar when the expeditionary force had landed in Kolvin. It was an ordinary thing. "Lots of soldiers wear the sign."

As if following Iaf's thoughts, Fra Ystram laid a finger on the sword symbol. "I did not mean this. I meant the sign of His favor. The soldiers say you took command after Colonel Kensie died. They believe they would all have died had you not saved them. We all might have died, had you not pushed the regiment to action. Your actions saved more than your fellow Scoths."

"Then the force was not destroyed."

"Mauled, but not destroyed. We are retreating."

"And the drakkenree?"

"They and the hillmen follow in small numbers, keeping contact, but they are not pressing us. It is as if they have other concerns now that they have shown us who is master in the forest."

Teletha's patrol encountered the outriders of Baron Yentillan's force, which put her in a position to escort the grim Baron and his knights into the king's tent. It wasn't her place, but no one forbade her. That suited her; she knew the arrival of Yentillan meant that something important had happened—or was about to.

Peyto, excluded from the private conversation of King Shain and Yentillan along with the rest of the scribes and hangers-on, came over to her. "Did the Baron say what brought him here?"

"And a good day to you, Master Lennuick."

Peyto scowled at her.

"No," she said. "But it can't be good news."

"Yes," Peyto agreed. "Shain's already reaching for the fortified wine."

"A little early."

"Even for him." Peyto's gaze turned to the baron's knights. "Perhaps the less lofty would have words for the even less lofty."

Teletha left him to pry information from the knights by himself. If he could. They were soldiers like her, higher in social rank, but soldiers still, and she knew a soldier's moods; she could see from their faces that they wouldn't be talking.

Janden and one of his men arrived within minutes. She followed him back inside. He stopped by the entrance and swept the tent with his eyes, whispering a few words to his companion before moving in to greet the king. The companion departed.

Almost immediately, the king called for Baron Jost and the knight commanders to be summoned. Shain, Yentillan, and Janden sat in silence while they waited; Janden didn't look happy about that. When the commanders had assembled outside the tent, King Shain gave the order that the walls be drawn back. Yentillan rose and spoke.

"My lords, I have already given his Grace the news I carry. You have been called here to hear it all at once. The Imperials have fought a pitched battle in Gremaire Forest by the Loramigonne River."

"Your face says the news isn't good," Baron Jost observed.

"Disastrous," Yentillan admitted. "The Imperials are defeated and scattered. Their general is dead or captured. The enemy is in pursuit of their army's remnants and is marching on Jost's town."

"From what source does this news come?" Janden asked.

"A messenger from Honistonti reached us, calling for support. His force had been ambushed. We saddled and rode at once, but were ambushed ourselves by a pack of Turtle and Cragcat warriors. We scattered the hillmen, but it cost us most of the afternoon. It was near dark, and moving in the forest at night would only have asked to be set upon again. Before full dark had fallen, my outriders met stragglers from the Imperial force. The battle was done and the Imperials defeated. I knew we would be no match for a force that could rout the Imperials, and so we rode at once to bring the news."

"Even in the forest in the dark?" Jost asked in an accusatory tone.

"At the time we were not moving into territory held by the enemy," Sir Bryyan said in Yentillan's defense.

"Away from the battle," Jost said.

"Away from the battleground, aye," Yentillan said heatedly. "But not from the battle. That was already lost."

"I am sure that Baron Yentillan did what seemed wisest at the time," Janden said. "Certainly it was important that we hear this most unfortunate news. The defeat of the expeditionary force means that the drakkenree are stronger than we believed. It also means that we no longer face simple raiding forces and scattered pockets of strength. Clearly they have assembled into an army of considerable strength, possibly sufficient to overwhelm your army as well, your Grace. It might be advisable to move east and join with the forces under your son. The combined armies should be more than sufficient to put paid to the lizards."

"And abandon my town?" Jost objected.

"It is unlikely that it can be held," Yentillan said.

"We held it against them all winter."

"The enemy's numbers have grown since winter," Janden pointed out. "With the defeat of the expeditionary force, our position has been dangerously weakened."

Jost snorted. "The Imperials fought the enemy in the forest. The hill monkeys and the lizards can't stand before Kolviner knights in the open. Besides, the levy can hold the town while we take the fight to the enemy."

"Open battle would be fine if it were only monkeys and lizards. They have the great beasts as well," Yentillan said.

"Walls are the best remedy against their beasts," one of the knights said. "The things can't climb."

"But the monkeys can," said another.

"You will starve behind your walls while the drakkenree make free with the countryside," Janden said to Jost.

"That is why we must attack them as soon as we may," the baron responded.

The wrangling went on, King Shain sitting back and listening, wine cup in hand. Teletha couldn't decide if the king was being shrewd or indecisive. Some of the Kolviner knights were all in favor of moving to fight the invaders at once. Knights and lordlings who held land not already occupied by the invaders objected; they saw no reason to abandon the defense. Others, either knowing the loss themselves or fearing it, supported those who thought the fight ought to be sooner than later. Finally, Shain spoke, siding with his more aggressive knights. Janden's face went black.

The king called for maps and started to discuss the best place to meet the enemy.

Teletha had heard enough. If the Kolviners were intent on battle and the invaders now willing to oblige, as it seemed they were, the drakkenree and the hill tribes would be drawn away from their hiding places; the forest would be empty and easy to pass through, especially for a single rider like a scout familiar with the terrain. Such a scout was now of small use to the king's effort, for an open field battle had little role for scouts. She wouldn't be needed. Not by the king anyway.

She slipped out of the tent.

Dantil and three of the other riders stood by outside, talking with the king's guard. They looked up as she emerged. She tried to give the impression she was on an errand, giving them a cursory nod and passing them by without a word. It seemed to work; none of them tried to wring from her word of the doings in the king's tent.

Stopping by the tent she shared with her patrol, she grabbed her gear, then headed for the corral. She kept telling herself that she was doing the right thing all the while she saddled her horse. The cord of the Sword Guild weighed heavily on her arm. She stopped and stripped it off, but she couldn't bring herself to throw it away. She tucked it in the saddlebag.

There were duties and there were duties.

Saddled and ready, her horse seemed anxious to be gone. She led it to the gate of the corral, slowing when she saw Dantil and the three riders loitering at the edge of the light cast by the gate's torch. She passed through the gate, refastening the rope barrier behind her.

As she gathered in her mount's reins, Dantil stepped up to her. He stood close, closer than his usual wont. Something hard poked her in the side. Looking down, she saw the pistol in his hand. Janden's pistol, cocked and ready.

Dantil's face was expressionless. Although they had ridden together, she knew Dantil was Janden's man first and foremost. If the captain had given Dantil the pistol to use on Teletha, he would use it. Though she had never seen Dantil use a pistol before, even a novice couldn't miss with a muzzle almost touching his target's belly. The other riders formed a semicircle around them, tense and ready for her to try something.

She wasn't that stupid.

Janden appeared out of the darkness behind Dantil. "Going somewhere, Sergeant Schonnegon?"

"Doesn't look like it," she replied

"The guild code calls desertion a capital offense."

"I wasn't deserting."

"No?" He tugged her right arm up where the torchlight could fall on it. "Where's your bond cord?"

"It must have fallen off."

"Not good enough, Schonnegon. Take her away."

25

RAFF JANDEN RODE ALONG with the vanguard of King Shain's army, but his mind was not on his immediate surroundings. His failure to convince the king of the wiser, longer-term strategy still galled him, but it was only a part of the complex situation surrounding him. There were many aspects to the problem, small and large, and all fought for his attention. All made his stomach sour.

He was not one to rely on others when it mattered; he'd learned the folly of that in the past. Unreliable subordinates were the bane of the best plans. Unpredictable subordinates were almost as bad, especially the ones like Schonnegon, who were prone to acting rashly in precarious situations. And this was indeed a precarious situation. Fortunately, Raff had guessed how she would react to the news of the Imperial defeat and laid appropriate plans.

She claimed that she'd only intended to seek out her friend the magician. Her trip was to be a rescue attempt, and given what he knew of her capabilities, she might even have had a chance, as unlikely as it seemed for a single person to succeed where an army had failed. Such a noble motive, and so out of place here.

This was no ordinary conflict, just as the man that she wanted to rescue was no ordinary man. Her magician friend had never been useful to the cause; in fact, Tanafres had been treacherous right from the start, given what he'd

done at Yentillan's stronghold. His secretive and traitorous
exit suggested that he was a pawn of the drakkenree, an
association possibly dating to before the first raiders wearing orb talismans had shown their ugly, muzzled faces.

And now that the Imperial cause here was in jeopardy,
Schonnegon had been caught trying to slip away into the
night as Tanafres had. Perhaps she intended to join her
friend in treachery, perhaps not. Raff was surprised to find
himself hoping that she might merely be misguided, or
even fallen under the magical sway of the magician and
therefore not responsible for her actions. Raff was not com-
petent to judge that last possibility. He knew her as a soldier under his command; she'd been a good cavalry leader
and a good fighter. She had shown herself a sturdy and
quick-thinking independent operator. She had earned his
respect. She was ill directed, but then, she was self-directed.

Or, he reminded himself, deluded by the magician.

Still, properly motivated and directed she might be very
useful. The Coronal Empire was always in need of the sort
of person she appeared to be. For the moment, his threat of
execution would remain a threat. As ever, he was loath to
waste a useful tool.

But Schonnegon could not be allowed to go roaming
Gremaire Forest on her own. The risk was too great that
she would end up in the hands of the enemy, willing or not.
She knew too much of the Kolviners' strength and too
much of the king's plans; too much about Imperial military
practice as well. Best she be mewed up until matters
resolved themselves.

The ignominious defeat of the Imperial expeditionary
force had not been a part of Raff's plans. Even better than
Honistonti, he had known that the strike into the heart of
the Gremaire Forest was dangerous. However, he had also
had a better appreciation than the general of how important such a probe would be; almost anything would have
been worth the risk—if they uncovered the drakkenree
mage and destroyed it. But Honistonti had failed, and lost
most of the best troops in the Kingdom of Kolvin in the
process. Raff couldn't destroy the drakkenree threat with
an army composed mostly of Shain's feudal fighters.

Honistonti was lucky he wouldn't have to answer to the empire.

New plans needed to be laid, new strategies decided. Foremost, they needed a way to stem the rushing tide of drakkenree advance.

A shouted order to halt brought Raff out of his troubled thoughts. The vanguard had just reached the crest of a small hill. Before them a broad plain spread outward toward the river. With a quick look to the hills behind them and the forests around them, Raff decided it must be the River Daige; the marsh tucked into the sweeping bend of the river was his best clue. The village they overlooked would be Rastionne. The village was far from deserted; hundreds of men camped nearby.

"What do you make of it?" Shain asked.

Spotting the tattered unit standards, Raff said, "The Imperials."

"What's left of them," Jost added.

"Unfurl the banner," Shain ordered. "Trumpeter, let them know we come to their aid."

"Is that wise, your Grace?" Yentillan asked. "The enemy might hear."

Raff was glad to see that months of wilderness skirmishing had taught at least one Kolviner some caution.

"Let the enemy hear," Shain said. "We are not skulkers like them. Let them hear! Let them come! We will welcome them and feast them on Kolviner steel."

The knights cheered their king.

Banner flying and trumpeters blowing, the Kolviner vanguard advanced on Rastionne. A small party of soldiers rode out to meet them, Fra Ystram at their head. The Vehrite commander was alive, so at least some of the early intelligence was faulty. Things might not be as bad as they appeared.

"Well met, your Grace," Fra Ystram called as he came within earshot. "We had not hoped to see friends so soon."

"Well met, Eminence," the king returned. "We had not hoped to see yourself, nor so many of our allies. What we have heard has been grim. I am heartened to see you and would have the tale of the battle from your own lips."

"Grim it was," Ystram said. "We had a hard time of it, and it is not a comfortable tale. With your Grace's indulgence, I would ask you to await the arrival of the rest of our men, that the tale may be told more fully, and those upon whom Vehr has laid his hand be present."

"There are more survivors?"

"By the grace of Horesh and the blessing of Vehr, yes. They come on apace, but the care of the wounded slows them."

Hearing that, King Shain gave orders for the army to encamp.

As the remnants of the expeditionary force trickled into the fields around Rastionne, Raff moved among them. He observed their state and listened to what they said. Let Shain have his tale of the battle; Raff was more interested in what was left and what might be done with it. He also wanted a better picture of the strength of the drakkenree's military power and determination.

It became clear that a considerable number of troops had survived the battle. The foot had come through in better shape than the horse. Most of the Scothic regiment remained, and a little more than half of the other foot. The Baaliffite knights were destroyed as a fighting force, as were the Imperial regular cavalry; but nine out of ten of the Vehrite cavalry survived, although half of them lacked mounts. In all, there remained almost half of what Sorigir Renumas had sent on this mission. Less than Raff would have liked, but more than the first accounts of the defeat had led him to expect.

Used judiciously, the force could still serve. They would no longer be a decisive element, but as a supplement to the Kolviner army, they could be effective in a raiding campaign to keep the drakkenree off-balance. Here in this wilderness, foot troops sometimes were more effective than cavalry. The Imperial foot were far better quality than the Kolviner levies and mercenaries.

But first the force had to be reforged. They needed heart, for the defeat had sapped their confidence. Fortunately, from what he had heard, Raff saw that there might be a way to reform the battered companies into a useful tool. In the midst of its defeat, the expeditionary force had found itself a hero, the lieutenant of the late Colonel Kensie. Iaf Smyth was the hero of the day. And heroes were inspiring.

Unfortunately, like Schonnegon, Smyth was tainted by Tanafres. The Scoth had associated with the magician regularly during the winter in Jost's town, and had accompanied Schonnegon on her unauthorized rescue mission. Barracks rumor had it that Smyth had gone with Schonnegon because he was enamored of the woman. If true, it gave Raff a lever.

Whatever his motivation, Smyth had been instrumental in saving what had been saved of the expeditionary force. Some of the troops were saying that the young lieutenant had been touched by the gods. The way that the simpleton Vorsan had attached himself to Smyth enhanced that image.

Dantil found Raff as he sat outside the king's tent contemplating the situation. The gruff sergeant wasted no time in reporting. "Kammie's in from his scout."

"And?"

"Hain't good. They're moving along the Daige. Twenty clans, maybe more. Eight hundreds of lizards."

"Between us and Jost's town."

Dantil nodded. "Will be by noon tomorrow, anyway."

"Baron Jost won't be happy." King Shain and his knights had decided to meet the drakkenree forces outside Jost's town; that plan had just taken a fatal blow. Steps had to be taken to see that the Kingdom of Kolvin didn't fall apart along with it. "Schonnegon secured?"

"Aye," Dantil said sullenly

"Trouble?"

"Hain't been nothing we couldn't handle."

Thunder rumbled distantly in the southwest. Dantil looked up, worried. Raff was glad he didn't believe in random omens.

"Rain coming. It'll slow them down," Dantil observed.

It would slow everyone down. "Keep the scouts out." Dantil nodded and turned to go. Raff gave him a last order. "Have someone find Iaf Smyth and tell him that the king wants him."

It was time to get things moving. Raff went into the tent to prepare the king. Shain was still questioning Fra Ystram about the details of the battle in the forest. Raff listened for a minute to gauge the king's concerns; he didn't much care for what he heard. The king seemed obsessed with the fine points of combating the drakkenree in a melee.

Such a narrow field of view.

At a convenient break in the talk, Raff said, "A word for your ear, King Shain." Shain, as always, listened. The Vehrite started to excuse himself, so Raff added, "This is for your ear as well, Eminence."

The warrior-priest remained, and that proved fortuitous; without coaching, the priest enthusiastically fell in line with Raff's intent. All was arranged by the time Smyth arrived at the tent. The Scoth looked nervous as he entered. Raff let him advance a few steps before moving to stand at his side. Raff bowed to the king, holding it until Smyth joined him. Straightening, he said, "Your Grace, you remember Iaf Smyth."

Shain squinted at the Scoth. "I've seen him before."

"Indeed you have, your Grace, under less edifying circumstances. But I have called him here tonight to present him to you in a different light. This man is the one who saved the Scothic regiment and, thereby, the rest of the expeditionary force."

"Vehr smiles upon him," said Fra Ystram.

"As the good priest says," Raff agreed, for once thankful for an interruption of a planned speech. "Iaf Smyth has shown himself a brave and resourceful commander. He is worthy of honor, both from you and from the emperor. I cannot speak for your Grace, but in certain matters I may speak for the emperor. Here, today, I do that."

Raff pulled the *staliarm* out of his shirt and held it up for all to see. The time for subterfuge was long past. Calling upon his link with the talisman, he willed the sign of his authority to appear. The tiny chip of precious metron in the heart of the setting began to glow, shedding a light that rivaled that of the candelabrum on the king's map table. In the glow of the *staliarm,* Smyth looked stunned.

"By the right of this *staliarm,* with which I was invested

by the Emperor Dacel the Fourth himself, I hereby appoint and name Iaf Smyth as captain-general of the Imperial expeditionary force for the duration of this crisis, or until the emperor sends a chosen successor."

The young Scoth snapped his head around and stared openmouthed at Raff.

"What say you, Captain-general?" Shain asked.

"I—I—"

"I told you the hand of Vehr rested upon you," Fra Ystram said. "You cannot deny His will."

Smyth looked terrified, but managed to stammer out, "I have never denied the will of the gods."

"A good enough acceptance," Raff declared, willing the *staliarm* to revert to its normal state. "Now, your Grace and my lord commanders, we have business to discuss. There is word of the enemy."

26

IAF'S MIND WAS NUMBED BY the double blow of Janden's revelation as a man of the *staliarm*, and the scout captain's use of that authority to elevate Iaf to the rank of captain-general. The other commanders' easy acceptance of Iaf's presence softened the shock, but he still had difficulty believing that they thought him either ready for or worthy of the honor. He had never commanded even one regiment, let alone a force of regiments. Why did they think he could now?

At first he just listened; there was so much he did not know about how the council worked and about the situation. Janden seemed to take a lead role in the discussions, which made sense; since the captain held the *staliarm*, he spoke as an agent of the emperor, and who would not listen to the emperor's word? But the longer Iaf listened the more confused he became. It seemed that Janden had been the one who convinced Honistonti to launch the ill-fated Gremaire Forest probe. The justifications Janden gave to the council made a certain amount of sense, but Iaf thought that too much had been risked for too little. He was shocked when Janden said that he had been expecting the force to take heavy casualties. They had been sent to nearly certain death so that Janden could learn a little more about the enemy. Had it been a decisive battle, and had they been expecting it, all would have been different. As it was, Iaf felt betrayed.

But he said nothing. What could he say? The battle was

over and men, good men, were dead. Nothing could change that.

Janden went on, telling everyone about the latest moves by the enemy. Each time some plan was advanced, Janden waited until it looked as if the council was reaching a conclusion, and then he would introduce more information that showed the flaws in the plan. He seemed to have a total grasp of the enemy's options, to have fully mastered the complexities of the situation.

But if Janden truly was so knowledgeable, how had the disaster in Gremaire Forest come about? No honest commander would have deliberately sent his men to such pointless deaths. The others seemed satisfied with Janden, even Fra Ystram. They were all so much more experienced than Iaf. Were Iaf's feelings misplaced? Perhaps he just didn't understand.

But if Iaf didn't understand the logic of commanders, he recognized the brutal logic of the battlefield. The drakken-ree and the hill tribes were marching in force greater than before. There were other details concerning the enemy, all of them forbidding. Even if Janden were wrong about the particulars, the threat was real and imminent. There would be another battle soon. When Iaf pointed out that the survivors of the battle in Gremaire Forest were not ready for another retreat, the decision was made to fight on the plain where Rastionne village stood.

Iaf left the meeting with King Shain and the commanders more shaken and disturbed than he had gone in. He barely noticed when Jax Vorsan materialized out of the darkness and fell into step with him. The giant's presence was no longer strange, certainly not compared to what had happened tonight. Iaf walked through the camp, his head awhirl. Hearing the soldiers shout his name or his new rank as he passed didn't help. Obviously, the news of his elevation had spread.

He needed to talk to someone with a level head. Old Bert would have suggested Air Captain Schonnegon. Teletha Schonnegon was nearly a saint in Old Bert's eyes, and his solution to any problem that involved thinking. Iaf had come into manhood thinking the same, and finally meeting her hadn't changed his opinion much. Unfortunately,

Teletha wasn't available, being off on a courier mission. Master Tanafres was a wise man, despite what was said about him by others, but he was elsewhere as well. There really wasn't anyone he could talk to.

"How about you, Colonel Vorsan?" Iaf asked on a whim. "Have you advice for me?"

The big man said nothing. He might not have even heard.

Iaf decided to walk some more, hoping that the night air would clear his head. Too many things had changed tonight. He need to sort out his thoughts. To the southwest thunder rumbled, threatening a follow-up to the evening's shower. The air was humid and oppressive, but no more oppressive than Iaf's mood.

Colonel Kensie had taught him that a man must order his needs, that he must do first what must be done, that which ought to be done only after, and lastly that which it might be nice to do. Such was a commander's responsibility. A patrol riding out to the southeast reminded him of the greatest danger. The enemy was out there. King Shain wanted a plan to deal with the enemy, and Iaf had none. Feeling that seeing more of what lay around Rastionne might inspire thought, he took his path away from the camp.

An hour of fruitless wandering later, he had only vague ideas, none of which seemed satisfactory. A sharp-toned voice with a lecturing tone drifted to his ears from a nearby canvas stretched between two wagons. He recognized the voice as that of Peyto Lennuick, companion to Master Tanafres from his days in Scothandir, and now serving Shain as a clerk. Master Lennuick had come to Iaf's village as had Master Tanafres, a gift of the domarag. Maybe he was someone Iaf could talk to. Master Lennuick had a sharp tongue, but his mind was sharp, too, and Master Tanafres had listened to the clerk. Teletha had listened sometimes as well.

Master Lennuick was berating someone about the difficulty in allocating payment for the supplies consumed by the army. Iaf moved closer and saw that the object of Master Lennuick's lecture was the Einthofite priest Bern. Iaf remembered finding Master Tanafres in conference with Fra Bern more than once. Perhaps the gods did guide the feet of those who asked Them for help, after all.

Iaf approached, careful to make enough noise that he wouldn't surprise them with a sudden appearance. As he stepped into the lantern light, Master Lennuick greeted him.

"Ah, Captain-general Iaf and his shadow. You are abroad late, Captain-general. Is command not turning out to be the stuff of your dreams?"

"What do you mean?" Iaf asked.

"You look more like a man condemned than one promoted."

Did he? He was aware then of the tension in his face and at his temples. "Perhaps that's because I *feel* more like a man condemned."

"Is the army's situation that bad?"

"It's not good."

Fra Bern spoke for the first time. "But you are troubled by more than the threat of the enemy."

It was true, but which of those troubles could he tell to these men? He found himself saying, "I'm not sure who the enemy is."

"That is a problem," Master Lennuick agreed. "What causes such confusion?"

"Captain Janden says that Master Tanafres is with the drakkenree, helping them."

Master Lennuick scowled. "Does he? And how does he know that?"

Iaf started to answer, but Fra Bern spoke first.

"I am afraid that I am responsible." The priest told them of his dream and how he had told it to Captain Janden.

"Your dream is not conclusive," Master Lennuick stated when the priest finished his tale.

Iaf nodded in agreement. "Master Tanafres may be in the company of the drakkenree—but a renegade aiding them? I don't believe it."

"He is stupidly fascinated with the lizards and their magic, but he is not so empty-headed as to aid them," Master Lennuick said.

"The king and his council listen to Janden. They may believe that Master Tanafres works with the enemy, but I just can't." There had to be something Iaf could do. "I would like to prove that Master Tanafres is not a renegade.

If I could bring him back, he could show everyone that he is not a traitor."

"Do not be foolish, my son," Fra Bern said.

"The priest is right," Master Lennuick said. "You're a brave and resourceful lad, and if you could bring him back, I'm sure you could also prove him not a renegade. Our friend may be foolish and headstrong, but he knows what side he is on when the line is drawn between civilization and barbarity.

"These are not your younger and more carefree days back in Scothandir. As an Imperial military officer, you now have the responsibility of command. It may drag at you like a weight, but you know you must bear the burden. Your concern must be for the men all around us, the men who trust you. A captain-general cannot act like a common soldier, nor even as a lieutenant. You must put the safety and welfare of the entire Imperial contingent ahead of any one person, even an Imperial citizen. Or a friend."

"I know that." He really did, though Master Lennuick's lecture made it clearer. "*You* understand, Master Lennuick. And you, Fra Bern. But I don't think Tel—er, Capt—er, Sergeant Schonnegon will. At least not at first. I wish I could explain it to her, but she is away on a courier mission."

"She's as headstrong as Tanafres, but she was an officer once," Master Lennuick said. "She might manage to remember how it ought to be."

"A moment, please," Fra Bern said. "Captain-general, who told you that Sergeant Schonnegon was on a mission?"

"Captain Janden."

The priest's mouth collapsed in a frown.

"Well, what is it, Bern?" Master Lennuick asked. "What do you know?"

Fra Bern hesitated. The clerk started to prod him again, but Iaf shook his head and, to his surprise, Master Lennuick held his speech. Finally, Fra Bern found the words he sought.

"Sergeant Schonnegon is in Rastionne. She is being held at one of the houses."

So Janden had lied. Somehow, Iaf wasn't surprised. But why had Janden lied? What gain was there in this for him? More and more, Janden appeared as a man obsessed with his own plans. He seemed prone to keeping secrets, a tendency that had cost good men their lives. Such a man was dangerous to those around him.

"Who exactly is holding her?" Master Lennuick asked.

"And why?" Iaf added.

"Captain Janden said that she had tried to desert," said the priest.

"Trying to go after Yan again, no doubt," said Master Lennuick.

Iaf thought that she'd agreed not to. Had something happened? Was there something he didn't know? Something new that Teletha had learned? "Where is she?" he asked.

"I can take you there," the priest said.

"Do so."

Master Lennuick caught Iaf's arm as he turned to leave. "Is it wise to interfere?"

"Is it wise not to? Desertion in the face of the enemy is punishable by death. Usually the sentence is carried out at once. If Tel—Sergeant Schonnegon was really running away, Janden should have executed her on the spot. As seems to be his way, he is playing a more complicated game here. I want to know what it is. I think it unlikely that he would tell me simply for the asking."

Master Lennuick released his grip. "Be careful. Janden does have the authority of a *staliarm*."

"We are not within the empire just now," Iaf pointed out.

"I think he knows that well enough. Inside or out, however, the *staliarm* commands the loyalty of all good citizens."

Iaf chuckled bitterly. "Since when have Scoths been *good* citizens?"

Master Lennuick gave him a sharp look. "At least try not to stir up trouble you can't handle."

"I'll try to keep it to the kind I *can* handle, but I *will* see her free in either case."

Fra Bern led Iaf through the camp and across the village. Pointing out a small farmer's cottage, he said, "She is there. See the men by the door? They are her guards."

"Only two?"

"I have not seen more."

"How do you know so much, good priest?"

Fra Bern looked away guiltily. "I saw her taken by Captain Janden's men. I was surprised and asked the captain what brought it about. He told me of her attempt to flee. I feared for her soul and asked to be allowed to counsel her. The captain agreed. I had no reason to suspect the captain of duplicity."

"And she never asked you to carry a message to her friends?"

"I offered, but she seemed reluctant to speak before the guards. You see, they never left us alone. I thought at the time that she felt guilt at what she had tried to do. I see now that there might have been other reasons for her silence."

"Well, I intend to find out what's going on. Stay here, Fra Bern."

"I wish to help," the priest protested.

"You have helped. From here on, you will be more of a hindrance, especially if there's trouble."

Iaf approached the house along the hedge surrounding the property. The greenery was even tall enough to hide Vorsan. Through a gap in the hedge Iaf caught a glimpse of the guards. He didn't recognize either of them. From the cut of their coats, they were from the Third Foot, Vorsan's old regiment. Would that be trouble? Or would Vorsan's presence at Iaf's side be helpful? He hoped it would be the latter; the less fuss this stirred up the better.

Squaring his shoulders, he rounded the corner and started down the path to the cottage. The guards saw him coming; they couldn't miss him. One nudged the other. Pointing a thumb to Iaf's right, where Vorsan walked, the man said something in a low voice. His companion laughed. Iaf walked up to them.

"Do you know who I am?" he asked

"You're the Scothic kid, the big hero," the taller one said. "So what?"

Iaf tried to ignore the man's sneer. "Janden set you here, didn't he?"

"So?" said the shorter one, mimicking his fellow's tone.

"I must presume that you know he is a man of the *staliarm*, and that is the reason you follow his orders. You are both loyal servants of the emperor."

"Yeah, we're loyal." The tall one spat on the ground near Iaf's feet. "Loyaler than any Scoth ever born."

The man's hateful attitude was palpable. Iaf forced himself to ignore it. It would be best if this could be done without violence. "By Janden's own word as a man of the *staliarm*, I am now captain-general of the expeditionary force. In that capacity, I order you to hand over your prisoner."

"You're a lying scut," the tall guard accused. "You're no general."

Vorsan reached out past Iaf and laid a palm on the man's chest in what looked like a casual gesture. The man seemed to fly backward into the wall. His head banged against a beam, knocking off his hat.

"Captain-general," Vorsan said.

"You've witched the colonel, you Scothic dog!" the man snarled. "But I know how good a spell is when the magician's dead."

The man started to pull his sword. Iaf went for his own, but Vorsan was faster. The giant stepped forward and grabbed the man's coat with both hands. Lifting the soldier from his feet with contemptuous ease, Vorsan slammed him against the building. This time the man's head struck the beam with a resounding thunk. He slid slack-limbed to the ground. Vorsan turned to the other soldier.

The guard backed away, hands held up and open. "She's in the root cellar," the man said quickly. "Don't want no trouble, Colonel. Call him off, Captain-general. I'm a good soldier."

"Good soldier," Vorsan said.

"Show us where she is," Iaf ordered.

"I will show you, if he will not," Fra Bern said.

Iaf had been too focused on the soldiers and hadn't heard the priest approach. "I told you to wait."

"The deed is done." Fra Bern held his chin resolutely forward, daring Iaf to object to his presence.

Their brief standoff gave the guard a chance to back away from the door. As Iaf noticed the man's retreat, the soldier took to his heels.

"Good soldier," Vorsan repeated.

Fra Bern led them inside and pointed at the large chest in the middle of the chamber. The box sat on a trapdoor of weathered boards. "It took both of them to move it," he said.

Vorsan stepped up to the chest and slid it away. With one hand he tore open the door. A yelp of surprise echoed up from the darkness.

"Fear not, lady," Fra Bern called.

"Are you all right?" Iaf asked.

"Get me out of this hole, and I will be," Teletha answered.

Vorsan crouched and extended a hand down into the cellar. He straightened, hauling Teletha out and lowering her gently to the floor. She stepped away from Vorsan, eyeing him as if he were some kind of strange and possibly dangerous animal. Turning to Iaf, she threw her arms around him.

"I'm so glad to see you," she said. "I thought they'd be hanging me in the morning."

Iaf let his own arms enfold her. Somehow he'd never envisioned himself rescuing the great Air Captain Schonnegon as if she were some maiden in a balladeer's tale. It didn't feel quite right. He knew he ought to say something, but the only thing that came to mind was, "Fra Bern told us where you were."

She left Iaf's embrace and gave the priest a hug. A briefer one, Iaf noted. "You are a faithful friend, Fra Bern," she said.

"I am glad of your goodwill, lady, but it is the gods to whom I must answer in the end."

"As do we all, Fra Bern," Teletha said.

"Sergeant Schonnegon, I need to know why Captain Janden arrested you," Iaf said.

She narrowed her eyes at his formality, and he felt uncomfortable again. He steeled himself, waiting for her answer. At last she said, "I was going after Yan."

It was the answer he expected, but it stung anyway. How had the magician inspired such devotion in her? She needed to know how her actions looked. "The situation is grave, Teletha."

"Yan?"

But how could he tell her? "There is still no reliable word."

"No *reliable* word? What is the rumor then?"

"One of the scout patrols reports a merin marching with the drakkenree."

Her brow furrowed. "A merin? Yan?"

"So it would seem."

"He must be a prisoner."

"He wears no chains and carries no burdens. It has been said that he has transferred his loyalties to the drakkenree."

"You can't believe that," she said.

"I do not. But some do."

"Yan would not help them of his own will. Something else must be at work." She smiled conspiratorially. "If they think he's gone bad, we'll just have to show them otherwise."

And they said Scoths had narrow vision? "It isn't that simple. The drakkenree and the hill tribes are marching. Some of them are already between us and Jost's town, and their main force will be here tomorrow or the next day."

"Well, if they're close, Yan is close."

"You can't be seriously thinking of trying to take him from their midst." She'd be throwing her life away.

"Why not?"

"Don't be ridiculous. How can you sneak your way through their entire army? Master Tanafres is the magician, not you."

"I'll find a way," she said resolutely.

"You'd be going to your death," Iaf warned.

"He may be going to his if we don't help him."

She was probably right. Part of him wanted to see Yan Tanafres dead, for the way he held her in thrall and made her want to throw her life away. Part of him remembered the man in Scothandir whom a young boy had recalled fondly for years: a kinder, smarter man than Iaf had become. Yan Tanafres was a good man, and his call on Teletha's affections was clearly stronger than Iaf's would ever be. How could he hate a man she loved so well?

"I want to go with you." Before she could answer he rushed on. "But I can't. Did you hear what I said to the guards?"

She nodded. "A little. Couldn't hear much down there. Something about being a general now?"

"Captain-general," Vorsan said.

"It's true," said Iaf. "A little crazy, I think, but true. I know you no longer owe your allegiance directly to the emperor, but I do. For years I heard how Air Captain

Schonnegon always knew her duty, and always did it. How could I aspire to less? But I can't go with you"

She looked him in the eyes, and for a moment he thought that he detected a faint smile on her lips. She seemed soft and vulnerable then, more a woman than an air captain, and he almost reconsidered his decision not to hate Master Tanafres for owning her heart.

"And I can't stay," she said.

She clearly knew what she wanted, but did she understand the impossibility of success? "Then you love him more than your life."

"I—" She looked away.

They stood there awkwardly for several moments. Fra Bern continued to direct his attention elsewhere as he had through the whole conversation, but Vorsan just stared. Iaf felt his face grow hot. Just now, he wished he'd left the big Islander to the drakkenree.

"If the enemy is approaching, you will have much to do," she said, without looking at Iaf.

It was true. There was nothing he could say that would change things. She would do what she had to do, as would he. "A scout of the forest might be useful for the army," he said. "A lone rider would be unlikely to attract much attention from the enemy. Do you think any of the king's scouts could take on such a task for the benefit of the king's allies? It would be very dangerous."

Teletha sighed. "Thank you, Iaf."

"Captain-general," Vorsan said.

"Thank you, Captain-general," she said.

She walked through the door, pausing to relieve the unconscious guard of his weapon. Iaf watched her walk up the path.

"See Fra Ystram," he called after her. "Tell him I said to give you a horse."

She waved—in thanks or dismissal or good-bye, he didn't know. She said nothing. In a few more steps, she turned the corner and was gone.

Out of his life forever? He prayed it would not be so. But in any case, the Teletha of his dreams was gone. In a strange way he was glad. Well, not glad—relieved.

There was nothing more to do here.

There was, however, much more to do elsewhere.

Trailed by Vorsan and Fra Bern he marched back to the king's tent. He didn't want to talk, and shut down every attempt the priest made to get him to. By the time they reached the tent, the king had retired to his sleeping chamber, but the maps were still there. Iaf lit a candle and pulled up one of the stools. He'd had a few thoughts earlier in the evening and wanted to study the maps again. Perhaps there were things that might be done to improve the situation.

The *military* situation.

Janden was an unfeeling man, and, for the moment, Iaf envied him that. "Work is the antidote, my boy," Old Bert had said. "Hard work makes the mind clear and the heart light."

Sometimes Old Bert had lied.

The king's tent was quiet, and no one disturbed Iaf as he studied the maps. Fra Bern left at some point, but Vorsan stayed by Iaf's side until the walls of the tent turned gray with the coming day.

When Raff rose, he got the word of Schonnegon's release and subsequent departure. He was considering how it would affect what was to come when Dantil's patrol rode in with the word that the enemy main body was less than a dozen miles away, leaving Raff with far more immediate things to worry about. He sent out more patrols, probing for the flanks of the drakkenree advance and seeking to learn as much as possible. They came back with nothing but bad news.

Raff had mixed thoughts when he saw how the young Scoth was throwing himself into the role of captain-general. Smyth was ordering units about and putting men to work, preparing as well as he could for the coming battle. Too bad all the effort was likely to be futile. While Raff awaited his scouts' reports, he watched the boy, impressed at his energy, and feared that he had found another good tool that was about to be wasted.

All activity on the plain stopped when the first elements of the enemy force emerged from the forest late in the afternoon. Anxious eyes watched as they began to deploy. Raff knew then that the most pessimistic reports from his scouts had actually been optimistic.

Of course, Shain wanted to strike at once. It took the combined force of argument by Raff, Fra Ystram, and the fledgling Captain-general Smyth to restrain the Kolviner king. As it turned out, the Imperials were the wiser, for the drakkenree did not attack that day; it was too late an hour by the time most of their ill-disciplined allies managed to array their troops. It gave the Kolviners a reprieve of at least the night.

The saurians were in no hurry, now that they had the Kolviners pinned here. Their bregil allies might even now be urging a night attack, for they could see better in the dark than merin. But Raff judged that the mixed force relied on the drakkenree for most of their striking power, and the lizards disliked night fighting. And, of course, the general of that army was a lizard. The enemy would wait for the light.

The reprieve was only a postponement of disaster. Come the morrow, things would not go well for the Kolviners. The river at their backs prevented an organized withdrawal, which meant battle, and battle favored the more numerous enemy. Worse, what had once been an Imperial advantage, the presence of a trained battle wizard, now lay with the lizards. They still had their black-scaled mage. And possibly Tanafres as well. The situation looked hopeless.

In the here and now.

Shain's Kolviners and the remnants of the Imperial expeditionary force were going to engage the drakkenree here. They could make the enemy pay a substantial cost to defeat them. A serious, hard-fought battle would weaken the lizards and limit their future operations. A battle could buy precious time. Perhaps enough so that other steps could be taken.

One had to consider how events affect the long term.

There was little more that Raff could do here. The battle would be lost whether he remained or not. But there were still things that he could do, still steps that *had* to be taken if the drakkenree threat were to be crushed.

That night he took his horse across the ford, and by the time the sky grayed he was well on his way on the road to Brandespar.

27

BY THE TIME HE'D FINISHED STUDYING the maps, Iaf was sure that the camp around the village of Rastionne was indefensible. With double the number of troops, there might have been a hope. The village existed here in part because of the nearby ford in the broad River Daige and in part because of the low, flat fields of rich soil fenced by the river, hills, and forest. The extent of the open ground was not great, even by the standards of these wild parts of Kolvin, but more than enough for a battle.

And battle was approaching closer by the hour. Janden's scouts were in and out all morning, conferring with the captain. As usual, the man kept his counsel to himself; Iaf hoped that any significant change in the situation would motivate the man to say something.

Iaf knew the expeditionary force wasn't up to another retreat. And if they were, where would they go? The forest to the east and south already belonged to the drakkenree. The hills to the south and west were open and rolling, inviting but deceptive; the tired Imperials could not outpace the drakkenree for long, and would be run down and killed. The river and a broad band of marsh blocked them to the north, and where the river ran through firmer ground to the west it was too wide and deep to cross save at the ford. Beyond the ford lay most of Kolvin, and wisdom suggested a retreat toward more defensible ground. A small force might even hold the ford against the oncoming army for long enough that the rest could escape safely. But King Shain had closed the route as effectively as if he had raised the level of the river by his height, for the king had sworn on his family's honor to crush the invaders. No Kolviner would run now, no matter how prudent it might be.

Once some Kolviner lordling had tried to make this plain his own. Near the bend in the river, hard by the marsh, was a low hill topped with the remains of a timber keep. It would have been a good place to survey the fields and guard the ford. But the lordling was gone and the place long abandoned. Little remained of his handiwork beyond the ruins of his tower, just what had once been a moat skirting the hill from the marsh to a place near the ford. The villagers used it as an irrigation ditch.

The hill and its barrier ditch was the best defensive site available. The river completely guarded one side, and the marsh, which the scouts reported as so treacherous as to be uncrossable, another. The ditch protected the other two sides, making a rough rectangle big enough to hold their arrayed forces.

It also bid fair to become a trap. There would be no retreat with the river at their backs. But King Shain's insistence on standing to fight was trap enough; a battle in the open part of the plain would see them surrounded and annihilated.

At the morning conference, Iaf suggested that the combined army take up its position using the ditch to cover their front. Fra Ystram and the other Imperial commanders nodded in agreement, but King Shain said, "We need no ditches. They will only impede the horses."

Without Janden to support him, Iaf was only able to win the concession that the ambulance wagons, the camp followers, and such ordinary folk as had gathered under the army's protection be emplaced behind the ditch. Iaf would have preferred that those not involved in the fighting cross the river to the safer side, but the king wouldn't stand for the suggestion that his army was in danger of defeat.

Around midmorning, the first bregil scouts appeared at the forest's edge. Using the excuse of protecting the innocents, Iaf moved the Scothic regiment to the ditch and began work to improve its defensive qualities. He had the other Imperial units stand to arms for inspection. Shortly thereafter Janden appeared with reports from the Kolviner scouts. The drakkenree were advancing on them. Iaf sent an armed detachment to the forest to cut wood for stakes.

About two hours after noon, the detachment returned in haste, carrying the word that the enemy was upon them. Shortly thereafter, the first elements of the enemy's main body emerged from the forest. Tribesmen in their barbaric trappings clustered at the edges of the forest. Entire companies of drakkenree soldiers marched onto the field. The bellow of a *terriserpens* echoed from among the trees.

King Shain wanted to strike at once.

"The combined army is no more ready and arrayed for battle than the enemy," Iaf told him. The king countered that by having the trumpeters blow the call to arms. The troops of the combined army slowly came to order. Fortunately the enemy were slower still. Iaf spent the early afternoon continuing to argue against forcing the battle. Fra Ystram and Janden backed him, but only when Baron Yentillan spoke on their behalf did the king listen.

"See their numbers, your Grace," the Baron said. "Our men had not thought to fight this day. Though they are brave, their hearts are not prepared to face such a mighty array. Were we to attack, we would be overwhelmed."

"The moment has passed," the king finally conceded.

If it had ever existed. An impetuous charge by the knights over the soggy ground would have been disastrous. The Kolviners might have dispatched the vanguard of the enemy, but they would have gone no farther. Horses mired, the knights would have been overwhelmed by the rest of the light-footed tribesmen. Possibly by the drakkenree as well; Iaf wished he knew the enemy's capabilities better.

The men of the combined army nervously stood their ground. It was obvious to all that they were outnumbered, and that the odds were growing worse. One of the bregil clans started an impromptu attack, but a shift of Ystram's cavalry aborted their movement. An advance by Baron Jost's knights quelled a second clan's attempt before it came to hand strokes. The armies remained poised, shifting fretfully like barnyard curs before a fight.

And more bregil and drakkenree emerged from the forest.

It was too late to send the noncombatants away; their crossing the ford could set off a panic in the combined army. Alternatively, it might trigger an aggressive reaction from the enemy, tilting the armies into immediate conflict. The risk was too great.

They needed time if they were to have any chance. Time to ready positions, and time to convince King Shain of the wisdom of using such positions.

As a blessing from the great, good god, the drakkenree gave them time. As Janden had predicted, the lizards did not attack that afternoon. For hours, the enemy general seemed unable to get the ill-disciplined tribal groups into the positions he desired; they shifted back and forth in unruly bunches and occasionally an argument would break out. Such nonsense wasn't enough to disrupt the enemy ranks, opening them to attack, but it did hinder their deployment.

A late afternoon thunderstorm was the prelude to the end of martial endeavors for the day. Both armies hunkered down under the lashing wind and rain, and when the sky cleared again, Iaf saw that several of the hill tribes had retreated from their positions in the battle line to take shelter in the trees. The drakkenree made an attempt to chivvy them back again, but the sun was lowering in the western sky. By the time Horesh touched the hills behind the river, tf'she enemy units began to stand down.

The Kolviners and the Imperials knew they had been given a reprieve. No one in the combined army was under the illusion that the enemy would be going away. They all knew that dawn would find the drakkenree still out there. With a full day before it, the drakkenree war leader would have enough daylight and time to satisfy its desire for battle.

At the evening conference, King Shain at last acceded to Iaf's plan to defend from behind the ditch. Iaf was pleased; the king had chosen his plan over Janden's continued insistence on retreat. It wasn't that Iaf thought that accepting battle was wise; he just didn't think they could execute a successful withdrawal.

Under the cover of darkness, the units of the combined army began to move across the ditch. Iaf set every able hand to improving the site. He had the men scavenge what wood they could, even ordering the ambulance wagons broken down. The wounded wouldn't be going far in any case. The only wood he didn't allow touched was the lordling's tower; it provided too good an observation point, allowing him to watch the whole of their defended front at once.

For another night Iaf got no sleep beyond the briefest of naps. Fortunately, Janden stayed out of his way. The *staliarm* man had made Iaf captain-general and, by Vehr, Iaf intended to do the job. With King Shain finally agreeing to his idea, Iaf didn't need Janden any longer to back his arguments with the king. Which suited Iaf just fine. If Janden had shared what he'd known of the enemy's strength sooner, they could have started preparing the defenses sooner or found a better site entirely. Iaf had no use for the man's secretive ways.

Iaf wanted to be everywhere at once. Knowing he couldn't, he tried anyway. He arranged and rearranged the disposition of the troops as new ideas occurred to him. He checked the improvised defensive works, often skipping across the ditch to see if they were well concealed. He moved along the ditch, talking to the men, encouraging them, acting as though he was confident they would meet and overcome everything the enemy threw at them. He did his best to do what Colonel Kensie would have done, and tried to display the confidence that Old Bert had always said was a part of Air Captain Schonnegon.

Teletha had flown, and wouldn't be with Iaf for this battle. He hoped he'd make her proud. He hoped she was safe.

Iaf made the final deployment as the sky began to lighten. He wanted all the troops within the ditch to be in place before Horesh's light made them visible to the enemy. The enemy was on lower ground; they wouldn't be able to see much beyond the combined army's front ranks, a minor advantage.

From his vantage point atop the lordling's tower, Iaf was the first to see Horesh that day. The sunlight crept down onto the arrayed army, all in position. Iaf took out Honistonti's spyglass; the device had been one of the few things belonging to the general that had been recovered from the Gremaire battlefield. Putting the glass to his eye, he surveyed the surrounding terrain. There was fog on the fields, and all was quiet save for small disturbances here and there to the east. He focused on one of those spots and caught sight of a bregil scout, heading back to report to his master. Bregil had excellent night vision, and Iaf had suspected that scouts for the drakkenree had been watching through the night. Had his efforts at subterfuge been in vain? He had done what he could with the troops to hand. Vehr grant that it was enough.

The Scothic regiment held the right flank, along the short stretch of ditch that turned from the main section and ran toward the river. They faced the flank rather than forward, toward where he expected the enemy to deploy. He could not leave the flank undefended, for the enemy had more than enough troops to overlap the longer stretch of the ditch.

The Kolviner soldiers were arrayed in three equal battles along the longer stretch. Their missile troops, bows and crossbows only, were grouped into two wedges between the battles. The battle line covered the whole frontage, but only thinly. For each battle, there was only a small reserve of fifty or so men to its rear.

King Shain commanded the center battle, the position of honor, Baron Jost the right, and Baron Yentillan the left. Yentillan's flank lay against the marsh; with their wilderness experience, his troops would be best suited for a fight there if the enemy somehow managed to make an attack across the swamp. It had taken some coercion, but the proud Kolviner knights had agreed to dismount and fight with their footmen. It helped the morale of the soldiers, and anyway, the waterlogged fields on the other side of the ditch were bad for cavalry.

Close by the lordling's tower, screened by the hill, the Vehrite cavalry stood in reserve. Horses from the regular cavalry had allowed their knights to be horsed, but they still numbered fewer than twenty. Their unmounted brothers and the other cavalrymen were scattered among the battles, the better to give heart to the Kolviners. The Vehrites were less heavily armored than the Kolviner knights. Their lighter harness made them a less powerful shock force, but it meant they were less hindered by the poor ground. More importantly, they were more disciplined and better trained to function as a unit. If any cavalry were to be employed this day, the Vehrites were the best available.

Across the fields, the enemy was stirring.

Two companies of lizards moved out, taking positions two bowshots from the ditch. A half dozen clan groups soon joined them. For a time, no further troops advanced. Then another company of lizards took up a position on the enemy's left flank. The troops remained in tight groupings rather than adopting battle formations, which puzzled Iaf. It puzzled him further when the enemy made no more troop movements for over an hour.

It began to seem that the drakkenree war leader was waiting for something. A flanking maneuver? More reinforcements?

Iaf's answer came when a column emerged from the forest. There were lizard soldiers and bregil warriors leading the column, but most of the newcomers were bearers, merin and bregil. The merin wore bonds. There were also a full dozen *terriserpens* with the column and more than twice that number of some other kind of saurian beast. Fortunately these new monsters were only beasts of burden, if the packs slung on them were real.

Iaf searched among the humans, but the quality of the spyglass was not sufficient for him to distinguish individuals. He spotted a merin man standing near a large black drakkenree. From the way the man moved, it was clear that he was not restrained like the others. The man's clothes were unfamiliar, but the way he wore an assortment of leather satchels about his person stirred Iaf's memories. It seemed that Janden had been right; Yan Tanafres walked freely among the enemy.

Surprised that Janden was not here to make a point of the issue, Iaf realized that he hadn't seen Captain of Scouts Janden since the last evening's conference. Scout reports were still being made, but they were being delivered by Janden's second. Iaf sent a runner after the man.

Janden's second returned with the runner while Iaf was in conference with Fra Ystram. "There's nothing new, Captain-general," the scout said.

"Dantil, isn't it?" Iaf asked.

"Aye."

"Where's Captain Janden?"

The man set his jaw in a peculiar way before answering, "Hain't seen him since yestereve."

Iaf suspected that wasn't the whole story. "But you did see him yesterday evening. What was he doing the last time you saw him? Truth now, the good priest here will know if you're lying."

Dantil gave a look at the priest and seemed to consider whether the priest could tell a lie from the truth. With a shrug, the scout said, "Crossing the ford."

"Deserting?"

"Hain't a witch, to know a man's mind," Dantil said with a sidelong glance at Fra Ystram.

"Do you know what he intended to do?" the priest asked.

"No."

"Or where he was going?"

"No."

Iaf asked, "Did you know he was leaving before he did?"

"No."

"You were Baron Yentillan's man once, weren't you?"

"Still am."

"Then have him find you a place in the battle line. Dismissed." Iaf turned his back on the man.

After a few moments, Fra Ystram said, "We must not dwell on the foibles of others. Vehr has set us a stern task, and we must devote ourselves to that."

"Janden ran." And he had imprisoned Teletha for her intentions. *She* hadn't run like a coward.

"He is gone," Fra Ystram agreed. "But many brave men are still here."

"Yes," Iaf said. What had Janden known that he hadn't told anyone? And what among those secrets would affect today's battle? Iaf didn't know; he couldn't know. And he couldn't allow himself to worry about it. He had made the best plans he could. They would just have to see the day out. If Vehr smiled upon their efforts, he could worry about Janden then.

Iaf returned to his perch in the tower.

Across the floodplain, near the edge of the forest, the enemy was building something. At first Iaf thought it was a siege tower, but such a machine would never cross the soft ground, and it would be of little use in any case. Then he realized that it was an observation platform, something similar to what he occupied. The enemy's tower was finished by early afternoon. It was not so tall that it commanded a view into the combined army's position, but it would allow an observer a clear view of the drakkenree army's deployment. The black drakkenree mounted the ramp to take up a position on the tower. The man Iaf felt sure was Yan Tanafres accompanied it.

In the fields, the clan warriors began to straggle out into a battle line. The three companies of drakkenree spread out with considerably more precision. More hillmen joined the line. Such a screen would mask the drakkenree from observers on the same level, but Iaf's tower offered him a view that negated their precautions.

More of the enemy units moved onto the field. Iaf watched them array themselves into two double battle lines, each with bregil in front of drakkenree. The lizards were the better warriors, but Iaf understood what they were doing; leading with irregulars to preserve your own troops was a common tactic. He wished that the drakkenree war leader had not used it; the combined army's shot was limited, and Iaf would rather have used it on the lizards. They were a greater threat in close than the tribesmen, making it much preferable to kill them at a distance.

The enemy began their advance, moving cautiously across the fields. To Iaf's relief the *terriserpens* were held back from the initial attack. He'd thought that the ditch would be little obstacle to the monsters, and he'd feared the havoc that the great beasts could wreak in close quarters. In the past, the drakkenree had used them mostly against cavalry, since the beasts panicked the horses and threw even the most disciplined unit into chaos. Maybe they were saving them against a cavalry threat. Iaf hoped so; a score of Vehrites would be no match for the beasts on the field. But if the threat of a cavalry action caused the drakkenree war leader to withhold the *terriserpens* from battle, twenty cavalrymen withheld from the battle was a small price to pay.

The enemy line reached the first row of stakes, and Iaf nodded to the trumpeter at his side. Those stakes marked the first target point for the shot; the archers were trained to make a shot to that point. The trumpeter's call rang out. Seconds later, a flight of bolts and arrows lofted from the Kolviners. A few of the enemy fell, but most of the missiles struck harmlessly in the dirt, yards in front of the advancing line. The bregil skulkers must have moved the stakes. The Kolviners' most effective volley had been wasted. First score to the enemy.

The second flight, arrows only this time, scythed down dozens of the leading bregil. Some of the missiles flew past the front line, and Iaf saw one lizard go down. Not enough to make a significant difference. The enemy picked up the pace of the advance. Some of the crossbowmen got off another shot, and most of the bowmen two. They took down more of the enemy, but didn't stop them. The bregil swarmed into the ditch, splashing through the muddy water. The Kolviners surged forward to meet them, standing among the stakes and striking down the hillmen as they tried to scramble up the bank. The fighting was fierce.

The enemy battle line didn't overlap the Kolviners' front, and Iaf saw why. The *terriserpens* were moving forward on the enemy's left flank. The attack Iaf had feared was coming after all, and likely to fall against his fellow Scoths. Bonny fighters that they were, they would be shredded by the monsters. Once the beasts were through with the Scoths, the combined army was doomed.

"They come," Fra Ystram called up to Iaf.

The Vehrite had ridden his horse up to the base of the tower to give himself a view of the battle. The bobbing heads of the giant reptiles were visible to anyone not engaged in combat. The progress of the *terriserpens* was slow; the soggy ground seemed little to their liking.

"There's time," Iaf shouted back.

The priest nodded. After a few quick words, the runners waiting with the Vehrite were off, carrying Iaf's prepared orders.

The slow progress of the *terriserpens* would give the noncombatants a chance to escape; their departure now would not affect the army, for the Kolviners were too busy to notice. Iaf hoped that all who now ran for their lives would be fleet enough.

In response to the orders carried by the runners, the Scoths shifted ranks, opening corridors for the frightened camp followers and civilians to pass. The mob foundered its way across the ditch in a hubbub of yells and splashes. Some few were mounted on draft animals, and as soon as the beasts caught sight of the advancing monsters, they began to scream and shy. One riderless horse leapt the ditch and ran for the ford. People streamed after it.

"Release all the spare horses," Iaf ordered.

"We will have no remounts," Fra Ystram complained.

"All of them," Iaf insisted. "Give them to the women and the slowest. Get them out of here."

Fra Ystram obeyed.

The *terriserpens* caught sight of the throng and came on faster.

The mob began thrashing its way across the ford. Iaf noted the speed of the *terriserpens*. Too fast.

A cry from below took his attention. A company of drakkenree had forced the line and was moving in on one of the archer wedges. The first of the archers was already engaged by the time Yentillan's reserve unit hit the drakkenree and began forcing them back. The breach seemed under control. Iaf turned his attention back to the ford.

One *terriserpens*, smaller and lighter than its kin, had forged ahead and was snapping up stragglers who had been unable to keep up with the rest. The other monsters followed hard on its trail. The beasts were pursuing the fleeing civilians.

As Iaf had known they might.

Fortunately most of the noncombatants—could they be called that anymore?—were across the ford and tearing away across the countryside. A few still struggled out of the river.

The lead *terriserpens* was halfway across the ford, the last just entering the water.

"Now?" Fra Ystram called up to him.

Iaf didn't answer. The Kolviners were holding, barely. Several of the hill tribes had decided they'd had enough and were pulling out of the fight, but the drakkenree still fought. The leading *terriserpens* had almost reached the far bank. There was no doubt what it would do should it catch those it pursued.

"Sound the call," Iaf told the trumpeter.

The brazen sound rang in his ears. For a moment, he thought that he had misread his troops. Then, from their concealed positions along the bank, the Imperial Third Regiment of Foot stood. Thunder rolled across the water as they discharged their arquebuses in a massive volley. The smoke from the weapons billowed out in foul-smelling clouds, concealing the river; but Iaf, and all the men of the combined army, heard the screams of the *terriserpens*.

A cheer rose from the Scothic regiment and rippled along the line. The Kolviners struck harder, battering the enemy before them. The drakkenree and bregil wavered.

The smoke of the first volley began to break up. At least six of the monsters were down and thrashing the water to a bloody, muddy foam. The fleet one lay stretched and still at the far side of the ford, its head on dry land. Stripping the Imperial troops of their guns and massing them on the flank had worked. As monstrous and powerful as the *terriserpens* were, they were still flesh and blood. Flesh and blood withered before massed shot.

The Third Regiment fired again, more raggedly this time. Some of their gunners had only the barest of training, and had yet to reload.

More of the monsters screamed and another fell.

A small group of drakkenree broke from the left flank of the enemy battle line and rushed toward the ford. Iaf was surprised. These lizards didn't look like the soldiers he knew; they wore no armor and carried no weapons. And they were gray. When he saw that no further maneuver seemed imminent on the flank, he pointed them out to Fra Ystram.

"Take them," Iaf said.

The warrior priest turned his horse and led his men toward the flank. The Vehrite trumpeter sounded his horn. The Scoths shifted aside again. This time they opened different avenues for the troops passing through them.

Ystram's cavalry thundered over the makeshift bridges concealed beneath the muddy water. The ground across the ditch was firmer than almost anywhere in the river's floodplain, but still some of the horses foundered in soft patches. The losses did not prevent the Vehrites from riding down the gray drakkenree.

28

YAN FOUND HIMSELF WITH a much better view of the battle than he cared for. The platform built for Yellow Eye commanded a clear view of the floodplain contained within the bend of the River Daige. From the vantage of the makeshift tower, Yan and Yellow Eye had watched the drakkenree force spread out into their double battle line. To Yan's inexpert eye, each of those lines seemed to contain twice as many soldiers as the knot of Kolviners and Imperials crowded behind their ditch.

"You may rest," Yellow Eye had said as they took their place on the platform. "There will be no magic today. *Grm'lktn* has asked me to refrain; he is eager to teach your people a lesson without my aid. It is a good decision, and so I have agreed, although it will encourage him to think yet more highly of himself."

Despite Yellow Eye's comment about Gremlekten's eagerness, the drakkenree war leader had seemed in no rush to begin the assault. Gremlekten had consulted with other soldiers, inspected groups of drakkenree, and parleyed with hill chieftains before finally ordering his forces into battle array. He had moved with the deliberation of one confident of victory.

And why should he not be confident, with such overwhelming numbers? Nearly a quarter of his force were drakkenree soldiers, each able to outfight two or three merin. His bregil allies outnumbered his merin foes by three or four to one. Then there were the fourteen drakkenkain, according to Yellow Eye more than twice the number yet employed in one battle. Yan had seen too well what just one of those monsters could do.

Finally all was arranged to Gremlekten's satisfaction, and he gave the signal to advance. The soldiers moved forward, crossing the fields in a steady, squelching march. The first flight of the defender's missiles fell short, but the defenders held against the initial shock of combat. The keepers sent their drakkenkain charges forward. The sight of the monsters moving up must have pushed some of the defenders over the edge. Yan observed a wavering in the defender's right flank. A trickle of people trying to cross the ditch became a flood, a disorganized mob fleeing for the river.

"It will be over soon," Yellow Eye said.

Yan wasn't sure. His eyes weren't good over distance, but he didn't think that those fleeing wore armor; there were none of the flashes of reflected light he saw in the turmoil by the ditch where the fighting was going on. The troops were still fighting. Which meant that the runners were those who did not fight: clerks, priests, craftsmen, and all those who follow an army.

Was Peyto among that mob? If he was, Yan hoped he would escape. Someone ought to get out of this disaster alive.

Horses, mostly riderless, joined the flight. The drakkenkain began to close on the fleeing people. The Kolviners defending the ditch seemed to be wavering.

In a sudden roll of thunder, the situation changed.

Yellow Eye hissed and stamped his foot when the drakkenkain were caught by the Imperial ambush. Blunt toe claws ripped furrows in the wood of the platform. The mage hissed louder when the Vehrite cavalry emerged from behind the Kolviner lines and caught the keepers in the open. The keepers were not trained soldiers like their green brethren; they were slaughtered by the Vehrites.

"This is intolerable," Yellow Eye snarled. His fingers began to writhe in energy-focusing gestures.

"You told Gremlekten that you would not use your magic."

The drakkenree's fingers froze. Yellow Eye turned glittering eyes on Yan. "It is so."

Out on the field, the second line was moving forward; by themselves, the troops in that line still outnumbered the Kolviners. Gremlekten and the drakkenree around him seemed unruffled, still confident. But Yellow Eye was not satisfied.

"My *grrff'tn* with the gray ones demands action. I cannot ignore the calls of their spirits. But word-bond must bind, even to a soldier." Yellow Eye rocked back a little, jaws slightly opened. It was a pose Yan had come to recognize as a thinking stance. After a moment, Yellow Eye snapped his jaws closed. "By my word-bond I am bound to refrain from using 'my spells' this day. *Grm'lktn*'s own words free me to act. There is more to magic than spells, and sources beyond mages."

Yan knew that well enough. Spells were formulae for controlling the mana safely. A magician could use the energy directly, but the results were not always predictable. Using such energy was difficult at the best of times, and the middle of a battle was almost the worst of times for such dangerous tricks. The gates of Baron Yentillan's stronghold loomed large in his mind. Yellow Eye, however, was a far more accomplished mage; he might be able to handle the energy.

To the detriment of the Kolviners.

What could Yan do to stop Yellow Eye? He'd seen what the drakkenree had done to Fasolt? Yan had far less experience than the Imperial wizard. Opposing Yellow Eye would be suicide. It wouldn't help the Kolviners in the long run; Yan would die pointlessly.

It was soon apparent that Yellow Eye had in mind something other than the manipulation of raw mana. The drakkenree reached back along his side and snagged one of his straps with a claw. A tug shifted the leather around and brought the casket dangling from the strap within reach of Yellow Eye's hand. The Serpent's Eye was in that casket.

Yellow Eye meant to unleash the power of the artifact!

Yan didn't know of what the Serpent's Eye was capable, and neither did Yellow Eye; there had not been sufficient time to study it. Yan did know that he could not oppose the strength of the artifact's magic. He also knew he could not stand idly by and let Yellow Eye use magic to devastate the Kolviners and their Imperial allies. He had to do something! But what?

The Serpent's Eye might be the answer as well as the threat. Since Yellow Eye was no more familiar with it than Yan, the drakkenree would be grappling with forces and energy patterns that he did not understand and might not be able to control. Uncontrolled magic could be very destructive. Often its first victim was the presumptuous fool who unleashed it. If Yan could manage to disrupt the mana flow at a crucial moment, Yellow Eye's own ambition might be his undoing.

What would happen then was unknowable. Nevertheless, this might be his only chance to prevent the Serpent's Eye being used against honest, innocent men and women.

While Yan fretted, Yellow Eye released the wards on the casket. He laid the box on the platform before unlocking and opening it. As the lid swung back, the Serpent's Eye was exposed to the first natural light it had seen since it was placed in the cavern, possibly the first natural light ever. The ocher orb seemed insubstantial, a sphere of misty transparency, yet it was solid enough for Yellow Eye to take it in his hand.

The drakkenree mage bowed his head over the orb and began to make passes across it with his free hand. Yan did not have to try to feel the forces gathering around the platform; their strength was enough to penetrate into the physical realm. Though no cloud showed in the sky, the air took on the feel of an approaching thunderstorm.

A storm surely approached, but not a natural one. There was little time left for action.

The earring the drakkenree had put on Yan was more than mere jewelry. It was a talisman that the mage had used to channel spell energy, encouraging Yan's obedience with physical pain. In working with Yellow Eye, Yan had also seen hints of the mystic link between the earring and his *claviarm*. Could he even use the *claviarm* anymore without Yellow Eye knowing? Did he now need the drakkenree's permission to perform magic?

He would find out. Pulling the amulet from under his shirt, he took it in his hands to maximize the physical contact. He focused his physical senses on the *claviarm*, renewing his acquaintance with its physical existence. His palms felt the smoothness of the metal, warm from his body heat. His fingers traced the shape of the decoration, the roughness of the incised script. His eyes drank in the soft gleam of light playing off its surface. It seemed all it had ever been and no more. Gently he extended his arcane senses. At first he did no more than confirm the *claviarm*'s arcane existence; he did not dare channel any energy through it. His caution was wise; something that he could only envision as a chain hung on the amulet's spirit form. He had no doubt that the alien spirit form had been set there by Yellow Eye.

Yan recalled the simplest protections he had learned from Gan Tidoni. Those charms were designed for an apprentice's first touch of magic, to focus and protect the novice as he followed his master into *præha*, before the apprentice had built his *claviarm*. Yan wove those charms now, not with the blind faith of the novice but with the surety and strength of a magician. Once those elementary precautions were in place, he worked his way through each protective charm his master had taught him, and then through those he had devised himself, building the best defenses he could without drawing on the *claviarm*. None would be as strong as the sorts of defensive magics he could employ while linked to the mana through the *claviarm*, but he hoped that Yellow Eye would not detect them.

Having done all he could to ward his actions, Yan shifted his awareness into *præha*. In the mana realm, the platform was awash in ocher light. The surging energies of emotion and death from the battle washed around them. Other energies swirled down from the sky in a rainbow whirlwind and rushed in a vortex around Yellow Eye. The drakkenree's spirit form spread its arms wide and welcomed the energies. Where in the physical world he held the Eye in his hand, here his hand was empty. Here, the Serpent's Eye glowed on his forehead, just as it had on the statue in the cavern.

Yan felt himself in the presence a power unlike anything he had ever sensed before.

Yellow Eye turned his head to regard him. The drakkenree's eyes glowed with the same ocherous shine as the Serpent's Eye. "Do not be foolish, mammal."

"You're the foolish one," Yan told him. "You don't know what you're tampering with."

The drakkenree's eyes turned dark with amusement. "You cannot see what I see."

"I see how dangerous what you're doing is."

"Return to the physical."

Yan did not obey the order.

With a contemptuously casual gesture, Yellow Eye constrained the mana to his will. Yan's earring burst into fierce fire, scorching hair and flesh. He screamed. He screamed louder when the energy arced from the earring to his *claviarm*. The metal grew hot in his hand, burning hot. Unable to bear the searing pain, he unclenched his fingers. He might have had hot coals on his chest. His shirt charred, filling his nose with the stink of burning fiber. It was immediately replaced by the smell of burning flesh. Yan twisted violently away from the pain. The thong parted and the *claviarm* fell. Metal splashed when it hit the wood of the platform.

Yan's mind reeled and his body with it, smashing hard against the railing. The wood bent, but held. His *claviarm* was gone, and with it a part of his soul. He collapsed to his knees, feeling as if someone had shoved a red-hot nail into his skull. Darkness nibbled at his mind.

But the charms Yan had woven had an effect. They had not protected him from Yellow Eye's attack, but they had done something else. His *claviarm* was a fused lump, but he remained in *præha*, in touch with the mana. The glorious, wonderful stuff of magic that had been his joy since he had first touched it. The sublime beauty of the magic, the wonder and mystery of it, was all that saved his mind.

He'd lost his *claviarm*, but he refused to lose the magic.

He armored himself in his desire for magic. He strengthened himself with memories of calmer, happier days when he had first come to know the magic, and his heart had opened to it. He had given his life over to understanding magic, and now, in the aftermath of Yellow Eye's attack, he knew he had come to a better understanding of his relationship to it.

He could still feel the gentle touch of the mana, still see its flow and hear its passage. Experimentally he extended a finger, and felt the magic shift in response. The touch warmed him. He opened himself to the mana stream, letting it lift his spirit with its caress. The song of the bright energy uplifted him. He felt comforted, reassured.

Beyond the pool of tranquillity in which he stood, a storm was growing. All around him the mana was coursing, rushing to take a shape at Yellow Eye's urging.

Yan moved his bubble of harmony into the swirling whirlwind. He rode surging currents, whirling wildly as the mana streamed in tighter and tighter circles. He had no control, but he didn't need control; he felt the power and was content to know that he could touch it. That knowledge renewed his strength. His body lay damaged on the platform, but that didn't matter at the moment; his essence was stronger and more alive than it had ever been.

He watched as Yellow Eye's spirit form rode up the column of the power he had gathered. Yan knew the mage's surprise at sensing him there.

"How?" asked Yellow Eye

Yan answered with his own question. "Is this what the Eye can do?"

Radiating pride, Yellow Eye said, "This is what I would have it do. This is strength to obliterate the *maah'nn'kun'yee* infestation from this land. This is power to do all I wish. All I wish and more."

"More?" Yan could feel the destructive potential of the magic. He could hear the rumbling in the earth below, see the winds beginning to rip at the trees of the forest. Quivering with excitement and strain, Yellow Eye was almost ready to unleash the energy he had gathered. It was too late to disperse the magic.

Yan saw the only chance he could conceive.

"Let me help you," he said, pouring his newfound strength into reinforcing Yellow Eye's summoning. Yan opened floodgates, bored bigger holes, threw open shutters. All that was, he reinforced. Where a seam of the spell was stretched he repaired it, and made the stitches smaller for strength.

Yellow Eye staggered under the impact in the mana surge.

"You wanted more," Yan yelled over the roaring energy.

"No! It's too much!"

Yan gave the drakkenree still more.

Energy rammed into Yellow Eye and Yan reinforced the doorway, made it larger. The drakkenree fought the power bulging and swelling against the walls of his control. Yan sensed the drakkenree falter. Bending the magic to his own will, Yan slammed it into Yellow Eye. The drakkenree reeled, but Yan was relentless. He smashed in, driving Yellow Eye's will down, bludgeoning his spirit form to its knees. But drakkenree didn't have knees like merin, and Yellow Eye's legs snapped under the assault. The mage's physical pain colored his spirit form. Unsparingly, Yan hammered at him. The drakkenree's protections cracked under the inexorable pressure.

Yellow Eye's resistance collapsed.

Yan flayed his defenses and stripped away his shields until all of the drakkenree mage lay open to him and Yan was in control. Yan dared do no less. Once he was satisfied that there was no deception, that Yellow Eye could no longer mold the magic to attack, Yan reached out and took the Serpent's Eye from the drakkenree's hand. The Eye vanished from the forehead of Yellow Eye's spirit form.

Yan felt an eye open into his own mind. New vision showed him things he'd never understood before. Awed by the vision, he said, "This is not what you thought it to be."

Yellow Eye only whimpered.

"Why? Why did you seek it?"

A new vision filled Yan's head. It was Yellow Eye's vision, a dream of the world as it ought to be. It was a world in which only drakkenree and their minions and beasts walked Aelwyn. There were no men, no bregil, no sign of their works. All, save what the drakkenree made, was gone. Beyond their makings, the world was as it had been before any being dreamed of harnessing, building, or leaving a mark. It was a powerful dream, an idyllic vision.

Yan could not accept it.

Aelwyn as it ought to be?

Without merin? Without bregil?

How could it be?

In Yellow Eye's heart, such a land not only could be, but had been. In Yellow Eye's mind, it could be again. *Would* be again.

The Eye throbbed in Yan's hand, hot against his burned flesh. The Eye pulsed in his brow in sympathetic vibration. Yan was frightened. Open to the magic as he was, he sensed the hand—the taloned and scaled hand—that had formed the Eye in a distant past, in a world not unlike that of Yellow Eye's dream.

Yan had felt that magic before.

He tried to thrust the vision away, fearful that the magic might be strong enough to turn Yellow Eye's dream into reality. But in his fear he had no control. The mana crackled around him, spiking out in a thousand directions. One of those spikes pierced Yellow Eye's mind. The drakkenree's scream tore past Yan like a hurricane wind, exploding with an almost-physical violence. The air howled louder and louder, booming with violence expended and impending.

Yan felt Yellow Eye's mind wink out. In that last moment Yan sensed the strength of the drakkenree's mind, the depth of his intelligence. Yan knew with a sad certainty that he had extinguished a brilliant scholar.

What had he done?

That was clear enough. Intentionally or not, he had killed by magic. Yellow Eye's body still breathed, but all that had made the drakkenree mage more than a beast was gone. Murder by magic, one of the crimes by which the Triadic Church would judge him a dark magician.

As he looked down at what was now a mindless animal sprawled on the platform, the Church's judgment seemed unimportant at the moment. Gusts of restive power coiled around him, obscuring his view of the physical world. The wild energy that Yellow Eye had raised and Yan had enhanced continued to crackle around him. Whatever Yan had done in overwhelming Yellow Eye's capacity was still building, threatening Yan himself now.

He wished that he were somewhere else.

And he was.

Supported by the mana, he floated above the battlefield. The entire floodplain lay beneath him. He might have been one of the moons, or the sun—or a god.

Fra Bern's shaking voice describing his dream echoed in Yan's ears. The great yellow orb in the sky, like an eye looking down. An eye looking down upon the world as Yan was now doing.

Fra Bern had sensed an otherworldly power in his dreams, a power as foreign to the Celestial Court of the Triadic faith as it was to the Court's enemies. The priest hadn't thought magic was involved, but he might have been wrong. What if the priest had foreseen this moment?

It couldn't be.

The priest had feared a god, and for all his godlike view, Yan was no god. He'd had similar views before, lofting his spirit form above the world while in trance. Even as he tried to explain it away, he knew that this circumstance was far different.

It seemed to him that he could see everything below him, all at once and each bit separately. Spirit voyaging had never offered such clarity and comprehensiveness. He saw it below him: the Kolviners and the drakkenree, the Imperials and the hillmen, the dead and dying drakkenkain. On the far side of the river, people fled the carnage, and Peyto was there running with them. Fra Bern hid behind the soldiers of the Third Regiment. Small bands of bregil and drakkenree, late for the battle, still hurried toward the site, all unknowing of the events unfolding. Farther away, across the river, a lone horseman rode westward. Closer to where Yan's body stood there was turmoil among the drakkenree leadership as they watched the first battle line complete its disintegration. Gremlekten led his bodyguard forward to join the second line's advance. Panic ripped among the bearers and prisoners. In the confusion Threok found a knife and began cutting the bonds of merin prisoners. At the edge of the woods Teletha crouched, watchful and waiting.

Yan was buffeted by the battle beneath him. The surging emotions clashed in jangling discord. Pain and fear roiled in clouds. Hate for the enemy and love for friends warred and jostled within the combatants. Flashes of light marked the release of life energy as one warrior killed another; the mana flared and churned around such spots. Yan saw now how to twist and amplify such emotions, harnessing them into destructive energies to rip across the battlefield. With the strength flowing through him, such magic was now his for the molding.

He remembered what he had done at Baron Yentillan's steading, and how the results had not been what he had intended. Today, too, his control of the mana had not been complete. Intending to subdue, he had extinguished. He dared not contemplate what might happen if he shaped the magic to destruction and unleashed it.

The harsh and horrific magics of the battlefield were not for him. Destruction was not the answer. How could it ever be?

He had already been the destroyer today, the searing fire, and he had not been enlarged by it. Empowered, yes, but what was power? *The will constraining the world*, was Gan Tidoni's definition. Today, Yan's will had constrained the world of one being to the point that the being was no longer a part of the world.

This was not why Yan had studied the Art.

He wanted to make, not to destroy.

He recalled the harmony he'd felt earlier when he'd used his earliest lessons to protect himself in his attempt to touch the magic. That peace had shielded him from Yellow Eye's violence. The memory of it calmed him now. In reflection, the mana storm swirled with less violence, its colors muted.

While he steadied his mind, below him the battle made lifeless meat of thinking beings. Drakkenree and hillmen fought their way across the ditch. Ammunition gone, the Third Regiment forced their way across the ford to join in the hand strokes. Iaf came down from his tower and, Jax Vorsan at his back, led the reserves into the fray. The drakkenree and bregil forced the defenders away from the ditch.

A world in which only drakkenree and their minions and beasts walked Aelwyn, was Yellow Eye's vision of the world.

The world was as the world was. To force it to be otherwise was a fool's task, a child's dream. The world could not be made to fit one person's willful idea.

He saw a path.

Gathering the strands of power, he wove them into a net to cast over the battlefield. Having formed the power to his will, he launched it. His cast touched the merin, Kolviner and Imperial alike, and wrapped them in the magic. He touched them, he touched them all, and for a fleeting moment he was all of them.

Or so it seemed.

To each he offered new strength, a second wind, renewed resolve. They needed only to put their will to their task. They needed only to be what they were. Desperate men and women accepted, and he poured the strength of the magic into them. They took it to their hearts.

One fought to see his child again, another her husband. One fought for the honor of the regiment she'd served for a decade, determined to die well. Another fought to kill those that threatened his land and all he had striven to build. Whatever reason they found, they fought as fresh troops just come to battle.

Some who couldn't accept Yan's offer died, distracted by his touch. Others died despite their newfound strength. But many rallied who would have fallen as their weakened arms could no longer withstand the blows of the enemy. As individuals rallied, so did the army.

Its energy focused and spent, the mana storm quieted.

There was still turmoil, of course. The battle still raged. But Yan's piercing vision lost its sharpness. Yan bid the Eye slip deeper into quiescence. Shaky hands of flesh rolled the orb into the casket and closed the lid.

Yan returned to his body, and knew at once the pain of the physical manifestations of his magical battle with

Yellow Eye. His head was afire and his hands and chest raw with agony. He tried to scream, but nothing emerged from his abused throat. While his mind had been elsewhere, his body had been doing a lot of screaming.

Under the misery of his suffering, he felt a pressure on his brow; the magic still buzzed in his head. For all that his physical body was depleted, he was charged still with energy. His awareness of his surroundings was spotty, but he knew there was still danger. While he still could, he tweaked the mana flow, enfolding the platform in a cloaking spell. The spell would shield him from the attention of the drakkenree.

It would shield Teletha as well, for she was coming up the ramp.

Somewhere on the battlefield Fra Ystram was wounded.

Reaching the top, Teletha gave Yan a quick glance before turning hard eyes on the twitching from of Yellow Eye. Sword ready in hand, she advanced on the drakkenree.

Yan forced his voice to work.

"No," he said.

His word was his will, and she stopped as if she'd hit a wall, held by his desire. Her eyes shot arrows of disbelief and outrage at him, but he ignored them. He would explain later, and she would understand.

Merin died at drakkenree hands and drakkenree were slain by merin.

Gripping the rail sent spikes of pain into his hands, but he couldn't stand unaided. He managed to reach his feet and stagger forward. She did not resist when he took the blade from her hand. More of his magic, or her intention? He couldn't tell.

Gremlekten was wounded but he killed his attacker. He slew like a demon, but the merin bore him down. The war leader died in agony from a dozen wounds.

The world spun in dizzying circles as he turned toward what was left of Yellow Eye.

"I hadn't thought you one for revenge," Teletha said to his back.

Fra Bern called upon his god to give healing to a wounded bregil.

No healing here. "Not revenge. Mercy."

He thrust the sword into the drakkenree's body, using the magic to guide his hand so that he struck cleanly to the heart. It only took a little more magic to ensure the wound was instantly fatal.

He felt the life leave Yellow Eye's body.

Iaf saw the wavering in the drakkenree ranks. Calling the Scoths to follow him, he led them in a charge. Leaderless, the drakkenree and bregil forces slipped into rout.

Yan's vision narrowed until he could see only the dead mage at his feet. A bloody sword lay across white bones protruding from Yellow Eye's splintered left leg. Teletha had said something but Yan had missed it. He tried to ask her to repeat what she had said, but he mumbled. She responded anyway.

"I said, I guess you didn't need me after all."

Yan's arcane resources ran dry, leaving only his worn and insufficient physical self. He crumpled. To his surprise, he didn't slam into the wood of the platform. Teletha's arms were around him. Gently she lowered his limp, gangly form to a restful position.

Who said he didn't need her?

She would guard him. He was safe now. Hoping to escape pain in the realm of the dreamless dark, he let go of his consciousness.

29

YAN WAS IN TERRIBLE SHAPE. Teletha had done what she could to bandage his mangled ear and burned hands, but she wasn't even sure whether what she'd done was the proper thing for such a wound. Yan was the one who knew about wounds. She sat beside him, wishing she knew better what to do.

At the sound of a footfall on the ramp, she left her place by his side and scrambled across the platform to get her sword, abandoned on the body of the dead drakkenree. The grip was slimed with blood and other fluids from Yan's hand, which would make it difficult to wield. But she managed to keep the point steady as she whirled to face whoever came.

It was Fra Ystram. He carried his sword in his left hand, for his right was wrapped in a bloodstained bandage and strapped to his chest with a leather thong.

"Peace, Sergeant," the Vehrite said, carefully lowering his own weapon.

Teletha relaxed her stance with a sigh. The priest was no enemy, and she was grateful. "I am very glad to see you, Eminence."

"And I you, Sergeant. I saw the troops, including my own, pass by this structure as if it were not here. I thought that curious and came to investigate. I had been expecting to encounter the enemy's wizard." He inclined his head toward the dead lizard. "The drakkenree mage is dead?"

She nodded. "Yan stuck him."

"Then the spell that hides the tower is Master Tanafres's work?"

Teletha didn't know anything about a spell, and said so. She gestured toward Yan's supine form. "Yan's in no shape for spells. He needs a healer. Are you one, Eminence?"

Fra Ystram's eyes filled with sadness as he looked at Yan. "That is not my gift. I would that it were. I see that the magician has suffered to aid us this day. At least you have found him again."

"Perhaps too late," she said

"Not too late," Yan croaked.

Trust him to contradict her. She crouched by his side. "Too stubborn to die?"

"Very stubborn." He tried to smile at her. At least she thought the grimace he was making was intended to be a smile.

"It seems we have much to thank you for, Master Tanafres," Fra Ystram said.

"I don't want to talk about it." He coughed in a spasm that racked his lean frame. "Tell me, priest. The battle. Is it over?"

"The hillmen are fled and the drakkenree retreat in disorder. The enemy is broken, and we hold the field."

Yan didn't say anything, but made his grimacing smile again. Teletha saw tension go out of his body, the way it did from a ground crewman releasing the last line on a lifting balloon. He closed his eyes again and slipped away into unconsciousness.

There was nothing practical they could do. Fra Ystram kept vigil with her by the side of the magician, helping her pray for Yan's survival. It lifted her heart to have the priest there, since Yan was now in the hands of the gods. Below them the moans and cries of the wounded made an eerie song of mortality.

Nothing had changed by time Iaf arrived. The lad looked older than he had the last time Teletha had seen him. Then he was just learning the worries of command, now he had weathered his first battle as a leader. Weathered and won.

Iaf didn't look happy as he took in the scene atop the platform with a glance. With a nod to Teletha, he approached Fra Ystram and crouched by the priest's side.

Jax Vorsan, silent and grim, followed Iaf up the ramp. Like most of the warriors she'd seen today, including Iaf, he was wounded; but his animal vitality showed no sign of having been lessened. When Iaf stopped near the warrior-priest, Vorsan took another step toward Teletha and stood looking down at Yan. The big man's face was unreadable.

Teletha listened in on the soft-voiced exchange between Iaf and Fra Ystram.

"Will he live?" Iaf asked.

"As the gods will," the Vehrite answered.

"The lizard mage?"

"Dead by the hand of Master Tanafres."

"That ought to be enough proof for anyone."

"Proof of what?"

"That Janden's a slanderer as well as a liar and a coward." Iaf leaned over the railing and shouted orders for a string of horses to be gathered and made ready for travel.

"What is your intent?"

"My job as captain-general is done here."

"Not yet," Fra Ystram said. "The enemy still has a sizable force."

"Their leaders are dead; they won't stand." Iaf shrugged. "King Shain can harry them back into the hills."

"As may be, but the Imperial force is still charged with aiding the king, and you are still the captain-general."

"There's a whole army to chase them," Iaf snapped. "One more man won't make any difference."

"You are the captain-general," Fra Ystram said stolidly.

"Someone else can lead them. Why not you, Eminence?"

"I was not appointed commander."

Iaf started to snap a reply, then paused. A sly smile ghosted across his face. "If I'm still the captain-general, then I can still issue orders. Correct?"

Teletha suspected she knew what was coming.

"It is your duty to do so," Fra Ystram said.

"Then take these as your orders, Eminence. I charge you to take command of the pursuit. That is a lawful order, is it not?"

"It is," the Vehrite said.

"King Shain has regard for your word. He will accept you in my place."

"He should not have to."

"Well, he's just going to have to," Iaf said. "I'm going after Janden."

"You need me." Yan's creaky voice commanded their attention with a completeness beyond its strength.

"You're in no shape to go anywhere," Teletha said.

"You look worse than when old Gormen dragged you home from the sea," Iaf said.

"It is unwise," Fra Ystram concluded.

Yan ignored them. "You don't know where he is going. I can find him."

"How?" Iaf asked

"Bring me the casket." Yan pointed a trembling finger at the object he wanted. Teletha moved it to his side. Yan fumbled at the latch until she brushed his hand away and opened it for him. She lifted the lid to reveal a dull ocher sphere.

"Is that the fabled Serpent's Eye?" the Vehrite asked.

"It doesn't look like much to me," Iaf said.

"It is more than it appears," Yan told him. "I can use it to follow Janden."

"Just tell me where he is, and I'll go after him."

Yan shook his head. "Not without me."

"You can't ride in your condition," Teletha objected.

"Tie me to the horse."

Stubborn mule. "You'd never stand the jostling."

"I'll manage." Pain whitening his face, Yan struggled up onto an elbow and stared at Iaf. "You won't find him without me. Not in time, anyway."

"Not in time for what?" Teletha asked suspiciously.

"I'll tell you on the way."

Brandespar was a city by Kolviner standards, which meant that it was larger and finer than the Scothic towns Iaf had seen as a boy, but far less than the Imperial cities he'd visited. The ride from the city gates to the waterfront was not long.

Stopping to leave their remounts at a stable added some time, but not enough to make much difference. By Iaf's estimate, they were not far behind Janden. Janden had only the one horse and couldn't have traveled as quickly as they had, having spare horses.

Master Tanafres was on the edge of collapse. His parlous state tore at Iaf's heart, almost as much as the worried looks Teletha gave the magician. There could be no doubt Master Tanafres had won her heart. Could the magician not know how much it hurt her to watch him risk his life this way?

The magician had said that Janden was currently in Brandespar. They had come to the end of the trail, and the magician was no longer indispensable to the hunt. They no longer had to allow him to continue pushing himself past his endurance. As he watched the slumped magician walk his horse slowly along the quay, Iaf knew that the man had gone as far as he could. Iaf resolved to see him rested.

Master Tanafres's horse clopped to a stop in the shade of a shed. Iaf hadn't seen the man so much as twitch the reins to give the horse direction. Iaf rode up beside him; Teletha and Vorsan brought their horses in behind. The magician raised a trembling hand and pointed at a row of buildings. One was a two-story building with a weathered sign hanging over its open door.

"The inn?" Iaf asked.

The magician nodded weakly. More than ever he looked like a man with a limb already entangled in death's net. In a voice that was little more than a strained whisper, he said, "He's there now."

Iaf looked him in the eyes. "Do you listen better than your friend Fra Bern?"

Another nod, slower this time.

"Good. Then stay here." It felt strange giving orders to the magician, and Iaf couldn't help wondering if he'd dare try it if Master Tanafres looked less like an animated scarecrow with a bad case of the plague. "Teletha, you'd better stay with him."

"You may need help," she said.

"I'd rather you not be involved," he said, adding, "Air Captain."

She straightened and shot him a hard look. He stood up to her icy stare, and, just when he was sure he would wilt, she said, "I understand. Vehr guard you."

"As He wills."

Iaf dismounted. Vorsan was at his shoulder a moment later. Iaf would have preferred leaving the big man behind as well, but he had already learned the futility of ordering the giant to do anything but stay at his side. They walked across the street to the inn.

Soldiers were normally good trade for a public house and, though they were not wearing all of their armor, their buff coats and helmets marked them for soldiers. However, the innkeeper didn't look at all happy to see them. Iaf suspected the man knew grim intent when he saw it.

"We're looking for a man," Iaf said in his best Kolvinic. "Janden's his name."

"Don't know no Janden," the innkeeper said.

"He's an Islander. Tall man, lean. Hair cut like a Kolviner. We know he's been staying here."

The innkeeper started to shake his head, but froze when Vorsan raised a hand and took a step toward him. "His room's upstairs on the left," the man said quickly.

Iaf thanked him and headed for the stairs. He didn't know what would come from this confrontation; he only knew he had to have it. Janden was a proven liar and manipulator, and his schemes had gotten good men killed. Needlessly, in Iaf's eyes. How could such a man be a holder of the *staliarm*?

Then the door was in front of him, and there was no more time to sort things out. The moment was upon him. He nodded to Vorsan and the big man threw himself at the door. Metal screeched against wood as the hinges ripped free and the flimsy wooden panel collapsed inward. Vorsan's bulk filled the frame for a moment, then he was through. Iaf followed in his wake.

To find disappointment.

The room was empty. Had the innkeeper lied? Could the magician have been wrong? Iaf knew whom he trusted. The innkeeper had spoken quickly, perhaps a little too quickly. He could easily picture Janden bribing the innkeeper to lie for him.

Iaf spun and headed back for the common room. Vorsan, slower going down stairs, had just started down when Iaf hit the packed earth floor of the lower story. The common room was empty, the innkeeper nowhere in sight. Iaf stepped to the open door and found him, running full tilt down the street. It was the run of a fearful man rather than that of a messenger.

Behind him he heard the squeak of a hinge and a woman's shrill laughter belled in his ears.

As Raff opened the door to head back for the common room with the whore, he saw the two men. It was the middle of the afternoon, and he was surprised to see anyone in the common room, much less a mismatched pair of dust-covered mercenaries. Though bedraggled and looking a bit worse for the wear, they looked employable. By Baaliff, there'd be work for them soon enough, and what Kolviner lord wouldn't want a man like the big one? The fellow was almost of a size with the addle-brained Jax Vorsan.

Even off the battlefield, these fellows might prove useful soon. The whore he'd bought for the afternoon hadn't been as good as her promises. He wanted better if he was going to be spending some time in this squalid little Kolviner town; which he was, since the next ship to Sessandir wouldn't be leaving for another week or more. With luck, he could scrape the whore off on one of these two.

The pair turned to look at him as he started to smile in preparation for making their acquaintance. He aborted the gesture when he saw the big one's face. Gods! The big one *was* Vorsan! Which meant that—yes, the smaller was Iaf Smyth, the boy he'd made a general. What were the two of them doing here? Raff had a good idea he knew, but it was always better to be sure.

There was no point in opening a conversation with Vorsan; the big man still had the same befuddled scowl he'd worn the last time Raff had seen him. Before his wounding, Vorsan's face had been mobile, and he'd had a sharp tongue little held in check; the Vorsan he knew would have been already running off at the mouth. No more. Raff addressed the boy.

"You surprise me, Smyth. I thought your sense of duty would keep you there to the end. I didn't expect you to run."

"I didn't run."

Scoths had such a prickly sense of honor. "You don't need to lie to me. I can see that you're alive. How many died before you ran?"

"Too many died! And I said I didn't run."

"All right, you didn't run. But how else would you be here?" He hadn't figured the Scoth for a practical fellow, but here was the evidence before him. Add practicality to the flare Smyth had shown for command and there might be uses for such a fellow, beyond soaking up a mediocre whore's attentions. "I have to give you credit for being brighter than I thought you were, though. Maybe if you buy me a drink and take care of my friend here, I'll think about taking you back with me to Sharhumrin. I'm sure we'll be able to find work for a man who knows when it's time to cut his losses."

"I don't think so. You left us all to die."

"Don't be absurd," Raff advised. "I made the same decision you did. I just saw the inevitable result sooner. You'll learn in time."

"You never expected us to do other than lose."

"The odds were too long, boy."

Raff's words seemed to settle something for the Scoth. He nodded slightly, the kind of gesture one makes to oneself. "I have spoken with the king's son, Prince Shain," he said as though revealing a great secret. "I know what you told him. He knows the truth now."

"And what truth is that?"

"We defeated the drakkenree. They are dispersed."

"Impossible."

"The gods don't think so."

"What about their battle wizard?" Raff asked. "Do you mean to tell me that you defeated their magic as well?"

"The wizard is dead, killed by the hand of the man you said was a traitor."

Could Smyth be lying? No, he looked totally sincere. Besides, he wasn't really the sort—and if he were, there were more believable lies to tell. How could the Kolviners and the remains of the Imperial force have defeated more than twice their number? What about the drakkenree mage? It couldn't be true. Could it?

"Hell of a story, Smyth. Man tells a story that good, he deserves a drink." The innkeeper was nowhere in sight. "Innkeeper? Get your butt out here and pour some for my friends!"

No one came running from the kitchen. No one stirred in the common room either except the whore, finally disentangling herself from his arm. Like a squal sensing a predator and looking for a new tree branch.

"It's not a story," Smyth said. "It's the truth. And you're going to choke on it."

Raff looked at the Scoth out of the corner of his eyes. The fellow was stony-faced. His stance was rigid with righteous anger.

This was bad news. Raff had stopped to take time to prepare the prince; someone had to hold ground until more forces could arrive. He had sent a messenger ahead to Brandespar because he'd wanted to get the word to Sorigir Renumas as soon as possible. Renumas would act on Raff's letter, not knowing the information was wrong; and when the real news reached the capital, Renumas would lose face. At the very least. If Sorigir Renumas fell from grace with the emperor, he would surely see to it that Raff suffered as well.

Raff knew about Renumas's concept of suffering, and he had no intention of facing that.

"What exactly are you proposing to do?" he asked the Scoth.

"I intend to expose you to the emperor for what you are. A schemer, a liar, and a coward. The whole Imperial court will know your falsehood before I'm through. You will no longer be a disgrace to the men of the *staliarm*."

"A big boast. You're just a boy, and a Scothic boy at that. What do you know of the court?"

"The emperor is an honorable man."

"The emperor's honor doesn't matter. You'll never see the emperor! You'll have to deal with the court, and you have no idea what that's like. You'll have to convince one official after another just to gain entrance to the palace or the court. Do you have recommendations or letters of introduction? Even if you did manage to see anyone of importance, what match is your word against that of a holder of the *staliarm*?"

"It won't be just my word."

"Vorsan's not the best of corroboration," Raff pointed out.

"There are others ready to denounce you. King Shain for one. Fra Ystram for another. Master Tanafres for yet another."

Even the damnable magician? "They survived as well?"

"By the grace of the gods, they did."

The gods had no grace if they had let this come to pass. Still, the situation might be salvaged, but only if the Scoth didn't hold to his plan to challenge Raff's account of what had happened here in Kolvin. Something had to be done. And quickly, if Raff was to salvage the situation. He turned to Vorsan.

"Colonel Vorsan, you can't be going along with this fool. He's a *Scoth*, for the sake of the gods! You know what liars they are. They're natural-born rebels and traitors. *You* know. You've fought them. You're as loyal a man as ever pledged to the emperor. How can you stand beside a Scothic traitor?" Was that a crack in the big man's scowl? "Step away from him now, before he taints you. Think about your honor, man! Think about your pledge to serve the emperor! There is no mercy for those who consort with traitors and malcontent rebels like the Scoths. The emperor will be grateful that you helped stop this traitor."

Vorsan opened his mouth as though he might be about to say something.

"You're finished, Janden," the Scoth said. "I'll see you exposed. At the least, I'll see you hanged as a deserter."

Smyth took a step forward, and Vorsan made no move to stop the Scoth. But at least the idiot made no move to aid him either. There was a chance. Raff grabbed the whore and shoved her at the Scoth. She squealed as she slammed into him, and the two of them went down in a tumble. Raff spun and headed for the back room where he'd lain with the whore, and where he'd left his pack. Behind him he heard the Scoth cursing. The whore was screaming.

Raff reached the pack and pulled out his pistol. He flipped open the pan cover and cocked it as he stood. There was only one way out of the room, and that was back into the hall to the common room. The pistol would be his safe-conduct. And if the Scoth was stupid enough to object, Raff would demonstrate what happened to people who meddled with their betters.

The Scoth met him at the door, skidding to a stop as he saw the pistol in Raff's hand.

"What's the matter, Smyth?" Raff grinned at him. "Not so interested in death all of a sudden? Yours is not so pleasant to contemplate as another's, is it?"

The Scoth backed up. Raff pulled his second pistol and stuffed it into his belt. Snatching up his pack, he slung it over one shoulder. All the while the Scoth watched him with hatred in his eyes. Let him hate. A good hatred built character. It wouldn't matter for long anyway.

"Back up," Raff said, gesturing with the pistol.

The Scoth did as he said, slowly enough to be aggravating. Vorsan waited in the hall. The Scoth had to back into him before he'd move. When they reached the common room, neither of them moved very far from the archway; but there was a clear passage to the door. The whore crouched by the fireplace, whimpering.

"You won't get away, Janden."

"Who says I'm going?" He raised the pistol.

Vorsan moved faster than Raff would have thought possible for a man of his bulk. The giant's hand closed around Raff's, grinding his fingers against the trigger guard and smothering the action of the lock.

"No," Vorsan said.

Raff was infuriated. He couldn't allow this man, this *idiot*, to ruin him. Raff bent down and drew the knife he kept sheathed in his boot top. He brought it low across his front and stabbed upward for Vorsan's heart. He felt the blade slide through the leather of the buff coat, only to catch on bone and skid. The tip skipped out and tore through the flesh of the giant's left arm in a spray of blood.

The whore started screaming again.

Vorsan roared. His meaty fist lifted and came crashing down on Raff's shoulder. Agony splintered into being there and his arm went numb. Baaliff, the idiot was strong!

The whore kept screaming.

Vorsan tightened his grip on Raff's pistol hand and Raff felt the bones snap. Damn the man! Raff would be crippled in both limbs now. Snarling, Vorsan lifted Raff from his feet. The shattered bones in Raff's shoulder tore through his flesh in an explosion of torment. Damn, damn, *damn the man!* Raff felt himself flying through the air. He hit a beam crossways, so hard that he didn't feel it. He fell to the dirt. Though he could taste the dust and blood in his mouth, he couldn't feel his legs. The last thing he saw was Vorsan's booted foot rushing for his face.

30

THE INN WHERE JANDEN DIED wasn't the best in Brandespar; but given Yan's condition, the others had decided he needed a place to rest as soon as possible. In a small bit of compensation, Janden's money paid for the place. It was nearly a week before Peyto finally arrived; the clerk had delayed to collect letters from King Shain and Fra Ystram detailing the conduct of the campaign against Yellow Eye's drakkenree prior to the Battle of Rastionne.

"You are just in time, Master Lennuick," Iaf said when the clerk entered the common room. "The ship for Sessandir is leaving on this evening's tide."

"I am aware of that," Peyto said, though Yan guessed it was bluff. "I would have been here sooner, but my search for you took me to a few, somewhat more noble, establishments before I was directed to this one."

"It was to hand," Teletha said.

"And one of the rooms was already paid for," Yan said. "A thrift I am sure you will appreciate."

"You look terrible," Peyto told him.

"You should have seen him when we got here," Teletha said. "He looks a lot better since he's gotten some rest. You look like you could use some yourself."

"Travel at speed is never kind."

"Has there been trouble?" Iaf asked anxiously.

"None more than was expected. The drakkenree are not

compliant about leaving the Kolviners' lands, but King Shain is insistent," Peyto said. He proceeded to tell them of what had happened since their departure. In return, Iaf told him of the confrontation with Janden. When the telling was done, Peyto asked, "What now, then?"

"I must go to Sharhumrin and tell the tale," Iaf said. "I would take it as a kindness if you could convince Master Tanafres to follow when he is well enough to travel. He seems deaf to our arguments."

"Deaf, is it?" Peyto gave Yan a calculating look.

Yan tapped a finger on the air beside his bandaged ear. "I am a casualty."

"The other ear looks fine to me. Perhaps you do not hear because you do not wish to."

"Perhaps that is so," Yan agreed.

"What kind of a fool are you, Yan Tanafres?"

"Hush, old man," Teletha chided. "Yan's no fool."

"I will not hush! No fool? What better chance could we possibly have to go to the capital? When the tale of this campaign is known, you will be a hero. The emperor will be grateful, and the Imperial gratitude can be very generous."

"I'm no hero, and I do not desire the emperor's gratitude. What I am is a very tired scholar of magecraft. Janden has taught me the lesson you've been trying to pound into me for some years."

"Which lesson—of the many—is that?"

"It is clear that Janden had the favor of the emperor. If it takes a man like him to survive at the court, I have no wish to be there. I am not an intriguer like him."

"He is not the best example," Peyto said.

"But you do not deny that he is an example," Teletha said.

"A bad one," Peyto said.

"A very bad one," Iaf said.

"One bad example is no reason to deny yourself the advantages of the court," Peyto said.

"But the advantages of the court will deny me what I desire," Yan said. Peyto narrowed his eyes in suspicion, but Yan went on as if he hadn't noticed. "I find that there is much for me to learn here in Kolvin. Yellow Eye had barely begun to scratch the mysteries of the place where we found the Serpent's Eye."

"This place, is it the city of Ul-Schuttariat that you've sought?" Peyto asked.

Yan shook his head slowly. "I don't think so, but it might be better for my purposes. It will take some study."

Peyto harrumphed. "You can't be planning to waste *your* life in this wilderness as well, Mistress Schonnegon."

"I've never *planned* on wasting my life," she said. "It just seems to happen."

"So you're staying with him?"

"For the moment."

Peyto harrumphed again and glowered at Yan.

"You don't have to stay," Yan told him. "I'm sure Iaf will be able to get you a position at the court, if that's what you want."

"Aye, Master Lennuick," Iaf agreed. "As you say, the emperor's gratitude is expansive. So, will you at least come with me? I could use your advice."

Peyto slipped the satchel from his shoulder and handed it to Iaf. "It's these letters you need, not me. There are other fuzzy-minded folk who are in greater need of good advice."

As Iaf accepted the satchel, Jax Vorsan appeared at the door. In his hand he held the reins for three horses. Iaf said, "It's near time to be off."

"Three horses?" Yan asked. "Were you so sure that one of us would be going with you?"

"I'm escorting him to the ship," Teletha said.

Iaf wouldn't meet Yan's eyes. Yan waited patiently until Iaf looked up, then he said, "I wish you a good journey. We shall meet again."

Iaf shook his hand. "A prophecy, Master Magician?"

"A promise, my friend. I leave prophecy for the priests; it's not a sufficiently rigorous practice."

"Unlike magic?"

"There is nothing like magic."

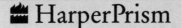